MW01051027

She could feel the onset of an intense sexual tension between them. It was thrilling, so acute that she was trembling long before they reached the door to his suite. She tried to suppress her restless sexual hunger for him. It was the same hunger she had experienced in front of the Venetian mirror in her bedroom that afternoon. Barbara was just a little frightened that her libido should take over her life. She had never till that moment realized how compelling her sexual drives were. Always she had thought that it was her lovers who were more powerfully sexual than herself. She saw it all so clearly now. That had not been the truth of it.

Avon Books are available at special quantity discounts for bulk purchases for sales promotions, premiums, fund raising or educational use. Special books, or book excerpts, can also be created to fit specific needs.

For details write or telephone the office of the Director of Special Markets, Avon Books, Dept. FP, 1350 Avenue of the Americas, New York, New York 10019, 1-800-238-0658.

HUNGRY HEART

Roberta Latow

AVON BOOKS ◆ NEW YORK

If you purchased this book without a cover, you should be aware that this book is stolen property. It was reported as "unsold and destroyed" to the publisher, and neither the author nor the publisher has received any payment for this "stripped book."

All characters in this publication are fictitious and any resemblance to real persons, living or dead, is purely coincidental.

The poem on page vi is taken from *Collected Poems*, C.P. Cavafy, edited by George Savidis, translated by Edmund Keeley and Philip Sherrard, and reprinted by kind permission of Chatto & Windus and the Hogarth Press and The Estate of C.P. Cavafy.

The poem on pages 313-314 is taken from *Collected Poems*, George Seferis, translated by Edmund Keeley and Philip Sherrard, and reprinted by kind permission of Jonathan Cape.

AVON BOOKS
A division of
The Hearst Corporation
1350 Avenue of the Americas
New York, New York 10019

Copyright © 1993 by Roberta Latow
Published by arrangement with the author
Library of Congress Catalog Card Number: 93-90635
ISBN: 0-380-77414-3

All rights reserved, which includes the right to reproduce this book or portions thereof in any form whatsoever except as provided by the U.S. Copyright Law. For information address Curtis Brown Ltd., 10 Astor Place, New York, New York 10003.

First Avon Books Printing: March 1994

AVON TRADEMARK REG. U.S. PAT. OFF. AND IN OTHER COUNTRIES, MARCA REGISTRADA, HECHO EN U.S.A.

Printed in the U.S.A.

RA 10 9 8 7 6 5 4 3 2 1

For my friend Bibi, a Polish countess who claimed her father's dream, and her husband, Rodney Harris

On hearing about great love, respond, be moved like an aesthete. Only, fortunate as you have been, remember how much your imagination created for you.

C.P. CAVAFY

Prologue

He was not handsome, more a colossus of a man, with his six-foot-plus height and massively broad shoulders and chest, his dark hair, thickly Eastern European accent, formidable hooked nose, and kind brown eyes. He humped hundred-pound sacks of potatoes, crates of lettuce, boxes of apples, baskets of peaches and plums as if they were weightless. He was among the last of the traditional Yankee peddlers, even if not a Yankee himself, nor even born in his adopted country, the United States. He drove an imposing, bottle green Mac truck, with its powerful motor and hunky Goodyear tires.

Cassandra was not happy having to work for a remote and gruff if not unkind father. But this was 1942. There was a war on, no young men at home to take on the summer job. Worst among the things she detested about working on the truck was having to peddle with him into the Blocks in Chicopee. The Blocks, were filth and poverty, a foreign land.

The area was the size of two football fields, with not a blade of grass, a single tree. The hard-packed earth had not a hint of life in it. On it perched row upon row of weathered houses, little better than double-decker shacks with steep wooden outside staircases. They formed lines of depressing, sinister, barracks-like accommodation running the length of that barren place, with ample room between buildings for the peddler's truck to park and serve its inhabitants.

Here hardly a word of English was spoken. The place even smelled foreign. This pocket of near-poverty, mid-European peasantry, seemed an oddity in Cassandra's beloved New England. She didn't know what to make of the peddler's jovial, even affectionate, manner with the pudgy-faced, big-breasted, wide-hipped and massively soft and wobbly-bottomed women who waddled out in their flip-flop sandals and threadbare cotton flower-printed dresses. Dresses that clung to their sweaty nakedness.

The middle-aged women looked slovenly, loose and raunchy. Base. There was about these women, devoid of prettiness and artifice, no form of femininity. Not as the American dream depicted it and the girl understood it. What they did possess and exhibit was a kind of animal sexuality. It was here for the first time the girl saw the outline of a woman's pussy; enormous, fully-rounded, jiggling breasts with frighteningly large nipples. Over-ripe, broody females. No girdles or bras in the Blocks to hold the body and sexuality in check. The smell of garlic seemed to emanate from the very pores of a woman's skin. One smelled of raw onions, and another carried the aroma of staleness. Another had taken on something of the strong Polish sausage she gnawed at. They were all, one way or another, like that. They smiled with teeth missing or capped in gold. With hands like hams they pinched or prodded the fruits and vegetables, hands rewarded by the peddler with a smack and a sharp reprimand, then a smile. With shrill voices they bargained for pennies, and spat out their demands.

It was all so ugly.

The last customer walked away laden with brown paper bags. Cassandra watched the peddler stride across the dry, dusty ground, an orange crate containing a customer's order balanced on his shoulder. He knocked at a door and disappeared through it. Ten minutes later he emerged, the empty crate in one hand, a glass of cold milk in the other. He returned to the cab and his daughter, handed her the glass of milk. The glass was worn away with scratches and chipped in several places. She felt revolted to have to drink from it. Even the glass was an icon of poverty. She refused the glass of milk. He drank it down for her. Why couldn't he see the filth and poverty of the Blocks as she did? Why didn't his soul wither as hers did when they visited?

He put the crate away, took her empty glass and disappeared into the house once more. The cab was stifling in the 99 degrees Fahrenheit. She sweltered. Felt the grime of dust and sweat, and was dizzy from the oppressive heat and misery of the place, its unrelenting ugliness.

She hopped down on to the hard, dried earth. A cloud of dust rose around her ankles. She was parched. The dust irritated her mouth. Desperate to escape the sun, the heat, Cassandra crossed the yard to find her father. She heard voices, her father's and a woman's. They were talking in Polish. A rank smell of stale cabbage and raw onion, rancid butter, sour milk, greeted her when she finally knocked on the screen door.

With the adults engrossed in their conversation, her knock went unnoticed. Cassandra, too distressed to be polite, opened the door and stepped into the room. A shaft of light from a window streaked across the small room, dark and dingy but surprisingly neat. She was mesmerized by what she saw in the channel of light. In an old chair sat her father, his arm around the waist of a child, sometimes speaking to her, at others to the woman across the table from him. Never had she seen such a look of affection in his eyes as he had for that child.

He addressed her as Mimi. She was a hauntingly beautiful, elegant-looking child, though skinny in the extreme, standing in her bare feet in her dress of near-rags. Cassandra could hardly take her eyes from the child. The long, golden blonde hair in ringlets, the violet eyes, a creamy white, unblemished skin. There was a luminescence about the child that held Cassandra's attention. A very female frailty that one expected to see only in a woman, not in a mere child, and certainly not one who lived in the Blocks. Mimi realized someone else was in the room, and turned to face the peddler's daughter. Cassandra was stunned by the pathos in Mimi's eyes.

Reluctantly she stepped away from the peddler, Mimi and Mashinka's only friend, their only link with a world outside the Blocks. The woman, who looked neither better nor worse than any other woman on the Blocks, pulled out the empty chair next to her and offered it with a gesture to Cassandra. Reluctantly she accepted the chair. Seated next to the woman she was overwhelmed by her scent, whiffs of garlic and neat gin, so strong and sweet in the heat, Cassandra felt quite queasy. The woman drew from her bosom a grimy, wrinkled handkerchief. Bending forward she mopped Cassandra's face. She cringed.

"Your father a good man. Our friend," Mashinka told her in passable English.

The woman's words were slurred, presumably from the effect of drink. Covered in a white oilcloth that was yellowed and cracked with age, the table looked mean. It bore a chipped saucer of sliced sausage, a heel of stale bread, some green pickled tomatoes on a cracked flower-patterned plate, the inevitable bottle of cheap gin and two glasses. The woman offered her a slice of sausage. Cassandra declined but asked, "A drink of water, Daddy. Can I have a drink of water? Then can we go?"

She watched horrified as a fat, ugly, amber-colored cockroach climbed up the apron of the oilcloth and scuttled across the table. The woman casually swept it away with her bare hand. Cassandra heard it crunch under Mashinka's shoe as she ground it into the floor. She watched Mimi wash an old, chipped jam jar and fill it from the tap. As she handed the glass to Cassandra, she caught for the first time a look of envy in Mimi's eyes. Envy and a kind of hunger that lurked beneath a façade of pride.

Neither girl spoke. But for the remainder of that afternoon the fruit peddler's daughter was haunted by Mimi's beauty, the air of mystery she sensed around her. Mimi had shone like a lustrous pearl in the ugliness of the Blocks, in the gloom of such poverty. How luckless, thought Cassandra, for her to have such a life. And yet the peddler's daughter felt no pity for the beautiful child. Mimi did not inspire that particular emotion. She radiated a special kind of charm, a seductiveness, a kind of power that in itself was a mystery, and mightily attractive. And Cassandra resented being swept up in it, just as her father had been. It worried her that she lacked the charisma of that mere urchin girl.

New England
New York City

1942

Chapter 1

Six o'clock in the morning, and it was already unbearably hot and humid. A Berkshire Mountains day. Cassandra was waiting, in her usual place in front of the Post Office, for the Mac truck to round the corner, stop and pick her up.

She had already hoisted herself on to the running board and was swinging herself up on to the leather seat when she saw Mimi slide across it to station herself between father and daughter.

Surprised, she almost lost her balance. A strong arm shot out and caught her. Joe Pauley's vise-like grasp lifted her to plunk her firmly next to Mimi. Bending across both girls now, he slammed the truck door closed and pulled the door handle forward as far as it would go, locking them firmly in.

"OK, girls?"

They nodded. Grabbing the stick shift, the peddler threw the gears into first, and the heavily laden truck lumbered forward. "Good. We have a big day ahead of us."

For fifty-five miles, there was silence in the cab. The two girls sat, feet on the box of chains, bouncing up and down at each pothole in the road, trying to remain upright among the peddler's paraphernalia and Mimi's pathetic belongings: a small cardboard suitcase tied with a piece of clothesline, a patched but clean cloth bundle tied in a knot, and a never-worn pair of black patent leather shoes. These she held tightly in her lap. Contact between herself and Cassandra was limited to when the truck, climbing steeply, took a sharp bend in the narrow winding mountain road at an ill-judged speed, so that the girls fell against each other.

The climb was long and beautiful. A stream gushing over

rocks and fallen trees on one side, the steep rise of the mountain on the other. Luscious and varied shades of green from the dense forest, broken by the sun, dappled the road. Mimi pinched hard the skin between her thumb and forefinger to make sure this ride was not a dream. She felt the pain, and, reassured, gave an inner sigh of relief. Still hot and humid, but less so because the temperature dropped with every few miles, they traveled up the shaded mountain road. It shocked Mimi that she had forgotten that life could be as beautiful as this mountain road. She felt that no matter what happened, whether the lady who was to take her in liked her or not, she would at least have escaped the heat, the smell of poverty in the Blocks, for one day.

But once they left the wooded mountain, and the road turned to open hills and farms, and the sun was hanging unrelentingly hot in a cloudless sky, Mimi sensed how important it was that this stranger with whom the peddler would place her really did want her. Mimi remembered Mashinka's last words to her: "Be brave and good, do what you're told, and work hard. Then one day your father will come and find you." No he won't, she had wanted to tell Mashinka. He was lost to her. So many losses she had forgotten how to cry. Mashinka was the last person on earth whom she knew and loved, and soon she would be gone. Dead like Tatayana. But in her heart Mimi knew that Mashinka was right. One day her father would come and find her, and only that eased the pain of her aloneness, of being a wanderer dependent on the kindness of strangers just to stay alive. Her love for her father was all the life Mimi had, the rest was mere survival.

She sensed the strength and power of Joe Pauley the peddler, the excitement he felt hurtling up the mountains in the huge truck, and the anger and jealousy of Cassandra even though she didn't understand it. Nor did she want to. She was too busy trying to adjust to being free from the Blocks and bracing herself for what was to come.

First stop Ida Hall's General Store: gray-painted, wooden farmhouse with a long, deep porch hung on the front, and two old-fashioned red pumps, one for gas, and the other for kerosene in the yard in front of it. It was variously a grocery, an ice cream parlor, a candy store selling hard liquor, a fresh fruit and vegetable market. The peddler pulled up to the entrance. The screen door opened. A boy carrying a basket of green beans walked out on to the porch. Having placed it among other boxes and baskets of produce, he ran back through the door, shouting, "The peddler's here, Mrs. Hall."

"How many times do I have to tell you, Herman, he's Mr. Pauley to you? So you call him that, boy," ordered Ida Hall as she pushed the screen door open and strode on to the porch. It slammed behind her, and the tall, slim, stern-looking woman, plain and shining as if she had just been scrubbed, stood peering at them with hands on hips. She had a spinsterish quality about her: hair of silver gray pulled back off her face and pinned into a tight, hard bun at the nape of her neck, three yellow pencils with red erasers on the ends pronged into it. Mimi thought her formidable, and although she didn't cringe with fear she did harden to face this woman in case she was spoken to.

From the cab it was all eyes on Ida Hall. The peddler sighed. Never easy, she was still one of his best customers. He whispered rather loudly to Mimi, "You and Cassandra can go and sit on the steps. She makes the best doughnuts, fresh, maybe even still warm. Be good, and I'll get you some."

His daughter watched him take the shoes from Mimi's hands and roughly push them on her feet, smile at her, stroke her hair and pat her on the shoulder. He said something in Polish, and she nodded her head. Then he opened the door and slung himself down. Walking around the front of the cab to open the door for the girls, he called, "Morning, Ida."

"Mornin', Joe. You're runnin' kinda late."

"Had to pick up this little girl. Delivering her over to Beechtrees. That put me behind," answered the peddler. He walked to the rear of the truck, let down the tailgate and hung up his scales.

The two girls scrambled down from the cab. The peddler's daughter greeted Mrs. Hall politely from the bottom of the steps. Mimi said nothing.

"Oh, brought a friend, have you? What's your name, child?"

"She won't understand you. She doesn't know English, and she's not my friend."

Both Cassandra and the woman looked surprised when the child answered in near-perfect English and without a trace of accent, "That's not true. I do speak English, and my name is Mimi."

"Well, you're a pretty little thing, Mimi. Got some spirit, too. I like that in people."

"What did I tell you, girls?" boomed the peddler from somewhere among his boxes and baskets. They jumped at his words and ran up the steps to sit on the top next to each other, silent and staring straight ahead at the truck and Herman and the peddler unloading Ida Hall's order.

Mrs. Hall laughed. "Nice fresh milk. Just cooled from the cow, half hour ago. Frosted doughnuts. How 'bout that, girls?"

They nodded. Mrs. Hall opened the screen door and turned to look at the still-surprised peddler's daughter. "Well, fancy that, Cassandra Pauley. Ridin' fifty-five miles sittin' next to somebody, and never sayin' a word to 'em. Not even knowin' they speak English. Ain't you got no curiosity?" She disappeared into the store, the screen door closing lazily behind her.

Mimi wished that Ida Hall had not said those things to the peddler's daughter. She had sensed the girl's hostility towards her. Would it be worse now? What must Cassandra be thinking? What Cassandra was thinking was: Why does this stranger from the Blocks get so much attention? First from Father and now Ida Hall. Cassandra looked at her. Mimi, sensing her angry gaze, turned around to face her, so that their eyes met.

Here, away from the monstrous Blocks, sitting in the sun, the trees and green fields around them, Mimi looked unhealthily pale, pathetically skinny in her cheap, pale blue flowered cotton dress with its little puffed sleeves. More refined, maybe, and even prettier than Cassandra had thought her the last time they met. But there was a sadness in her eyes that made Cassandra feel sorry now, not only for herself but for Mimi as well.

"You should have said you spoke English," Cassandra told her angrily. Mimi remained silent, but kept her gaze on Cassandra. "How old are you?" she asked.

Mimi hesitated. She was trying to decide whether she

wanted to talk. Now there's pride for you, thought Cassandra. And what a nerve, coming from where she did, and with a mother like hers, to think twice about talking to *me*. Mimi had made up her mind. "I'm nine years old."

"What grade are you in at school?"

"I don't go to school."

"Well, when you did. I mean, before the summer holidays."

"I've never been to school. Any time."

"Of course you have. Everybody has to go to school, that's the law. Then where did you learn to speak English?"

"I learned my languages at home, all my studies . . ."

They were interrupted by Mrs. Hall with the plate of doughnuts, a jug of milk and two thick glasses, the kind that come free with grape jelly. "Languages? You speak more than English and Polish then, Mimi?" She was bending down and handing the tray to Cassandra, who slid away from Mimi to place the tray between them.

"English, Polish, French and . . ." Mimi stammered.

The peddler joined them with a crate of corn on his shoulder, about to sling it down on to the porch at Mrs. Hall's feet. He added, "That's a lucky thing, too. Ida, just look at this corn, sweet as a nut." And the peddler ripped one side of a husk down to expose the bright yellow kernels. Mimi watched and listened to the business transaction at hand, riveted by the two adults' sparring.

"One ear don't make a box, Joe." The peddler gave her a look bristling with annoyance. He tore down the husk of a second ear of corn, then a third, staring at Ida Hall defiantly.

"Six boxes," she told him, pulling one of the yellow pencils from the bun of hair at the nape of her neck. She wrote something on a sales pad extricated from the pocket of her dress. "We'll settle price later, Joe. Now let's see your lettuce." And Mimi was forgotten. Cassandra wondered why it was a lucky thing that Mimi spoke several languages. She had almost ceased wondering what the girl was doing there with them. And now this.

Mimi was hungry. She nearly always was, but usually pretended she wasn't. She waited for Cassandra to take the first doughnut, to pour glasses of milk for them. Such self-control had become habitual. Even in the worst of times, Mashinka had found food for them. Maybe not feasts, but food enough to sustain them. Then the peddler had entered their lives and had befriended them, and their money, what there was of it, seemed to buy more food.

Mimi held the glass of milk in her hand. It trembled: she had less control over her hunger today than usual. She raised the glass to her lips. The scent of the rich sweet milk filled her nostrils. She drank from the brimful glass. First a sip, most delicately, so as not to spill a drop. She closed her eyes for a second, an expression of relief when the gnawing sensation of hunger was stilled. Then she began to gulp down the milk in great long swallows. The glass was almost empty when she caught herself, stopped, and looked around to see if anyone had observed her.

Cassandra was quick to lower her eyes, pretense prompted by shock at the look on Mimi's face. Cassandra had never seen hunger like that before. She instinctively avoided creating the embarrassment Mimi must feel at having been caught out. Not knowing what to do about it, Cassandra gulped down more than half of her own glass of milk. Turning to Mimi, she told her, "I'm so hungry and thirsty." She filled their glasses again, and handed Mimi a doughnut. That moment of anguish—Mimi was usually a master at hiding it—vanished from her face. For a few hours Mimi had a friend, her very first girlfriend.

The two girls understood that they were friends. But what to do about it? Mimi was aware of being able to draw people to her, and that was a comfort, but always short-lived.

She was wise, survival-wise, beyond her years. A series of traumas had ensured that. She no longer took the chance of feeling too deeply for anyone. A deep fear lingered that they might vanish the way Tatayana had, and her mother and father, her brother . . .

Mimi carefully wrapped the second doughnut in the coarse paper napkin still lying on the tray. Cassandra watched her. "For later," explained Mimi.

Cassandra took the doughnut from her and began unwrapping it. "You don't have to save it, Mimi." Smiling she handed the partially unwrapped doughnut back to her. "We have a whole truckful of food to eat, and my daddy always buys the biggest and best lunch. You'll never be hungry again."

Mimi stared at Cassandra and took the doughnut offered. How innocent, how lucky, how dumb about life this spoiled daughter of the peddler seemed. But she was, too, kind and generous. And what would happen to me, Mimi wondered, without the kindness of strangers? She wrapped up the doughnut again. "Just to be safe," she told Cassandra. She remembered too well her hunger. Not all strangers were kind.

It was three o'clock in the afternoon when the truck pulled up. The massive ornamental iron gates were set into a fifteen-foot-high wall of stone that extended as far as Mimi could see. The peddler stopped, idling the motor, and leaned from the cab, calling out, "Open up, boys, it's Joe Pauley."

Two men appeared at once. "Right on time as usual, Joe."

Mimi watched, half in trepidation and half in excitement, as one of the men slipped a key into the huge padlock, and the two men pulled on the heavy chain, dropping it on the ground. Each took one side of the massive gates of elegant but rusting curves and twists of heavy metal. They lugged them open just enough for the truck to pass through. Once inside the gates the peddler stopped the truck and cut the motor. He hopped down from the cab and gave a hand with the closing of the gates and the chain. The two young men had gunbelts strapped to their waists. Rifles leaned against the wall. He shook their hands. "All quiet, boys?"

What an adventure, thought Mimi. Have courage, don't be a baby, she told herself in an effort to enjoy the sights and sounds that continued to amaze her since the peddler had taken her from the arms of a weeping Mashinka, who had, even through her tears, kept assuring Mimi that all would be well.

"Nothing but quiet, Joe. Gotta check you out anyway. You have an extra passenger."

"That's right, a little girl."

"I sure do know that, Joe. The children have been down here at the gate twice, looking for your truck. Those kids are hankering real bad for a playmate, something else to amuse them. Well, let's have a look at her and her luggage."

Mimi seemed neither surprised nor puzzled by the men guarding the gate, and Cassandra was quite used to them. To pass through the gates of Beechtrees was the highlight of her working day in the Berkshires. "Mimi," she whispered, "this is the best place we come to. Any moment the Queen might come out to the truck as she has done several times with her cook and the young princes and princess. She has been so nice. Nothing like as grand as she looks in the newsreels with her diamond tiaras and ball gowns. She fled her country with her Prince and their children only at the last moment, with the Germans on their heels marching into her kingdom. So here she is sitting out the war in Beechtrees instead of being captured and used by Hitler. I find it all quite unbelievable. This actually happening in New England."

Mimi felt relieved to think that even a Queen could be a displaced person in times of war. She was about to tell Cassandra "It's not unbelievable to me," when the peddler spoke to Mimi in Polish. Mimi was reluctant to do as he asked, but she trusted him and finally allowed one of the FBI men to open her cardboard suitcase. Most of the little that was in it was utterly threadbare. The men, like the peddler, seemed embarrassed. They tied it up again with the piece of clothesline and then untied the patched cloth bundle. Books and photo albums, a locked flat leather envelope wrapped in an aged piece of oilskin.

Mimi tried to rally herself as the men rifled through her things. She felt upset and downtrodden that she should be subjected to this search. The gloom on Mimi's face was unmistakable, her silence heartrending. The peddler picked Mimi up by the waist and swung her from the seat to set her on the ground. She looked pathetic. Even the FBI man felt foolish for having rummaged through her belongings. He squatted down beside her. "Don't look so sad. My name is Jack, and this is Ernie, and you don't have to be afraid of us or our guns. We're only here to guard the gate. We just protect the family. We're kinda friends. We go out shopping with them and for long rides and picnics. We all have a good time. You'll like living here." Uncertain that he'd got his point across, Jack looked up at the peddler. "Not gonna cry is she, Joe?"

"No, I'm not going to cry," answered Mimi having bounced back from some dreary dark place where she had been. She had had enough of people speaking about her as if she wasn't there. No one missed the note of assurance in the tone of her voice. The three men looked relieved.

Mimi listened to one of the men tell her, "Hello, I'm Jack's partner, Ernie." He put out his hand to shake hers. "This is a great place. You got everything right here in these grounds. Even a little house in the orchard where the children go to school. It's small, mind you. Used to be a dovecote. But it's big enough. There are only three of them. There's tennis and swimming, and horses to ride. So put on a happy face." And she knew he and Jack were nice people, but wondered how to put on a happy face when she didn't feel happy.

Ernie patted her head, and told Jack he was going to ring through and tell them the child had arrived.

None of what the men told her came as a surprise to Mimi. The peddler had already told her most of what she was to expect. She suddenly thought, what if they don't like me? What will happen to me then? She began wringing her slender, delicate hands. That was more than Jack, the younger of the two, could stand. Yet again he stooped down. Gently taking her hands in his and separating them, he said, "Are you worried about working in the kitchens with cook? You don't have to be. She is a very nice lady, when you can understand her. Now that's not going to be a problem for you, 'cos Joe tells me you speak the same language."

The peddler returned from the far end of the truck. He had dipped a clean handkerchief into the melted ice collected at the bottom of a lettuce crate. Brusquely he wiped Mimi's face and then her hands, one at a time, while conversing with her in Polish. "And what if they don't like little girls who smell like a summer salad?" she asked. The peddler laughed and patted her on the head, and then took some of her hair in his hands. Had she a brush? She climbed up on to the running board and leaned into the cab for her case. There were a brush and a comb. The peddler adjusted the wing-mirror. Balanced on the running board she combed her hair. It sprang into lustrous curls. She tied a pale-green satin ribbon in a neat bow around it.

Cassandra sat silent. How come Mimi had the attention of the three men, and the good fortune to have come to live at Beechtrees? Finally she asked her, "Are you going to live here with the Queen and the Prince and their children?" Mimi turned away from the mirror, perching still on the running board. She looked at Cassandra.

"The cook. I'm going to live with the cook. I'm going to be a scullery maid while I learn. I'm allowed to attend school and play with the princes and be a friend for the princess after all my chores are done. Mr. Joe and Mashinka have fixed it for me."

"Mashinka is your mother. Won't she miss you?"

Mimi felt a hint of tears in her eyes, suppressed at once. Just at that moment she was whirled around by the peddler. He attacked her shoes with a dirty rag, giving them an extra burnish. He pulled on the hem of her dress and smoothed the wrinkles with his hand. Again in Polish, "What more can they expect? You've been riding in a truck since before six this morning." Then, tossing the damp handkerchief to Cassandra, he told her, "You clean up a little, too. Your hands. The cook might offer you something. Maybe comb your hair?" From the shelf above the seat, reaching under a box heavy with the weight of his extra stock of brown paper bags, he withdrew a clean, well-pressed shirt. He stripped off the sweat-stained one he wore, and passed a comb through his own hair. He turned away from the girls, distancing himself by several steps, to undo the wide, worn leather belt, tucked his shirt neatly in, buckled and re-buttoned his trousers, before turning his attention again to the two FBI men.

They walked together to the rear of the truck whence the peddler snatched a large brown paper bag. Snapping it open, he filled it with peaches, plums and cherries. "Be good to her," he told the two FBI men. "An insurance policy." And he waved four large yellow bananas at them before he popped them into the bag.

"Jesus, Joe, that's great, thanks. But this kid, Joe? What do you think it'll take to get her to smile? Have you ever seen her smile?"

"Never. Years I know her. And the mother, a drunkard. Never lets the kid out of the house. No school, no nothing.

But a good woman. Poor as a church mouse. Crazy she is for
Mimi, worships the ground the kid walks on. She comes not
twenty miles from where I was born, but like me she's a long
time away from the old country. Not even when Tatayana was
alive did she smile. She was a woman, a teacher, who lived
with them. A lot a tragedy there. It's some story. They're
only in America since maybe three, four years. The brother,
he was a no-good drunk. Took 'em in, and then died. So they
lived off his pension. And now Mashinka hasn't got long to
live. Cancer. Believe me, our children should never go
through what Mimi has. But what can you do? That's life."

He handed Ernie the bag. "Jesus, Joe, you gave us too
much."

"Never mind. Just be nice to Mimi. She needs friends."

"It'll work out, Joe, but the cook will work her hard." The
three men walked back to the cab where Mimi now stood
looking up the avenue of beech trees. Mimi felt her heart racing. Could it be true that this was to be her home?

"OK, Joe, you go on ahead. Jerry's stationed at the entrance to the back drive. He'll take you in."

The drive from the front gates up the beech avenue to the
mansion house was just short of a mile. The grounds, over a
hundred acres of them, were not especially well tended and
were overgrown: paths wove through high grass where wild
flowers mingled in abundance. The beech trees themselves,
though neglected, were still impressive. The road boasted as
much dirt as patches of gravel. There were ruts and potholes.
Beechtrees' parkland had about it an air of comfortable wildness. It was a place of nature to which man had applied his
hand, cutting a path through it without actually spoiling it.
The afternoon sun filtered light through the leaves. Its dappled pattern across the road reminded Mimi of the mountain
road. She could imagine how birdsong would be woven into
the silence here once the rumbling of the truck ceased. It
would be the sweetest song she had ever heard.

She tried to still her heart. Impossible. Her happiness, its
sheer improbability. Memories were flooding back of another
wood, barely remembered. But how could she have forgotten? Home, she was coming home. Maybe not her own home,
but such a home as the Blocks had never been. She began to

cry. She was thinking of Mashinka and Tatayana, her teacher. Poor Tatayana. Of the three of them she had suffered most in their wanderings to find a home for themselves. And she had died of a broken heart, or so Mashinka said. Her tears were for Beechtrees too because it was so beautiful and because it was true, her father would come and find her, and they would be together for the remainder of their lives.

The peddler was thinking of his schedule. How quickly he could decently get away from Beechtrees. The summer camps? And the furriers on vacation from New York? Several houses of them, four or five families to a house. His toughest customers. Now that they were inside Beechtrees, Mimi, though not quite forgotten, was relegated to the back of the peddler's mind. As far as he was concerned, she was settled. He had done his bit for poor Mashinka and Mimi. More than his bit. A good deed was a good deed, but charity still began at home.

Commerce made him oblivious to Mimi's tears. But not so Cassandra. She placed an arm around Mimi's shoulder and pressed a clean handkerchief into her hands. The two girls looked at each other. After taking a deep breath, Mimi composed herself and dried her eyes. For a few seconds she covered her eyes with her hands. When she removed them, the crying was over.

The three, strangers to each other in their various ways, bumped along over the rutted drive. All her life Mimi would remember the peddler and what he had done for her and for Mashinka. Most especially for taking her fate in his hands. That ride from the gate along the avenue of trees gave her the first real sense of comfort since she had been sent away from home with Tatayana and Mashinka, to become a refugee, a casualty, a mere item amid the flotsam of war. It was the road to new beginnings for Mimi. This displaced child of nine knew it. She could feel something stirring in the very marrow of her bones. The comfort of strangers.

Chapter 2

Half a mile up the avenue, a pair of winged stone griffins, the more menacing for being pitted by time, wind and rain, stood on ten-foot-high stone plinths. Like sentinels they appeared on either side of the secondary road that led through the stable courtyard to the kitchen gardens, the kitchen itself and the service entrance to the mansion house. At the turning the peddler slowed for a man to hop on to the running board. A head poked through the window. "Hi, Joe, Cassandra, and you too—can't keep calling you 'you too.' Got a name?"

"Jack, she's called Mimi," the peddler told him as he shifted gears and picked up speed again.

"Well, Mimi, look over there."

All eyes in the cab looked in the direction pointed out to them. They could just see, parallel to the truck and a good distance from it, running through the tall grass and its spattering of wild red poppies, three children of various ages and sizes wildly waving at them. They were shouting and jumping up as they ran, to get a better look at the truck and a glimpse of cook's new helper.

Mimi's heart was racing. She watched them and remembered fun, happiness, what it felt like to run wild and laugh and play. The Blocks and Chicopee, years of imprisonment in those grim, smelly rooms—now it was just a bad dream, a long nightmare through which only Mashinka's and Tatayana's love for her had sustained them all. The poverty that had ground their spirits had alienated them from the niceties of life. At the beginning there had still been laughter between herself and Mashinka, first her wet-nurse then her nanny, her second mother, and Tatayana, her governess and tutor.

But that had been in the early days of their exile, shortly after her father had engineered their escape from the war to safety. When they had thought Mimi's father would follow them and build a new life for them all. She could hardly remember those days when they still had hope and dreams.

The children racing the truck were too far away for their shouts to be audible, but a game was most definitely on. The peddler shifted gears again and picked up more speed. Jack hung on, Cassandra waved with both arms. She got into the spirit of things, even turned to Mimi and raised her arm, making her wave. Cassandra knew the children from previous visits. The peddler's arrival was always an excitement for them. For security reasons, few callers were allowed on the estate and the entire household and their FBI minders felt the strain of seclusion, no matter how comfortable it was. Now the children would have another refugee from Hitler like themselves as a playmate. This was a real event.

The truck stopped in the cobbled courtyard long before the children arrived. A nine-year-old child could hardly expect to understand the power that places can exert upon a life, but Beechtrees and its whole ambience exercised a comforting power over Mimi. The displaced child felt a sense of security, of belonging. With every minute that passed she gained confidence in herself and her future. She climbed down from the cab to stand next to the peddler, her few possessions spread on the cobblestones next to her. She was ready to confront fate with more hope of happiness than she had expected.

"Cassandra, go tell the cook we're here."

Cook was a large, soft-looking woman in her thirties with kindly eyes, a downy lip, a sharp tongue. She could be a hard taskmaster. A blubbering string of assistants who had left could attest to that. Although Cassandra liked her, she did not envy Mimi having to work for cook. She was from Czechoslovakia, like Mimi, fluent in French, and with Polish learned from a long-forgotten husband. Her English was practically nil. She detested America, Beechtrees, and being in exile. But she loved every one of the royal family she cooked for. And so there she remained, a part of their lives, a significant member of their household. And willing, with many reservations but on the peddler's recommendation, to save a life and get some help in her kitchen. A week's probation, that was all she had promised, and even then Her Highness and the children would have to approve the child as a fit playmate. But the peddler had paid no attention to that condition. He was sure that Mimi, once seen, would not be turned away.

Cook arrived in the courtyard almost simultaneously with the Queen. As one, sovereign and cook granted audience first to the peddler and then to Mimi. It was not difficult to understand why the Queen was so beloved of her people. She was a down-to-earth, courageous and generous soul who had governed with a sympathetic and caring hand. Though now in exile, she would rather have faced the occupation of her country and remained with her people. Prudence and diplomacy, an inability to be the puppet of so evil a regime, made her no less a refugee than the child standing in front of her. More illustrious, a wealthier refugee (she was known to be one of the wealthiest women in the world) but in exile from her home and her people, just like little Mimi.

More often than not she shopped at the truck with cook. She unaffectedly played the housewife in her unpretentious cotton dresses, usually with a scarf around her hair. She appeared to enjoy very much the role of country lady and family on holiday in the Berkshires.

Mimi had no idea what the two women had expected, or indeed what the peddler had told them. But whatever it was, they were not prepared for her. Though they tried to hide it, surprise was evident in their eyes. Mimi, for all her certainty that fate had at last dealt her a better hand, was full of anxiety. Unconsciously she joined her hands and began wringing them as she made her curtsy. Mashinka's instructions had been automatically put into effect. It was quite obvious that the two women were distressed by the condition of the beautiful child standing before them, and by her plight. They spoke to Mimi, giving the child reassurance that she would be happy here. They were interrupted by the royal children who swooped down on Mimi as if she were some long-lost friend. They appeared to be pulling her in five different directions, wanting to show her everything at once.

Cook insisted they first pick up her belongings and show her to her room: a small, sparsely furnished, very clean room, just off the kitchen. Two windows overlooked the courtyard and the stables. The eldest boy of about fifteen dropped her suitcase on the bed. She barely had time to admire the window-boxes filled with a profusion of summer flowers at their best before they pulled her from the room and out to play. Play meant first climbing all over the peddler's truck, in and out of the cab, to help Cassandra weigh the onions and potatoes, to insist that peaches, plums, some grapes be purchased. A tour of Beechtrees, they told her, was to be given after family tea on the lawn.

Mimi was lost to her peddler-benefactor long before he took down the galvanized metal scale, freshened his more fragile load with blocks of ice from Beechtrees' ice-house, pushed up the tailgate, and had his cup of coffee with the cook. But not so lost that, when Cassandra climbed into the truck's cab and the peddler leaned in to it to honk his horn several times, announcing their departure, she didn't run back with the children to say her farewells. They had been speaking in French, but said goodbye to the peddler in English. When cook called them to her, they obeyed, watching as Mimi said farewell. Mimi and the peddler spoke, as they always did, in Polish.

"You be good," he told her. "Remember, you must work hard for cook. I'll see you next week. And I will bring you news of Mashinka. But don't expect good news. You know how sick she is, what she told you about going to heaven to meet Tatayana. This is home for you now. Cook will take care of you. You have friends to play with, a school, a beautiful place to live. You'll be happy here."

"I will be happy here, Mr. Joe. But who will talk about the old country with you, the way Mashinka and I did? Who will read us those wonderful stories from *The Forward* by Mr. Singer? You will be lonely without us."

Cassandra watched her father pull Mimi toward him and pat her on the head. There was affection in that action. And what would she have thought had she known that he was fighting back a sense of loss? The child and Mashinka had afforded him companionship.

"No, not lonely. But just like you, a naturalized American citizen who should forget about the old country, give up the old ways, become more American, *be* more American. You have to learn from any Americans who come your way. This is the most wonderful country in the world. The Blocks was no place for you. Hard it will be, but you can do it. Mimi, I have to go. Here." He peeled off five one-dollar bank notes from a wad of bills and shoved them into her hand. "Put this away, a present. It's always good to have a little money in your pocket. If cook doesn't offer you pocket money, you come and tell me. You understand? Now go and play. Too long it is since you had children to play with. I don't say you have to be happy, Mimi, but at least enjoy yourself."

He left her standing there and climbed into the cab. Jack stood on the running board to ride with them back to his post. Cook called Mimi to her. The child hesitated, but when the motor burst into life, walked slowly back to join cook and the children. The peddler made a wide arc in the courtyard with his truck. Mimi watched it lumber away. It had gone only a few yards when she charged after it. Running alongside the truck, tears streaming down her cheeks, she called out in English, "I'll always remember, Mr. Joe."

The peddler did not slow down, never looked back. Cassandra did. She leaned out of her window and watched the girl chase after the truck, the other children not far behind her. Mimi stopped only when she was no longer able to run, the dust from the road rising up around her skinny legs. The children caught up with her and watched the truck disappear down the road. Cassandra felt at that moment that she might never see Mimi again. She felt a sense of relief, but also a need to acknowledge her, to bid her Godspeed. Cassandra waved and kept waving until, at last, the children responded to her frantic appeal and all waved back.

No amount of comfort, kindness, time, could dissolve that feeling of separateness Mimi felt as a displaced person. It showed in her eyes, even as the smile came back into them. Those things that made her life sweeter were fast becoming a solid foundation to build on. They acted like scar tissue over a wound. But the scar remained. No matter how faint, it remained. And for a nine-year-old constantly blocking out the pain of too many traumatic losses sustained in a young life, for a child made wise beyond her years, Mimi was doing just fine at Beechtrees. She had cultivated the ability to live from moment to moment and to expect nothing to last.

The family, their cook, and every other person in service at Beechtrees, even the FBI men, all swept her swiftly into their world, filling every minute of her waking hours. The children: Juliet, almost the same age as Mimi; Pierre, twelve; Maximillian, fifteen, gathered her to them as a new toy to be played with. They sensed at once her hunger, her need to belong, her separateness. Right from that moment in the courtyard when they had first set eyes on her, it had been so evident as to have overwhelmed the children without their even realizing what it was that drew them so quickly to her. Mimi inspired instant love, that appeared to answer deep needs within her benefactors as well as herself. So strong were they that all barriers crumbled. Mimi experienced friendship and family, laughter, caring and comfort. Eagerly she lapped it all up.

She was graceful and agile in both body and mind, and very female, with a seductive personality that vied with a certain remoteness that intrigued. Her sense of self was strong but confused. So she was unaware of being a nine-year-old femme fatale, or anything else. She had, too, a generous spirit, and gave whatever of herself she could, making it easy for her benefactors to gather her to their bosom, this strong-willed child. She rose at five in the morning to work in the kitchens until eight o'clock, when she joined the children's world of school and play. Then she would return to the kitchens and the cook to work from six in the evening until bedtime.

In a matter of days it became obvious to everyone that Mimi was not the child they had thought they were taking into their home. This could not be the offspring of an alcoholic Polish peasant woman, who was dying of liver cancer, leaving her a penniless orphan—which was what the peddler had told them she was. But no matter how discreetly they probed, Mimi maintained this version of her background. There were her American naturalization papers to confirm it.

The family's affection for their scullery maid and intermittent playmate was as strong as her pride. Had she had a better background and had not been a kitchen worker she would, at the very least, have been adopted as a companion or surrogate sister for Juliet.

Several weeks after her arrival the peddler was approached by the Queen. They conferred at a distance from the truck and Mimi and the children. The Queen came immediately to the point. "Have you told us all you know about Mimi and her background, Mr. Pauley?"

"Yes, ma'am. All that they would admit to, ma'am."

"Ah. Then you suspect there is more to Mimi's story? I think you had better first tell me all that you know for fact, Mr. Pauley."

"There is not much, ma'am. I knew the brother for years, a worker in the wire mill in Chicopee. I used to leave his order at the door every week, he'd pay me once a month. He never mixed with his neighbors. He was a solitary man, a drunk, though a good worker, never missed a day. But he wasn't a nice man. He could be mean when he was drunk. Then he tells me his two sisters are coming to live with him, and a niece. I should call in to them and give them what they want. So I do. And that's the story he told, and that's what they stuck to. In all the years I know them, they never changed it."

"But you never believed it, Mr. Pauley?"

"No, ma'am. You see, they was all afraid. They, like the brother, never went out, never mixed with the neighbors. They thought they were too good to live in such a place, among such common people. I used to buy most everything for them and bring it in. That's how I got to know them so well. They needed a doctor, I sent the doctor. A funeral, I sent the undertaker.

"I knew one thing for sure—the two women were not sisters. Impossible. One had Russian blood in her, I am sure of it, and was very educated, very sensitive, delicate in her looks and ways. The other was Polish, from peasant stock. I know, our villages were not very far apart near Bialistock. At the beginning, when they had more money, it was easier for them. They would sometimes leave the Blocks for a day. But that didn't last long. Tatayana, the teacher, could not adjust to the life they had there. She used to say, 'If the Count knew, oh, God above, if the Count knew.' And Mashinka, who turned into a worse drunkard than her brother, used sometimes to whisper to me, 'My brother lied. We thought he was a rich man with a house with many rooms, educated, running a business.' I suppose that was what he wrote to the old country. Wanted to be a big shot. Some big shot! A drunkard, that's all he was."

"The Count? Mr. Pauley, what did that mean, do you think?"

"I don't know, ma'am, it could mean anything. I know only that as time passed they all grew more strange and reclusive, never left the house. Mashinka used to say it was because they didn't belong there, Mimi was too good to play with the children of the Blocks. After Tatayana died, Mashinka went to pieces altogether. Only drink and keeping Mimi safe mattered to her, and that one day Mimi's father should come and find them. Many times I asked Mimi about her father. Never would she talk about him. All she would tell me was that after the war he would come for them."

"Mimi will not talk to us at all about herself," said the Queen pensively.

"Maybe some day. I know her for years now, and she seems a different child here. She belongs here, among people. Who knows? Maybe when she's not so afraid and miserable. I have to go, ma'am. I'm running late."

The Queen watched the truck roll away, the children racing against its speed. She kept her eyes on a now healthier-looking Mimi, a more nourished child, with color to her skin, wearing one of Juliet's hand-me-downs. The white cotton gloves covered the chapped, not-yet-healed hands. Her heart ached, not just for Mimi but for the hundreds of thousands of displaced children Hitler and his murderous war had produced. Mimi in fact was a lucky one: sanctuary was rare. They would be her first priority on her return to her country. To heal them, to help them find their parents, or at the very least new homes. Not often did this sovereign without a country succumb to despair, but the sight of one child saved among thousands brought hopelessness momentarily closer. The war was not going well, Hitler was devouring Europe, pulverizing England. One day she would return. But when, dear God, she thought, when? And to what? In time she pulled herself together, placed her hands for a few seconds over her face, took a deep breath and called the children to tea.

Each day of those first few months at Beechtrees, Mimi was strengthened by the changes she was experiencing. The paranoia instilled in her by Mashinka, Tatayana, and her father, to ensure her safety away from a war-torn Europe, was quickly vanishing. Almost as if it had died along with Mashinka. What was surfacing in its place was a Mimi less afraid to remember who she was, where she had come from to America and her ugly, unhappy life in the Blocks. Her uncertainty about who she was slowly dissolved along with her fear of being discovered.

The family was Roman Catholic and devout. One of the dilapidated round stone pavilions on the east lawn served as a makeshift chapel. Makeshift but ornate—it was hung in red and royal blue silk, and had several golden candelabra. On its gold embroidered altar cloth stood a jewel-encrusted cross. A stone statue of the Virgin Mary, always surrounded with fresh flowers, had been brought with them from their fallen country. It was the focus of the serenity and power that dominated God's little acre here. It had been consecrated by a visiting cardinal who traveled for the ceremony from New York, and who returned often to comfort the exiles. Every Sunday a mass was celebrated and confessions heard, and everyone on the estate attended, no matter what their faith, to pray for peace. Every day, each member of the family made a visit to the chapel: their faith encouraged it and adversity demanded it.

One day Mimi was taking a shortcut to bring a basket of cakes from cook to Jack and Ernie when she saw the Queen emerge from the chapel. You might not have called her a beautiful woman, but something about her transcended physical beauty, something that seemed to Mimi very powerful. Her kindness? Her goodness? And there was too, for all her simplicity, an unmistakable grandeur. It wasn't often the girl saw her alone. Today, something attracted Mimi to her. She walked through the falling leaves under the afternoon sun and watched her benefactress sit down on the top step of the pavilion-chapel as if waiting for Mimi to join her. They smiled. Mimi sat on the bottom step and looked up at her.

"What a lovely autumn day, Mimi."

"Yes, ma'am," Mimi answered her. They remained silent for some minutes, the Queen looking out across the parkland and enjoying the sun on her face, the peace and quiet, and the presence of this charming child. Mimi did not take her eyes from the woman. The Queen realized how close they had become. She raised Mimi's hand and removed the white cotton glove. She caressed the hand, turned it over, and taking a pair of eyeglasses from her pocket looked at it.

"Oh, Mimi, your hand is looking so good. Soon, maybe even in a few days, you won't have to put on the ointment or wear your white gloves. Only in the kitchen, to keep them pretty and smooth." She turned the small hand over in hers again and remarked, "Mimi, you have the hand of a lady. Somehow I don't think it was meant to be a worker's hand. I think you have the hands of an artist, a pianist . . . yes, maybe you have musical hands." She replaced the glove on the child's hand.

"I was born in Prague. And our house had a family chapel, too. Would you like to see it? If you would, I could show you my pictures."

And that was the breakthrough they had all been waiting for. Once Mimi had spoken of the chapel in Prague, she was able to put the pieces of her life together for herself and the family. She continued on her way to deliver her basket to Jack and Ernie at the gate, once she and the Queen had decided that she should bring her pictures to tea for everyone to see.

At the gate the two men greeted her and she told them all the news of what was happening at the house. She asked, "Jack, you keep telling us, 'The FBI always gets its man.' Is it true?"

"That's right, Mimi."

"You never miss?"

"Never. We may not get him right away, but we never give up. We always get our man. Just like I said."

"Then you could find my father?"

They might not know the details, but the agents were not

insensitive to what this child had been through. They had seen every day the changes in her. They sensed this was an enormous thing she had come to do, asking them to find her father. Jack and Ernie looked at each other. Then Jack, who was sitting on an old wooden chair, called her to him. Placing an arm around her, he told her. "Yes, but ... er ... you would have to give us all the information you have about him, and then time to get everything ready for our search. Can you do that?"

They saw the hesitation in her face. Then she nodded. And for the first time since they met Mimi, she smiled for them. She smiled, and they worried. They had remembered the "dead or alive" part of the FBI formula. The man they eventually got was as likely to be dead as alive. It was something they had not stressed in their lighthearted boasting to the children.

Chapter 3

He was handsome, tall and slender. His dark hair was worn maybe too long for a military man. He had enormously sexy, violet-colored eyes, the more so for their hooded lids, shape and the ever-so-slight slant to the way they were set. Bedroom eyes that simply devoured women. Everything about his square-shaped face complemented everything else. The Roman nose, the high cheekbones and sensuous lips, the cleft in the chin. The body spoke to women and his every action, when centered on a woman, was a promise of lust, sexual delights, a possibility of love.

He cut a dashing, romantic figure in uniform. An officer and a gentleman. Provenance: one of those occupied foreign countries Americans hardly knew existed before Hitler had their populations heil-ing him in terror, recipients of the vague charity of high-society war-relief balls in New York.

He stood with Gertrude Lawrence and a sleekly-uniformed Clark Gable, the more handsome and exciting for belonging to real life, not some movie. A matinee idol stepped down from the silver screen for the duration of the war. The party—several colonels, a brigadier general, a much too pretty WAC officer, and a scattering of luscious ladies in elegant gowns or smart little black silk dresses, sporting tiny, teasing cocktail hats with fetchingly seductive veils just covering the eyes—glittered with vivacity like spectacular jewels.

They were only one of the parties in the five-deep crush of beautiful people laughing, flirting, drinking at the bar in the Stork Club, awaiting a table. The room rang with chatter, a humming energy, much glamor and bravado, an intense excitement befitting heroes bent on a victory over evil. St. George targeted on the old Teutonic dragon. The kind of extreme passion to live, laugh and love that occurs in a capital city in wartime, free for the moment from the fray and destruction. Hardly a man in the room was out of uniform: the vibrancy of military power added a frisson of danger held in check. Mostly high-ranking officers from all the services, managing to forget war and their fragmented lives for a few hours, to make contact, find a place for themselves in a city where it was impossible to locate a hotel room, a restaurant, a lady not already taken. New Year's Eve, New York City. The dying hours of 1943.

Barbara Dunmellyn was a tall, willowy blonde with the looks of a showgirl: wealthy, very New York Upper Fifth Avenue chic, cultivated and intelligent. Not the usual credentials for a Smith graduate with aspirations to be a great American painter. She had been standing for some time searching the sea of people for her uncle's party before she spotted the man and labeled him a lady-killer. She could not, for all the noise and shoving of the crowd, stop staring across the room at him. He had a magnetic quality that was relentlessly drawing her to him. She must get closer, know what it would be like to feel his lips upon hers, be caressed by such a man, devoured by him.

She was not alone in her carnal lust for Count Karel Stefanik. Were not two beauties already in thrall of him? She watched him flirt, amusement in his eyes as he played with the women. She was jealous. It was mad, insane, but there it was. She wanted him, and for no other woman to have him. She tried in vain to keep herself in check.

He hadn't as yet seen her. For him she didn't even exist, but she was in love. She tried to rationalize such madness. Impossible. The men in her life usually fell wildly in love with *her*. She didn't much like this reversal of roles. She was a woman accustomed to control her relationships with her men, the lovers who lost themselves to her. She had a penchant for great men who somehow continued to cross her path, men of letters, passionate, sensual men. Men of genius and power, with legendary purpose in life. She was attracted to nothing less.

Barbara Dunmellyn was an enchantress who knew how to tame men like that, and, once tamed, was clever enough to keep them. Men adored her for that rare combination in women: beauty, courage, unselfconscious sexual passion, a finely developed creative soul, a fiercely intelligent mind, an ability to subordinate herself to them without losing herself. She was a woman with whom heroic men of genius fell fatally in love. Such men for her were an aphrodisiac, a necessary drug.

Once in love, she was capable of great sacrifice. The sacrifice of self. She enjoyed loving men, being part of a man's life—especially a demanding man with greater talents than her own, someone of enormous ambition, mesmerizing power, destined for monumental success. A man who might change the world, make history. She enjoyed playing second fiddle to such men and paying homage to that something special that heroes have. Her unswerving interest in her lovers and their work bound them to her. Such men are seldom immune to the flattering attention of a beautiful woman.

They were like fodder to her. Imperceptibly she devoured them. They were what nourished her own, very private, creative impulse. Her lovers reaped many rewards from loving Barbara, none greater than the brief glimpses afforded of her soul. She never allowed more. She was an egocentric and yet self-sacrificing woman, who could be capricious yet fiercely devoted. Men loved her for that, and for her never being shrewd or reckless in her relationship with them. She was as ruthlessly honest in love as she was in all aspects of her life and work.

When she fell out of that state of being in love, she found herself again. A stronger self that quickly moved on. She was a heart-breaker, and she sensed, when her eyes met those of the handsome mesmeric figure across the tense hedonism of that room, that she had met her match. Maybe even her destiny.

Someone pushed against her. An accident. One she was grateful for. It broke the spell, jolted her into making a move. But she had hardly made any headway through the crush of people when Sherman Billingsly, the owner-host of the Stork Club, New York's most famous, elitist nightclub, spotted her. Pushing his way through the revelers, he greeted her, took her by the arm, cut a path through the crowd and delivered her to her uncle, the brigadier general, now talking to the man she wanted.

He took her hand in his, lowered his head to place his lips upon it. It was more than a courtly kiss, that first grazing of his lips on her skin. She felt a shiver of pleasure. It made her smile. His eyes, by the smile they returned, showed that he understood the erotic interest he had aroused in her. Their introduction by the brigadier was brief, hardly audible against the din of laughter and chatter. She didn't catch the man's name before she was swept away from him and into a greeting from Clark Gable.

She accepted a glass of champagne, let herself be dazzled by his open, sexy smile, the Gable dimples—and not for the first time. Gable and her uncle were long-time hunting buddies. Now they were sharing a war. Clark and Barbara had met on several occasions. Theirs was always a ten-minute flirtation, nothing more. Tonight, in the crush of revelers eagerly bent on seeing out the old year, her flirtation with cinema's current male icon appeared to be just what was needed to buoy her up. It was she, Barbara Dunmellyn, who made the first move on Count Karel Stefanik.

At just the right moment she turned from Gable to Gertrude Lawrence, the brigadier's close friend, the charming and glamorous singing star of London's West End and New York's Broadway, who had the Count captivated by her seductive charisma. She intruded upon them by planting a kiss on Miss Lawrence's cheek.

"Happy New Year, Gertie."

"Barbara!" The star, delighted to see her, returned the kiss.

"You can't have him, Gertie, he's mine," Barbara whispered in the lady's ear. Then she made a gesture: a shrug of her shoulders, the raising of her hands as if to the gods. Insinuating that it was beyond her control, that fate, or some god indeed, had ordained it. She quickly slipped her arm through Karel Stefanik's and gazed into his eyes, ensuring that her gaze transmitted the intensity of her need for him.

He removed the glass from her hand and placed it with his on the bar. Then, never taking his eyes from hers, he disengaged himself from her. They were apart for only a few seconds before he pulled her slowly toward him, savoring every nuance of taking control, drawing her into an embrace. She was surprised by his strength, his fingers biting into the flesh of her arms. Their bodies touched. His first words to her were, "This cannot be a love story. There will be only a beginning, no middle and no end. I don't want to deceive you about that."

It was a deep rich voice, his English perfect but graced with a foreign accent, sensual, with seductive, honeyed overtones. Not quite a French accent, nor one as soft as Portuguese: something in between, impossible to place because of an occasional guttural sound. It was the accent of a man who spoke several languages fluently. There was, too, a sexual undercurrent in every word of warning he uttered.

This was not the man she had expected to encounter when she fell in love with him across a crowded bar. Barbara Dunmellyn was not the sort of woman to steep herself in an obsessive affair, certainly not interested in unrequited love. She had to admire his astuteness in knowing that she expected love. No, not expected, demanded love from her men. This was no mere warning that she wasn't going to get it from him. Nor was it made as a teasing ploy in the game of seduction so congenial to certain men. This was a statement of fact. And something else. A message: I'm yours, sexually yours, for as long as it lasts. I want you in just the same way as you want me.

That was quite a message, and one rarely spelled out so directly even now, two years after Pearl Harbor. Barbara mused on the idea that this was 1943, and things a great deal different from before the war when American sex was for the most part still dressed up as love. Wartime excused promiscuity, the fulfillment of sexual needs and attractions. These days there was an immediacy that placed courtship on the back burner of life. Romance of the moment, rather than love, was the order of the night. Pent-up erotic passion expressed itself in relationships never meant to last. They had become acceptable, indispensable even, at least for the duration of the war.

"Are you so sure about this?" she asked him.

He touched her long, blonde hair, held some of the silky tresses in his hand and, bringing them to his lips, kissed them. "Quite certain."

The intimate gesture sent a shiver of erotic delight through her. It changed him from stranger to lover. No matter his declaration that they would never be a love story. One brief moment in their lifetime: she could live with that, if he could.

She was mesmerized by him. It was a fight against submission to his magnetic charm. But Barbara Dunmellyn was strong, as strong a girl as he was a man. She won her brief but intense fight against his becoming an obsession. She stood up to the reality of the situation he had created. She told him, "I'm different from the other women you make that speech to. I'll not succumb to you in a lie, as I am sure most of them do when they tell you they accept you on those terms."

They were jostled by a passing woman, a beauty. She apologized to them. Barbara caught the flirtatious look she gave Karel Stefanik. The time, the place, the night, inspired flirtations. They were running through the crowded bar like wildfire. They way he assessed the woman did not go unnoticed by Barbara. It told her something about him. He was a lover of women. He had the kind of adoration for them that the most exciting womanizers have. It was the eroticism, the physicality of women, that excited him; the way the female mind worked through the body. It was his passion for women that made him so attractive, quite apart from his sensual good looks, his very special persona. He confirmed what she was thinking when he reacted to the newcomer by pulling Barbara even closer to him. "You have a far more sensual beauty than she does. And you feel right in my arms," he whispered.

"Let's go somewhere where we can dance. I bet you're a hell of a dancer," she suggested with a seductive smile.

"But what about Miss Lawrence's party? Surely we can dance there?"

"I know a better place."

"We are expected." He grazed her cheek with the back of his hand. "But I don't always do what is expected of me."

"I am quite certain of that," she assured him, and accorded him a knowing smile.

"I'll take care of it."

She saw him make his way past several people to talk to Gertrude Lawrence and the brigadier, and watched him kissing Miss Lawrence's hand. It was only a few seconds before they looked over at her. The brigadier waved, Miss Lawrence threw a kiss.

The doorman apologized for the shortage of taxis, but assured them that cabs were arriving spasmodically with new revelers. Why didn't they wait in the bar until the several couples before them were accommodated? "An hour should do it, sir," he told the Count. Barbara and Karel eyed each other, and there was an urgency in the look that passed between them. "We won't wait," she told the doorman. He put on his cap and pushed the door open for them.

They stepped into the crisp cold air. Gusts of wind with the promise of snow in them swept down the street and swirled around them. They stood under the canopy for a few minutes watching couples wrapped in finery braving the elements to make their destinations before the New Year was rung in. Even in the dark street, in the cold, there was that special kind of gaiety that New York always generates over the Christmas holidays, with its passion for dressing up in silver tinsel, golden snowflakes and red ribbon, forests of pine and spruce cut into miles of Christmas boughs and trees.

"It's not all that far. We can walk it," she assured him.

They stood looking at each other for several minutes, seemingly unable to go forward into the night. That thing that can sometimes happen to two strangers who have become intimate before they have become friends. In those few minutes they were able to come to terms with that. It had not been possible in the crush of people all around them in the Stork Club.

He wore no hat; his overcoat, a military affair with wide lapels and a belt dangling through the loops, was worn over his shoulders. He looked to Barbara even more charismatically attractive than when she had first seen him. Standing away from the crowd, there was about him that winning combination to be found in some men: hardness, a macho toughness, sensitivity, softness. He cut a romantic figure not only because of his sensual, mature good looks and magnetic charm, but because there was, too, an intelligent, complex personality there. It was all in the face, the way he carried himself. He was a man with a secret. A man of mystery. That was as obvious to Barbara as his good looks and the promise of sexual bliss he insinuated. The lust in his eyes told her at least that much about him. She believed what she saw in his eyes, what he had told her. She would always believe what he said.

Barbara was not exactly dressed for a winter night in her gunmetal gray silk taffeta. A gown cut on the bias with string-like slip-straps over the shoulders. A glamorous evening dress that accentuated the fullness of her breasts, the long slender torso, small waist, slim hips. She wore white gardenias in her hair, and no jewelry. Her fashionable waist-length silver fox jacket lay open. He reached out and pulled both the jacket closed and her into his arms. He held her there and moved his hands down her back to caress her full, rounded bottom. "You're not dressed for this cold night." He removed his hands to take her face in them, caressed it, and kissed her on the lips. It was a kiss that built slowly into passion. A kiss that lit a fire in her.

"Where do we go from here?" he asked.

She knew that was a loaded question. But she was too warmed by the fire he instilled in her and the sensual sound of his voice to be bothered with some trite, teasing answer. "Dancing. I am going to take you dancing. You do like dancing?"

"Very much."

"But not at Gertie's or a club where I will have to share you with a lot of strangers, making merry and waxing sentimental over the end of a dreadful year. I know the perfect place where we can dance and dine, and where we can make love."

She enjoyed the pleasure she gave him with her suggestion. It showed in his face, in a smile that inspired her to touch his face with the back of her hand. He took it in his own and brought it to meet his lips. It was she who felt the urgency, she who broke the spell when she took him by the hand and started running up the street. He struggled into his coat as best he could while on the run. When they turned the corner on to Fifth Avenue she slowed down and flung her arms around his neck. After turning his collar up against the wind, she gave him a wildly passionate kiss.

All her life she would remember how he threw back his head and laughed. It was a kind of joyous expression of pure pleasure. He placed his hands on her hips and lifted her off the pavement and swung her in a circle several times. When he placed her down again, he told her before he took her hand in his and they half-ran, half-walked up Fifth Avenue, "Tonight we forget the war, the world. We'll be selfish for each other and our erotic dreams. We'll live as all great lovers do, to satisfy our hungry hearts."

For blocks they rushed on, only to stop suddenly for a kiss, a look, a hug, then raced on again to their destination. The night was crisp and cold, and the wind now carried large, fluffy snowflakes that fell to the ground and vanished, leaving the pavement wet and the lamplight like so many moons shining up at them from it. Several times Karel broke away from her to try to catch a taxi. Impossible. They didn't care.

The Avenue, the night and New Year's Eve were working a kind of magic on them. In that dash up Fifth they were accomplishing miracles. A closeness, a kind of loving and admiration, a certain togetherness that usually comes to lovers with time. But they knew there was no time for them so time became irrelevant for Barbara and Karel.

Near the Sherry Netherlands an old woman selling flowers, bunches of violets tied with red ribbons, huddled in a doorway. He bought Barbara a bunch of violets. They were the color of his eyes. They rushed on past the Pierre, but not before he crushed her against the stone façade of the hotel. He tried to pick the snowflakes from her hair. He tilted her face up. The light from the lamppost played upon it. He studied it. She shivered from the cold, and he pulled her roughly into his arms and kissed her. He bit hard into her cold lips and sucked on them. She savored the warmth of his mouth. He found her tongue: passion burned bright for them in that kiss. She returned it by biting even harder into his lips. She was more hungry for him than even she had realized.

She gathered her skirts up above her ankles now, as they hurried through the now-settling snow. Her satin pumps, stained with wet, stuck to her ice-cold feet, and she seemed almost to hop from one foot to the other as she ran.

"How far?" he called.

"Just there. And it's a good thing. My feet are so cold I can hardly feel them."

It was only a few yards. He scooped her up off her feet and into his arms. The doorman rushed to open the door and then through the walnut-paneled entrance hall to put a key in the private elevator that went directly up into Barbara Dunmellyn's penthouse flat.

Karel placed her on her feet and they were immediately overwhelmed by the warmth of the overheated lobby. She shivered and he placed an arm around her shoulders. They walked toward the now open elevator and the doorman standing at attention next to it.

"Happy New Year, Miss Dunmellyn. And you, sir."

"Happy New Year," they chorused in reply. Barbara reached for the doorman's hand and shook it, Karel followed suit, and they realized as they entered the elevator that they did feel happy. Very happy. And on such a night: New Year's Eve, which they both usually dreaded for its false *bonhomie,* and most especially this 1943 war-torn one, dreaded for so many public and personal reasons.

The doors slid closed and Barbara turned the key. The elevator carried them upward. The heat, the quiet, except for the dull hum of its motors, seemed to sober them up. Karel opened his coat. She slipped out of her wet shoes. He reached for her hand, she ran her fingers through his hair and leaned in against him and licked the cleft in his chin with the point of her tongue. He closed his eyes for a few seconds, and she reached up and kissed first one, then the other. She stepped away from him, just enough to give him an adoring smile certain to melt any man's heart.

Noiselessly the doors opened and they were greeted by a middle-aged Chinese man wearing gray pin-stripe trousers and a white jacket. "Lee, we've come home to dance in the New Year." There was a surprised look on Barbara's houseman's face. She began to laugh as he helped her out of her jacket.

"And why are you still here? You should be long gone to your own celebrations."

"I'm on my way," he answered. "I was just putting the last touches to your New Year's Day dinner."

"Lee this is . . ." She flushed with embarrassment.

He came to her rescue. "Karel Stefanik. Happy New Year, Lee."

"Happy New Year to you, sir." Lee helped Karel off with his overcoat.

They were standing in the entrance hall, a balcony several steps above the vast sunken living room. Half a dozen French windows overlooked Central Park where it was fringed with a haze of light shimmering through the snow showers from the surrounding buildings. The room was bathed in soft warm light from ivory-colored silk lampshades dotted around it. Karel leaned on the rail of the white marble balustrade and surveyed the room. It had the kind of cosmopolitan chic he had never seen before. She slipped her arm around his waist and they looked at each other. "You're not surprised?"

"No, more pleased than surprised."

"Then you like it?"

"Very much."

Now they surveyed it together and watched Lee put a taper to the open fires laid in the pair of impressive white marble fireplaces at each end of the room. The folded tissue paper and kindling burst into fire. Bright orange flames flared up and caught the pinecones and applewood logs. In the dimly lit room the pink glow of the flames danced in reflection in the windowpanes.

Ching Lee turned on another lamp, only to be told by Barbara, "No, Lee, no more light, thank you." She all but skipped down the stairs, pulling Karel behind her and walked him to the windows overlooking the park.

"There, I give you New York."

She left him standing at the window admiring the spectacular view and walked to the far side of the room to warm herself by one of the now blazing fires. She watched him walk from the window around the room, taking it all in.

"And the most warm and perfect ballroom for two."

He smiled at her from across the room before he bent down to take in better the sweet fragrance of white lilacs from one of the many bouquets of spring flowers. It was on the tip of his tongue to say, "New York steams in the luxury of central heating while London burns and Prague freezes." But he quickly wiped the thought from his mind. It sounded too bitter, too crass. Had he not promised her for their time together to forget the world and its wars? He knew what their hearts hungered for. Karel felt a surge of sensual pleasure while looking at her. She was an erotic, sublimely exciting woman. He liked her the more for not concealing the voracious appetite she had for him. He was filled with admiration for her and the ambience with which she surrounded herself.

Persian carpets of great age lying on a dark polished wooden floor. Seventeenth-century Chinese lacquered cabinets, French and Italian silver-gilded consoles with sumptuous marble tops, bronze and silver gilt candelabra and Venetian wing chairs. Chinese Chippendale sofas, and deep, comfortable, tapestry-covered French chairs with elegantly curved walnut arms and legs, all of the same period. Tables, Directoire, of ormolu birds, whose spread wings carried upon them circular tops of luscious black marble. Roman and Greek bronzes sat comfortably on them. A life-size ballerina cast in bronze by Degas and a Rodin male torso stood on black marble pedestals near the windows. The splendid draperies and cushions and walls were covered with white silk damask. Paintings alone splashed color about the room. Soutines, De Chiricos, Picassos and Braques, a Seurat, several large Matisses and Gauguins in ornate carved and gilded frames.

They were hauntingly exciting and beautiful in the dim light. They turned the comfortable, luxurious room into an island of creative energy. A room of fabulous passionate paintings, works of art that set the senses aflame. He looked again at Barbara and wondered what lay behind this very sexy lady, this privileged young woman who surrounded herself with a world of high art, and the illusion that the world was a place of tranquillity and beauty.

He listened to her giving Ching Lee instructions, but heard nothing. He was distracted by the way she kept her eyes fixed on him. He could feel Barbara giving herself to him, willing herself into his psyche, stripping him down to his naked self, setting him free. He was flattered by her desire for him to take her into an erotic world where they could lose themselves in lust. The firelight reflected on the silk taffeta of her gown. The glow seemed to accentuate even more her magnificence, a body that yearned to be tamed by him, that he would make his own.

She lit two tapers and handed him one and they walked through the room lighting dozens of candles and switching off the lamplight. They danced to the music of the big bands—Glenn Miller, Guy Lombardo—before they broke off to dine at the table Lee placed in front of the fire. He served them champagne and caviar, sizzling crispy duck in a black cherry sauce, mangetout, potato puffs. Then he discreetly vanished.

Chapter 4

Over dinner they did not speak about themselves or the war. No personal or political small talk either. They spoke about sex, their erotic desires, their sexual fantasies. At one point he thought he might have gone too far in relating the pleasures of having two women, or of sexually enslaving a woman until she abandoned herself first to him and then to the bliss of sexual orgasms and beyond. At some point he asked her, "Do I shock you when I tell you that's the way I want you?"

"No. It excites me. That's where I want to be." He rose from his chair and removed his jacket. Circling the table he went to her and took her hand in his and helped her from the chair and into his arms. Together they chose more music to dance by: Jimmy Dorsey, Cole Porter, the piano of Eddie Duchin, the seductive voice of Billie Holiday. They hardly spoke to each other except with their bodies. It felt so good, so right, that dialogue.

Enveloped in his arms, Barbara felt him taking her over, herself slipping into a vortex of desire that was pulling her down and away from all the realities of life save sex. She kept pressing harder, always harder, against his body, as if she wanted to melt into oneness with Karel Stefanik, whoever that might be. His powerful presence had about it a kind of danger that excited her imagination. His silences—and then, when he did speak, the sensual voice—rubbed her raw with sexual innuendo. She visualized herself impaled upon his rigid cock. She closed her eyes, the better to keep hold of the pleasure she so acutely sensed from that vision. She came in a long and luxurious orgasm. He stopped dancing and tilted her chin up and smiled, and then he laughed. He sensed that she had come for the first time with him. Pleasure for her shone in his eyes. "And so here are our beginnings," he told her.

She licked his lips with her tongue, loosened the knot in his tie and slipped it slowly from around his neck. He removed his shirt: she ran her hands over his chest and kissed his nipples with a hunger he liked. He slipped the belt through the loops of his trousers and placed it in her hands. She watched him undress. When he stood naked before her she was surprised at how muscular he was, how broad in the shoulders. For all his slimness, he had a powerfully strong, robust body. A man in his late thirties, yet he had the body more of a man in his youthful prime. There was about him a virility that excited thoughts of debauched, depraved sex.

If she had surmised by her physical attraction to him that here was a libertine, now, seeing Karel standing naked before her in the candlelight, she was certain of it. Sexually he was better endowed than any man she had ever had: a knobbed penis, beautiful for being thick and long, a scrotum large and luscious-looking. He was a man to be admired naked as one would a Roman god carved in marble; a mature man cast in bronze like the Poseidon in Greece. A nude man of flesh and blood who was an Adonis, whose sexuality was as much a part of his life as breathing. Here was a man by whom to be made love to, worth giving oneself up for, with whom to explore the extremes of Eros, and pass into sexual oblivion. Such thoughts were thrilling but frightening, too. Dangerous. Like swimming with the sharks.

He hadn't touched her, and yet she knew there would be no holding back in the sex they would have together. That very thought excited her own sexual nature. And there was something else: the man standing before her, whom she hardly knew but to whom she was sexually committed, who had a powerful presence not only erotically but as a man, was subordinating her to him. That he should be able to do that was not only intriguing but thrilling to Barbara.

She crossed her arms in front of her and, bending down, raised her gown from the hem up and over her body, her head, and discarded it. As he reached out and straightened the white gardenias in her hair, plucked with one sharp tug the delicate, black lace panties from between her legs, he told her, "You're lovely. More than lovely, and very sexy."

That accent again. The voice, the look in his eyes: they made her tremble. When he roughly pulled her into his arms and caressed her body with searching hands, they touched, thigh to thigh, bosom to chest, skin to skin. She felt a sensation she had rarely known before, as if they were being scorched by each other.

He was tantalized by her breasts: heavy but firm and high, and fully round, capped by a nimbus as pale as a peach, with nipples thick, long and erect. They were raunchy breasts that begged to be handled by a man, sucked on. Provocative breasts that excited a man's passion. He held them in cupped hands, and caressed them, at first tenderly, and then the excitement was too great: tenderness turned to a rougher handling of them. They were breasts that demanded a mouth to suck hard on them, sexual ardor, the unbridling of a man's lust. He obliged her. Karel listened to her protestations of pleasure. Then his own urgency made him swoop her off her feet and into his arms. She placed her own arms around his neck and clung to him with her legs wrapped around him. He carried her thus toward the open log-fire while searching out that place between her legs where he wanted to be. Hungrily, he kissed her on the mouth while his fingers thrust unceremoniously deep inside her warm, moist slit. A sharp cry of pleasure escaped her. He caressed that place he knew from the moment she had approached him was to be his. "Lovely," he repeated again and again.

She watched him rise. The size and power of his erection took her breath away. She wanted to caress him with her hands and yearned to have him inside her mouth, her cunt, but was frightened by the very size and splendor of him. Her fear died, was killed by desire. She caressed the knob, folded her fingers around the pulsating organ. "No," he told her. It was an emphatic no. She retreated.

"I want to make love to you first. To pleasure you. Later. You can do what you want with me later," he told her in that honeyed voice of his.

He placed her on her feet and kissed her. Then he put his

fingers in her mouth, inviting, "Lick them, a taste of yourself." She licked her fingers, and then he kissed them. They walked together the remainder of the way to the far end of the room and the fireplace there. Now his kisses and caresses were more aggressive, incited by a need to get inside this woman and feel her to be his. While pulling her down with him on to the white marble hearth, he licked her with an eager tongue, kissed flesh with a hungry mouth. He sucked on her fingers and licked her wrists. She felt as if she were being devoured by him. He held her foot in his hand and kissed the arch, licked it, sucked on her toes, kissed her ankle, rose to the inside of her thighs.

On his knees between her legs now, he buried his face in her mound of silky blonde pubic hair. She was like an aphrodisiac for him. He spread her luscious long limbs as far apart as possible, the better to view her most intimate self. He reveled in her ripe femininity. Quite tenderly he raised those long shapely legs and placed them on his shoulders, then lowered his mouth to the cleft between them. He searched out her clitoris with his tongue to tease and tantalize it.

He was ruthless in his desire to give her pleasure. His was a rough and passionate sucking of her moist fleshy labia, those seductive outer lips of cunt. He bit into them and heard with pleasure her groans of ecstasy. He ravished her with his mouth. With deft fingers he wrenched open those lips and placed his tongue as deep as he could into the opening.

He found the taste of Barbara's now-repeating orgasms ambrosia. He felt her squeeze on his tongue with her cunt as she dug her long red fingernails into his back. She writhed with pleasure under his sexual generosity. She came with an orgasm so powerful that her body shuddered. So sublime was the sensation of this orgasm with him that she wanted it never to stop.

She asked him, "Take me. Please. I want your cock inside me, to feel it moving in and out of me. Fuck me, Karel." He held back. She begged.

"No," he told her. "Soon, sexy lady. Soon, glorious Barbara."

He left her only for a few minutes. When he returned he lay down next to her and gathered her in his arms, rocking her gently, and whispered in her ear, "Ours can never be a love story, but I will always love you for tonight, for your lasciviousness, because we share a lust and a sexual freedom that allows us our erotic fantasies and the courage to change them into realities. You're a luscious lady, Barbara, sublime."

She reached out to take his cock in her hand. He stopped her with a tap on her hand, a playful slap on her cheek, and sharper slaps across her breasts, interspersing the chastisement with passionate kisses. It was sexy, and he incited her to give in to him. She liked being enslaved by his sexuality. She told him in a husky voice, "Whatever you want, so long as I come, and we are together in our depravity."

He smiled. How quick she was to understand where he was taking her. How clever to show him she still retained command in their relationship. It excited his desire to tame her further, to break her down until she was his unconditionally.

He slipped out of her arms and on top of her. Holding her face in his hands while he rubbed her body slowly and seductively with his, he teased her into an ethereal state where she felt as if she were floating through twilight. The feel of his magnificent erect penis rubbing against her made her burn for him. He inched his way down her body with kisses, and was once again on his knees between her legs. They were now both lost to all else but erotic pleasure. She bit as hard as she could into the hand that held her chin. Then he sucked her tongue into his mouth with terrifying passion. She bit into his lips and drew a drop of blood. He laughed at her when, pushed into a violent state of passion, she went for him with the leather belt he had handed her when discarding his clothes. He felt the sting as it cracked across his hip and his buttock. He wrenched it from her hand. With one quick flick he whipped her across the breasts with it, then threw it across the room. Placing his mouth over one of her breasts he sucked on it so hard she called out in frenzied pain and passion. Then, squirming in his arms, she came.

He felt frantic with sexual ardor for her now, and grabbed some of the cushions scattered on the floor around them and propped them up under her. "So you can watch as well as feel." He reached for the silver jug of thick cream that he had fetched from the dining table when he had left her for those few minutes. Still lost somewhere in the aftermath of orgasm she had hardly recovered as she watched the cream dribble slowly from the jug in a thin trail around the nimbus of her breasts. With his fingers he spread it over them until she shone slippery smooth in his hands. He kneaded her breasts and licked them and kissed her: she tasted the cream and laughed, telling him, "How delicious. Crazy, sexy and delicious."

He dipped the jug and trickled a lazy stream of cream between her breasts, the flat of her belly, trailed it over her curly-haired mound. She watched him pour the sensual liquid into the cupped palm of his hand and bathe her cunt lips, her slit and her clitoris in the cream. She was slippery in his probing fingers. It was an exquisite sensation. He filled his hand again and pushed more easily inside her. "Use your cunt, Barbara. Suck in the cream," he ordered. He moved now easily in and out of her satiny cunt, stretching her more open as he went deeper in with his hand. Roughly, he raised her bottom. She felt him induce the remainder of the cream into her open and yearning vagina. She watched him fuck her wildly with his hand, and felt a painful thrust when he entered her up to his wrist. She screamed and came and nearly fainted. When she felt him caress the tip of her cervix with the cream and her come, she surrendered: she was his. She lost control and kept coming. She lay open and relaxed and ready for what she knew was all she wanted: the large and pulsating cock he had prepared her for.

He pulled his hand from her: she felt the cream trickle from her cunt to her anus, between the cheeks of her bottom. He caressed and teased her open there too, making her ready for him. What bliss as he moved his fingers from one place to the other. He was a magnificent lover, irresistible. And the more she gave in to him the more she climaxed. Sexually she was over the edge, ready for as many little deaths as he could bring her to.

"And now, we go where you want to be. But this time together," he promised her.

It seemed as if she had lived her whole life for this one night with him. The excitement and pleasure he instilled in her brought her to tears. Her heart yearned for more. For him to enter her with his raging penis and make their orgy complete. All sense of ego and self were gone. His fingers moved in and out of her two most intimate places freely now: she no longer knew which of the sensations brought her to climax again. Nearly all her body was wet and slippery with cream and come, most especially her genitals, the inside of her thighs, the crack between the cheeks of her buttocks.

The tip of his penis, its large and beautiful throbbing knob, rubbed up and down against her pussy's silken slit. She thought her heart would stop in her moment of terror for the pain she imagined was to come with the onslaught of his penis. Her emotions, already shredded by the sexual delights he had already heaped upon her, were to take on yet more experiences. She held her breath so as not to weep when he gently placed his arms under hers and up over her shoulders, then gripped her tightly and whispered in her ear, while he slowly but firmly thrust his cock between her wet cunt lips that spread open to receive him with a relative ease she could hardly have imagined. "I never again thought that I would feel as alive as I do with you. I thought the war had destroyed me, until you found me. Until I recognized your heart is as hungry as mine is. It's your hunger that has restored me, set me free to pursue the ultimate in sexual pleasure again. I will always love you for that. Don't move, just stay the way you are, I want you to feel me take possession of you, not to miss one sensation."

Those were his last words to her before, with one eager thrust, he was deep inside her. He muffled her cry with passionate kisses. Her heart beat quickly, his penis throbbed inside her, he made her mouth his own. He fucked her with his kisses and his cock. She felt the throbbing of his whole life inside her. She was filled by him. They were in possession of each other. She wanted to weep with joy.

He whispered first beautiful things to her while he fucked her, and then, as his rhythm and thrusts quickened, he became more base, more obscene, before losing his English and assaulting her with sexual instructions in a confusion of languages. She obeyed his every impulse. They mastered each other, lost themselves in their lust, became violent. She inflicted great weals across his back with her fingernails, bit him. They were locked together, and her pelvic movements matched his. They were in a sexual frenzy. Finally he had the stamina to master her, to bring her to a point of no return. The sensations kept invading her, no matter how much she begged him to stop. She fought against losing consciousness during a stream of orgasms she experienced when he fucked her in turn from one orifice to another. They were both lost in the wilderness of sensation, and it was then—when instinct alone told them that they were giving each other more than they had ever given another human being; when at last they sensed there was no separateness between them—that they came together in a crescendo of utter bliss. It was a long and luscious orgasm that seemed to go on forever and to sweep them away with it.

Barbara lay in his arms drifting somewhere between the conscious world and some ethereal place. She sensed in herself a femaleness, not just her own but that of all her sisters under the skin. She wished for them all, at some time in their lives, to find themselves at that place where she had been with Karel Stefanik, where she was now. She understood her search, their search, for the right man, now as she had never understood it before. That need to find the man who inspires complete trust, who has in him both lust and love for women. How easy, when you find such a man, to give yourself up to him, to die to the world, to live for nothing but those moments of sexual ecstasy with him, as she was doing at that very moment.

But how many do find the Karel Stefaniks of this world, so they can lose themselves in them and sex? Feel safe enough, secure enough, to relinquish their hold on life and vanish into orgasm? she wondered. How many women, especially intelligent women such as herself, with fierce pride, in control of their love and their life, do find the man who wants to make real their sexual desires, fantasies even, as Karel did? How often, if ever, did they, as she did now, love a man enough to want to bathe in her lover's come, to have quenched her thirst with it, to hold within her that special elixir and enjoy sexual enslavement?

Lying entwined in each other's arms, the firelight playing over their bodies, she watched him dozing and thought about

those things. Her heart was as full of him as her body. She
reveled in the miracle of finding and experiencing such a
man, a stranger. She dozed off and even in their sleep they
did not lost the tight grip they had on each other. Twice more
he came and she climaxed with him before they fell into a
deep sleep.

The room was bathed in bright sunlight, the fire no more
than a mound of white ash when they awoke. Even that they
did together.

"Good morning," he wished her.

She touched his face with the tips of her fingers. Ran one
of them over his lips. He opened his mouth, and sucking the
finger gently between his teeth, gave her a love bite. There
was about him a new tenderness she had not seen before: it
touched her deeply. She shivered. He assumed she was
chilled and reached to draw the white, fox-trimmed cashmere
blanket over them. He was wrong, she was not the least
chilled lying in his arms.

"You're a wonderful dancer. Thank you for last night. And,
yes, it is a good morning. Good morning. Good morning, to
you." And she smiled and kissed him lightly several times on
his lips and face. Barbara felt happy.

Cozy, a strange word to use with him, but that was exactly
how she felt, still entwined in his embrace, their nakedness
now covered by the luxuriously soft blanket. They remained
like that for some time while they struggled from their sleep
into real waking. Finally, taking her in his arms, he carried
her through her bedroom and into her bathroom.

They sat facing each other in the green marble sunken bath
that steamed with the scent of almond and apple oils. The
water was slippery smooth and caressed their skin sensuously.
They bathed themselves and each other and allowed the luxury of their bath to take them over and deliver them into yet
another kind of oblivion. Liquid notes from Bizet's *Pearl
Fishers* filled the room from next door.

He raised the sponge and squeezed. Rivulets of the steamy,
scented water ran over her breasts. Again and again he repeated the exercise. He seemed mesmerized by the action.
When he came to himself, he wrung the water from the
sponge and very carefully washed away the remnants of her

makeup from the night before. The tips of her long blonde hair trailed in the water. He played with them lazily. He asked her, "Happy?"

"Very. I feel I want to sing. All of me wants to sing. My heart, my toes, my nose." He began to laugh at her. "And you? I want so much for you to be happy too."

"I had forgotten what real pleasure could be like. What extraordinary sex could do to me. That there are still in this horrible world beautiful, luxurious women such as you, who can give me pleasure. Am I happy? Am I glad? I feel like springtime. Young and new, fresh and full of blossom."

With that, in one swift action, he pulled her roughly towards him, spreading her legs around his body. He thrust his erect penis, still immersed in the deep bath water, into her and pulled her down on top of him, careful to arrange her legs so they did not disengage. There they lay, covered to their necks in the satin-smooth hot water. Kissing, making love, this time with words of affection while they explored each other, they searched for new sexual sensations together and found them.

They made love all day and the following night. They remained by choice in the grip of Eros, and laughed and played with their appetite for sexual excesses. And the more sex they had, the more secure they were in taking that next step further. Nothing fazed them: no sexual fantasy that was expressed, no sexual request. And now it was her turn, and he became *her* sexual slave. She tied him to the bedposts. He was to be the passive partner, teased and tortured sexually by her. She was to be in control of their lovemaking, and that was what their sexual excesses had become. How clever and imaginative she was in this new role she played with him. It was a new kind of excitement for him. So he gave himself to her in sex no less than she had given herself to him. He had no need for bondage to give her what she wanted. So he slipped the knots easily, and she watched him submit to her voluntarily, and that passionate act on his part became for them yet another form of arousal.

Passion, desire, took them over yet again as it had so many times during their days and nights of wild, unbridled indulgence. When he had played the passive role long enough, it

was with a degree of violence that he took command of her
and control over their sexual liaison. And they entered that
world of sexual abandon that they were so happy in. For one
last time they stilled their hungry hearts.

They lay exhausted on the silk sheets and among lace-
trimmed pillows, each in a personal silence trying to ease
back into a world other than the one each had created. A
world where they would have to deal with themselves as responsible individuals, confronting people and places and
time. It was he who broke the silence, the spell they had
woven around themselves. "Out of necessity, not out of
choice—may I use the telephone?"

When he replaced the receiver, he turned on his side to
face her. He smiled. She knew that sort of smile. She had after all seen it on other men's faces, had used it herself. It was
a smile that was meant to be a compliment. One used in place
of words that might cause embarrassment, or even worst suggest love and commitment now that the sexual tryst was over.
Karel's smile may have told her that but his violet eyes told
her something else too. He was no less hungry for her than
when they first met. He did indeed have a hungry heart. He
placed his arm around her shoulders and drew her close to
him. Though she was in her lover's arms, feeling warmth and
affection, adoration even, she could also feel him drifting
away from her. Neither of them made any attempt to stop
him. She turned to face him. With crooked finger she rubbed
lightly the stubble shadowing his face.

"How long do we have?"

"I fly out sometime this evening."

"I think you'll want to do something about this." And she
rubbed her chin against the roughness of his, and placed an
affectionate kiss on its cleft.

"Yes."

"Well, I can do something about it. My brother keeps a
room here in my flat. You can use his shaving things. Wait
here, I'll bring you one of his robes."

The banality of life was moving in on them, planes, shaving, a robe, separating them. She should have felt some anxiety about that, but she didn't. She felt closer to him for it.
Was that perverse on her part? she wondered. A trick of the

emotions to compensate for his leaving her? Somehow she thought not. He had warned her: only a beginning, no middle, no end. And in the few days they had been together they had lived a whole lifetime more intimately than many couples who have years. What need she be anxious about?

Karel watched her walk from the bed. He wanted to remember every inch of her naked body, a voluptuous body he had loved so well, one that had given him a taste of life, a will to love again. There was something in the way she moved, a certain power that only women have and that he adored. Every step she took was self-assured and provocative, exclaiming, "Look at me. Love me." She turned, as if she were hearing his thoughts. He could see in her face how close they really were. She loved him. He experienced a tremor of delight. He liked being loved by such a remarkable woman.

She turned back to the cupboard to pluck from her wardrobe, a dressing gown, and felt his eyes still eating into her flesh. But not just her flesh this time: her soul as well. She closed her eyes and allowed herself for a moment to feel the pain of losing him. And then the pain passed, and she turned around as she slipped her arms into the honey-colored cashmere dressing gown with turned-back cuffs and a hem of rich sable. She walked back to the bed and her lover.

"How grand, how splendid a robe. It looks so Russian. Yes, you look like a Tsarina. Leave it open," he commanded. "Just a little while longer. Instead of my own Naked Maja, I have my naked Tsarina, my bare Contessa. If only I still had a palace staircase for you, a great painter at hand ..."

"And where would you exhibit me?"

"Where everyone could see you. The dining room. Yes, I would hang you over the gilded console there, and the men would all want you, and envy me. The women would simply be jealous of you and your place of honor."

She sat down next to him on the bed, and ran her fingers through his hair several times. He kissed her hands and her breasts. She closed her eyes and he kissed them and licked her lashes. When she opened them she saw and felt even closer to him. Neither needed to say the word: happiness. It was theirs, and it was as simple as that.

"And who would you choose to paint me?" she asked, enjoying his little fantasy as much as he did.

"I don't have to think twice about that. Henri Matisse. He would adore you, your sensuality. He would find you very beautiful. Yes, Matisse could paint you so. Then every man who saw his portrait of you would want to lick you, the very paint of you, off the canvas."

They both laughed. "How amusing. You have a delirious imagination."

"You seem surprised?" He gave her that charming, hurt, somewhat-innocent look she had seen before.

"No, not surprised. I have after all experienced several imaginative moments with you."

That appeared to please him. It also silenced them both. He raised her hands to his lips and closed his eyes while he kissed one hand and then the other. He was hiding his emotions, and she was thankful that he could not see hers. When he opened his eyes, he reached out and began hooking up her still open robe.

"Ching Lee is back today." She reached for the telephone and arranged for their breakfast. Then she showed him to her brother's room and bath. When she turned to leave he asked, "Must you go?"

She watched him while he shaved and bathed and dressed in the uniform that had been found scattered around the living room: the shirt laundered, the jacket and trousers pressed by Ching Lee. He wore his Royal Air Force uniform with great style. It nearly prompted her to ask how a Czech happened to be an English officer, but she thought better of it. Of asking him anything. Questions were not part of their affair. Was that not evident, he having not asked her a single personal thing about herself?

When he was dressed they walked arm in arm into another room, the library, a handsome place furnished in rich dark mahogany. An English partner's desk set in the middle of the room had on it a silver tray and a pitcher of Bloody Marys, a plate of curled prosciutto and warm squares of buttered toast. He seemed delighted with the room. He went directly to the shelves and began examining the books. She filled two cut crystal goblets for them, and stuck a stick of celery in each, presenting him with his after kissing him on the back of his neck.

He took the goblet from her and asked, "What other surprises lie in this flat? This is a wonderful library." He touched the rim of his glass to hers. They drank.

"Not too much prosciutto. That American breakfast you asked for is in the making. I'm going to dress while you browse. After breakfast I'll surprise you and open another door." And she was gone.

When she returned to the library, she lingered at the entrance and watched him for a few minutes. He was standing at the window looking pensive. He appeared to be a million miles away. It was several minutes before he realized that she was in the room and turned to face her. For the first time she saw incredible pain in his eyes, a sadness of extraordinary depth. She marveled that, at the sight of her, the despair she had seen in him simply slipped away, was replaced by a smile in the eyes, that seductive charisma he possessed in such abundance. Neither spoke. The magic of attraction that can happen to two people spoke for them. They walked toward each other and kissed. With his arm through hers, they left the library.

They had their breakfast in the brightness of a winter sun in a conservatory off the kitchen. Bacon and sausage patties, eggs scrambled with cream, stacks of blueberry pancakes dripping with butter and pure Vermont maple syrup. Endless cups of coffee. She watched him eat when she was not attending to her own plate. He had obviously been ravenous for the luxury of fresh food, virtually unobtainable now in England.

The door that Barbara opened for Karel was at the top of a curved staircase off the conservatory. It opened into an artist's vast studio whose entire movable roof was of glass and a series of white canvas shades that were adjustable for shifting the light where it was needed.

Chapter 5

This was not the studio of some wealthy dilettante, nor were the paintings those of a talented amateur.

The large wall-size canvases were impressive, serious works of art. More than good. She hung back and allowed him to view them on his own. Watching him Barbara realized that she had brought him to the studio not because she wanted to impress him with her work, but because she wanted him to know all aspects of the woman he had loved for a brief period in his life.

She had no idea that his presence in the studio would affect her in any way, but it did. She sat on the edge of a work table and was very still, not wanting to distract him. Seeing him there brought her closer to him: it seemed to round out the intimacy, the oneness she felt with him. It was very odd, but as he walked through the studio absorbed by the paintings she realized that while not in the least a shadowy figure, he lived in the shadows of his own life. Her instinct had been right from the beginning when she had first laid eyes on him in the Stork Club. He was a remarkable man, but a man with many secrets, a man whose life was cloaked in mystery. She felt privileged, as she sensed he did, that they should have given themselves to each other so completely. They were a part of each other's lives: they always would be. Though she doubted they would ever meet again. She felt such a rush of life within her that there was no room for sadness about the imminent parting.

He was in the middle of the studio now. Karel turned from a painting to face her. "You should have told me."

"Well, we used our time a different way, I guess."

"You are a fine artist, maybe even a great painter."

"Yes," she assented matter-of-factly.

"Come to me." He opened his arms.

She walked into them and he hugged her. "What a many-sided woman you are." Together and in silence they walked through the studio viewing the paintings. She knew instinctively that these were not mere compliments: he was not only impressed, but truly understood her work.

She was a powerful painter of sensual images in abstract forms. Her paintings had sensitive souls. The overly-large canvases were in themselves yet another form for her subjects and the various media she used in her work. Her paintings had integrity, a quality they shared with Barbara herself.

Barbara Dunmellyn was one of the better-kept secrets of the art world. Admired by Peggy Guggenheim and Max Ernst, Hans Hoffman, Pierre Matisse and several dealers, she refused all offers of a one-woman exhibition. She had the support of four of America's finest museum directors. Immensely successful painters were her friends. The art critics who had seen her work praised it and prodded her to take a dealer and exhibit. But Barbara bided her time. She never sold, traded or gave away her paintings. She worked and waited. Waited for the war to be over, for a new art direction to emerge from the old one, like the new world that was bound to rise from the ashes of war, evil, and mass-destruction. Then, and only then, would she exhibit in New York and Paris and London. She was grateful that she and Karel had no need to talk about her work. He understood her paintings and liked them. She sensed that they were as personal for him as they were for her.

"Let's go downstairs and sit in front of the fire," she suggested, though she sensed that Karel would have been content to remain in the studio looking at her paintings.

"Yes, let's do that," he was quick to reply, understanding that she was communicating more to him than was merely spoken. "My work is a great part of my life, and I want you to know that. But it has nothing to do with the few hours we have left together."

In the living room they stood looking out the window. New York spread out before them was a mesmerizing sight. She could see how much he admired it. She felt quite selfish wanting to keep him to herself and not offering more of the city to him. "A walk in the Park, would you like that? We could go ice-skating, would that amuse you? Or is there something else you would prefer to do?"

"I'm too content just being here with you to indulge myself any further with New York City. Let's just spend the remainder of the time we have here, in front of the fire. Alone. Just you and I. No Ching Lee, no calls or callers. Wouldn't you like that too?"

She smiled and took his hand. They walked together towards a sofa in front of the blazing fire. To answer him seemed such a trite response when they both knew what she wanted. She changed the subject.

"I'll drive you to the airfield tonight."

"They'll be sending a car for me."

"Even better, then I'll accompany you and save my gasoline stamps."

"I think you'll need clearance. It's that kind of airfield."

"Brigadier generals' nieces get clearance."

"Then get clearance," he told her, evidently delighted: he would not have to leave her until the last minute.

She kissed him. He liked the relish sensed in her quick kiss before she left the room to make the call to her uncle and dismiss Ching Lee.

When she returned he was sitting comfortably on the sofa in front of the fire, his jacket now open. He was reading something by Voltaire, in a French edition he had found in the library. Barbara felt relaxed and happy, not at all sad about a lovers' parting. She tossed a cushion on the floor and then sat down on it between his legs.

He looked up from his book and asked her, "Do brigadier generals' nieces have the influence they think they have?" He stroked her long blonde hair.

"Oh, yes. I'll be going with you. But we have less time than you think to get deliciously tipsy." They were not facing each other. She put her hand on her shoulder, wanting him to cover it with his. He obliged by grasping it, bending forward and kissing first the back of her neck and then the hand he held. She snuggled up tight between his legs. He abandoned his book to sit with her thus and watch the magic of a log-fire's leaping flames.

They sat for some time enveloped in an opulent silence that seemed to speak volumes. The sort of hush that touches the soul, enriches it in some mysterious way. The silence was made even more poignant by a life-enhancing force the lovers felt within themselves. It appeared to beat like their hearts. In the tranquillity of the room they could sense, too, a voiceless chorus of beauty and passion. The Matisse painting of a nude reclining on a chaise in a Mediterranean room filled with sunlight sang to them from above the fireplace with its own colorful silence.

Ching Lee appeared carrying a silver tray with a decanter of fifty-year-old Scotch whiskey, a siphon of water, a pyramid of bite-sized sandwiches, chunky crystal glasses and crisp, white linen napkins edged in lace, a crystal ice bucket. He poured drinks for Barbara and Karel and then made his exit. They touched the rim of their glasses and sipped their drinks. Barbara turned back to watch the flames.

That profound silence had not eliminated the sounds and signs of life going on not only within them but all around them. A change in the weather: the sound of the wind, the patter of sleet against the windowpanes. The almost inaudible tick of a clock from the far end of the room merely accentuated the calm. Karel found it, although completely different, as exciting and provocative as the sexual excesses they had for days been indulging themselves in.

He leaned forward, reached around Barbara to remove the glass from her hand, and lifted her up and on to his lap. He cradled her in his arms and kissed her affectionately on the cheek. And then, with her still in his lap, he straightened her legs out. He took her shoes from her feet, placed them on the sofa to make her more comfortable, and handed back her glass.

"That's better. The other wasn't bad, but having you in my arms is better," he told her.

She liked the happiness in his voice. She rubbed her cheek against his face, touched her glass to his and they drank. She was not unaware that he was studying her. She guessed that he was doing what they had been doing for days: observing each other so as never to forget. She was right of course. He confirmed it now. "I want to remember you always naked and in flagrant orgasm with me, and after that how you look now. I love how you look now." He took her free hand in his and, turning it over, kissed it passionately in the palm and licked it with the tip of his tongue. Delighted, she closed her eyes for a moment and sighed.

She had taken great care in dressing, wanting him to think she was beautiful. But she hadn't wanted him to forget what a lustful creature she was either. She had put on a pair of wide slacks that hugged her hips and her provocative, well-rounded bottom, the flat of her stomach. Fashioned from the sheerest of camel-hair cloth, they seductively covered her thighs and fitted sensuously up against her cunt and across her pussy. Tucked into them she wore a white organza shirt, its pointed collar and turned-back cuffs of antique, white Belgian lace in a pattern of chrysanthemums. It was a particularly feminine and seductive contrast, the well-tailored shirt and the semi-soft, five-inch lace cuffs that moved floppily, enchantingly, with every turn of her hand, the collar with every movement of her head. The semi-transparent silk organza only enhanced Barbara's beauty and the blouse. With her pale nimbus and nipples it was the full, rounded shape, the heaviness and voluptuousness of her naked breasts that incited, the hint of nipple that tantalized. And, against her skin, under the blouse, a strand of huge pearls to match those in her ears. Brown alligator shoes. A large square-cut diamond on one hand.

Her shoulder-length blonde hair shone silkily. Her velvety brown eyes were filled with contentment and love for him. He missed nothing. He took it all in, flattered that she should love him so well, as several men before him had been flattered and seduced by the attentions of such a lady. She sighed. Contentment. He recognized it. His own state of mind exactly. He hugged her to him. Together they were oblivious of time and place.

When their glasses were empty he eased her off his lap, placed more logs on the fire, and refilled their glasses. He helped her to her feet and to remove her blouse, then lay down with her in his arms. She loved his hands and the way he caressed her breasts. He felt the weight of them in his hands. He stroked her arms and her shoulders, caressed the hollow under her arms, felt her ribs under his fingers. It was as if he were giving her a ritual bath with love instead of water. His tenderness was so sweet, like that of someone petting a favorite animal or a cherished object. He eased his hand under the waistband of her slacks, and she mellowed even further into his arms when he caressed the flat of her belly, the bone of her hip, plied with his fingers her mound of soft golden hair. He was satisfying not mere sexual hunger for her this time but his hunger to love someone.

The light was dying, the setting sun cast a pink winter glow all through the room. He kissed her on her nipples, and then as tenderly on her lips. He said, "Let's have some light."

And she understood he didn't want the day to die. She slipped from his arms after kissing him on the shoulder. For a second she laid her head on his lap, then gave him another kiss. She liked the feel of the rough wool fabric of his fly on her lips, the hardness pulsating within. She caressed him with a gentle touch where her lips had been, and then, bending over him, took his head in her hands and kissed him on the lips.

He watched her naked to the waist except for her pearls, walking around the room putting on lamps. When she returned to him he was standing in front of the fire. He kissed her breasts, and then lightly her lips. He held out her blouse ready for her to slip her arms into. He adjusted the shoulder line of the blouse. Turning her around to face him, he first buttoned the cuffs, then the front. He poured them yet another drink, and they sat again next to each other in front of the fire. He eased himself away from her, not far, but it was deliberate, as if he had to put some space between them. They turned to face each other. There was no sadness in his voice when he told her, "If only we could keep the world at bay and stay where we have been for the rest of our lives. But life moves everyone on. Maybe in another place and another time."

She stopped him by placing her hand over his mouth. "I don't think that I can bear to hear this. There is so little time left. There is no point in filling it with 'if only's.' You don't

believe in 'if only's' any more than I do. The hell with another place another time, it couldn't be anything better than
what we have here and now. If you're creating those senti-
ments for me, forget it. I promise you, you don't have to. In
fact I don't want you to. I'm all right. I am with you, and will
be until that plane disappears from sight."

"I've never met a woman like you."

"Well, I did tell you that when we met, remember?"

"Yes."

"But you didn't believe I accepted your warning that ours
could never be a love story with a future in it."

"Was I as harsh as that?"

"The warning was, but said with more European charm—of
which you are a master, by the way." She smiled, to let him
know she had never taken offense at his declaration but had
merely accepted it. "I believe your exact words were, 'This
cannot be a love story. There will be only a beginning, no
middle and no end.' "

They had never been mere words when he had first told
her that. Now, after they had become lovers, one might have
thought that repetition of those words might distance her
from him. But they had the opposite effect on Barbara. She
felt closer to him and remembered how wonderful it had all
been. How nice it would be to begin all over again. She felt
sexually excited by the idea. It came as a surprise to her that
her body should still want him so much, when her mind and
emotions were happy and content with what they had had together. That made her restless. She found it impossible to sit
still. She rose to her feet. He was right at her side pulling her
roughly into his arms.

It was as if he wanted to crush her into his very own body,
make her part of himself. Their kisses were passionate and
violent, and after several minutes she became breathless with
ecstasy. He loosened his grip on her and watched her close
her eyes and sigh. He knew that look, that sigh: he had seen
it, heard it so many times in the last few days when she had
come in exquisite flushes of orgasm. He was mad with lust
for her. He found his way into her slacks, she wore no under-
garment. With great urgency he searched out with grasping
fingers as much of the warm silky stream of orgasm as he

could. He brought his hand to his mouth to lick his now luscious fingers clean. His lips were shinily coated with her. She wanted to weep for the pleasure she saw in his face, and for her own. His heart was beating like a drum. She thought he might be close to tears when, more calmly now, he took her in his arms again just to hold her while they composed themselves. He whispered in her ear, "I adore you. I revere you."

"Karel, one of the best things about us is our hunger for each other. So let's, for the time that's left to us, continue to enjoy being the selfish lovers that we are."

There was a tremor in her voice that she wished had not been there, not for her sake but for his. She sensed that he might have spoken from some sense of guilt, and that would have been abominable. Emotions were running high for them both, and so she had no doubt that he would understand her, and that it was not weakness on her part of a desire to cling to a love story she had already been warned could never be.

He was much more in control. He raised her hand to his lips, kissed it and told her, "You are magnificent. The most beautiful thing that has entered my life in a very long time. Maybe ever. I will always hold you dear to me. And you are quite right: my heart will always be hungry for you."

She listened to Karel Stefanik. There was no maudlin, cheap sentimentality in his words. They were an expression of genuine feeling. Once again silence enveloped them. For a time they sat together, savoring that something special that great loves are made of.

Karel began reading aloud to her from the book he had taken from her library. Then their idyll was shattered by the intrusive buzz of the intercom. It silenced him. He placed the book on the sofa and they looked at each other.

"I'll go." Rising from the sofa he touched her shoulder, and she placed her hand over his. "But where," he asked, "is that terrible machine?"

"It's the black telephone on the table near the window."

If that small enclosed world that they had created for themselves was shattered, certainly the feelings they had for each other were not. She was resting on her knees on the sofa, leaning against its back, her arms folded across the top and her chin resting on them, watching him walk back towards her. She could not help but smile when she told him, "My goodness, you look the most handsome, romantic figure of a man. No wonder I picked you up at the Stork."

He gave her one of his charismatic smiles, and laughed. "Now what should I say to that? What can I say except thank God you did? How frightening to think that we might never have met."

His words hit her hard. They made her realize what she had not until that moment. It would have been more than frightening, for then she would not have met the great love of her life. She quickly recovered herself, more grateful than ever for the courage they had shown to love each other for one brief period in their lives.

"The driver says he's early. We have a little time."

"Then one last drink—for the road," she told him, and mixed their drinks. Then they sat in another part of the room in a pair of Venetian wing chairs that faced each other, near one of the windows overlooking the terrace and the view of the city beyond.

"It's a fairy-tale city. I've always thought of it like that. I've always liked it. Its energy. Its opulence and its fragility. The slums, the ugliness, all that incredible hardness. It has a kind of madness that doesn't exist in Paris or London or Rome. It's so uncivilized, and I don't know how people can live here, really live here. But I have met you, and so now I'm learning that it can be done. New York is unique, and so has been this four-day trip to America, although I don't know that I have accomplished what I came here for. Only time will tell that.

"What I do know is that, since we have been together, you have made me forget the war and devastation I am about to return to. Barbara, you are so removed from all that, so safe. You can't begin to understand what insanity this war has brought upon Europe and England. And may you never know. You're so alive and rich in yourself—but never take that for granted. I have for years been so busy trying to survive, I had forgotten that there *is* more to life than mere survival."

He went to sit on the arm of her chair, to place an affectionate kiss on her lips, to slip his hand through her blouse and caress her bare breast, to lay it over her heart. It was as if he wanted to feel her warmth, the beat of her heart, life pulsating in his lover for one last time.

They held hands and listened to the wind driving sleet against the window. He was entranced by the sound and the sight of it streaking down the glass. She was losing him. She could feel him drifting away. It seemed as if the storm was transporting him to some place far from her. She tightened her grip on his hand, trying to hold him back, keep him warm and safe and with her for just a little while longer. Too late. She watched him slip his hand from hers. He was gone. She had lost him to the life he lived beyond their idyll when it came flooding back to him and he told her, "I was a very different man before this war. I was living a life quite alien to the one I live now. And then one morning I woke up. Scales had fallen from my eyes. I faced the reality. My country, my life, the world, were no longer being merely threatened—they were being shattered. Almost too late, I became ruthless about my country, about my daughter and myself just staying alive.

"There could be no betrayal of a loved one, no collusion with the enemy for me. The loss of my home, freedom, my country, became an unbearable thought. From that moment when I lost my illusions and faced the reality of Hitler and Nazi Germany, everything that I did, everything that I do now, every breath I take, has been and still is for the survival of those things and my daughter. But it has been survival bought at a price.

"Self-denial: my child, my homeland, my estates, my identity. It has had a corrosive effect on me. My life has lost the capacity for even the most extreme emotion. Cunning replaces feeling. That, I am sorry to say, is the romantic figure you think you see before you."

He was less lost to her than Barbara thought because he rallied himself, broke away from the mesmerizing sleet trying to beat its way into the warmth and safety of the flat. He turned to look at her and tell her, "It's temporary. Until the war is over and I find my child, till my country is free and my land and houses are returned to me.

"There are not thousands nor hundreds of thousands but millions, Barbara, millions of people more hurt than me. Millions who have suffered unspeakably, and perished in this war. Innocent Jews, gypsies, the Poles, the Czechs, Hungarians. I feel no guilt about those who have been hit harder than me. My shame is for having sold my child's identity to preserve her life. That's my pain, my anguish.

"I live with that pain every day, every waking minute of my life. It will always be there until this war is over and I can return here to America to reclaim my daughter. I wanted her to grow up with a childhood she could bear to remember, and not have to invent one, as the hordes of concentration camp children, ghetto children, the hungry and lost orphans roaming the streets, begging for bread, rags for shoes, will have to.

"I ease my conscience about my child because I know she is safe here in America with a mother who adopted her, a woman who was her wet-nurse. She loves her as her own child. And the girl has a tutor who loves her no less. These women are devoted to her and care for her. She lives secure in their love and the comfort I have provided for them all until my return. And yet, with all that, she is a victim of war, a displaced person. My hope, my dream, is that she is too young and too innocent and happy to know it.

"I try not to think about her. But, when I do, it is in a lovely house with a garden where she has not a worry in the world. Where no one can reach her, hurt her, or use her to get to me. It assuages my guilt for the danger I put them all through before I took action to ensure their safety, for abandoning her.

"Czechoslovakia, my country, has a government in exile in London. I flew to Washington on a mission for them. It was to be London, Washington, London. I am only in New York because weather delayed my flight back to London. A romantic figure, you see? A ruthless bastard, more like! These days with you have been more than perfect, more than any man has a right to expect. We've been selfish for each other, and reaped fantastic pleasure from our selfishness. Maybe even sparks of love. But love is not my game. Survival is what I'm playing for. I can only hope you understand, and that you will forgive me."

Barbara was stunned by all that Count Karel Stefanik had chosen to reveal about himself. She had not expected it. Nor had she expected that he would fall in love with her. In spite of his words, the coolness with which he had spoken, she sensed that he did love her, no matter that he didn't want to. She had had other men fall in love with her. The signs were there now: she read them clearly

"Forgive you for what, Karel?"

"For walking out on you. No. That's not quite right. For walking out on love. That's more the truth of it."

He pulled her up from the chair and held her in his arms. Then he sat down again with her on his lap. They kissed. She stroked his hair, and he kissed her hands. There was nothing to forgive, and therefore nothing to say about his departure. Nor about understanding that they would never meet again.

The intercom buzzed. They let it carry its irritating tune for some moments while they sat silent looking into each other's eyes.

Chapter 6

Mimi's change of fortune began with the kindness of the fruit peddler, Joe Pauley. But real change began in her life on that autumn afternoon in 1943 when she and the Queen met on the steps of the chapel. When she felt secure enough to cut through the tissue of lies she had been living with since she had been parted from her father, and mentioned that she too had a chapel in the house where she lived in Prague. Always looking for diversions to keep the children amused, the Queen had suggested a tea party where everyone could view the child's precious photographs. Those were the first details Mimi had voluntarily given anyone about herself. Neither Mimi nor anyone else could possibly envisage how a tea party could change her fortunes.

Until that day Mimi's life at Beechtrees had been a happy but hard one. She worked tirelessly and with a willingness to please in order to remain at Beechtrees that was exploited by everyone. The family and cook treated her as what she was supposed to be, a poor waif from the gutter who was there to serve and learn. Every job that was too low, menial or dirty in the kitchen: the rubbish details of scrubbing the floor, the pots, cleaning the stove, the endless potato and onion peeling, fetching the heavy bags of charcoal. Even the cleaning ladies used her to fetch and carry for them. The children thought nothing of making her do their chores and pinched her as a warning not to tell. She never ate until the family's meals had been served and then, the "waste not, want not" theory was the excuse for her having to eat scraps. By the time she was allowed to go to bed she was trembling with exhaustion. And yet, as her first year there wore on, she etched herself into their hearts. Not enough, however, for them to think of her as an equal. She ran, she fetched, and was thrown the occasional bone, some small treat that showed her they would have liked it to be different. The tea party to view her photos was a gesture long overdue because, in spite of her position at Beechtrees, she had wormed her way into their hearts. Everyone sensed Mimi deserved better than what they were giving. That made them uncomfortable.

Tea was always the gathering time of the day, and whenever possible turned into a party. What they had seen as a breakthrough for Mimi was all the excuse they needed to make a party of looking through her photographs. The tea table had been set in the library in front of the fire and covered with a linen and lace cloth. It was resplendent with silver pots for coffee and tea and hot chocolate, cream, sugar and jams: apricot, blueberry, strawberry. Cups, saucers and plates in a sparkling white porcelain edged with a lacy pattern of gold. Cook filled the table with her delicious thin-cut sandwiches that melted in the mouth, filo pastry-squares filled with chicken and mushrooms in a thick, white, buttery-tasting sauce. There were tarts and cakes and scones, and crispy hot fried apple-fritters sprinkled with powdered sugar. When Mimi and the maid, Bessie, and cook had set the table, and the Queen had done the flowers, Mimi had asked permission of the Queen for Jack and Ernie to be allowed to come because they were going to find her father. Another breakthrough? It was more than anyone could have hoped for.

The excitement of Mimi breaking out of her shell put everyone into top gear. The two school teachers prepared little entertainments: a song, a poem, a reading of a scene from *A Tale of Two Cities* were to be the children's contribution to the party. Then would come Mimi's: the showing of her photographs.

Jack and Ernie had come, Jim was posted to cover the gate, and cook had joined them after serving. It was Mimi's party: she asked if everyone could dress up for tea. They had, with Mimi herself in one of Juliet's prettiest party frocks, her golden hair tied back off her face with a ribbon embroidered with flowers.

Much laughter and applause for the entertainments, much

eating and refilling of cups. Lots of chattering about the weather, school, going skiing in the winter, whether they could find a toboggan-run in the area. They were trying to pretend the war did not exist, although it kept slipping in and out of the conversation going round the table.

With tea declared over, and the table removed from the room, the children sat in a circle on cushions on the floor in front of the fire. The adults were in chairs behind them, except for the Queen who sat in the center of the sofa, Mimi alongside her. Next to Mimi was her broken and squashed cardboard box of photographs held together with a selection of colored rubber bands, and the leather envelope lying in her lap.

"May I show you my chapel now, ma'am?" she asked.

"Yes, now would be a perfect time, Mimi. And maybe you could give us a little talk with each picture."

"Oh, yes. I could do that," she answered with some enthusiasm.

Then very carefully she removed one rubber band at a time, and the lid. "I'll hold those for you, Mimi," offered Jack and took them from her.

The next fifteen minutes had been both a revelation and a disappointment for the tea-party guests. The revelations were the claims that Mimi made on the commercial photographs that could be found in any tourist shop in Prague. Beautiful, colored reproductions of one of the finest rococo chapels in Czechoslovakia, complete with frescoes and ceiling-scenes of unimaginable beauty. The altars and niches displayed images of Christ on the cross, sunbursts of gold hung on the painted and gilt paneling, some encrusted with jewels. Cherubs flung themselves from the opulent deep carvings everywhere, or flew down from the celestial ceiling.

"I will pass them to you first, ma'am, and then please will you pass them on around the circle? This is my favorite," she said, smiling, "but I like this one in our country house almost as much."

There had been less than a dozen such photographs: a baroque palace in Prague, another (or so Mimi claimed) family chapel in Hacha, worthy of a pilgrimage for the paintings of Christ on the cross in richly carved gilt frames alone. A palatial house on the edge of a lake, an aerial shot of an ancient wood with a herd of deer on the run. A large, rustic hunting lodge on the side of a mountain, a magnificent formal garden with a stone gazebo in the middle of it. Any identification once printed at the bottom of these photographs had been carefully cut away.

When, with a certain composure and childish pride, Mimi had shown the Prague chapel to her sovereign benefactor, she had said, "I know how much you like the little chapel here. Maybe some day you can come to our chapel. It's very beautiful, don't you think? You could pray there with my father and me, and perhaps you could come at Christmas. Then it's all draped in gold and white flowers. All sorts of white flowers."

Mimi's openness, her enthusiasm about the chapel, a future, had been spontaneous, as any child's would have been who wanted to say, "Look, I have something and I want to share it with you and to say thank you for your friendship, generosity, and hospitality. Maybe, even, I love you."

The adults in the room were touched by her display, but not unaware that, after she had shown several of the photographs, she seemed to lose her enthusiasm, to become less informative about them. She had been pleased to be sharing her box of treasures, but they could actually feel her receding from them, pulling back into herself before she was halfway through them.

The adults hardly knew what to say, because they were having to question Mimi's claims. Were they true? Was this part of the life she had before she found her way to America? Or were they just postcards and commercial photographs of her country that she had fantasized about in her need to create some kind of a life, a home, a background that could lift her out of the trauma and poverty of her life? And so what they did say was admiring but cautious, to their own ears banalities. But, to a nine-year-old desperate to have something to share with them, banalities were good enough.

If the Beechtrees adults had that problem, the children certainly did not. Privileged children, born and brought up in houses such as those Mimi chose to claim as hers, were innocents, with no reason not to believe what she told them. It had been their gullibility, the happiness they felt because Mimi was not the poor waif they had all thought she was, that prompted questions. "Can we come to visit?" asked Julia.

"Oh, yes, and stay, all of you, for as long as you like."

Pierre asked, "Have you a boat on the lake?"

"Yes. You can come for a summer."

"Then the next summer you can come to us," suggested Maxi.

"Do you have a stable?" Julia had become obsessed with riding.

"Which house shall we visit?"

"The lake," answered Pierre.

"No, the hunting lodge." That was Maximillian, preoccupied with anything that had to do with guns. "That is a deer park, isn't it, Mimi?"

And so it went on, while the adults worried whether this was a child's fantasy or a real life lost, and maybe lost forever if it had existed at all.

There were two photographs left in the box which Mimi had seemed hesitant about showing. For one brief moment she had the most wonderful feeling in the world. That she did belong, that it was true that it was all going to come right. That her father would come and find her, and that her real mother, who had vanished so long ago, would reappear, and they would all go home.

The photos, having been passed from hand to hand, were now coming back to Mimi. She had been about to replace them in the box (she was very careful in handling them, almost neurotically so) when Her Highness asked, "Mimi, won't you show us the last two photos you have in the box?" The chattering seemed to die down. All eyes were on the box.

Everyone in the room was aware that Mimi had suddenly come under some pressure: unconsciously she was wringing her hands. She lowered her eyes. Catching sight of what she was doing, she stopped abruptly, removed one of the pictures from the box and handed it to the Queen. It was of Mashinka holding Mimi in her arms. Mimi was wearing a luxuriously long christening dress of antique lace studded with tiny pearls. The second photograph was of a five-year-old Mimi, looking far less emaciated than she did now, wearing a beautiful party dress of silk whose hem was trimmed in roses cut of the same material. She had ribbons in her hair, and a face full of laughter.

"Who is the lady holding you, Mimi?"

Again, the wringing of the small, elegant, now healed, hands. A look of confusion had showed in those large violet eyes before she lowered them. "My mother . . . my mother Mashinka."

Not for a moment did any adult in that room believe that Mashinka was Mimi's natural mother. But they all pretended they did because that was what she wanted. Jack broke the awkward silence that prevailed. "No picture of your father? It would help me, Mimi, if there was."

"No. No picture of my father."

Pierre had gone and sat on the floor in front of Mimi. He helped her to arrange her possessions in the box, and replaced the rubber bands, while asking her a stream of questions about Czechoslovakia. She had sat back, regained her former composure and answered whatever she could.

She felt happy once again, good about being able to talk to Pierre about her country. It felt exciting to have once again a heritage that she could talk about. But always in the back of her mind were her father's words, his warnings about talking to strangers about herself or the family. She had played his game now for years: Mashinka being her real mother, her only family. Talking about anything else was like dreaming aloud or making up a story. She pondered: were fathers always right? She was reminded of how horrible it was, that almost too late flight from her homeland. Maxi poked her gently out of her thoughts when he asked, "Can I bring my friend Anatole? He's French."

"Yes, bring anyone you like. There are lots of rooms."

"Mimi, I'm looking for clues. The FBI always looks for clues. It helps find the man they're after. You still do want me to find your father, don't you?"

"Oh, yes. My father said he would come and find me after the war. But I can't wait until after the war. He said I would be safe with Mashinka and Tatayana, and I would live in a big house with Mashinka's brother, who would take care of all of us. But there was no big house for us, and now they're all gone, and my father would be very angry that I am left alone. I think I have to find him and tell him what happened. Clues—where will we find clues, Jack?"

"Maybe we will find some in that yellow oilskin packet, Mimi. What's in there?"

"I don't know. Daddy gave it to Mashinka. And Mashinka gave it to Mr. Pauley to give to me before she went away."

"Your mother?" asked one of the teachers.

Again hesitation. Then she answered them, "Yes, my mother."

"Why do you call your mother Mashinka, Mimi?"

Mimi looked uncomfortable with this question, but bravely answered, "She liked to be called Mashinka, and not Mother."

Mimi was lying. It was so obvious, it confirmed the conviction of every adult present that Mashinka could not be Mimi's natural mother. Doubts about Mimi's photographs suddenly seemed unkind. They might indeed be pictures of a life she had had to flee from when the Germans marched into Czechoslovakia.

Mimi picked up the parcel. She looked at Jack, "Maybe there is something in here that will tell us where my father is."

"That's right, Mimi, and that would be called a clue."

"Oh." Hope seemed to brighten her face, and she began attacking the knotted string. Julia rushed to the far side of the room to the sewing basket to find scissors.

Scissors in hand, Mimi seemed reluctant to cut the string. Ernie asked her, "Did your mother ever tell you anything about the packet, or whether you should open it or not, Mimi?"

"Mashinka said it was only to be opened if we were in desperate circumstances, because it's all my father had left in the world now. She used to look at it a lot and say, 'I wonder if we are in desperate circumstances yet.' I don't think she really knew what to do about this packet. Now it's mine, I don't know. Am I in desperate circumstances, Ernie? Do you think I am?" she asked Sophia the cook. They all turned their eyes on the sovereign sitting next to Mimi, seeking an answer.

"I think you should open the package, Mimi. I am certain your father would approve. And you should remember what Jack said: there might be clues inside."

She seemed still to be hesitant, pondering what to do.

"Poppa gave this to Mashinka when he said goodbye to us on the ship when we sailed from England."

"Did he say anything else, Mimi?" asked Jack.

"I don't remember. It was so long ago, and so many terrible things have happened since then."

An uncomfortable silence had fallen over the room. They were snapped back to the reality of this child's plight, and of the other lost children like her. For all the present chatter and laughter, the worn pictures, she was still a child alone in the wilderness of war, and only on a sabbatical from that because she had been taken in by them.

The Queen seemed more affected than the others, projecting yet again in her mind the hundreds of thousands of Mimis in her own country who were even less fortunate. The silence was broken by Jack who finally took control of the situation. "Why don't I open that for you, Mimi? This is after all my case." That seemed to relieve everyone. They all started talking at once. Mimi handed the packet to Jack, who, with the permission of the Queen, sat down next to her to open it.

He took the scissors from Mimi and was about to use them. She stopped him. "I think we must save the string."

Jack was not going to dispute her wishes. He worked on the knots with the help of the pointed end of the scissors.

Mimi watched Jack struggling with the knots. She caught the excitement and enthusiasm of everyone in the room about her parcel. She listened to them chattering about her pictures and offering silly guesses at what the parcel might contain. There were giggles, laughter even. She wondered what all the excitement was about. Why didn't she feel the same way? All she could feel was utter relief to be rid of the parcel. She had never felt much curiosity about the yellow-wrapped leather envelope. Too much anxiety from her life with Mashinka and Tatayana was focused upon it. How could it be anything good, anything important? Now Jack had suggested that there might be clues in it to reunite her with her father. In seconds the parcel would be open. Another reminder of her past agonies would be removed. That seemed more important than any hope of clues. She could feel herself drifting away from all the fuss going on around her. Memory took over. She could almost see, almost hear, her father, recalling that last time she had been with him. When she had begged him not to send her away, he had told her, "Nothing is more important to me than your being safe and out of this hell. You will want for nothing. There will be laughter and fun with Mashinka and Tatayana. None of the struggle for survival that war brings. When I come to get you, I will find a happy child, who has been made as safe as possible. Then it will all have been worth it. That's why, Mimi, you must never tell anyone your real name or my name. Nor who your daddy and mummy are. Pretend, it must always be pretend for us until after the war when we can return safely to Prague. Pretend, always make believe that you are Mashinka's little daughter. Then we will all be safe. I promise I will come to find you, and make up for all these years of separation to you. You must be Mimi Kowalski now. Pretend I am a Kowalski, and your beautiful real mummy never existed. That we are Kowalskis, just like Mashinka and her brother."

She shook her head, trying to excise from her memory his last words to her. How could he have been so wrong? Safe, yes. Away from the bombs, yes. He had done his best. She imagined the upset he would feel to know how hungry they had been, how awful life in the Blocks had been for her. How his plans for her had all gone so wrong. Except one: she was safe and still very much alive. And Maxi, with his obsession for the war, had made her understand as she had not done in the Blocks how lucky she was to be even that. She vowed that, when she and her father found each other again, she would never tell him of the agony of those years without him.

She caught herself wringing her hands. She watched herself for a few seconds. It took all her willpower to stop. At last the string had been removed. While being undone the oilskin cracked. The thick, red leather envelope with its brass lock was revealed. It held everyone's gaze.

"I'll have to break this lock," declared Jack.

"Do you have to?" Mimi appeared concerned.

"Got a key?"

"No."

"Then what choice do we have? Sorry, Mimi."

She shrugged. Ernie was sent to the kitchen with cook. They needed something strong and sharp.

It was more a cosmetic lock than a safety device. It broke without too much effort. Jack lifted the flap and placed the leather case on Mimi's lap.

One deed was for a property: the house and garden at 45 West Eleventh Street, New York City. A second was for an apartment building on Central Park West in the same city. A Morgan Guarantee Bank of New York savings account book. All three documents were made out to Mimi Alexandra Kowalski.

Jack looked up from the slim, folded property deeds with their red wax seals and narrow satin ribbons tied through the silver grommets. The room was quiet. Everyone was waiting for him to tell them what the documents meant.

"Are they clues?" asked Maxi.

"They might be," answered Jack.

"Well, what exactly are they, Jack?"

"Will those papers find my father?" asked Mimi.

"Whoa, hold on there. One question at a time. Pierre, they could be clues. They're not exactly clues that are gonna tell me where Mimi's father is, but they could lead us on to further clues. The great thing is now we've got something to go on."

"Are they not property deeds?" asked one of the teachers.

"That is exactly what they are." He passed the documents over to Ernie. Turning to Mimi, he asked, "Maybe we should talk about this in private, Mimi. Would you prefer that?"

"Not really."

"Don't look so glum. I think we have incredibly good news here."

"We do?"

"Yes, very good news. Ernie's going to read through these documents, and then we will explain it all to you. The best we can before we talk to the lawyers in New York who have drawn them up. As for the bank book, it has only one entry, and that's dated October 1938, the amount one thousand dollars. But that doesn't mean anything. Deposits might have been made over the years and not entered in your passbook. It is your passbook, Mimi, because it's made out in your name."

"Does that mean I have a thousand dollars?"

To Mimi and the other children that was a fortune. When Jack said, "Yes, and I can't promise but I think probably much much more," the whooping, the hollering and the children dancing around her made Mimi laugh. Ernie took advantage of the moment and pressed on. "Let's go through the rest of this case. Maybe it has other surprises in store for you."

In the zippered compartment Jack found two black velvet pouches and a long, narrow, two-inch-deep tin, its once garishly painted lid no longer a picture but flaked paint. Jack had seen such tins before. They normally contained long, slim, hand-rolled Havana cigars. There was usually the distributor's name and address, a date, on the bottom of the box. Eagerly, he turned it over, but his hopes were quickly shattered. The stamp read, Augustus Phillipe Ltd, Rue Bonaparte, Paris, October 1935, No. 411. The name and address of the purchaser were certain to be recorded, but the swastika was flying over Occupied France. No hope there of tracing Mimi's father. At least, not until after the war. Only Jack seemed preoccupied with the box: all other eyes were riveted on the velvet pouches.

He placed the box in his lap and handed one of the pouches to Mimi. She untied the silk cords, opened the pouch and withdrew from it a diamond and black pearl necklace. The stones and pearls were enormously large and beautiful. There were gasps of astonishment from all around the room.

"I forgot all about this necklace."

"Was it your mother's, Mimi?" someone asked.

"Yes, but I didn't know we had it with us." She turned to Juliet and asked her, "Don't you think it's beautiful?"

"Oh, yes."

"Now I've got something for you to wear when we play dressing-up."

"Oh, may I, Mimi?"

How could either child understand the value of the necklace, or the significance it had in Mimi's life? The second pouch contained another necklace, a long chain solidly set in diamonds, and from it hung a cross. A priceless object of art. Made of twenty-two-karat gold, it was inset with nine emeralds, square-cut, each stone more than an inch across and surrounded by round-cut diamonds. "Walnuts and peas."

"What did you say, Miss Tolset?" the Queen asked the teacher who had spoken.

The still-astonished teacher answered, "Walnuts and peas, ma'am. They are the size of walnuts and peas."

"And Russian, I think," added the sovereign. And to Mimi who had brought the cross to the Queen so that she might have a closer look at it, she said, "Mimi, how very beautiful. They are yours. And you now have in your hands a treasure worth a great deal of money. A not-so-modest fortune."

A fortune? They had had a fortune in their possession during all those years when they went hungry and wore rags. When Mimi had been a virtual prisoner of poverty and the Blocks, dependent on the kindness of a fruit peddler for understanding and company. None of it made any sense to her. This treasure in her hands, living at Beechtrees. It was too unreal. Reality was her years in the Blocks, isolation and poverty, and the drink that destroyed Mashinka's brother, made her crazy and unable to cope with day-to-day living. Reality was the wasting away of Tatayana, who had slipped into a deep melancholia from which she never returned except for short spells when she resumed her role as tutor to Mimi.

She passed the jewels around for her friends and benefactors to admire. She felt strangely detached from the excitement the contents of her envelope had created, but happy. Everyone was having such a good time. After the initial dazzle of the jewels, clearly Mimi was the least impressed with her newfound wealth. Each of the people there tried to make her understand the significance of these discoveries for her. Everyone spoke at once. A buzz like a swarm of chattering birds filled the room. "You are no longer poor, Mimi."

"You have money for anything you want, Mimi."

"Clothes, lots of clothes. And you can buy a horse, your very own horse." That was Juliet.

"I'll teach you to shoot, and you can buy a matching set of guns." Everyone laughed at Maxi's suggestion.

"A house, all your own, although we would want you to still live with us. And we could all go there on weekends."

"Your future is secure."

They all meant well, and she appreciated that, but it never penetrated the wall of fear still surrounding her. Her fear of loss had been with her for too long for her to believe a real change of fortune had come to her. It was the Queen who finally made her understand that, while the search went on for her father, she would have financial security and be able to live in comfort with someone to care for her. That her father had indeed provided for her. The puzzle was that her guardians Mashinka and Tatayana had been so devastated by their emigration to Chicopee and what they found there, they had not seen that their destitution and misery could have been avoided. They needed only to have been brave enough to face the reality of their situation and to have opened the package. It was a desperately sad story, a stupid waste of life and resources.

Mimi understood what the Queen was saying, but she was preoccupied with thoughts of her father. They had all suffered the shame of having failed this brave and handsome man who had done so much to make them safe and happy and preserve them from war. "When you find him, tell him I am here, and safe and well. I am happy, and life has been very sweet. I have the leather case, and he mustn't worry." That's what she would tell Jack to tell her father. She owed her father that. Mimi thought that she should tell that white lie, not for herself alone but for Tatayana and Mashinka as well.

Ernie, having read through the deeds, went to Mimi. She was now sitting on a cushion on the floor at the feet of the Queen, Juliet next to her. He squatted down next to her and reassured her. "Mimi, remember the FBI always gets its man. We'll find him. But you have to help. You can begin by remembering the past is gone forever. Wipe it from your mind. No more scrubbing floors for cook, or getting up at five to do your work in the kitchens. You do understand?"

"Yes, yes, yes." A note of annoyance in her voice. "I am not stupid, Ernie. I can understand, but you don't. I can't forget running away from Prague, being chased across countries that didn't want us, hiding and being hungry, and leaving my father, my mother." She hesitated at that point, then recovered herself and continued: "My mother Mashinka, how could she not have known we were desperate? Enough to open this case. Our lives would have been so different, and Tatayana and Mashinka wouldn't have died in misery and unhappiness, crazy and lost. Just the way I was when Mr. Pauley brought me here. We could have lived in a house like my father thought we were living in, one like this. My poor father ... if he had ever known what happened to us, what would he have thought. Maybe that's what killed Tatayana and Mashinka, knowing we had all let him down. He thought we were strong. We were weak and very stupid. Why didn't we live the way he wanted us to? I will never let him down again. I know what has happened here today and I know it's all real and true. But in my heart I can't believe that I won't be hungry again, that I will have a beautiful, sunny room like Juliet that's all my own. Not until my poppa finds me."

Her distress was obvious. Everyone in the room tried to dampen their enthusiasm, to make it easier for Mimi, who had not the least idea of the value of the things in her possession.

"One last look into that tin, Mimi," suggested the Queen, "and then, in celebration of your good fortune, we will all have a sherry, even the children." That relieved the tension in the room and brought smiles to the children's faces. Childish giggles rippled through the room again.

Jack struggled with the lid. It appeared to have rusted tight. His tussle was watched by everyone. There was no lack of suggestions of how to prise it open. But it was cook who finally snatched it from Jack's hands. She cracked it hard several times on the marble hearth and managed to yank the lid free. She gasped with astonishment, and crossed herself three times. Then, walking quickly to her mistress, she handed over the tin container with its loose lid.

The Queen removed the lid. Long ago the box had been filled with a soft clay substance. Pressed into it were four diamonds, a square-cut, a round, an emerald-shape and a pear-shape, not one of which was less than forty carats in weight, the size of small plums. By anyone's standards, even a Queen such as Marie Caroline, who owned one of the largest and finest collections of jewels in the world, they were gems of undeniable beauty and quality. And dotted around the dark, now dried clay were smaller stones of various sizes and shapes. They shone like stars around celestial moons.

Chapter 7

Juliet and Mimi were inseparable during the winter of 1943. The thirteen-year-old Pierre was a constant companion for the two girls, and they joyously followed his every whim. He was slavishly in love with Mimi. But then everyone was in love with her, even sixteen-year-old Maxi, who was always on the verge of running away, wanting to join the army, any army, to fight and even to die to win the war. Mimi foiled his plans with a counter-suggestion that kept him amused for a while every time the urge came upon him to be a freedom-fighter. The children were what made life in exile for the adults at Beechtrees more bearable.

But no matter what joy there was at Beechtrees, it was always overshadowed by the war. The household hung on every smattering of confidential information sent through to them from the State Department. They read every account of every battle in the newspapers several times over. They worked as hard at economizing and keeping to the ration books as their neighbors, and they prayed and hoped for victory every day. The Queen's consort left them after Christmas to work in Washington in some capacity no one quite understood. Jack, Ernie and Jim, the three FBI men, grumbled: they had not joined the FBI to miss the war.

Mimi was happy, life for her was less of a hardship. Cook and the family knowing her new circumstances were able to treat her, if not like family, as a close friend, but Mimi never took her happiness for granted. She often suffered a tremor of anxiety. Those nervous moments served as a reminder to the child that the wonderful homely people who had taken her in could all vanish and leave her behind. She remained still a displaced child, roaming the world alone, waiting for her father. A victim of the fortunes of war. Courageous, a clever child, she would quickly shrug those black feelings off before they could take hold. Mimi had learned from bitter experience not to expect too much from life.

She was the only person at Beechtrees who never thought about the future. She could only think of now. The future, tomorrow even, was the unknown, a mystery, a no-man's-land of nothingness for her. To imagine a future would have confused her. But as for living in the here and now, she was an expert at that. And this remarkable ten-year-old had the admiration of everyone for it.

If Mimi was unable to contemplate or worry about her future, there was not a person on the estate who didn't do the worrying for her. Because everyone in the household knew one day that call would come and they would all—the family, the staff, Jack, Ernie, Jim—leave Beechtrees to go home. Unless Mimi's father did return to find her, or the FBI found him as Jack had promised they would, what was to become of Mimi? Every member of the Beechtrees community suffered her isolation for her. Behind closed doors, numerous Mimi-plans were hatched. But there was so much to be done for her before that day came. She was a child who hid the scars of her hardship well. Maybe too well. It was difficult to tell just how much psychological damage Mimi had sustained from living in such dreadful poverty and in semi-isolation from people and the world for so long as Mimi Kowalski, daughter of Mashinka.

The family had come to understand what dreadful mistakes had been made by those in charge of Mimi's welfare. Their human frailties and downright ignorance had caused this child so much anguish, pain, and separation from people and society. But Mimi had not understood it. She appeared to be blocking out her change of circumstances ever since the day it had been revealed over tea, when she showed her photographs and the contents of her treasured leather envelope in its yellowed oilcloth wrapper.

The war was going badly on two fronts for America. Young men were dying a long way from home. The reluctant giant roared. Resources were committed to the fight. It was

America's war now, not just England's or Europe's, or the Far East against Japan. America became preoccupied with its own tragedies, its war efforts, its sufferings. It lacked only bombing raids on the home country or an occupying army.

The small enclave of foreigners living at Beechtrees in the Berkshires of New England felt the changes in the American attitude. The war had all but come home to Americans. All foreigners, even allies, were still alien to them. The local New Englanders had always seen them as unfortunate victims of war seeking refuge in the peace and tranquillity of their homeland, yet also as a race apart. People to be treated with cordiality, respect; a topic of interest, spoken of in whispers so as not to be seen as New England nosey. Now they were more reticent about than interested in the royal foreigners at Beechtrees. They were more attentive to war bonds, rallies, the fresh gold star in a family's window, symbolizing the loss of a son, a father, a brother.

The Beechtrees residents became more isolated that winter of 1944. It was a bitterly cold one, characterized by blizzards. Their weekly excursions to the cinema in Pittsfield, to stop and lunch in Lee or Lenox, or walk through Stockbridge, were no longer carefree jaunts but hard work. The townsfolk still traded with them, were still cordial, but smiles were hard to come by that winter. Though it was never discussed, once they were beyond the Beechtrees gates, there was always a sense that they were guests who had remained too long, that their welcome had run out.

Joe Pauley never failed them through that winter. Only the snow drifts kept him from reaching them. But after they buried Mashinka in a grave in Chicopee his relationship with Mimi was never as close as when they had been friends in the Blocks there. Mimi's change of circumstances, though neither she nor the peddler was aware of it, distanced the child from her adored friend and most important benefactor. But in her young heart she never let him go.

Life at Beechtrees had not changed at all after Mimi's tea party. The sovereign and her consort ran the family with a frugal hand. Everyone had his chores, his entertainments, his schooling. Mimi still rose at five in the morning and did her work for cook. She still kept the room off the kitchen given to her on arrival. An alternative had been offered, but she had declined. The Queen and her consort insisted they should all remain as normal a family as possible under the circumstances, believing that normality and a structured life would give them all a base to cope with their predicament, the ravages of a world gone mad. Isolated and troubled by the anxieties of war they may have been, but their efforts at happiness were well rewarded. It was as happy a house as the children could have lived in. From that standpoint Beechtrees was a great success. Memories of it would kindle a lifelong gratitude.

Jack and Ernie's investigation into Mimi's affairs was fruitful, financially certainly, and interesting to the two FBI men. All their leads in the search for Mimi's father came to a dead end, but they were getting a picture of a clever and responsible man who went to great lengths to cover his tracks. Before long, Ernie and Jack realized their work would be doubly hard: all indications were that Mimi's father was using the name Kowalski to hide his real identity. But was that only in America?

So surprise and disappointment met Mimi's refusal to reveal her real family name. They persevered, but to no avail. Then an edict arrived from Washington: Close Kowalski file, immediately. At least until after the war. That directive proved to the two FBI partners how close they had come to locating Mimi's father. By the sound of the letter from Washington, maybe even too close. But Mimi was to know nothing about that. It occurred long after she had gone to Jack and Ernie and told them, "I thought about it, Jack. I still want you to find my father, but not until after the war. That's what he said: 'I'll come and get you after the war.' I don't think I should do anything before that. And especially not now since I can afford, with all that money I have, to take care of myself. All those things he did for me, and all that money, those houses and jewels, and all those arrangements I don't understand that he made to take care of me. To take care of him when he gets here. You must see, I have to wait."

Between the tea party and Christmas Mimi made a journey to New York. Only an inordinate amount of coaxing persuaded her to go. The Queen and her consort, Jack and Ernie, even the Naval Attaché, set about convincing her that she must deposit the contents of the red-leather envelope in a bank for safekeeping. A child's logic—"I've had it with me all these years—why do I have to put it away now? Is it because I know what's in it? That doesn't make much sense"— had to be overcome.

Eventually they did win her over. She boarded a train for New York City with Ernie, Jack and Miss Tolset, her teacher. They were going to see the lawyer who had drawn up the deeds, and the banker who was handling her financial affairs.

It was dark when they returned to Beechtrees, but that didn't matter to the children. They were all waiting for her in the kitchen, eager to hear about her adventure into the big city. "You won't be leaving us, will you?" asked Pierre, looking very concerned.

"No, of course not. Why would I leave you?" She seemed genuinely puzzled.

"Don't listen to him. He's stupid." That was Maxi.

"What's New York like?" asked Juliet. "Was it fun?"

"Well, it's better here. But there's something exciting about the place. It's all so, well, speedy. Everything's so fast. It's overwhelming. Sort of gigantic, like a city in a movie. Not very real. Lots of tall buildings. I never saw so many people rushing up and down the streets in bunches. And the cars, they can only move by inches."

"Did you see the houses?"

"Well, they're not exactly houses. One of them faces this park, not just a normal park but one bigger than I have ever seen, like a city all on its own surrounded by the real city. And it's a building with many floors, and different families living on each floor. It has these big windows that are two floors high. The lawyer who took us there, Mr. Wilson, says it has a fanciful 'façade,' " mimicking the lawyer's broad New York accent. All the children thought that worthy of a burst of giggles.

"What exactly does that mean?" asked a still laughing Juliet.

When Mimi got her own giggles under control she answered, "A fancy front, I think." This merited a new round of chuckles.

"You children are being so silly." But Miss Tolset couldn't

help smiling: a teacher could only approve their eagerness to hear all about Mimi's adventure. That was all it meant to them, an adventure. Such innocence was refreshing.

Mimi picked up where she had left off. "You can actually see the balconied studios behind the windows. Mr. Wilson was very proud of the building. He kept telling us that every single apartment had 'elaborate and lavish spaces.' " More New York mimicry evoked more childish laughter. The adults around the old, wooden kitchen table joined in.

"Oh, Mimi, that's very funny, but it's not nice to make fun of people. Please don't do it again. Mr. Wilson is a product of an environment—New York. They have their own way of talking, just as you all do." The admonition somehow lacked conviction: her imitation had been on target.

"I'm sorry, but he did sound so funny." Turning back to the children she told them, "He was so nice to me. He really wanted me to know that it was a special place in the city, and that many famous people had lived there and still do. I forgot their names."

"Isadora Duncan, Alexander Woollcott, Norman Rockwell, Noël Coward, Fannie Hurst, to name just a few," offered Miss Tolset, a mine of superfluous information. No magazine escaped her.

Mimi shrugged her shoulders and carried on. "We did go in. And it was very big and unusual, sort of exciting, and we went into one of the studios—that's what they call the apartments in that building—and looked out. And it was different from any house I had even been in. I felt just like a bird looking down on the city. It was a lot different to being in the streets. They are *so* dirty."

"What about the other house?" asked Pierre.

"Oh, much more like a real house, although it's divided inside into four flats, one on each floor. It's in a place Mr. Wilson says they call either Lower Fifth Avenue or the Village. Greenwich Village, on the edge of it, is what Mr. Wilson says. That's a more cozy house, and the Village a more cozy place."

"Did you get to see a newsreel?" asked Maxi.

"No time."

"No time! What else did you do? Why couldn't you go to a newsreel?" Much disappointment in Maxi's voice.

"We spent a long time at the bank. The man in charge seemed very nice. They took my bank book and made so many recordings in it that they had to give me another one."

"They're called deposits," contributed Jack, who was at the table with a cup of coffee, forking up pieces of mocha cream cake.

"Where did the money come from?" asked Maxi.

"Shall I explain or will you, Mimi? They won't be happy until they know everything."

"They should, they're my friends. But explain what?" She seemed genuinely confused.

"Just what Mr. Peabody at the bank told you about the money."

"Oh, that."

"You do understand?"

"Yes, Jack. Well, sort of."

He was now used to Mimi's vagueness when it came to her newfound security. So was everyone else who knew her. They understood it as exactly what it was: a defense mechanism created by her to protect herself from disappointment, from her fear of loss. "You understand it better, you tell them, Jack."

"OK. Now listen carefully. Before the war, Mimi's father bought the two houses and gave them to her." A look of astonishment on the children's faces. This was truly a grown-up present. Jack felt prompted to add, "But he didn't tell Mimi or anyone else. It was a secret, a surprise for her for the future. All the people in them pay rent to live there. They give the money to a man that's called an agent, and he gives the money to Mr. Peabody at the bank. He puts it away for Mimi, and someone writes it down in her little book so she knows how much money she has saved."

"How much?" asked Pierre.

"Pierre! What a rude question. It is none of your business. Apologize at once," demanded Miss Tolset.

Alert to his embarrassment, Mimi came to the rescue of her friend by leaping in before he could answer. "There is a flat in the building facing the park. It's way up high. The man who lives there does so only until father or I want to move in. Mr. Wilson says that's 'the terms of the lease'."

"What does all that mean?" asked Juliet.

"It means I have a place to live, and money to take care of myself, if anything should happen and I have to leave you all. That's how the man at the bank explained it to me."

"Mr. Peabody, not the man at the bank, Mimi."

"Yes, that's right, Mr. Peabody will arrange things. A school for me to go to, and everything."

"What do you think it would be like to live there, in the city?" asked Pierre.

"Oh, terrible I should think. Lonely and hard. You would have to know a great many people and go to a lot of places to find some friends. And there would be no one in the flat to talk to, to play with. Not even cook to talk to and to watch out for me."

"Oh, Mimi, that's because you don't know the city and all the advantages it offers. For me it is the most exciting city in the world, and I would give anything to live there." It was said as Miss Tolset was leaving the room. The children shrugged their shoulders and dismissed her opinion in favor of Mimi's.

The winter continued, harder on the adults than the children. For them there was always a birthday or a party, an American holiday or one of their own country's to celebrate. Their projects and amusements were the most important things in their lives. Being so isolated from other children they were dependent on each other and their imaginations to sustain them. And they were happy. So much so they missed the subtle changes going on at Beechtrees.

At last the days grew brighter, the weather warmer. What was left of the snow drifts melted away under April showers. The trees began to bud, the new grass to turn green, the crocus, daffodils and wild tulips were pushing their way up from the dark towards the sun. Spring in all its glory was bursting out all over. And with the season the old iron gates were creaking open more often.

Cars of high-ranking officers from the various armed forces of several countries came to consult with the Queen and her consort. Several men from Washington, representatives from the President and the Secretary of State arrived for lunch one day with diplomats from London, France and Belgium. There was a buzz in the air, which the younger children enjoyed because it was "company." Only Maxi saw the visitors as signaling intrigue in high places. He spent most of his time trying to gain access to their meetings. Frustrated by living between two worlds, those of childhood and manhood, he felt half in and half out of the adult world at one of the turning points in history.

Chapter 8

Closed gates at Beechtrees was something new. Odd to see those grand old iron contraptions manned by armed security guards, FBI ones at that. For as long as she could remember the gates had remained open. Beechtrees had been a wild and wonderful place where she and her brother had played and run free.

Since her royal guests had taken up residence she had not been there. Poor old Beechtrees. Built at the turn of the century, like most of the other robber barons' country houses around the Stockbridge Bowl, it had only come alive with people for short seasons: the summer months, a week at Christmas, some years at Easter. It was faintly bewildering to ride up the avenue of trees as a luncheon guest in your own house. She felt even more out of sync to see, as the car maneuvered the graveled, crescent-shaped drive in front of the limestone mansion, the sovereign and her consort standing at the front door. Lined up on the white marble stairs, flanking either side of the Palladian portico to the house, her staff, her cook, and Beechtrees' housemaids, estate manager, gardener, stable lads. And there was Hyram Walker, the caretaker and overseer of them all, who had come to the house long before she had been born.

It was an unsolicited and generous gesture by her house guest. Even more so when the sovereign stepped aside for the real owner to enter her house. In the drawing room, they spoke of many things before finally coming around to discuss the family's exile at Beechtrees.

"I do not know how we can ever thank you for your generosity in lending your home to us during this very difficult time. And now it is so kind of you to make that journey from the city to us here for lunch, when in fact it is we who should have gone to you. But security, and our reluctance to make ourselves conspicuous, has prevented that. I hope you understand," the Prince told her.

"If Beechtrees has the luxury of a family in residence for more than the short visits we always used it for, that suffices for me. When it is empty, I tend to think of it as a depository for my ancestors' shopping sprees for antiques and paintings during their grand tours of Europe. And that always makes me sad, because Beechtrees is a place dear to my heart. I have always been happy here. As I told you when I offered the house to you, I make no apology for the genteel, somewhat eccentric, shabby grandeur of the estate. It has always seemed to me to add a special kind of romance to the place that Beechtrees yearned for. Fanciful, you might think, but now you have lived here, I hope you agree."

Until that moment the adults in the room, the Queen, her husband, the American Naval Attache, an ambassador from their New York embassy, all seemed very stiff, on their best and most formal behavior. Their tension now visibly dissipated.

"Oh, yes. I do know what you mean. We have been most comfortable, and have had the luxury of living a simple family life. My children have been very happy and, though isolated and in exile from all that is dear and meaningful to our lives, we have found something here that has sustained us and kept our courage up." The Queen spoke with a genuine gratitude in her voice, though regally unruffled by emotion.

The conversation seemed to collapse after she spoke. And the Naval Attache, a tall handsome blond man, who seemed just a little in awe of the attractive woman sitting opposite him, rose and cleared his throat before he addressed her. "I am afraid I must ask you to keep in confidence what we say to you here today, ma'am. I have been assured that that will not be a problem for you. It is a matter, you see, of the family's safety, and a degree of secrecy is necessary for various reasons."

She thought it all just a bit too much double-talk, but did understand, having been around people in sensitive political and diplomatic circles since a child. She answered, "You have my word," though saying so sounded silly.

The Prince told her, "We will be leaving Beechtrees, your hospitality and indeed America behind us—but not forgotten—within the next few days. I am afraid where we go and how is all very—how do you say it here?—hush-hush. So we can say no more about that."

"We could not leave without thanking you," the Queen told her. Again the awkward collapse in the conversation that tended to follow a royal pronouncement. But the Attache recognized his cue. "Her Majesty and the Prince find this all somewhat embarrassing, but nothing is served by beating about the bush. They feel the need to impose once more on your generosity. But, before they ask a favor of you, they would like you to understand that you are under no obligation to help them with a problem they have taken upon themselves. You must feel free to refuse them, otherwise they would not wish to discuss the matter with you."

"What is the problem?" she asked directing her words to the Queen.

"As William has stated, I have created a problem. Her name is Mimi Kowalski. She was nine years old when she arrived here at Beechtrees. Since then she has had a birthday, and she is now a beautiful precocious ten-year-old. We took her in as a playmate for our daughter Juliet, and as a part-time helper in the kitchens. We had only a vague idea of the terrible circumstances she had been living in for the past few years since she fled from Europe. She is one of those hundreds of thousands of displaced children. She won us over at once, and we are the only friends that she has, the surrogate family that has helped to heal some of the many wounds that fear and loss and poverty can inflict.

"A few months after she arrived here, and as a result of some discreet sleuthing (as I think you term it), we have found that unbeknown to her, her father had provided handsomely for her. So she is all right financially. However, we do not know what to do with her until her father is found—if indeed the man is to be found at all. You see we cannot take her with us, much as we might like to. The wrench of having to separate from her is difficult enough for us: what it might do to her is too horrible to contemplate. So we have come up with a solution. Not the best, but the best that we can do under the circumstances. Our cook Sophia adores the child and is willing to stay with her until her family is found. We would like to leave them both here, at least until the end of summer, if you would agree to that."

"You see," the Naval Attache continued, "that would give Mimi some time to adjust to having lost once again the only friends she has, this family. And to get used to Mr. Peabody, at the Morgan Guarantee Bank of New York. He has agreed to act temporarily as her guardian, so he can handle the day-to-day running of their lives. School, funds, staff, that sort of thing, because, frankly, in such matters, Sophia is likely to be as much a babe lost in the woods as the child.

"The idea is eventually to move them both into a flat on West End Avenue that is available to Mimi. It all sounds good for her now, but you have no idea what the child has gone through, how those with whom she was put in care failed her and themselves. A tragic story with a Cinderella ending, we hope. Well, I guess that's about it. Except that all she lives for is her father's coming to find her. We have done our best to try to find him, but to no avail. It has not helped that the child is most reluctant to talk about him or anything to do with her life before she arrived here at Beechtrees. She does on rare occasions, but we do not press her about her past. We feel that as she grows more emotionally strong and secure, she will be able to face up to it and talk about it."

The woman felt discomfited. She rose from her chair and walked to the window. She thought, no wonder they were embarrassed. What an extraordinary imposition. Of course she would say yes, but she was not happy about it. Although she liked children, she lacked the maternal instincts that all women were supposed to have. Her life and her work lay outside those roles foisted upon most women. And beyond all else she was a very practical woman. She turned to face these people to whom she had surrendered her house. A gesture of hospitality had now evolved into a responsibility.

"I can see your predicament," she told them, "but no matter how you look at it, you are abandoning the child. And what about the child and the cook? What kind of life will they have here when you are all gone?"

"Mimi loves Beechtrees. She feels at home here. She has told us she is happier here than she has been since she left her own home. She will have to understand that only a world war has forced us to do this to her. We have taken her into our hearts, and she will be with us always until we meet again. And I will promise her that we will meet again."

Clearly the Queen had hardened her heart to do what she must do. Her time of playing families instead of the role of sovereign was nearly over. Some things must be going seriously right in the war, the woman thought, or were about to, or else this move would not be happening. Certainly they would not be crossing the Atlantic for a destination closer to the conflict if that were not true. Hence the secrecy. Something big was going to happen that must not leak out. Oh, what did it matter? "If the child is happy here, of course she can stay in the care of the cook," she told them as graciously as she could, having realized how churlish her thinking had been.

There were no smiles, but their relief was obvious. "I am genuinely grateful to you. You will understand better how difficult a thing this is for us to do when you meet Mimi. But first let me introduce you to Sophia. She is normally a trojan of a woman. Today, however, she has a slight case of nerves that I am certain will vanish when she hears you have agreed to Mimi and her staying on. In anticipation of your consenting to our plan, she has prepared a small speech of thanks. I am afraid I cannot dissuade her from this oratory."

It was now obvious that she had been invited to Beechtrees for a takeover of her own residence. Although it was still a somewhat bizarre situation, she did feel less strange about being there than she had on her arrival. She walked from the window to the fireplace, and studied for a few moments the handsome John Singer Sargent portrait of her grandmother, one of the great high society beauties of her day. Then she turned her attention back to the people in the room.

It had gone quiet again. She found these silent lapses where all conversation went dead particularly disconcerting. One had to begin all over again. Although she could talk as banally as any drawing room conversation required when she had to, she found it exhausting. Fortunately the cook's arrival spared her the exercise of her banality.

After introductions had been made, and Sophia informed that she and Mimi might reside in Beechtrees, everyone but she seemed to relax. Sophia, whose English had improved enormously since Mimi's arrival, seemed to the rightful mistress of Beechtrees to be tough and resilient but kindly on the whole, though very much the tyrant in her kitchen. Everyone listened while she struggled valiantly to say how grateful she was for the opportunity to live at Beechtrees with Mimi. Then, approaching the lady at the fireplace, she told her, "I am very good cook. While I am here, you come, I cook. You come with plenty people, I cook. I like to cook for party. I am free for you wishes."

She was all politeness with a charm that belied the simple woman she was. But when she said, "You understand!" it was with a sharp tongue and a command in her voice. And that amused the real mistress of Beechtrees. She liked the cook immediately, was seeing in her a tough old bird who had gone soft on the child.

She was saddled with the cook and the child at Beechtrees, and that was that. There was no point in resenting it. Nor in thinking any further of the matter. Their happiness was not her concern. She was not going to take on that responsibility as well.

The children had been told nothing as yet about a departure from Beechtrees. The news had been deliberately kept from them until the Mimi problem had been sorted out. Now there would be just a few days between the news and the departure. Easier to deal thus with the excitement and explanations, the inevitable sadness at having to leave Mimi behind. The demands of security clinched the decision.

There was high excitement among the children over meeting again the mistress of Beechtrees. Endless talk of the movie-starrish lady from New York who had so impressed them the first time they met her.

Mimi listened to them. She caught their enthusiasm. Who was the lady the merest mention of whom could reduce Pierre to blushes? From Juliet she heard of her elegance, her very

American chic. She talked of her Rita Hayworth beauty. Every eye was on Maxi, who now insisted they call him Max. "Maxi" no longer sufficed. He was lady film-star crazy. And his favorite was Rita Hayworth. Her colored photos were plastered all over the inside of his wardrobe. Juliet and Pierre transferred their relentless teasing of Max about his Rita Hayworth crush to the lady. His pleasure at the mere prospect of dining with her was blatant. Giggles and teasing, whispers that went out of control, what to wear to lunch so as not to let the side down and to look as pretty as possible.

A serious discussion was held by the four children in Mimi's room. "Mummy is the best mummy in the world, but most definitely not glamorous, not even a little chic. Grand when she is wearing one of her tiaras and all her jewels, but she won't do that until after the war. I overheard Miss Tolset tell Miss Quinn Mummy was lovely but dowdy. If it means what I think it does, too bad. But I'm afraid it is true, Mimi. You see, Mummy doesn't understand glamor, nor the movie stars, nor how exciting glamor and chic can be. But we must do our best, don't you agree, Max?"

He did, and so the children took great care with their appearance. By the time they filed into the drawing room, luncheon that day had become for them the social event of the year, after Mimi's tea party.

She would not quickly forget her first sight of the woman, that special kind of beauty, so still and cool and sophisticated. So seductive and sensual. But Mimi at ten years old could only find there an attraction, without knowing what it was or why it was so appealing. Nor did she have a name for that kind of female power. She only knew that she wanted it too.

Mimi and the other children were besotted by the woman. They missed nothing. Later they would talk endlessly about her hair, so long and sleek under an ivory-colored straw sombrero with a red, white and blue-striped band of glass beads around the crown. Her figure outlined under a silk dress of the same ivory color, simple but chic, with its wide shoulders and long pleated sleeves, a soft bow at the neck, the skirt finishing an inch below the knees. The woman's bosom, and whether she wore a brassiere, were topics for endless conversation between the children that night before they went to bed. As were her long legs and high-heeled shoes, her ivory-colored silk stockings, the ivory alligator skin handbag. They had never seen a woman dress all in one color before.

The way she moved, her gazelle-like walk ... every gesture, when she did use her hands, slow and elegant, like those of a Balinese dancer. And her stillness: the girls would later decide that the lady's stillness was an illustration of why they would never fidget again.

One look, one luncheon in her presence, and the impressionable Mimi had found her role model, consciously or not. She was quick to understand there was another world out there, embodied in this lovely visitor. She wanted to embrace the world that a woman like that lived in. Mimi could understand why the children were so fascinated by her. This was another kind of woman, one maybe Juliet, Pierre and Max had never seen, but Mimi had. Her own mother had been a glamorous femme fatale, and Mimi had seen no other woman to match her, until now. She was dazzled.

She was the last of the children to curtsy and be presented. "And this is our friend, Mimi. Mimi, this is the lady who has been kind enough to allow us to live in her house. I would like you to meet Miss Dunmellyn, Miss Barbara Dunmellyn."

The child was an enchantress with a magnetic quality about her. She was special, and Barbara understood at once how difficult it would be to abandon her as the family must.

And she was no stranger to Barbara. She had recognized Mimi as Karel Stefanik's child the moment she entered the room. The cleft in the chin, the shape of the face; she had his seductive violet eyes. When Mimi had stopped staring at Barbara and her lips curled in a smile of delight, she recognized that smile. And she heard Karel in Mimi's voice when the child spoke. The accent, the touch of honey in the voice, it was all there in the beautiful child standing in front of her.

Good sense, control, surprise, prevented a faux pas. How dreadful had she blurted out that she knew the child's father. That she thought he might be the great love of her own life. That she had spent the best three days ever with a lover-*extraordinaire*, a very special man, maybe the best man she would ever know. That, though they had not met or spoken since she had watched his plane soar through gusts of sleet into a New Jersey night sky, he loved her. Such things were beyond a child.

How and arranged by whom she would never know—but periodically three dozen white, long-stemmed roses had appeared during the six months since that night she had picked him up at the Stork Club on New Year's Eve. Along with them always the same blank white card with a raised crest engraved in gold; and written in a strong distinctive hand, the same message:

The heart is a lonely hunter

Never a signature. She knew instinctively that Karel Stefanik was saying in the most romantic of ways, I love you. You are not forgotten.

She grazed his child's cheek with the back of her hand. How disturbing for the child if she learned her father had been in America yet had not made contact with her. What a hardening of his heart to have done that. She remembered what he had told her about abandoning his daughter to ensure her survival, and bearing ever after the guilt of having done so.

Mimi placed her hand over Barbara's. Just for a second, a child's impulse to touch. In that brief moment they became friends.

Chapter 9

"When do they leave?"

"The day after tomorrow. I had no idea you would be here to lunch. It seems an age since I've seen you, my dear." He hesitated as if he were trying to remember just how long it had been.

Barbara helped him. "Don't rack your brain, Uncle. It was . . ."

He stopped her. "No, don't tell me. I've got it. Not since New Year's Eve at the Stork Club." He gave her a knowing smile. They were walking arm in arm toward the pond.

What Barbara had thought was going to be a rather sad, dull lunch turned out to be nothing of the sort. Once the other guests had arrived and were seated around the table, and the food, exceptional even by her very particular standards, was served, the party seemed to take off. She had been unkind in her thoughts about lunch. Having met cook, she half-expected stodge and dumplings, a Central European cuisine, palatable and filling, but prepared by a heavy hand. How could she have known that Sophia had been trained by the Queen's French chef? Every resident at Beechtrees must have skimped for months for such a meal to be presented that afternoon. What quantities of ration stamps hoarded! But then, they did have friends in high places.

They had begun with a lobster mousse. That was followed by a salad nicoise, spring lamb, roasted in masses of fresh rosemary and Pernod until it had a dark, rich crust and was pink inside. A gravy like nectar. Paper-thin slices of potato, layered one on top of the other, baked to a crispy top in cream and Emmenthal cheese, and baby carrots cooked in honey and sesame seeds. That dish was followed by an apple and pear sorbet, to clear the palate. Cheese, a splendid selection, was served with thin homemade oatmeal biscuits. Then, the meal having been accompanied by a brilliant Montrachet and a Chateau Margaux that elicited rave reviews from the men at the table, Yquem was served with individual hot raspberry souffles, so light as to melt on the tongue.

Replete with food, all the luncheon guests went on a stroll to the pond in the windless and warm spring day. The sound of childish laughter, the hum of chatter, the birdsong, the feel of the sun upon their faces, charged sore and frightened hearts. So much so Barbara had almost forgotten about the nasty shock Mimi was about to receive. This wonderful world of Beechtrees—how would she feel about it once she had lost her benefactors and friends yet again? She wondered about that for a moment as she watched the child happily chatting to Juliet not fifty yards from her. Her uncle stroked her hand affectionately. She smiled at him, somewhat relieved that he had forgotten New Year's Eve and her sweeping Karel Stefanik into her life for a sexual idyll.

"Are you working well?" he asked.

"Very well."

"And who is the lucky man currently in my favorite niece's life?"

"Why do you always assume that there is a man in my life, Uncle Harry?"

"Because I know you so well, my dear. You are that kind of woman."

"And what sort of woman is 'that kind of woman'?" she asked.

"You're fencing with me, Barbara, and looking for compliments."

She laughed and kissed him charmingly on his cheek. "You see, a perfect example: a peck on the cheek, and men want to dance to your tune. 'That kind of a woman' is one who can seduce the hardest of hearts. Even an uncle to adore you. Fortunately, I am an uncle and so I have my prize, you, forever. The tie of blood protects me from being dumped when you're bored with this old codger. You know very well the kind of woman you are: one who is like a siren, who calls men to her. One kiss, and the poor unfortunates can never let you go. Barbara, you're a femme fatale, like your mother was, and she was my favorite sister. You, of course, are my favorite niece. Now 'fess up to Uncle Harry: who are you seeing these days?"

She laughed. "A concert pianist with a dull Russian wife, a painter, and the most handsome and brilliant bachelor, a visiting conductor of the Boston Symphony orchestra, are all in the running."

"You see what I mean—'running.' I think that has to be the operative word here." He smiled admiringly at his niece. "Well, at least the amours you do allow to enter the race for your heart are rarely less than interesting."

The children kept looking back at the adults and waving. Juliet and Mimi were gathering wild flowers. Her uncle held her firmly by the elbow while they descended the steep slope that ran down to the pond. "Clever of you to bring practical shoes to change into. But then you are clever in most things, always looking forward. I am inordinately fond of you."

While the others took the long way to the pond, the children, with Barbara and the brigadier behind, negotiated the slope cautiously. Once at the bottom and walking alongside the pond, she called, "Max, why don't you and the children run on ahead and take the cushions out from the boat house? Get the canvas off the boat and we'll all go out."

Max puffed up with pride not to have been included as a mere child. Taking control of the situation, he rallied his crew to ready the barge for his Cleopatra. At least it felt that way.

"You know, Barbara, you have been truly wonderful about lending Beechtrees to the government to accommodate the Queen and her entourage. The President is grateful to you. I know he will not forget your generosity. Their exile here had posed us a few problems. But it has all come off rather well." Then, because she thought he had forgotten about Karel Stefanik, the brigadier quite took her by surprise. After they had walked in silence for some minutes just listening to the sounds of spring, he said, apropos of nothing, "I wonder what happened to that remarkable man you went off with the last time I saw you? What a charming fellow. What a heroic guy. I hope he makes this war. A handsome, dashing kind of chap with brains and courage. And, dammit, what passion to see his country free." The brigadier snapped his fingers several times trying to conjure up Karel's name. "Stefanik, that was it—Count Karel Stefanik. I really liked that man. Real guts. A fighter for what he believes in. A freedom-fighter in the true sense of the word. You've never heard from him again, have you, Barbara?"

"No."

"Neither have I. But then I never really expected to. It haunts me, what he said to Franklin. That's what he was doing here, seeing the President. We flew him over from London to get vital information on what was going on in occupied Czechoslovakia. His and other opinions from men like him working in their government in exile in London. He was leery about the Russians."

"Why do you keep speaking about him in the past tense?" Barbara asked bravely, without a flinch of the nervous emotion another woman might have shown for a man she had loved so well, albeit for only a few days.

"Yes, now why do I keep saying 'was'? He *is* one of the loyal supporters of Dr. Benes, once the President of his country, now the man heading the government in exile. Now there is some guy! You won't find many statesmen like Dr. Benes around. Czechs like Benes and Stefanik are what this war is all about in the end.

"The Czechs, you know, were taken off guard by the speed and surprise, even the mildness of the occupation of their country. Hitler made it a Protectorate and shrewdly allowed the people to retain their own President, Prime Minister and government. Giving the illusion to the people that they were free. While expelling, of course, those peoples he didn't want in the country. He was anxious to exploit Czech resources, some of which our friend Stefanik was determined the Germans would never have. The incentives Hitler offered the Czech people resulted in an industrial boom in thirty-nine and forty. His clever manipulation of those early years of the Protectorate is what held up the small resistance movement that began the moment the German troops entered the country." He broke off here and asked her, "Does this interest you?"

"Yes, dear, do go on. I find it all fascinating."

"Right then. So where did I leave off? Oh, yes." He patted her hand and continued, "That made the work of Dr. Benes, who was already out of the country, very difficult. He needed the support of a resistance and the Czech people at home to be the heart and soul of his government abroad. It's really strange but for as long as I can remember Dr. Benes has always done better as a statesman abroad than he has in his own country. I may be wrong on that. It's just a personal opinion."

They walked on in silence. The brigadier picked up a small stone and skimmed it across the pond. They watched it skip over the water. He turned, smiled at his niece, and slipped his arm through hers. They resumed their walk. He continued telling Barbara about Dr. Benes. She found it interesting to hear about a country of whose war she knew almost nothing. Her lover's country. It was difficult to associate it with Karel. Theirs had been such a closed and self-centered erotic world, created exclusively for themselves. She found it odd to think of him in other terms.

She watched Mimi in the distance unlacing the canvas covering the mahogany and brass-fitted motorboat, her hair shining golden-blonde in the sun. Uncle Harry would have to be interrupted, no matter how fascinating he was about Dr. Benes, if the child joined them. For the moment the last thing Mimi needed to hear more about was her lost homeland. Barbara listened as the brigadier continued, "They were on French soil as early as 1939, most of the Czech army intelligence, a few of their generals, and Benes and his people. They were establishing an army of sorts, trying for a government in exile. But the fall of France was imminent. So by Christmas of that year, they were re-grouping on British soil. Benes was relentless in his will that his country should be a democracy and free.

"We're talking here, Barbara, of a remarkably civilized man. When asked in Hitler's early days of power what his opinion of Hitler was as a human being, he said that he considered him a completely vulgar man. Scarcely better than an illiterate. A man with no reason, no ability to reason. He refused to meet Hitler. How could he ever discuss anything with a man so animalesque? I don't think the word exists, but he did use it. Perhaps a new language needs to be invented for that bastard. Benes said he would never meet Hitler because it would be impossible to have a useful meeting. That made Hitler furious. On three occasions he sent men to return to Berchtesgarten with Dr. Benes. The last emissary was so insistent," here the brigadier laughed, "and concerned for his own life if he didn't return with Benes, that he put tremendous pressure on the Czech. The good doctor finally agreed to go, but told the men pressing him that they had to understand that in his jacket pocket he would have a revolver. In his other pocket he would have a grenade. If Hitler shouted at him as he had shouted down other statesmen, he would take the hand grenade from his pocket and simply throw it at him, and cause a European scandal. He saw no use in meeting such a man. He liked meeting people who were capable of discussion. He found intolerable the way Hitler treated even British statesmen who went to see him. Benes was mortified to think that such men exposed themselves to the ravings of a maniac. He felt that it was undignified. They should not have placed themselves in such a position. He had no intention of doing so.

"Benes' plans for his country ruled out any discussion with Hitler. He preferred to remain what he had always been, a human symbol of democracy. Hitler loathed democracy, and so there could be no rapport between them.

"Now how's that for a politician? A real statesman, a lover of democracy. Now a man like that, with an army and a legation in England, a country whose resistance in the first few years of their occupation hardly got off the ground, inspired men like our friend Stefanik to fight as his famous ancestors had for the right to be free."

The brigadier fell silent and bent down to gather half a dozen stones from the ground. He handed several to Barbara and said, "How's your arm? You used to be good at this." He skimmed a stone across the water, challenging her.

"Not bad," he told her.

"But not good enough, it seems."

They sat down on a stone bench on the edge of the pond. "You got sidetracked with Dr. Benes. You left me curious as to what Karel Stefanik said to President Roosevelt."

"So I did." He sat silent and thoughtful for a few moments, then asked her, "I don't suppose he spoke much about himself when you were together?"

"That's true."

"Well, that doesn't surprise me. He has to be a very cautious man. He's linked very closely with the Czechoslovakian Legation in London, and flies as an auxiliary pilot for the RAF. He's made four drops into his occupied homeland, funding the resistance. The Germans have put a price on his head. They want him badly, and alive. He comes to Washington—I'm actually the one who arranges it and brings him in—to see Franklin, and to liaise with me. There's vital information he gets through the resistance that could be, when the time comes, of great help to us or the Russians—whoever gets there first to liberate the country. He knows it like the back of his hand and can mark our maps. Where the arms factories are, military installations, railways, and so on.

"Anyway, I bring him to Washington. A quick job, in and out, here only to see the President for a talk at Dr. Benes' request. He spends a few hours with me and some of my army and air force colleagues and then we go to supper with Franklin. It's the usual martinis before dinner. Nobody mixes a martini like FDR. A smattering of his close advisers, Eleanor, and two rather pretty older women. Stefanik came here to the States with Benes. Like the doctor, he is a passionate believer in freedom and democracy. But he was always with though apart from Benes' government—if you know what I mean, Barbara. He was too much of a playboy in politics before the war for anyone to take him seriously. Handsome, a terrific ladies' man, a Count, a big landowner—the whole lot."

Suddenly the brigadier stopped and turned to look at his niece. She could see in his face that he had detected her real interest in Count Karel Stefanik. She placed her hand on his and told him, "It was nothing more than a New Year's Eve thing, a little romantic interlude." Her uncle smiled and looked relieved. "Go on, please, Uncle Harry. It's fascinating."

"And nothing more?"

"Nothing more, I assure you," she told him.

"Well, anyway, Franklin liked him. Remembered him. He

was *au fait* with what this man had done for his country, what he continued to do for his country.

"Drinks went well, dinner was very amusing. It was like being in the room with two of the great charmers of the world. Then the women went off on a tour of the White House or something, and we got down to talking about the war. Stefanik delivered several messages from Dr. Benes. First-hand information, grim, worrying talk, none of which I can reveal here, you understand. And some time later the President said, 'Count Stefanik, *we will* win this war.' And Stefanik answered, 'Yes, Mr. President, I have no doubts about that. My worry is whether my country will win the war.'

" 'I don't understand, sir,' said Franklin.

"So Stefanik said, 'The allies will win the war against Hitler and Germany. Deals will be made, Mr. President, deals are always made after a war. Victimized countries have a habit of being carved up after great conflicts. Or worse, being swallowed up one way or another by the victors. It would be a tragedy for Europe if that were to happen, Mr. President. With due respect, I would like to remind you that the wrong peace could be as dangerous as this war. You are dealing with Stalin, Russia and Communism. Once the armistice is signed, who will control those voracious Russians? The allies will be liberating occupied countries that have lost everything. Having been raped by Germany, they will be raped by Russia. That's why I pray when the invasion takes place, it is the Americans who walk into Czechoslovakia and not the Russians. It would be good to remember, sir, it is a terrible thing to give away another man's country. That is nothing but another kind of enslavement, a different kind of occupation than that of the Germans, but maybe not so different as you might think.'

"Well, you know Franklin, the consummate politician, always the leader with the large and open view of things, always in control, wanting to be right and fair, always the honorable elder statesman in peace or war. He went as white as a sheet. And a bell started ringing in my head, because Franklin Roosevelt for the first time in all the years I had known him, faltered. Let his iron-clad image slip. Why?

What precipitated it? I had to ask myself. Stefanik, something he had said, hit home to Franklin. Sure, Stefanik was out of line to issue a warning like that but the President is always open to people's warnings. In a moment of weakness I have never seen before, Stefanik got to him. The President recovered himself, and answered eloquently, as he always does, putting Stefanik more or less in his place.

"Stefanik is neither a politician nor a diplomat. I understand that before the war he was generous, overly generous even in his support of Benes and his cause, but always stayed in the background, never in the forefront of politics. He shunned always any responsibilities that might bring him to the forefront or lead him to accept any official position in the Benes government. And then, when it really counted, when it was considered almost too late, he marshaled the right men and against all odds pulled off an heroic act for his country. And he has been fighting for its freedom in every way he can ever since."

Barbara watched her Uncle Harry pull out a long, fat Havana cigar, roll it between his fingers several times, and clip off the tip with a tiny silver guillotine. He lit it and puffed, turning it in his fingers so that the cigar burned evenly.

The children were running in and out of the elegant but ramshackle wooded boathouse. She heard Mimi shriek with laughter over something and turned her attention to the girl. That child is in no position to hear any of this, she thought. Mimi waved, and both uncle and niece waved back. He said nothing to Barbara about her. Clearly he had no more idea than anyone else in the house that Mimi was Karel Stefanik's daughter. Barbara returned her attention to her uncle.

"The Germans were already on the march into Czechoslovakia, the country was falling. Everyone was making a dash to get out. The Czechs were ill-prepared to handle what was happening. Dr. Benes and his followers were in France. Stefanik saw that the Germans were going to grab his country's resources, and not least the national treasury and priceless public and private art treasures.

"The museums and churches worked day and night to crate and wrap their valuables. They turned a blind eye while Stefanik and the men he could rally round him looted. It was them or the Nazis doing the same thing for the Third Reich. He hid them, just as he did his own things, in quarries and caves, or buried them in gardens, or sealed them in secret passages under old palaces. He was way out on a limb with a stroke like that. To protect those who helped him, and the treasures, once the trucks were loaded he himself drove them to their secret destinations. Just a few men helped him, newly-made patriots like himself, who agreed to flee the country with him. He was meticulous in protecting the museum people by leaving an inventory and a letter saying the treasures had been removed for safekeeping.

"While all that was going on, with the help of the few remaining officers who wanted to get to France to join the army assembling there, he took as much of the treasury as they could handle. They loaded it into five buses and nine cars. He grabbed his daughter and two servants, formed a convoy of gold and people, and led it overland out of the country. The main body of men who helped him became the nucleus of the resistance. They placed in him all hopes of getting the treasury out and bringing help back in.

"But time was not on his side. Neither were circumstances. Hitler wanted that gold. You can imagine what happened when they found out it was gone. Someone talked, named Stefanik and told about the convoy. And the chase was on to stop it before it left Czech soil. I don't know how he made it, but he did. German fighter-planes found and lost them three times. The convoy was strafed and scattered twice. At one point they had a brigade of Germans no more than an hour behind them. They could actually see the German trucks filled with armed soldiers in a valley below. They lost several adults and two children in the strafing. It must have been agony trying to get real speed out of that convoy. Buses not equipped to carry that weight or move at high speed. Anyway, they made it out. But their problems didn't end there.

"Hitler was furious. He had the convoy tracked across Europe and exerted pressure on various countries to close the borders Stefanik was trying to cross with the convoy. Somehow, with Dr. Benes in Paris pulling what strings he could to assist them, without revealing what the convoy was carrying which would have meant disaster, they crossed into Hungary, traveled through Bulgaria, on into Turkey and finally made for Istanbul.

"There they almost lost the whole lot—would have, but for Stefanik's quick thinking. Somehow, by converting his family jewels into costly bribes, he hired a ferry and drove the loaded convoy aboard. In the dead of night they sailed not on the ferry's normal route across the Bosphorous, but far out on the Sea of Marmara. There they were met by an English frigate. They unloaded the treasury, and all the people, and sailed for England. To this day the Germans are hysterical about losing the Czech treasury and art treasures. No one more so than Goering. To him they were like personal property. They would dearly like to get their hands on Count Karel Stefanik, or anyone they could use as leverage to make him return to Czechoslovakia and divulge the whereabouts of what he left buried as he fled the country."

Chapter 10

Pierre ran up to them and interrupted the brigadier. "We're all ready to go, Miss Dunmellyn. Who's going to row the boat?"

"I'm in charge," announced the brigadier. "I once won a trophy, a large silver cup, for Harvard."

"But not alone, Uncle."

"No, that's true. I stand corrected. I once crewed for Harvard, and we won a cup," he good-naturedly told Pierre, patting him on the head. Uncle and niece walked with all the children to the weather-worn wooden dock. It tilted not dangerously but lazily to one side. "That dock, Barbara," chided her uncle, "looks as if it's at its last gasp, it's so old and tired." The children loved that and burst into giggles. "Beechtrees always looks like genteel poverty on a rather grand scale."

He loved to tease her about Beechtrees and the haphazard way she kept it going. She refused to rise to the bait: it was sport for him, and sometimes irritated her. Instead she changed the subject. "Can everyone swim?" she asked, and was greeted with proud and enthusiastic affirmation that they could indeed do without the cumbersome life-jackets stacked under the seats at the bow and stern of the boat.

She had not managed to dismiss as quickly as her uncle the story she had just heard. For her Uncle Harry it was just another wartime story. A row around the pond and a walk on the small island in the center was a favorite pastime for Barbara, but she seemed at that moment unable to feel the enthusiasm she had when she had suggested it. She was more distracted by what she had heard. It had answered so many questions that she had never felt the right to ask. It also answered those that she might have raised about Karel's behavior and how they related to each other.

What fate, she had to ask herself, had brought Mimi to Beechtrees? Fate or coincidence? Barbara was never sure about fate. She felt about it in the same way as she did about reincarnation—uneasy, in need of more proof. She gazed over at Mimi and felt a warmth for the child, the responsibility which had been foisted upon her by circumstances. Caution, she told herself. Sympathy is one thing, but taking on the role of surrogate mother is out of the question. Karel's story, Mimi's plight, served to trigger something in Barbara she had been suppressing: the realization that she was deeply in love with Karel Stefanik.

She watched Uncle Harry with the children. He was busy on the dock, removing his shoes and socks, rolling up his trousers, methodically, from the cuffs. His jacket had already been removed and was lying neatly folded on the dock, its array of bars and decorations gleaming in the sun.

The rowing boat was long and sleek, of polished mahogany elegantly trimmed in brass. The seats had arched, slatted backs, as did even the two smaller seats at the bow and stern. The larger ones were double, back to back, and the rowing bench a thick slab of ebony. All had cushions, a faded floral pattern in a worn chintz on the seats. The back cushions matched, and were cut to the same arched shape, and tied on with rather large bows. The period steam engine was housed in a polished mahogany cabinet in the boat's stern. Nailed to the side, close to the bow, in polished brass letters was her name, *Carlotta Sanchez*. No one had ever learned why a rowing boat in New England should have been named anything as exotic as *Carlotta Sanchez*. Barbara's great-grandfather, a robber baron and eccentric, had built and named the boat and left sufficient money in his will to maintain it. It was the best-kept object at Beechtrees. The oars were long, and the paddles shaped more or less like palm fronds.

Once the brigadier had barked out orders for the boating party, he took to the oars. The other house guests arrived at the pond just as they untied and moved away from the dock. The prow of the *Carlotta Sanchez* glided smoothly through the water, parting green lily pads. The smooth strokes of the oars carried the boating party parallel to the shore, from which the other luncheon guests called out instructions. Max, having organized the seating arrangements, placed himself next to Barbara. They faced the brigadier oarsman. Juliet was sitting back to back with them. Pierre and Mimi were placed behind the brigadier and facing them. They made a happy party. Juliet stretched out across her seat so she was able to sit sideways and face everyone, albeit looking over the shoulders of Barbara and her eldest brother.

"Just listen to them," said a very grown-up Max. "One would think we were children, and had never been in a rowing boat before." He cheekily edged himself just a little closer to Barbara.

"I always did like rowing the *Carlotta Sanchez*. She's a lovely boat. So easy to handle. They don't make them like this anymore. How about a song?" With a surprisingly beautiful tenor voice, he burst into one of Gertrude Lawrence's best Noël Coward songs. Barbara picked up on some of the words. Juliet added her sweet voice and knew all the words. "If you can't sing it, children, hum it. Let's hear you now. Let's give them a tune they can hear on shore." He rowed smoothly and swiftly, and they sang Gertie's hits at the top of their voices. The ducks were not impressed. They quacked and paddled away. They had circled a good distance around the pond, nearly an hour of rowing and singing (the concert had degenerated into silly nursery songs and giggles) before Uncle Harry beached the boat on the island, sending a flurry of birds high into the air. Everyone clambered out of the *Carlotta Sanchez*, eager to explore the island. They followed the path to the gazebo in the center, and Barbara related stories about the grand picnics her mother had hosted there. How her father used to row out to the island alone to play his violin. "How haunting it was to hear faint strains of Vivaldi and Brahms floating back to shore through the sounds of nature all around: the rustle of leaves on the trees, the sound of birds and the small animals of the woods, the lapping of the water at the edge of the pond."

They made their tour and the children read the labels on the trees and shrubs, rare species gathered from all over the world and planted there by Barbara's great-grandfather. After boarding the *Carlotta* again, with Mimi and Juliet now sitting next to Barbara, Pierre behind them, while Max and the brigadier shared the rowing, they aimed for the shore. Clearly they were all having a happy time together.

An amber hairpin fell from Barbara's hair. Mimi picked it up from the floor of the boat and replaced it, asking, "Why don't you live here?"

"Well, I do, but only for very short periods at a time. My real home is in New York City, and I have a place in East Hampton."

"Mimi's been to New York," announced Juliet proudly.

"Oh?" answered Barbara, showing great interest in that news by looking directly at Mimi.

"Yes, and she could live there if she wanted to. She has two houses there, all her own."

"But only a flat that I could live in, Juliet. Not a house. It's nothing like this house, if that's what you think."

"How exciting, Mimi. And are you going to live there?"

"I live here."

"But you can live in both places, just the way I do." Barbara realized that she had stumbled on a way to ease the pain that was yet again about to engulf Mimi when she was told the family was leaving without her. Barbara was not blind to the fact that all the children were besotted with her. Saw her as an object of glamor from a world they had yet to experience and wanted to. Her voice could influence these charming children hungry for experience. She saw her opportunity to point out to Mimi that she had options, and how exciting it would be for her to live in New York City. But then warning bells began to ring in her head. Instinct told her, don't get too involved and lead this child on another trail of false security and love.

"I don't know anyone in New York. My friends are here, so why would I want to go to a big, dirty city full of strangers?"

"To meet people. Make more friends. You could do that. Why, you already have someone to call on. You know me. You see, it's as easy as that."

"But whatever would I do there all by myself?"

"Well, you wouldn't be by yourself, would you? There would be a housekeeper to live with you, and you would make friends very quickly at school. Why, I know some children your age in the city, and they have the most wonderful time. They're busy running about all the time doing the most interesting things. I could introduce you to them."

"I can't think of anything I could do if I lived in New York, except go to the park to get away from the people and all that rushing around."

"That's because you don't know New York. There is so much to do. For one thing, you would go to school."

"Wouldn't I have teachers at home like I do here?"

"Well, you could, but I think you would have more fun in a fine school I know. You would meet lots of girls your age, and older and younger as well, there."

"I think I would rather live here."

This was clearly not going to be easy, thought Barbara. Then help arrived from an unexpected quarter. "I wouldn't," piped up Juliet. "I would like to be like Miss Dunmellyn and live in both places. If I did, I would go to—to—well, I don't rightly know where . . ."

"To the theater, and concerts, and ballet. You could go to galleries and look at beautiful paintings. I could take you there some time. Museums—there are all sorts of wonderful museums in New York to go to. Not just stuffy old places but exciting institutions with fascinating programs for young people just like you."

"Oh, how thrilling a place it sounds. And cinema, all those movie houses, we could go to and see Hollywood films and newsreels. Well, if you don't want to live there, we could all go down just to see it some day," interjected Max, while pulling on the oars in rhythm with the brigadier.

"Shopping. We could spend all day just going shopping for the latest fashions."

"You need money for that, Juliet," Pierre told her. That took the light out of her eyes. "But . . ." The light came back ". . . We could get a year's pocket money in advance if we were clever." Everyone fell silent for a moment. The idea was brilliant. How to accomplish it?

"But it's so big, so many people. I can't even imagine how

we would get around the place." Barbara could tell from Mimi's voice that she was wavering. In spite of herself there was an interest. The prospect was growing on her.

That was true. But it was more the prospect of having Barbara Dunmellyn for a friend in the city than the city itself that interested Mimi. The woman was everything the children had told Mimi she was and much more. She was kind, and wanted to befriend Mimi and take her around and show her a new world of which Mimi knew nothing. And that was exciting, to be with such a glamorous and beautiful lady. And Mimi sensed something else, safety, the possibility of some continuity in her life, a stranger who would not suddenly appear to sweep her up and vanish just as suddenly as she had appeared. And that was something she had not felt since the day she was parted from her father. Mimi listened, hung on to Barbara's every word.

"Mimi," she told the girl, "it's like a great many little villages all strung together like beads on a necklace, and the necklace is the city."

"One of Mimi's houses is in the Village," Juliet offered.

"Where?" asked Barbara.

"I don't know. And anyway I like it here."

"Wouldn't you like to visit Mimi in her house in New York?"

"Would I! But I like it here too."

Well, Barbara thought, she's no help. Then Mimi surprised Barbara.

"If I did live in New York, I would have to live in the flat in the big building on Central Park West?"

"That's just on the other side of the park from me. We could be friends, and sometimes you could come over and visit with me. And when I have time—I don't have much free time, Mimi, because I work—but when I do, I would take you out to do something. Or you might come to have a meal with me. And if you're lonely with nothing to do—which is almost an impossibility—I have a man, Ching Lee, who takes care of me. He would take you around and show you some of the city until you were settled. So if one day you should decide to live in both places, you must call me and let me know."

Mimi was now utterly charmed by the idea of having Barbara as a friend. That the other children could go somewhere to be a guest of hers for a change. It was something to think about, visiting this lady in New York City. She suddenly felt a pang of sadness. If only Mashinka and Tatayana and she had met Barbara Dunmellyn on their arrival in America. If only they had never gone to the Blocks. Mimi began to wring her hands. She felt her joy slipping away from her. She caught sight of Juliet staring at her. When their eyes met, the look of concern in Juliet's, and then the signal, a discreet tap on her own hand, for Mimi to stop. She did, at once, and blocked out those painful thoughts of the past. The two girls exchanged brief smiles and their attention returned to the boating party.

"Is it rude to ask what you work at?" That was Max.

"No."

"Well, what sort of job do you have?" asked Pierre. "Are you a shopgirl?"

"God, you're stupid, Pierre!" said Max. His younger brother sometimes disgusted him.

Pierre ignored Max and persevered, "Are you a teacher, then?"

"No, I'm an artist. A painter."

"A proper artist with a studio and a slanted glass roof?" The possibility clearly enchanted Juliet.

"You look more like a movie star than a artist." Max reddened to hear his thoughts escape him. The brigadier laughed and teased.

"Barbara, I sense you have a serious admirer here in Max. I reckon you'd have no trouble getting him to live in New York and accept your friendship."

He decided to brazen it out. "You certainly would not." He managed for Barbara a rather bolder look than she had anticipated from him. Awkwardness was avoided when Juliet, lost in the romantic notion of what an artist would be like, pressed on, "A studio, all your own, with an easel and a palette of paints?"

"Yes, a very large and beautiful studio with all the painter's tools. Mimi and you—well, all of you, if you come to New York—can visit me in my studio. Afterward I will take you all out. We could have an ice cream at a wonderful parlor called Rumpelmayer's on Central Park South. How does that sound?" She had them all hooked now, Mimi included. She could see it in their faces, hear it in the voices questioning her at length about her life and New York.

Max and the brigadier secured their oars. The brigadier shook Max's hand, congratulating him on his rowing. Pierre threw the line to his father who secured the boat to the dock. They were all there waiting to accompany the Beechtrees sailors back to the house for tea.

Mimi looked so pretty and happy walking next to Barbara. She saw the quality that enchanted everyone who got to know her, that combination of child and waif with maturing beauty and intelligence. A charm not unlike Barbara's own that had drawn men to her ever since she had been a child. An independence, and yet a streak of vulnerability. And there was, too, something else, a natural sensuality about the child. Barbara had learned how to use those things to her advantage and to protect herself from being taken advantage of, and so would this child have to, all her life. Well, that's not a bad thing, thought Barbara. It has done me no harm to be strong. On the contrary. The thought prompted her to a decision: she would, until Mimi was back in the bosom of her family, be as supportive as she could of her, while remaining ultra-cautious that Mimi should not become dependent.

She told her, "You know, Mimi, life is very strange. When one door closes, another always opens. Take today, for example. I have had the most wonderful day, and soon I will have to leave you all to go back to New York all by myself. Tomorrow is another day, and another door will open, and I will have a different small adventure. That's how you grow and develop and learn. You make changes and go forward. When you are young, as you boys and girls are, you usually have to wait for your parents or guardians to make those changes for you. But soon you will be making them for yourself, with adults in the background to guide and advise. That will be so much fun for you and the other children. Don't you think so, Juliet?"

"I hadn't thought about it that way. I don't think Mimi and I have begun to think that way. Maybe we have been too lazy in our minds, Mimi. We are always letting Pierre find doors to open for us."

Barbara tried to hide her delight in what she was hearing, wanting not to make too much of it for fear of frightening the girls off, and especially Mimi. Instead she pushed her advantage in the hope she was opening a prospect of some sort of a future for Mimi after the loss of the family hit her. "You would go to live in New York if you could, wouldn't you, Juliet? I mean, part-time. There would always be your other place, Beechtrees. Even if you had to go alone, the way I do."

"Oh, yes. I would want to try it out anyway. To really see what's there."

"That's called experiencing a place. Well, good for you. We all have lots of experiences. Not always good. But one has to be big and brave and keep going forward and adding to one's life. Every time I leave New York and come to Beechtrees, it's to experience whatever there is to offer here. Fortunately it is always a happy encounter like today."

"Not everyone is a free spirit, an independent creature with a voracious appetite for life like yours, Barbara. You get it from both sides of the family. In you it's innate. Your mother and father were both like you. But there are those who are happy not to jump into the fast-moving rapids of life, those who settle for the easy-running streams. I'm getting on my bandwagon again, about your settling down. Sorry about that. But you know me, an old army man. Like things to fit into the system. That's why I am always in conflict about you. I like you too much the way you are, but ..."

The girls appeared riveted by the intense exchange developing between Barbara and her uncle. Everything the brigadier said seemed to them to glamorize Barbara even more.

"Oh, hell, don't ever change. You're the best." He kissed her on the cheek and strode away toward the Queen, saying, "Ma'am you have given an old soldier a lovely day. May I take your arm?"

Barbara had not seen her uncle in such high spirits for a long time. He was not among those having a good war: it had been taking a toll on him. He had a controversial reputation as a top army man: hard, ruthless with his men, some said a maverick, insubordinate at times to his superiors. A genius in certain aspects of war, for which he was respected. He had the President's ear. Men of higher rank and position had to respect that. She had great affection for her uncle, but for the other side of his character, the non-army side. When Mimi asked, "May I visit you in New York some time?" Barbara felt quite relieved. She had, after all, gotten her point over to the girl. She had thought it might have become lost in her uncle's interjection.

"Of course, Mimi. And if one day you should find yourself living there, then we could see each other often. You see, you already have a friend in New York, though I hope you understand that, if I cannot see you one day, I will see you another. My work and the art world fill my life: it has to take precedence over most other things. I would have to be a friend who would be there for you, but one you must not be too dependent on. Now, if that's good enough, we can be fine friends."

Barbara felt she had said it all. Had done all she could to try to ease the blow that was about to hit Mimi, and without involving herself too much. The girl was no dummy, she had a clever mind, she was a survivor. She had got the message, even if she had no idea why it had been delivered. Hopefully she would remember that a new door could open for her if she gave it a little push. That things had changed for her. That though she might be a victim of circumstances, she need not be a mere victim. Barbara could not but hope for the child's sake that Mimi would want to take that step forward rather than live alone with Sophia at Beechtrees. Barbara would be no substitute parent for Mimi: she hoped that she had made that clear. Barbara would be the only thing she could be to Mimi: the best of friends.

It was a soft, warm, rosy and mauve dusk when the family stood on the stairs in front of the entrance to wave the last of their guests a final farewell. They watched the car circle the crescent-shaped drive and disappear down the avenue of beech trees now covered gloriously in small, tender new leaves. The avenue looked like a scene from a French Pointillist painting; a little unreal, enchanting, mysterious. They remained there silent, listening to the sounds of Beechtrees,

nature making ready for nightfall. The silence was broken by
the Prince. "Everyone into the drawing room."

The children, still high on excitement from their day, had
expected supper in the playroom and bed to have been the
last directive of the day from their parents. And then a post-
mortem about it in whispers after lights out. For Mimi, an order from cook to change her clothes, the supper had to be
done and the kitchen made immaculate before she could go to
bed. For all her newfound wealth and closer relationship with
the family, Mimi still had her chores to do. She still kept,
more or less, to the dictum that she had to earn her keep in
exchange for living at Beechtrees and retaining the family's
and cook's friendship.

Looks passed between the children, broad smiles appeared,
the day was not over. This was more fun. There would be
plenty of time tomorrow to hash over the grand party and the
guests without having to sneak around to each other's rooms
in the dark. They should have suspected something important
was about to be announced when on entering the drawing
room they found the house staff assembled and waiting. But
they were overexcited children, still wrapped up in the day's
events and the glamor of so many illustrious visitors. The realization that something more was happening outside their
own little world was missed. It was only when, for the third
time, the Prince broke in on their chatter and restlessness
with a request for everyone's attention, that the room went
quiet. Cook went to stand behind Mimi, and even before she
whispered in the child's ear, "Pay attention," Mimi sensed
something momentous was about to happen, but not for her.
She felt a nervous tremor and began rubbing her thumb
across the back of one hand, aware of the smoothness of the
skin. She began wringing her hands, but caught herself before
anyone could see, stopped, unclasped her hands and placed
them by her sides.

"What we have all been waiting for is close at hand." The
Prince's voice was charged with emotion. "It cannot be long.
Soon the war will be over, and so we are leaving Beechtrees
for England, the day after tomorrow, to await the end of hos-
tilities there and to be closer to home. At the right time we

will cross the Channel and return with the Allied troops to Europe and our country, liberated from its years of tyranny."

Ever since her arrival at Beechtrees, Mimi had expected that one day she would have to leave it. Later, when she became less a skivvy for the family and more a friend, that they would vanish from her life was a constant expectation. But no matter how she had prepared herself, expectation and reality are two different things. She had to fight back tears. The pain of seeing Max, Juliet and Pierre jump with joy, whoop and holler and dance round the room with excitement, of listening to their enthusiastic questions, hearing the excited laughter of everyone concerned, was hard for her. But worse: not once did they glance her way. She was forgotten in the rush of such momentous news.

Mimi felt the cook's hands on her bony shoulders. Sophia gave a squeeze of reassurance. The child sensed that she was telling her, it's going to be all right, you're going to be just fine. Mimi turned to gaze into Sophia's face. The cook's eyes were filled with tears.

"Not us," she told Mimi. "You and I, Mimi, we stay here at Beechtrees."

It took several minutes before the children could be calmed down. Then the Queen called Mimi and cook to her side and addressed herself to Mimi. "You must know that if it were at all possible we would take you with us. But it is not." Her words did little to ease Mimi's pain at being left behind. Nor the surprise to Max and Pierre, the shock to Juliet. They burst into a shower of pleadings with their parents that Mimi should be allowed to accompany them, but were silenced with severe looks. "Children, you are making this more difficult for all of us, mostly Mimi. Miss Dunmellyn has invited Mimi and cook to stay here at Beechtrees. She will be safe and happy, it has been seen to."

The sovereign turned to Mimi and took the child's hand in hers. Stroking it, she told her, "You do understand Mimi? Cook has asked to remain with you until your father returns. She wants to look after you, and you must obey her. You will for the time being live here at Beechtrees with her. You needn't worry about anything. Mr. Peabody has agreed to organize your life here, schools and finances and so on. Be happy for us all, child. We are going home soon, and one day soon, so will you. After the war, when we are settled, the children will ask you to come and visit. Until then you can write to each other, become pen-pals. You must think of our departure as something wonderful. Peace is closer than ever, and soon we will have returned to our normal lives."

What's that? Mimi wondered to herself.

The child struggled against her sense of loss by thinking of the beautiful and glamorous Barbara Dunmellyn waving to her through the oval-shaped rear window of the black Chrysler as it disappeared down the avenue of beech trees, swallowed into the rosy-mauve dusk of descending night.

Chapter 11

The house was in turmoil. Everyone seemed dizzily excited and busy. Packing, preparing themselves for the future. Happiness and hope had until now always been in the shadow of war, fear of the future, stalking them. But suddenly those fears seemed to vanish. The family was on the move, about to cross the Atlantic. For the first time, everyone believed that victory was closer rather than farther away.

Mimi tried to enter into the spirit of things but it was impossible. The only thing she was experiencing was a sense of being left behind. Some invisible wall had dropped between her and the family. They were wrapped up in a new life that she could not possibly be a part of, and it hurt. It was only when the last car was pulling away from the entrance to the mansion house to circle the drive and enter the avenue of breech trees that she was able to overcome her feelings of separation and dash after it, all waves and smiles, calling, "Goodbye, goodbye, and thank you."

The cavalcade of cars—three limousines, two station wagons and a large van carrying household belongings—was moving out slowly in the dawn light just breaking over the leaves of the trees. The headlights of the cars like yellow hazy moons pierced the early morning mist. Jack, on a motorcycle, was bringing up the rear as far as the gate, where he would join Ernie in the black Dodge, to make up the last car in the small convoy heading for the Westover Field military airbase. There a transport carrier was waiting for its precious civilian cargo. Jack stopped for only a second to sweep Mimi up and gave her a ride as far as the gate. There she burst in on the family in the Cadillac waiting for their escort to get into position. Mimi said more enthusiastic and affectionate goodbyes. The family was swept up by the charm she could exude, and for a few moments the invisible wall that separated them vanished and they were together, bosom friends, happy and excited about the future.

Finally the car door was closed and Mimi watched the four motorcycle Massachusetts State Troopers making ready to fall behind the black Dodge, as escort. They revved their motors and circled round Mimi. One of the tall, handsome, uniformed policemen winked at her, another patted her on the head as they passed by to shoot out after the Dodge. She remained standing there, the dust rising up around her spindly legs, waving frantically until the cars and the troopers were long out of sight.

Mimi placed her hands by her sides. It was very quiet now except for the birds. She stood for a long time looking through the entrance to Beechtrees on to the public road. This was the first time she had ever seen the great iron gates of Beechtrees left open. It seemed strange but exhilarating. She had been so unhappy ever since she had heard the news of the family's departure, but all that was gone now. Her relief at not being so deeply unhappy was to affect her from that moment and for the rest of her life. She made a vow to herself that, no matter what, she would never tolerate such unhappiness again. Mimi made her second independent decision right then and there. Until her father came to claim her, she would do what *she* wanted to do about her future. With, of course, the permission of Mr. Peabody and Sophia.

She stood there, in front of the open gates, one lone figure in the morning mist with the sun burning off the remnants of night, until she was moved to walk back to the house and Sophia. Mimi entered a kitchen that smelled of frying bacon, freshly baked bread, coffee, the sweet scent of hot chocolate. The sad face Sophia had shown as she curtsied and said her goodbyes to the sovereign and her consort, hugged and kissed the children, was gone, replaced by a more placid and content expression. She was standing over the stove, pushing bacon around in a frying pan with a fork and humming a bright tune. Mimi stood watching for several seconds. Sophia, sensing that she was there, turned to smile at Mimi, and ask, "Scrambled or fried? One or two?"

"Scrambled, two."

"Good, then we'll all have scrambled. Go and call the teachers. I left them with long faces in the small sitting room." Mimi was amazed at how quickly enthusiasm for change can take over and transform one's mood.

Those left at Beechtrees made an effort to make a new life for themselves, sometimes in vain. Mimi and Sophia moved into large sunny bedrooms overlooking the park, but Sophia was uncomfortable and, after three days, returned to her rooms off the kitchen. The house seemed much too big for Mimi and the two tutors. They felt lost in it without the family for back-up, but kept their rooms nevertheless. The tutors, contracted until the summer holidays, stayed with Mimi as their only pupil until they took on Sophia too, teaching her English and American history. The four women pretended to themselves that they could live there as happily as they had when the family was in residence, the pretense wore thin. The incredible quiet and beauty of Beechtrees was still there for them, but they missed the adventure, excitement and fun the family generated. No more mysterious guests or endless talk of the war.

As Mimi watched the FBI men pack up their surveillance and security systems and one by one leave the estate, it slowly dawned on her that so would she. Because she and Sophia had choices just as Barbara Dunmellyn had said.

Jack and Ernie were the last FBI men to leave. They were accorded a sumptuous farewell lunch by Sophia, served at a table set up on the south lawn, with a grand view of the lush green trees and wild flowers covering the surrounding hills punctuated with grand old mansions that glistened white in the spring sun. The women, the two young teachers and Sophia and Mimi, were dressed in their best to make an occasion of the men's departure. The lunch consisted of pancakes stuffed with lobster and shrimp and a cream sauce, a cold vichyssoise, luscious and creamy, with snippets of bright green chives floating on top; rib of beef, boned, stuffed and roasted, crispy, mahogany-colored on the outside, rare and pink on the inside, with roasted potatoes, a lacquered golden color, crunchy, but soft and buttery-tasting once opened with fork and knife. The beef was stuffed with wild rice, crabmeat and mushroom, and served with baby candied carrots and tiny individual molds of hot spinach mousse. For dessert, fresh strawberry pavlova. Sophia produced exquisite wines, a Montrachet first, followed by a Chambertin, and with the pavlova, a Sauterne that was unforgettable.

The Prince himself had selected the wines to be served. It had been he who had ordered the meal to be given to the two men as a parting gift. It was an enjoyable lunch, one impossible to share without reminiscing about the adventures they'd had during the years they had been together, and that of course included the children, the Prince and the Queen. It was to remind Mimi of how empty Beechtrees really was, how much more so it would be once Ernie and Jack left.

Over coffee and long, fat Havana cigars, Jack sprang his surprise. "We have good news, Mimi, it came through this morning. Our transfer, and it's official." A large beaming smile crossed his face. Ernie continued, "We were stuck here. Much as we like you guys, *we were stuck here,* and out of it, for far too long."

Jack interrupted. "Now we've pulled the plum out of the cake. Our transfer is to the New York office, and that's a great posting. Lots of real action. It also means . . ." And he smiled at Mimi and Sophia, only this time it was Mimi who interrupted.

"We can see each other, still be friends?"

"That's right, Mimi. And I can still eat your cooking, Sophia. The city is not all that far away."

Mimi felt a kind of elation, a strange excitement. She felt relieved at the idea that Jack wasn't going to vanish the same way the family had. He was going to that big New York. Barbara Dunmellyn was in New York, and there was Mr. Peabody at the bank, and a place to live, and money in New York. Nothing was the same as it had been when Mimi arrived at Beechtrees. Stop looking back, she told herself. You don't have to be left behind, Mimi Kowalski, you have something *and* somewhere to go to.

Quite calmly she announced, "Sophia and I will be in New York too." She looked down the table. Surprise showed on her guardian's face. "Yes, Sophia. I don't know if we'll like it there, but we'll give it a try. Because I have a house there, we have a home, and we can't stay at Beechtrees as guests forever." Mimi felt a surge of excitement now that she had said it. Only Sophia seemed astonished. The others seemed pleased, relieved even. The following morning Miss Tolset called Mr. Peabody for Mimi, and yet another new life began for her.

The next few years were to be happy. Though she might still have been a victim of circumstances she no longer felt that way. Though nothing fundamental in her life had changed, and she was still waiting for her father, she filled her time with real growth. Her spirit no longer trodden down by poverty, confusion, being a prisoner of circumstance. Mimi felt a certain security in herself, and her soul was able to take wing. She no longer felt dependent on strangers but appreciative of their kindness. Throughout that spring and summer she and Sophia lived at Beechtrees until Miss Tolset and Miss Rifkin, the two tutors, finished their contract. Mimi and Sophia studied hard, Mimi preparing herself for school in New York, the first proper school she would have attended. Sophia, an immigrant woman, quick with other languages, preparing herself with the help of Miss Tolset to learn English and become literate in it, wanting to be for Mimi a mother-figure until her father returned. There seemed no doubt in Sophia's mind now, anymore than in Mimi's, that that would happen.

The three women and Mimi took sorties into New York to see Mr. Peabody, to check on schools, and to stay in the West End Avenue flat, newly decorated with the help of Mrs. Peabody, who like her husband and their children had become enchanted with Mimi and her courage in taking on New York. The cook and Mimi eased themselves into the city and a New York lifestyle of a sort that neither of them understood or appreciated. It took time. At the beginning they fled back gratefully to Beechtrees for regular visits.

It was several weeks before Mimi made contact with Barbara Dunmellyn. She felt neither nervous nor awkward when she made that first call. She was only excited about telling Barbara that she was happy at Beechtrees, and she and Sophia were coming to live in New York. And for Barbara, to hear the cheerful lilt in Mimi's voice was to feel a sense of relief and, yes, delight that she had made the decision to move to the city. There had been no doubt that Barbara had been charmed by the child, certainly as much as she was fascinated that Mimi should be the daughter of a man who represented for her a memorable sexual encounter.

Mimi and Barbara took each other up. In Mimi's eyes, Barbara was not just her beautiful and glamorous friend, and an artist, but someone who knew how to do everything correctly. Barbara was the person Mimi was truly learning from. She was the most important influence forming Mimi. It seemed to her that everything Barbara did added to life whether it was ice cream at Rumpelmayer's on Central Park South (Mimi's for the moment favorite treat), a night at the theater, a visit to a museum, a concert, lunch at Barbara's house, a restaurant, shopping, meeting friends. Mimi treasured every visit to Barbara. They were not so frequent that the girl impinged on her beautiful, vivacious friend's work or privacy. It gave Mimi great pleasure, tremendous security, seeing how much Barbara too enjoyed the things they did together.

On arriving on the New York scene it was Mr. Peabody's wife—because she was helping with the furnishing of the West End flat overlooking the park—and the Peabody children who were Mimi's first city friends. They swept Mimi and Sophia up. From them the odd couple learned quickly about the pace of life in the city. And, just as Barbara had promised, friends led to friends, and there was so much to do. Experiences fill your life in New York. It was Jack who explained that to Sophia and Mimi. "To be a New Yorker, a real New Yorker, is to be an experience-freak. You have to go and look, and see, and try everything. It's all out there for you. No use living here if you don't take advantage of that."

Jack, who drifted in and out of the West End flat, took them to the circus when it came to town, to the Statue of Liberty, Grant's Tomb. Every day was rich and full and Mimi became more secure in herself. She was appreciative of the privileged life she was living, of every morsel of food and fun that now was her life. One day while shopping with Barbara in Saks Fifth Avenue's Young Miss department, Mimi walked from the dressing room wearing a navy blue velvet party dress with white lace collar and cuffs to do a twirl in front of her for approval. Barbara was clearly delighted with what she saw. Mimi fussed with the labels dangling from a string at the cuff while she took a long look at herself in the full-length mirror as the saleslady dropped to her knee to turn the hem up.

"It's lovely, Mimi. You look so pretty in this one. It's the color. It sets off your blonde hair and violet eyes. Do you like it?"

"Like it?" Mimi giggled. "It's just lovely, Barbara. May I really have it?"

"Yes, if it's the one you like best. Come over to me. I want to check the collar."

Mimi obeyed and Barbara rose from her chair and arranged the white lace. "It doesn't seem to sit quite right," she told the saleslady. Finally it lay perfectly.

"There, Mimi," said Barbara. "Look at yourself in the mirror. How pretty you are, dear. When you grow up, you'll be a knockout."

Like you, Mimi wanted to say, but was to shy. Not normally a shy person, she was sometimes that way with Barbara. Instead she gazed into her eyes and said, "I never dreamed I would ever have a fine dress like this again."

Pretty clothes, luscious materials, had long been forgotten, left behind in the house in Prague. Mimi delighted in her new clothes and the knowledge that the cheap and dreadful illfitting cotton dresses she had been obliged to wear for the last few years on the Blocks were a thing of the past. It was Lord and Taylor's Young Girls department, Saks Fifth Avenue, B. Altman, and any number of small boutiques and knowing salesladies on Madison Avenue now. It was pretty and warm well-fitted coats for winter. Mimi need no longer "make do" with one dress for everything. Tatayana's threadbare coat, cut down, worn for winter no more. It was sports clothes, party dresses, school uniforms, casual wear, pretty colors, and all sorts of fabrics. And, miraculously, Mimi had places to go where she could wear them.

Barbara and Mrs. Peabody were instilling taste in Mimi. Good taste that became the norm for her, and that would last all of her life. Mimi was fast becoming a stylish, pretty young thing with a unique seductive charm. Often Barbara thought, not unlike her father.

What delighted Mimi most was that Barbara loved her, respected her as her friend. Barbara thought of places to go, things for Mimi to see and do. If herself unable to give Mimi all the attention Barbara considered she needed, she sent Ching Lee to accompany her. Barbara was good not only to Mimi but to Sophia too. She included her in many things where she thought Sophia would be comfortable. Barbara saw Sophia as just the woman she was, a mother-figure, companion to an extraordinarily charming and interesting child who was growing up fast. A boon to Mimi's life.

Mimi traveled to East Hampton, Long Island to visit Barbara in her house there. It was Barbara and her friend Brandon who taught her to swim in the ocean, Barbara who took her out on a yacht, and it was Barbara who made her understand the things in a woman men liked, because there was always a man in Barbara's life. A man in love with her, a man who wanted her. That became the norm, was expected as far as Mimi was concerned. The impressionable young girl realized that that was what she wanted too, what she would one day have. Mimi flowered, life was very sweet. Only at night in bed, thinking of her father, how happy he would be to know that this was her life, did she feel a pang for the years that had been so cruel to her, the years that had almost overwhelmed her. Remnants of those years existed for Mimi, habits she would never shed, insecurities that she sensed would never go away. But she was good about the past. If she felt herself reliving those dark years, that they were overwhelming her, she blocked them out, put them far away from her, and thought about now, nothing either side of now. She hardly thought about the future, except to include her father in it.

For two years now she had been taking tennis lessons at Barbara's club. Today she sat on the sidelines and watched Barbara play tennis with one of the club's pros. Mimi was aware of the men watching Barbara. As of late several boys had been looking at Mimi in the same interested way. She liked that. It always made her pull her shoulders back and stick her now developing bosom forward. With a tilt of the head and a twinkle of the eye, a cool but sure manner, she charmed them, childishly seduced them into wanting to get closer. She had learned those gestures from Barbara and smiled as she performed them now to an admirer.

Barbara lost, tossed her racket up into the air, then caught it and ran toward the net to shake her opponent's hand. Several men rushed on to the court and surrounded her, looking for a game. She charmed her way past them, all smiles, still shaking her head. "It's unbelievable," she told Mimi. "One stupid fault and then another, and I simply lost my confidence and blew the game. Don't ever do that, Mimi, never lose your confidence. Fight on."

She slipped her hand through the young girl's and wiped her face with a white towel. They went down to the locker room to change.

They left the River Club to go to East Sixty-fifth Street to stop for coffee with Brandon. He was Barbara's latest boyfriend, and Mimi liked him very much. They window-shopped along Madison Avenue and stopped in front of a window. Barbara was attracted to a black evening dress. "What do you think, Mimi?"

"It's beautiful. Sexy."

Barbara turned to look at her. "Sexy? Mimi, what do you know about sexy?"

"Sexy's what attracts men. You're sexy, Barbara, and I certainly want to be." She began to laugh. "Brandon must think you're very sexy."

"How do you know that?"

"The way he looks at you, and he's always touching you." Barbara felt herself go pink.

"How does it feel to be sexy, Barbara?"

"Mimi, I had no idea you thought about these things."

"Of course I think about these things, Barbara. All us girls do. We talk about it at school all the time. But I must admit, most of the time we don't know what we're talking about."

Barbara began to laugh.

"Can I ask you about sexy?"

"Well, I guess so, Mimi. You've asked me about everything else. I doubt that Sophia talks about sexy."

"Oh, no, I don't think that she talks about sexy," giggled Mimi. "How does it feel when Brandon kisses you? I've seen him do it, and your eyes go a little bit squiffy, and the way you slip your arms around his neck and lean into him. Does that make you feel good? No, it must make *him* feel good."

Barbara tried to keep herself under control. But it was difficult. She kept wanting to burst into laughter. "Yes, it does," she managed without a laugh. "It makes me feel warm, tingly, it's nice. Some day you'll know that feeling, a long time from now—at least I hope it will be. You stay a girl for a while longer, Mimi. Has a boy ever kissed you?"

"Oh, yes, Pierre's kissed me, and Max. He was teaching us how to kiss. Then, at a school friend's party, Bob Chalker kissed me and bit my lip. He went all funny when I kissed him back the way Max taught me to do it. But nobody's kissed me like Brandon kisses you."

Mimi felt very adult talking to Barbara about sex and men, it quite excited her. "Once," she told Barbara, "Juliet and I took our panties down and lay on the grass and opened our legs. Pierre and Max investigated us, and Max told us what men and women do together, and how wonderful it felt, and how much we'd like it. But he couldn't do it to us because we were too young. His fingers felt good there, though. I always think when Brandon kisses you and touches you, you must feel like I felt that day when the boys played with us."

Barbara was speechless. They walked in silence for some time before she was able to recover herself enough to tell Mimi, "If ever you've got any questions about sex, you come to me, promise?"

"Yes."

"If there's a boy who wants to do that again with you, come and tell me and we'll decide what you should do, OK?"

"There's nothing wrong in it, is there?"

"No, there's nothing wrong in it, it's lovely. Men will want to do that and much more, like caress your breasts, kiss them. You'd like that wouldn't you, Mimi?"

"Oh, yes, I like the feeling. Do you?"

"You mean, Max managed that as well?"

"Yes, but just a little bit, as an illustration, he said. He said we were no fun because we were too underdeveloped both in mind and body. Max had a real crush on you, Barbara. He said you were the perfect sexy lady. That he thought you really liked making love with a man. Do you, Barbara?"

She began wondering how she had become embroiled in this conversation, but thought she had to see it through with honesty and consideration for Mimi and her obvious need to know about sex. "Yes, very much. And so will you one day, but you need not be bothered with that now. Forget sex, Mimi, for a couple more years anyway. But if it comes your way, promise to come to me and we will talk about it?"

"Or Brandon?"

"Yes, or Brandon."

"I like Brandon, I like the way he loves you. It makes me feel good."

That was so sweet. It made Barbara want to weep that Mimi should be so innocent, so loving. The child deserved so much to be happy. There was something valiant about her. Maybe that was what drew people to her.

They were at Brandon's town house and, as she watched Mimi rush up the stairs, Barbara hoped that Karel could get back soon, before he missed her entire childhood.

Chapter 12

It was three o'clock in the afternoon. The sky was black, the streets so dark they were lit by lamps and car headlights. New York City was having one of those cold November rainstorms that drive people off the streets. The water swirled in streams down the streets toward the overloaded drains. It was level with the pavement. The cars trailed plumes of water as they sped over flooded tarmac. The avenues were awash. A wind that rattled the cars blew out any umbrella that opposed its ferocity.

Barbara could barely see the terrace through the downpour driven on alarming gusts of wind. Rain cascaded against the windowpanes. A roll of thunder rang in her ears. A dazzle of lightning lit up the sky. The spectacular duet was repeated again, and yet again, in various parts of the sky. A pair exploded simultaneously, one over the park, near Central Park West, the other over the zoo. Immediately a streak hovered over Columbus Circle and, seconds later, the Metropolitan Museum of Art, another almost directly over her own building. Awesome pyrotechnics.

Barbara was too mesmerized by the show to move sensibly away from the window. She was wrapped up in the excitement, the danger, the passion of the angry elements playing havoc above the earth. The room was dark, lit only by firelight. She was warm and safe with a box seat at nature's display, and she forgot everything else. How long she had been standing there she had no idea.

Then quite suddenly the rainstorm blew itself out. The dark was split by a streak of yellow sky. In moments the streak widened, the afternoon turned bright with sunshine. Barbara pressed the palms of her hands against the windows. The glass was cold. She felt the chill. She pressed her forehead against it and closed her eyes. It wasn't often she felt such disquiet of the heart as she did now. The shock of the cold against her warm skin, would that jolt her out of it?

She had awakened that morning from a deep sleep feeling a restlessness, an *angoisse,* that had been haunting her all through the day. Why this dreadful unease? What was happening that made her feel such inner disruption? She sensed that was what was happening to her. Something deep within her was stirring, an emotion that had obviously long been dormant. It had been interfering with her painting all day, until she felt compelled to leave her studio and forget work. A lost day. From the studio she had gone to the library and had chosen a novel to escape into. It worked for a short time, but her concentration was shot; no hope of enjoying a novel that day.

Lunch out. A trip to the Cedars Bar to talk art. Someone would be hanging out there on a day like this. Take Mimi on a shopping spree? She posed those suggestions to herself. None seemed incentive enough to get her on the move and out of the house.

Restless and sexy, that was how she felt. She opened her eyes and marveled at nature: the sight now of her terrace sparkling under a winter sunshine. She rubbed her cold hands, yet had to raise one to shade her eyes from a bright sun that had streaked quite suddenly through her drawing room windows to tint the room a buttery yellow. The little heat there was from it felt good. Barbara walked to the fire to warm her hands.

She felt a strange awareness of her own body. She seemed inordinately interested in her own physicality: her limbs, her breasts, her round voluptuous bottom, the beauty and sensuous seductiveness of her cunt. She was unused to such self-absorption, such passionate admiration of herself and her sexuality. It excited her. It was as if she were picking up on one of her lovers' lustful yearnings for her. She felt an aliveness in herself, a sensuousness that was thrilling. So much so that she felt the need to play her own lover and caress herself as her lovers did.

Barbara was a sexy lady, but rarely had she so hungered to be riven by a man, or felt so receptive to that special erotic love that is uncommitted and delivered by a lover who breaks all rules for lust and love.

In the bedroom she stripped off her clothes to study herself in front of the full-length, sixteenth-century Venetian mirror. It was as if she were seeing herself for the first time, lascivious, downright raunchy, extremely sexy flesh and emotion all rolled into one. She was a kind of lewd yet sophisticated object of sexual desire, in her high heels and ivory stockings held to her thighs by lacy black garters, a long strand of pearls draped carelessly over and around one breast. Her long blonde hair was swept back to reveal a face coolly beautiful, yet hot with desire.

She felt such tremendous yearning in herself to be touched. To have a man caress her, respond to the fire that was burning in her loins. Who is that stranger I see so hungry for carnal love? she asked herself. She found it difficult to square this sexually hungry woman, this sensuous feline femininity, with the other sides of herself. Had she never looked closely enough at that aspect of herself before? Had she never understood that the woman reflected in the mirror was as important to her as she was to her lovers? It was as if that part of Barbara had flowered for her, just her, for the first time and she could admire her sexuality with a new respect and pride.

She took one of her breasts. Cupping it in the palms of her hands, she stroked it lovingly. The nimbus round her nipple puckered under her caress, the nipple grew erect. She experienced a sweetly different pleasure from her own caress. She ran her hands over her hips, her thighs, and bent forward, hands on her waist, to watch the movement of her full, rounded breasts, felt their weight as she swung herself slowly from side to side, and caressed once more those breasts, her arms, her neck. The sensation of being both lover and receiver of her own lust for sexual sensation was different, another kind of sex.

She sat down on the end of the bed. Her own reflection contemplated her from the mirror. She raised her arms out and slowly fell backward. The movement in her limbs felt good. She raised her legs one at a time into the air, stretched them straight and stroked them. Lowering them, she bent them at the knee. Her feet were flat on the bed. Even that felt sensuous, very sexy. She caught herself up short, less embarrassed by her behavior than surprised by it. She told herself, this is ridiculous. But in her heart she knew that it was not.

With hands on her knees she pushed her legs far apart. There in the mirror was the reflection of the inside of her thighs: that exquisite line where leg meets buttocks, the long seductive crack, that place of mystery and pleasure, hidden in the short, silky curls of blonde hair adorning a mound aptly named after Venus. The sight excited her as a magnificent, raunchy painting by Schiele might. Her portrait in a sixteenth-century Venetian frame.

She was as if mesmerized by the voluptuous display of female genitalia. She wanted to see more, to feel more. She parted the outer lips with her fingers. Shocking the excitement she felt at the touch of the soft, pink and moistly fleshy inner lips of cunt. But this did nothing to dispel her restlessness, her sexual hunger. Yet this extravagant admiration of herself was enjoyable, liberating even. No replacement certainly for sex with a man: simply something other, not to be denied. Sex, right now, in the afternoon. There were any number of men as hungry for that and her as she was for one of them.

Normally she would have had no qualms about calling for one, but on this strange day she did. Instead, she climbed into a bath of scented oils: tuberose and jasmine. She luxuriated in the satiny smooth hot water, the steam swirling from it. There was her work, her lover, Brandon, whether to marry him or not, to absorb her thoughts.

So many reasons to do it. They were incredibly well suited to each other. He was a fine painter, far better than she would ever be. Maybe a great painter. Only art history would confirm what the American art world already believed. As she did herself. Not in itself a sufficient motive for marrying him—but along with the many other unignorable reasons . . . ? He was sexy, with a superior intelligence which he used, ever constructively, in his work as well as for art. A thoroughly intellectual painter, distinctively cerebral, an abstract expressionist, spokesman for the less articulate of his fellow artists. He was as much the master of the creative word and thought as he was of the paintbrush.

And the sex with Brandon, that was good enough. Understatement. It went beyond good enough. He was a passionate and imaginative lover. He adored her. Admired her work. They were the beautiful couple of the art world. Other things, many, recommended marriage between them. Not least that he was wealthy, with old West Coast money. So he understood her own position as a rich girl struggling for survival in the art game. That was the way it was until you had "been discovered," made your reputation. But . . . he had a bad track record in marriage. Two former wives and five children to prove it. He was reputedly a devoted husband, an inordinately sensitive and loving father, altogether wrapped up in his marriages—until domesticity took over his life and smothered him. Then, almost too late, he would bolt. There was, too, his drinking. Brandon Wells was a serious drinker. Alcohol was important to him.

But for the moment none of those things seemed to imperil their love affair. He was obsessively in love with Barbara. She liked that, and him. Enough? she had to ask herself. And then, maybe domesticity would not suit her over a period of time any more than it had suited him. That had to be another consideration.

Her concentration was too fragmented to pursue her possible future with Brandon Wells. Once out of the bath, she dressed in a long cashmere cardigan, the color of cognac, that reached to her toes. She closed the many small horn buttons down the full length of the dress, and pushed up the sleeves. It felt sensuous against her skin, excitingly soft, deliciously decadent and rich. She sat at her dressing table and clasped around her neck several strands of pearls: long ones that reached to below her waist, short and medium strands of various shapes and sizes. And in her ears large baroque oriental pearls. Bored with her own restlessness and inability to do anything else, she carefully made up her face, brushed her hair. She was not displeased with what she saw. Aloud she told the face in the mirror, "Well, at least I am one of those women that does it for me."

In the drawing room again, she decided on a drink. No ice,

and no Ching Lee to bring it. He was out with Sophia and
Mimi. She smiled. They had become a somewhat odd trio
who enjoyed each other's company. Barbara thought about
them, and then about Mimi. She took great pride in her
friendship with the charming and precocious child. It had
done them both good, the child and she had a delightful and
uncomplicated friendship. Mimi was influenced by Barbara,
her charm and her beauty, her ambition to learn and create
and to experience all that was on offer. To Mimi she was
someone to emulate. And Barbara found in Mimi a child
struggling to put her past unhappiness behind her, and be rec-
onciled with life and all it had to offer. That excited in her an
affection for the child. Something else: the joy of turning a
beautiful, damaged child into an elegant swan of a girl.

Though Barbara and Mimi saw each other, it was never too
frequently. Thankfully life had taken on new dimensions for
Sophia and Mimi: New York and its over-the-top lifestyle, in
the three years they had been there, had swept them along in
its orbit. Barbara had watched it turn their timid, sedate way
of life around. Thinking of that strange duo, Sophia and
Mimi, brought a smile to her lips. She felt suddenly better,
less restless. She mixed herself a strong whisky and soda and
walked to the window to watch the Japanese pines dance to
the wind, the puddles on the flagstones ripple. She drifted off
to a mental no-man's-land, and felt, for the first time that day,
the contentment that was the reality of her life. How good it
felt to be back to normal. That restlessness, like the storm,
had blown itself out.

The stillness of the room, its quiet and tranquillity, with
only the faint sound of the wind whipping across the terrace,
beating against the windows. She liked that: safe and warm
while the world pounded at her door. The harsh bark of the
intercom shattered the calm of the room. She jumped, put her
hand on her heart and chastised herself aloud.

She placed her glass on a table and answered the telephone. "Miss Dunmellyn?"

"Yes, Melvin."

"There's a man here wants to deliver some flowers. Shall
I send him up?"

"If it's flowers, Melvin, send him up."

What a day, she thought. Without warning, a wild, first-class, violent, disruptive storm. "Storm," she said aloud. "Storm warnings." And then to herself, "Not a bad title for a series of paintings. For an exhibition." What a sensational show they would make. She had something, ideas about painting were happening in her head. "Storm warnings." And, as a part of it, the storm itself.

She often talked out loud when a strong idea was taking possession: "Brewing, active and black and wild, the aftermath, the sun, the future, eternity. And always lingering in every canvas a sense of the storm." The very storm that she had just experienced, that had shaken her more profoundly than she had realized. Large canvases, huge canvases, larger than any she had ever painted before. Great slashes of power in paint and color, texture and form.

She was lost in thoughts about painting the series. She heard the elevator. She'd found a pad and a pen and was quickly jotting notes, not to lose any of the ideas. Without looking up, she told the delivery man, "Come in. I'll be with you in a minute."

She heard his footsteps on the marble floor, but was too distracted to pay attention to him. He would simply have to wait. The man laid the long, clear, cellophane box wrapped in a huge white silk bow on the hall table and waited patiently.

"Just leave them there on the table." She looked up. He was wearing a fine gray felt hat with a grosgrain band of the same color around the crown, the brim pulled down. It was wet from the rain. A Burberry trenchcoat tied, not buckled, at the waist.

Her first reaction was to place her hand over her mouth, to take a deep breath and try to calm herself. She did, of course, recognize him at once. She tried to still her racing heart. Barbara was overwhelmed with gratitude that he was alive and safe and standing in her flat. She had not realized until that moment that he had been a constant factor in her life. In all those years she had barely given him a thought, except on rare occasions when she saw something of him in Mimi. There had been, as he had predicted, no love story for them. No middle or end. Only a beginning that had gone nowhere, simply been suspended. She had accepted that she had given him up from the moment his plane had soared into the dark sky that cold January night in New Jersey.

But now he was here again and the world was as it had once been before for them. How could she have forgotten the exquisite sense of pleasure she had experienced with him then, that she knew was awaiting her now? Seeing him again, the years rolled back. She was alive as she had never been since his departure. How could she not have noticed that? How deep must she have buried her feelings for him. This restlessness, the sexual hunger she had suffered all day. Had she been making herself ready for something that was as imminent as his arrival? She should have known something was pending.

"I am sorry. But, you see, I never had a telephone number to call. Only an address to return to."

That voice. How hungry she had been all those years to hear it, to see him standing there, and she had never known it. He was in her heart again, a place she had never even dreamed he had inhabited.

"I have an unlisted telephone number," she told him in a trance-like state, thinking how banal her words sounded. Then there was silence, neither able to find words. But silence was their friend, playing Cupid. Finally he found a word.

"Sorry." And the tremor of emotion in his voice was unmistakable. It took several seconds for him to gain control of himself. Then he continued, "Seeing you again has quite taken me aback."

His confession made it easier for Barbara. She smiled at him as he walked to the edge of the balcony and placed his hands on the balustrade. She told him, "It's lovely to see you again, Karel."

She walked around the table towards him. He took off his hat and threw it behind him. And now she could see his face clearly. He seemed, if possible, more handsome and sensually attractive than she had remembered him. Four years nearly, yet his face looked more youthful. Surprising, since his hair had gone white in wide slashes at the temples, and more salt-and-pepper everywhere else. He laid his raincoat over the balustrade on the stairs leading down into the drawing room. They walked into each other's arms.

"Don't speak. Please don't speak," he whispered in her ear, the warmth of his breath caressing the lobe. It sent shivers down her spine. The accent still with those honeyed overtones, a seductive bedroom voice that promised so much. He took her in his arms, tilted her chin up and studied her face. As he kissed her eyes he could hear her heart pounding. More kisses and their lips parted. She sighed, and was overcome by her feelings for him. She began to cry and to place kisses all over his face. All the pent-up emotion, love and passion, the carnal desire she had wrestled with all day, exploded into tears and smiles. It was an extraordinary way to behave, but he understood. He held her tight in his arms and caressed her. She could sense his sexual need for her. His desire, gone out of control. She yielded to him, wanting only to be riven by him, to submit to their hunger for each other. She tore at his clothes, like a voracious animal biting into the side of his neck, his chin. She bruised his nipples with her teeth. She was like a wildcat from the exotic dark of some green jungle.

He picked her up in his arms and carried her to the bedroom. He put her down near the dressing table, fumbled with the buttons on the cashmere dress, and then, unable to wait, tore it open. She covered her eyes, not out of fright or anxiety over the loss of a dress: it was more because she was unable to cope with the wild erotic joy she saw in his eyes.

She felt his hands on her breasts, his mouth devouring them. Then he found her lips and sealed her sighs of pleasure with a long and hungry kiss. He lifted her off the floor and she wrapped her legs around his waist. She could feel that massive erect penis probing the crack of her bottom. He fumbled with his free hand to find on the dressing table a pot of scented cream, and grabbed it. He walked with her thus. Between kisses he told her, "We are like the animals in the jungle."

"Oh God, take me, Karel," she begged in a voice husky with need. She was so ripe, so ready, and he knew it and loved it. He unwound her from him and bent her over the bed, her back to him. He would take her, in just that position, because he wanted her to feel the deepest of penetration, to achieve the greater orgasm. He removed the lid from the pot and tossed it across the room. He scooped out great blobs of the luscious, scented cream. She felt the cold smoothness and his searching fingers between her cunt lips. His fingers pushing it into her already moist cunt.

"Look into the mirror," he told her breathlessly. The scene was raunchily magnificent. He spread her legs wide apart, gripped her by the waist. No ceremony. He thrust swiftly and violently just once. Then he was deep inside her. She tried to bite her hand to stifle the scream. She felt pain and pleasure as his body slapped against her bottom. He could hear her muffled cries, the sounds of her uncontrolled pleasure at being fucked by him.

Once deeply inside her, they remained standing and were quiet, trying to ease off the wild abandon with which he had taken her. He bent over her and used his hands to caress her, whispering to her how delectable he found her, what joy it was to be inside her again. He placed his lips against her bare back and kissed it. He could feel his heart pounding. Then it began for them, long and steady passionate fucking, until he moved in and out of her with ease. She came, a series of orgasms. With each one, pure bliss, sheer ecstasy. His own desire to fuck her went out of control. He used the flat of his hands across her bottom. He used them roughly, holding her in his tight grip by her shoulders, all the time moving to a carnal rhythm that drove them further into sexual oblivion. Anything, everything, for their selfish lust. Never stopping, he managed to reach under her and to find her clitoris. Now they were both feeling the extreme anguish of lust. They came together in a crescendo of passion. And neither of them cared that he might crush her every bone to powder, so tight did he cleave to her.

They lay there spent, exhausted. Finally, somewhat recovered, he pulled her into his arms, caressed her hair and licked her lips and throat. "Make love to me." It was not a plea, but a demand.

He pulled her head back by the hair and looked into her face. And repeated, "Make love to me. I want you to master me, to take me sexually as you have never done any other man. I want to feel that there is no one who could ever go the sexual route we have trodden together. That none of your lovers can or would give themselves to you as I will, or take you as I have and brand you theirs with depraved sex as I intend to." She obeyed him.

He had never had a woman take possession of him as Barbara did that afternoon. He submitted to her mouth, her hands. She matched him in her violent passion to possess. They watched each other in the Venetian mirror. In oral sex she was as lustful and magnificent as when adopting the role of sexually submissive partner. Lying on top of him, her face over his cock, she opened her lips to lick and suck him, while dipping her fingers into the same pot of cream. She covered his luscious plum-shaped balls hanging in their soft sac. Reaching beneath them, she entered that small tight place with her fingers. He was insane with excitement. The woman controlled him, made him submit. They had the power of sex and each of them held that over the other for nothing more than their mutual sexual pleasure. Theirs was the desire of wanting to give and to please, to take everything that sexual lust and depravity had to offer. It was a kind of sexual insanity where excess and imagination took them over. They were using several jade dildos on each other at the same time, and their mouths and tongues, when their orgasms could be contained no longer. That special ambrosia, the taste of sperm, a woman's orgasmic nectar: they experienced it together and reveled in their lust. Sadly, reluctantly, they removed the jade and drifted into their unique haven of sexual ecstasy, that place beyond people and thoughts and dreams. They were there, one with each other, where the body and the ego die, that elysian field of pure, unadulterated sexual pleasure.

"I hadn't planned it this way. But then I saw you and I could feel your hunger was as strong as mine. I make no excuses—I came alive with a desire that was stronger than any I had intended for us."

"All day I have been restless, lost. I only came together when you touched me," she told him.

They kissed. She watched him climb into his trousers and walk barefooted, bare-chested from the room, only to return minutes later with his arms full of white roses and present them to her. Then he took her in his arms and kissed her.

"I can't see a white rose without thinking of you. I sent them whenever I could."

It was strange that Mimi never entered her mind. Nor could she equate anything she had heard about Count Karel Stefanik with this man to whom she felt so connected. She had no questions because she wanted to hear no answers.

Then he asked, "Dine with me. I want to sit among people and have them see you, watch their eyes as they admire you. I want them to look at us and know there is something special going on between us. I want to show you off, carry you on my arm, walk into a room with you, smile at you across a table, listen to you order a meal. I want to walk down the streets where we once ran, sit next to you in a taxi, feel the everyday things of life with you. I am as hungry for that as I was to fuck you."

She laughed. "You sound like a crazed lover."

"I am a crazed lover. I thought you realized that. Now dine with me. Say yes."

"Yes. Oh yes. Please."

"I must meet a man at the Plaza Hotel at eight. That gives you time to dress. It's important, but it won't take long."

How could she say no to him? She was tired, exhausted, but she didn't want to leave him any more than he wanted to leave her. How could she disappoint him?

They bathed together. He recited a long sensuous poem. Partly in Czech, partly in English. He told her, "If I could write lines like that, it would be because I once loved a woman like you."

She wanted to cry. She fought back tears. She knew he was telling her that at that moment he was loving her more than anything or anyone. More, maybe, than life itself. Was that why it was so sweet to die in orgasm with him and be reborn in his arms? He touched her soul in a very special way as no other man had ever done. He marked her forever with his lust for her. If she hadn't known that before, she knew it now. How could they sustain the power of their passion? The answer, of course, was that they would be unable to. Life would step in and cool it down. She knew how each of them would strive not to allow that to happen. They would do what they must to keep it as remarkable and alive a love as it was. Or settle for nothing.

She was standing in a black satin chemise trimmed in lace, looking in her wardrobe for something to wear. He walked up to her. "Choose something lovely, grand, very elegant. Then, when we get to the hotel, I'll change into black tie and my dress suit. This is a celebration I want us never to forget."

How could anyone be happier than she felt at that moment? He kissed her shoulder, then went to sit on the bed and watch her dress. She chose black lace, stunningly elegant with tight, long sleeves that only just covered the shoulder and clung to her breasts. It was backless to the waist and had a skirt cut on the bias. It was simplicity itself, pure, lavish elegance. Around her neck was clasped a slim necklace of square-cut diamonds, and she wore large square diamonds in her ears. Slipping into high-heeled satin shoes she glimpsed herself in the mirror and was surprised at how young she looked. She ran her fingers through her hair, gave it a side parting and let it fall girlishly.

"I shan't dress my hair."

"No, you're perfect."

She smiled. He even understood that.

"I need to look as I feel, young, a slip of a girl, when I am with you." She smiled teasingly.

She chose a black silk-velvet cape lined in mink. He raised the large, soft, dramatic hood and draped it over her hair. She held his coat for him and watched him place his hat at a rakish angle. Together they left for the Plaza.

Chapter 13

Barbara was sipping a perfectly chilled martini while standing at the window in Karel's suite. She was looking across the Plaza to the park and the car lights flashing up and down Fifth Avenue. Since Karel had walked into her life again her mind had been in limbo.

He opened the door from the bedroom and walked into the sitting room while buttoning his dinner jacket. She was able, for a second, to take an objective look at this man and his continental good looks, his devastating charm. With him she shared a special happiness, one that was indefinable. No woman had ever held him, she was certain of that. His temperament was not monogamous. Barbara may have sensed with what pride he walked with her on his arm, how much he enjoyed their closeness, the delight he took in his adoration of her. But she had no illusions about Count Karel Stefanik. Theirs was a living-in-the-moment kind of sexual love.

When they had walked through the lobby of the Plaza, she saw how they had attracted the attention of both men and women. Barbara Dunmellyn was a head-turner, and she knew it. But the looks they drew from other guests at the hotel that evening were not for her, but for them, and generated by Karel. His manner, his magnetic charm, had not dimmed with the years.

She viewed him now in his dinner suit. Very English, Savile Row, correct, elegant. He seemed so *different* a man in his dress suit to the lover who had arrived with white roses. She took several steps toward him, wanting him to take her in his arms, this new and strange man who was smiling at

148

her. She felt, suddenly, just a little afraid of the power of his charm.

There was a knock at the door. He ignored it, preoccupied with picking up on her thoughts. He went to her, tilted her chin with his hand, kissed her lightly on the lips and told her, "All this is something other than what we are. All this . . ." And he touched the lapels of his dress suit, the black lace covering her arm.

"All this," he repeated, "is fun and games and real life. It has nothing to do with what we have together." The knock again, louder, more insistent. "Neither of us must ever forget that. It's the outside world and, good as it may be, it's not so rich, so exciting as our own private world. I'll prove that to you later." The way he looked at her, she knew he meant every word.

"Now, this man. I apologize." He shrugged his shoulders, and added, "Seeing him is *very* important."

He walked away from her to answer the door. "Mr. Bensen?"

"Yes. You are Count Karel Stefanik?"

"That's right. Come in. At last we meet, Mr. Bensen. I hope you don't mind. A close friend." Karel put Barbara and Mr. Bensen through introductions. "I want to thank you and your department for expediting my papers. A drink, Mr. Bensen?"

He accepted the offer.

The Count was nothing like Mr. Bensen imagined he would be. Here were no signs of stress. To Mr. Bensen he seemed untouched by a long and hard war where he had been hunted both by Nazi bastards and by certain factions in his own country. The latest files had created in Mr. Bensen's mind a different profile of the man standing in front of him. He had always been curious about a man who chose to be a hero instead of a father, to abandon comfort and freedom and a chance to make a new life in a country away from war. How this guy must have hardened himself to give up his child for her own safety. And to have ensured it by staying away from her until he had set up a future solid and secure enough for them never to part again. He was a guy who knew how to be mean to be kind. That had to count for something.

Mr. Bensen took a swallow of his drink and placed the cut-glass tumbler on the table. He had been carrying a large brown manila envelope with him when he arrived. It lay next to him on the sofa. Now he picked it up, placed in on the coffee table in front of him and twisted the tiny metal clips to open it. He withdrew its contents and spread them out in front of him.

"There you are, Count. It's all there and all official. Signed, sealed, and now delivered. You are an American citizen, and so is . . ." Mr. Bensen hesitated and looked over at Barbara Dunmellyn, sensing discretion was in order ". . . your immediate family. Here are the papers." Mr. Bensen shoved them across the table toward the Count. "And here are passports. You and your family can enter and leave the United States any time you like." He handed the passports over to Karel. "As soon as possible you will have to update your family's photographs. The enclosed document will cover you for that for a year."

There was no doubting the significance of those passports and documents to Karel or how they affected him. For a few seconds he seemed to lose control of his emotions. A sadness, a kind of pain, crossed his face, settled in his eyes. He rubbed his chin with his thumb and forefinger. He seemed for a moment suddenly older, quite worn out. Barbara half expected him to falter, to take a seat in order to recover his equilibrium. But Count Karel Stefanik was made of sterner fiber. He drew himself up seemingly taller than his six feet two inches. The light in his face, extinguished for a few seconds, returned. He replaced the passports and papers to their envelope. At the drinks table he poured himself a generous whisky. Turning to face his guests, he raised his glass and said, "To a new beginning for me and my child. A new life. A family life. Mr. Bensen, you are here like a messenger from the gods. Until you arrived with the missing pieces of a new life for us, I daren't go to find my child."

He raised the tumbler of whisky and drank. Then he told Barbara and Mr. Bensen, "We have been separated by war and tyranny, and finally my own stupid faith in mankind's will to be free, live in peace and respect his neighbor. I turned a blind eye for too long, and then almost too late made an extravagant gesture for my beliefs and my country. It could have cost my daughter her life. Never again. Mr. Bensen, you've delivered the foundations of a new life for us to build on here in America. Until I had that to offer my child, I could not disrupt her life. Chicopee Falls, Massachusetts." He raised the tumbler to his lips and swallowed what remained of the amber liquid in the bottom of the glass.

The Count smiled. He looked and sounded incredibly happy, sure of himself again. Mr. Bensen rose from his chair. For the first time since Karel walked back into Barbara's life, she thought of Mimi. How Sophia had described to her that first day she met a wrecked child, painfully thin, biting her lip, wringing her slender, red and roughened hands. A displaced child, with hunger and pain in her eyes, sitting in the truck of Joe Pauley the peddler on a hot summer's day. How Mimi's dream was all that she lived for: that her father would come and find her. And how far Mimi had come from then until now.

Barbara had no idea what Karel meant, "Chicopee Falls, Massachusetts." A location, clearly. But how could she know that he thought that was where he would find Mimi? She knew nothing about Mimi's life, except what had been sketched in by the Queen the first time Barbara was told about Mimi. Mimi never talked about her life before Beechtrees. In fact, much to Barbara's surprise and relief, she hardly mentioned her father either.

Barbara had never told Mimi she knew Karel, or all about Mimi's past. What could she have said? I had a three-night stand, an excursion into sexual oblivion with your father, and fell in love? A few flowers, and he vanished from my life to fight a war, just as he did from yours. Such a confession was impossible on several counts: the obvious one, Mimi would be shattered that he had been in America and had made no contact, and for Barbara's own selfish reasons. She cherished the very private world she and Karel experienced with each other and wanted to keep her Karel interlude all to herself. That was part of what they had been all about, selfish, one to one, love that excluded the world and everyone in it. She had not been bound to give that up.

Now for those same selfish reasons Barbara found it impossible just to burst out with the news that a series of incredible circumstances had led her to befriend Count Karel Stefanik's child Mimi. She had rationalized her silence by recognizing the emotional traumas father and daughter had suffered, were still suffering. The emotional bond between Karel and Mimi was intense. They must be allowed to discover each other on their own terms, in their own time, and in their own way. She remained silent.

Barbara could not but feel that the war had taken a greater toll on Karel then she had originally thought. His few minutes of distress shocked her. She was experiencing at first hand and for the first time how the war had torn apart, partially destroyed, just two of millions of lives. To remain silent until after Mimi and Karel Stefanik had united their lives, caught up with their pasts, and begun their new life seemed as important as her own selfish reasons for silence. Anything else seemed too intrusive, too cruel. And remaining silent prevented her from shattering Karel's dream that he had done what he had done to Mimi to ensure her survival, his belief that he had cushioned the blows of war for her by surrounding her with comfort and love.

"Count Stefanik . . ." started Mr. Bensen.

"No, not here in America, Mr. Bensen. It sounds too phoney, too pretentious, and we titled refugees seem two-a-penny in New York. No, I think we drop the title from now."

Mr. Bensen tried again. "Sir, have you a plan of how to go about this reunion? If we can help, you have my number."

"I'll keep that in mind, Mr. Bensen. I've made no plans. For years I have been taking one step at a time, especially concerning my daughter. The last step was to obtain and have in my own hands the right papers to secure our future. I will now think about the next step." With those words Mr. Bensen was dismissed, politely but firmly.

Barbara and Karel dined in the Oak Room on oysters and a perfect Montrachet. It was followed by green turtle soup, roast partridge and wild rice, puree of celeriac, and tiny thin potato pancakes fried to a crisp. With it a Chambertin the color of garnets and rubies, with a nose that carried the scent of musky, sun-drenched grapes aged in oak and time, and made one think dark red damask roses and deep purple lavender. For dessert crêpes Suzette.

It was one of those meals that only happen when two people are totally in place for each other. Where anything else, even a loved child, is made to vanish by the sheer power of an intimate relationship pulsating with life. When every morsel of food is enjoyed ten times over, every sip of wine teases the taste buds and fills the mouth with an ambrosia fit to be served at Valhalla. The sensation of epicurean pleasure, sensual attraction that promises sexual delights, lustful abandonment of the body and soul, makes small talk redundant.

Each of them in their own way was wrapped up in the other. It made a kind of magic for them as a couple. They felt it and so did others in the room. The waiters, the maître d' and other diners caught themselves stealing glances at the beautiful couple enjoying the power of passionate love. They had to admire how Barbara and Karel were free and happy enough to wear their feelings like a cloak of diamonds for all to admire and enjoy. This was not just another couple out to dinner. These were lovers in the greatest sense of the word. Just to be in that dining room that night and sense erotic love, an aura of passion, lifted spirits throughout the room. It created an atmosphere, a buzz. That infectious something that people rise to.

"There are so many questions that I should want to ask, but I can't think of one. Not one that would matter," she told him, apropos of nothing.

"It occurred to me only in the elevator going up to your apartment that there might be a man in your life. That I might be making a fool of myself. That it had been years and that you might have forgotten me. But none of those things mattered. I had to take the chance."

Their conversation died. They savored instead the silence between them. It was like that for them all through the meal. Several times each tried to make conversation for several sentences. Then once more they would drift off course. A smile to replace words, a shrug of the shoulders, flippant laughter at themselves. Often through the meal he would raise her hand, take it in his and stroke it, kiss her fingers, place light, sweet kisses on her arm. The romance evident in them excited envy in every woman present. It is difficult not to respond to an awareness of love.

After dinner they walked through the lobby to the small, intimate night club. In a dark corner of the room they drank Calvados as he whispered, "You are that rare breed of woman that inspires lust *and* love. You're a dangerous lady, Barbara." And then removed her earring and kissed and licked her earlobe.

She took the earring from his hand and replaced it on her ear. "I like 'inspire lust.' Would you care to elucidate?" she challenged. Tilting her head back and to one side and teasing him with a seductive glance, a wicked smile, she raised her hand to stop him from speaking, "And love. Ah, I inspire that too. Tell me about that."

He was about to speak, but she silenced him by placing a finger over his lips, and caressed his lower lip with the oval tip of a long glossy red fingernail. "Dangerous? You see me as a dangerous woman. How dangerous?" But before he could speak, she took his hand and, rising from her chair, "I think I would like to dance."

He laughed, enjoying her seductive, provocative charm. She was taunting him with her sexuality, exciting his lust for her and they both knew it. She was playing with him and it worked. Holding her close to him, their bodies moving as one to the rhythm of the music, she incited him to tell her in a sexy whisper, "You're like an aphrodisiac. You set my sexual fantasies aflame. But you know that, don't you?"

"Yes." Barbara rubbed herself up against him. She moved sensuously in his arms. He felt her heat for him, her sexual hunger. It mingled freely with his own.

"What do you want?" he asked.

"Everything."

"Sexual? With me?"

"Yes."

"I won't fail you."

"I know."

"You are glorious both in and out of your sensuality. I adore you. That's why you are so dangerous. Because I sense that I will want you always, all of our life. I have never felt that about any other woman."

"And there have been many."

"Yes, very many. I have always lusted after woman. My libido demands it."

"And you always will."

"You know me too well. Well enough to deal with that?"

"I don't have to, darling." She kissed him on his chin, at the corner of his lips and slid the tip of her tongue between his and licked his mouth, under the cover of dim light and with other people dancing near them on the small dance floor. She felt him tremble under her sensual advances. He stopped dancing, slipped his hand from her naked back where he had been holding her to caress her breasts briefly before walking her from the dance floor to their table.

Their closeness overwhelmed them. They sat at the table listening to Eddie Duchin at the piano playing Cole Porter, Mabel Mercer singing romantic songs that put a catch in the throat. They hardly spoke except with their eyes, the warmth of their bodies, caresses. They knew how to excite each other in the most intimate way without being crass.

Barbara had no idea when it happened, the realization that they were still so very hungry for each other. That neither of them had been sated by their extravagant, very much out-of-control sexual encounter that afternoon. That that side of their nature had taken over. Their lusty feelings were not making a sham of their evening. That had been wonderful, equally exciting in its own, clearly romantic way. They had shared the evening, but it was growing dim in the light of another kind of need: the impulse to be more sexual, more intimate with each other.

He called for the bill. She could feel the onset of an intense sexual tension between them. It was thrilling, so acute that she was trembling long before they reached the door to his suite. She tried to suppress her restless sexual hunger for him. It was that same hunger she had experienced in front of the Venetian mirror in her bedroom that afternoon. Barbara was just a little frightened that her libido should take over her life. She had never till that moment realized how compelling her sexual drives were. Always she had thought that it was her lovers who were more powerfully sexual than herself. She saw it all so clearly now. That had not been the truth of it.

They entered his suite of rooms and Barbara was aware that Karel's own voracious libido, his passion for sex and love for women, an innate male sureness of his sexuality, triggered in her those very same things. He, as the supreme sexual adventurer, a libertine, gave Barbara sexual freedom to be those things herself. Only with Karel did she willingly relinquish her heart and soul to Eros. It seemed natural with him to abandon herself to sex beyond the control of either, to go as far as they could together in search of sexual oblivion.

She turned around to face him. He was still standing by the door watching her. He was aware of that. She divined it in his look. He knew exactly where they were with each other. It was no small thing, what they had together. It made her heart race. She bit her lower lip to remain silent, to hold back. They gazed into each other's eyes. There it was—lust. His every movement was a sensual tease, a sexual taunt, a subtle priming of her. She was stunned into standing rigidly still, like a fallow deer caught in a car's bright headlight. Just waiting for his move on her.

She saw him remove the "Do Not Disturb" sign. It needed to be on the outside now. She watched him close the door and actually jumped, she was so tense, when he double-locked the door. He walked toward her, removing his jacket and dropping it on the sofa. She kept her distance by continually backing away from him. He pulled on the black silk bow-tie, loosened it and left it hanging around his neck. He removed the sapphire studs from a plain, Egyptian cotton dress shirt and dropped them into an empty ashtray. She was riveted by his every movement, but continued to back away from him. She imagined she could feel the heat of his ardor. He all but tore his shirt from his body, so ready was he to be naked for her. She watched him step out of his shoes, raise his feet one at a time to peel off his socks.

He held her enthralled. He was stalking her, was going to take her as she had never been taken by any other man. The way he always took her, abandoning the norm for anything that excited their sexuality. He removed the remainder of his clothes. Breathless with desire for him, still she backed away. It was very nearly a shout when she called out, desperation in her voice, "I'm afraid."

He looked up at her and laughed, "Never."

"Yes," she told him.

"Of me?" He seemed merely amused, a smile lingering on his lips.

"No, not afraid of you. Afraid of me. How you affect me."

"And me? What about me?" he asked as he walked up to her. There was no more backing away from him. She had come up against the wall. He grabbed her tightly. "This was not in my plan. You have to know that. You have to know that I never planned what is happening to us. You have to believe that."

She could think of nothing, believe nothing, because after he spoke he placed a long, passionate and hungry kiss upon her lips. Then he swept her up in his arms and conveyed her toward the bedroom. Violently, he kicked the doors open and carried her to the bed.

Chapter 14

The two men stood opposite each other. For several seconds they said nothing. Finally, "It's been a long time, Karel."

"Long and tough, David."

They shook hands. David Rawlings Peabody and Count Karel Stefanik brought the formalities to an end with an emotional hug. They stepped back and took stock of each other. Maybe the years had not done too badly by them. Again a firm handshake. Karel told the banker, "There was never a time, David, that I didn't think we would meet again. I always believed the day would come for me to claim Mimi and begin a new life for us both. More modest than I had hoped for, I'm afraid, but a life nevertheless."

"Not so modest, Karel. You've done very well with us here at the bank. They have at least been financially prosperous years for you on this side of the Atlantic. Your buildings are safe and secure. They generate a more than reasonable income. The bank followed your instructions. We invested a third of the income in blue-chip stocks. You will be amazed how they have soared. Your money has been achieving compound interest for years. Some would consider it a modest fortune. Something substantial, anyway, to begin again with. How have things been in Czechoslovakia?"

"From a business point of view, disastrous. Financially, I'm wiped out."

"The lot?"

"The lot. And some."

"Are the properties still there, intact?"

"There, yes. Some intact, others needing fortunes to repair them. I still hold the deeds to my property, but that doesn't give me possession of my estates. The Germans occupied the palace in Prague and shipped most of its contents to Germany. The Russians helped themselves to what was left. All they could find, that is. And my own countrymen claim they have no idea what has happened to the rest of the family's possessions. I have heard appalling things from long-time faithful servants and farm workers. Until the country finds its feet again, men like me are going to be heroes to some, villains to others. Depends how they stand politically. I am not happy with the way things are going in my country. One day I'll go back, when it's the sort of democracy that will hand me back what's mine, gratefully, out of a sense of respect for a man's rights. Till then, I see Communism and Russia looming over our future. It's no place for Mimi and me to try to catch up with those horrible lost years. I'm leaving Czechoslovakia behind for a while. I'm going to try to put my family together again."

The charm, the intelligence, the good looks, the basic belief in man's right to live and be free, seemed still intact. But, for a few seconds, David saw something that had not been there before. Karel Stefanik was a deeply disillusioned man. He simply covered it up rather better than most. Others tended to carry their disillusionment like a cross on their back for all to see and weep over.

Several men were brought into David Peabody's office. They presented Karel with a detailed report of his assets. He was surprised when David estimated the value of Karel's holding assigned to Mimi at $1,650,000. It was beyond anything he could possibly have hoped for. So quickly and so recklessly had he moved to get money over to America in those few months before Hitler made Czechoslovakia a German protectorate, he had actually forgotten how well he had done. He tended never to look over his shoulder at what he had been through: the pain was always too sharp to live with. He had done what he had to for himself and Mimi to stay alive. It seemed to him a miracle that he had done so well under such horrendous circumstances. Others had fared catastrophically.

Once they had dealt with their business Karel relaxed back in the chair and lit a cigar. "And now I have everything: all the pieces put together to give me and my family a secure home."

"Will you remain here, then?"

"Oh, yes. That's why I wasn't in touch sooner. I had to make sure that, when I did find Mimi, I had everything in place for us to become a family. Thank God for the day you and I met in Paris before the war, David. A long time ago now. What were you then? A very unsophisticated New York trainee-banker on a two-year stint at the family bank in the Place Vendôme. I don't know where I would be without the advice and care you and the bank have given my finances since. Not to mention the security I have had about Mimi all these years knowing that if she, Mashinka or Tatyana needed anything you would have handled it for them. Tomorrow I will go to Chicopee Falls for Mimi. The address, David?"

"I never had an address."

"What?"

"They never sent an address."

"They never asked you for further funds? How did they live? By God, I owe that fellow a lot, that brother of Mashinka's, if he has supported them all these years."

Karel stood up abruptly. "If you have no address how am I going to find them?"

"Mimi's not in that place, Chicopee Falls. She's here in New York, Karel."

He sat down again. He seemed calm and unemotional about it. "You'd better explain."

"I never heard anything from them. And then, four years ago, Mimi arrived. She was holding a red envelope which she claimed you had given her for an emergency. She was with an FBI man. They had had a terrible time with her. They had almost to force the child to accept that the time had come for her to open the envelope. Then an even more difficult time getting her to come here to the bank and hand over the envelope for safekeeping."

"I don't understand. How did the FBI get involved with Mimi?"

"A coincidence. They were protecting an exiled European royal family. From what I understand, Mimi was a house guest. They helped her at the Queen's request."

They were interrupted by a knock at the door. The safe-deposit box was brought in. David Peabody felt relieved by the interruption. He did, however, advise Karel, "I'm Mimi's guardian. Made so by default, so to speak, but a guardian only until your return. Please don't press on about this until you have seen, and spoken to Mimi. I would prefer it that way, Karel."

He hesitated. None of this was as he had expected. But, as David Peabody suggested, he dropped the subject. The safe-deposit box was opened. The contents of the red leather envelope were handed over to him. He opened first the slim tin box. The jewels sparkled in the light on the desk. He opened the drawstring pouches and spilled their contents out on to the desk. It was all there. All that was left of four centuries of one of the finest collections of jewels in Europe.

He made no comment about the jewels. It seemed to the men in the room that it took him some time to collect himself. Seeing them again overwhelmed him. He asked for them to be replaced in the safe-deposit box. He stood up.

"Where is Mimi, David?"

"At half-past three this afternoon she'll be skating with my daughter in Rockefeller Center. Karel, she doesn't know that we were friends, even that I know your real name. When she speaks about you, she refers to you as 'my father, Mr. Kowalski.' It was a matter of confidences, you understand. Both the child's, to keep yours, and mine, to keep both of yours. And, of course, it seemed a better idea for your safety as well as Mimi's."

"It seems as if I have asked a great deal of a casual friend. I will always be in your debt for this, David. I'll not press you, but I don't understand any of this. I assumed they were safe and happy in Massachusetts, not living in New York."

"There is no 'they' anymore. But Mimi should tell you all about that, not me. I know hardly anything about it. She came to us a very secretive child, about you, and about her past. She confides in no one on all that, Karel. When you see her, how happy and well she is, what a good life and a good time she is having, you will understand why we never pressed her about her life before she arrived at Beechtrees to stay with that royal family. She is a quite remarkable and lovely child, you will be proud of her. She is the only one who will be able to tell you about her life. All that matters is that you did the best for her, and you will see she is really well, really happy. I promise you she is. There has only been one thing for Mimi: the day her father would come for her. That's what she lives for, and now you're here."

For Mimi the day was like any other day. She had no premonition that her life was about to be turned upside down yet again. She awoke at five in the morning as she always did, and sat with Sophia in the kitchen drinking hot cherry tea, a habit the cook and the child had never been able to break since they left Beechtrees. They talked about their plans for the day and then Mimi went back to bed for an hour. There Sophia brought her breakfast: poached eggs on toasted brioche, and slivers of baked ham, hot milk lightly flavored with coffee and a hint of cinnamon.

Mimi bathed, dressed in her school uniform and gathered up her books. With Sophia she waited in front of the building for the school bus to come by and pick her up. She talked to the doorman, Morris, and greeted people she knew from the building rushing through the entrance doors to get to work. She petted Mrs. Schermerhorn's three poodles, out for their morning walk with her maid Ruby, just as they were every morning. Then the school bus arrived, honking its horn and bearing her classmates, who were waving to her and Sophia, eager to see if the cook had a box of her bite-size buttery filo pastry apple pies for them, which she did. The door hissed open and Mimi climbed aboard. Only just in time did she pop her head out to remind Sophia to meet her at Rockefeller Center with her skates at 3:30 before the door hissed shut again. She passed the box to Debbie in the first seat and made her way to the rear of the bus where she always sat. She waved until Sophia was out of sight and continued chattering with her school friends until they poured out of the bus in front of the Upper East Side school just off Fifth Avenue.

At 2:30 she hurried with her best friend, Penny Peabody, to the Peabodys' East Side mansion. They changed their school uniforms for skating costumes, and the Peabody nanny and the two girls were driven by the family chauffeur to the Rockefeller Center. There she met Sophia, who gave her her skates and fussed over her. Nothing out of order there. Sophia would have afternoon coffee with the Peabody nanny in the glass-fronted restaurant and complain about the pastries while watching Mimi and Penny skate. Then they would all go home to Central Park West. Here Sophia would give them hot chocolate and petits fours. Sophia looked forward to these Wednesdays, and Mimi sensed nothing different about today from any other day.

David Peabody and Karel Stefanik stood above the rink watching the skaters go round and round to the music. David turned to him. "Do you know how you are going to handle this, Karel?"

"No, I have no idea."

David Peabody was uncertain. Had it been a good idea taking Karel to see Mimi at the skating rink? He felt concern for them, yes, but also anxiety about father and daughter. What effect might their reunion have upon each of them? It was too fraught with emotional danger. Something the New York Peabodys steered well clear of. There was not going to be an easy way for father and daughter to come together: anyone who knew Mimi's and Karel's story, or even a fragment of it, was aware of that. David looked at Karel. He actually studied him for several seconds and concluded that, if anyone was going to be able to handle such a moment, Karel and Mimi were.

Satisfied he was right, David finally gave in. "Over there." His heart ached for his courageous, heroic friend. He felt Karel's pain at having watched his own daughter for fifteen minutes and been unable to recognize her. Still Karel could not pick out his daughter from the crowd of young, pretty girls circling the rink. David touched his arm. "Karel, over there. The beautiful girl—she's laughing. With blonde hair. The girl with the soft white beret and the white velvet skating outfit with gold buttons. She is wearing white fur mittens, her hands chap very easily." And David felt embarrassed for having told him such an intimate detail about his daughter. How indiscreet. He sounded more like a father to Mimi.

"Mimi! God, it's Mimi. I was looking for her as she was, how stupid of me. She's beautiful, so grown up."

He started walking round the rink not taking his eyes from

his daughter. David followed close behind. He descended the stairs to get closer to her. And the nearer the two men approached the rink, the faster Karel walked. Now he was practically running. David tried to hold him back. "Easy, easy, Karel."

They were almost at the rails, and the two girls were on the opposite side of the rink, laughing as they practiced their figure of eights. When they had had enough of that, they linked arms and skated gracefully together, picking up speed as they went, faster, faster, until they were whizzing along at a quite dizzying speed. Then they broke from the skaters all moving in the same direction around the rink and skated into the center, which was almost devoid of people. There they practiced their ice-dancing. They laughed at two boys who were showing off, collided and went down in a crash on the ice. Someone bumped into David's daughter and she lost her balance and went down too.

While Mimi was helping her up, the two girls spotted David Peabody and began to wave. Mimi caught sight of Karel at once. She caught her breath. She had recognized him. Her eyes widened, and her heart beat with a happiness hither unknown to her in her young life. No trauma, no shock: pure happiness. It was her father. She forgot her friend and skated straight for Karel. She was frantic to break through the ten-deep ring of people circling in a solid mass around the rink. She must get to the railings. She tried one place and then another. He smiled and waved. He was thrilled: she knew him still. He broke into a run, rounding the rim of the rink, trying to get to her. He began to cry, pulled the scarf from around his neck. He was waving it at her and calling, "Mimi, Mimi." The wind ruffled his hair and he was laughing. He wanted her to see him, to know for sure it was he. They arrived at the rail together and banged into each other in an enormous hug. They drew away and she slipped under the rail and into his arms. He picked her up, and kissed her all over her face. He took off her hat, caressed her hair and kissed and hugged her. He tried, but it was impossible for him to stop crying. "Mimi," he kept repeating.

"Poppa, Poppa, you're here."

There were no tears for Mimi. No misty eyes. Her large violet eyes just shimmered with happiness. "Don't cry, Poppa. I'm fine, we're here, I knew you'd come. I always knew you'd come. You told me you would. I did everything you told me so you would be safe, and you are, and you're here, just as you said you would be. Don't cry, Poppa." Mimi hugged him and returned those many kisses.

A crowd gathered around them. They were standing quite still. One man, for some reason, was snapping pictures of them. They noticed nothing. Penny, David's daughter, was now standing at the rail next to Mimi. David pushed through the crowd. He had retrieved her beret. He saw how close to losing control Karel was. He tried to interrupt them, to offer them some privacy, but there was no point. Finally it was Penny who got through to Mimi. She was slipping the rubber guards on to her skates for her so Mimi could walk away from the rink.

That interruption gave Karel the pause he needed to regain control of himself. He wiped his eyes unashamedly and kissed Penny's hand. The New York crowd began to clap. Several men and women patted Karel and Mimi on the shoulder. Gradually the crowd returned their attention to the skaters going round and round on the ice.

Mimi would remember all her life those words, that moment at the edge of the Rockefeller Center skating rink. She said simply, "Penny, this is my father, Count Karel Stefanik, and my name is not Kowalski, I only borrowed that for the war. My name is Mimi Alexandra Stefanik. And today I have a poppa again, who is going to buy us hot chocolate."

Sophia had been standing on the sidelines of the crowd, weeping uncontrollably. She was only a few feet from Mimi. Holding on to her father's hand, Mimi pushed toward Sophia and introduced her father to the cook. "This is one of my best friends, Sophia. She takes care of me. We make cakes together. Sophia, this is Poppa, he has come to take us home."

The cook gave a little curtsy. Karel, ever the gentleman, kissed her hand in a perfect continental kiss. Sophia burst into fresh tears. Karel placed an arm around her shoulders to comfort her. Then he took them all to the Plaza, the Palm Court. There was champagne and hot chocolate and cakes for everyone.

The closeness was there and so was the love in abundance. That neither father nor daughter had a problem about that was obvious to everyone in the party at the Palm Court. It had all gone better than anyone could have hoped for in such an extraordinary reunion. Emotions were running high for all concerned: father, daughter, friends. Here was a long-awaited happy ending. A Cinderella story come true, Little Orphan Annie meets Daddy Warbucks, all mixed up with Peace in Our Time. The Peabodys and Sophia were torn between weeping with relief that Mimi's dream had come true, and laughing because father and daughter had beaten the odds, slain the devil, and could begin to live again, be a family.

Karel returned with Mimi and Sophia to the flat on Central Park West. It was inevitable that there would be surprises for them both. That was to be expected. They had after all been living lives neither knew anything about. But a surprise Karel never expected was to be greeted by silver-framed photographs of Barbara Dunmellyn, set on tables, the piano, one next to Mimi's bed. Some were of Barbara alone, others with Mimi. Others of Barbara, Mimi and Sophia. Yet others of people, all strangers, whom Karel knew nothing about. There was no photo of Karel, or of Lydia, Mimi's mother, or her brother. It was as if she had no family at all. That was, of course, to be expected. The child had never had any photographs of her past with the exception of a few of the family houses. They had been taken away with her real identity. And it had been he who had done that to her.

Karel had always known what he had done, and at times had questioned it, but the reality was right here, now, in front of his eyes and it hurt. It hurt badly. If he could feel that pain, then what must Mimi have gone through? What pain had she been made to sustain, a child without a family whose past, and real identity, had been denied her, a child who had trained herself to live every day of her life as a lie. Mimi had lived her whole childhood wrapped in a tissue of untruths. He asked himself, What have I done? And for both their sakes relegated those questions to the past, so that the pain of what had been might fade away. He thought only of the present and his reunion with Mimi.

Sophia retreated to the kitchen to make a welcome home dinner for Karel and Mimi gave him a tour of the flat.

"And this is your room, Poppa. We call it the guest room so as not to tempt fate. That was Barbara's idea. But everyone always knew it was my poppa's room."

At last, the tour over, they sat together. Mimi snuggled up next to her father on the sofa. They were silent for some time just watching the lights of New York through the large window overlooking the park.

"I think this is the happiest day of my life, Poppa."

"Mine too, angel."

"No one has called me 'angel' since the last time you did, Poppa."

Karel pulled her up closer to him and stroked her hair. He touched her cheek, the tip of her nose. He kissed her on the lips and then her hand. "You've been a very brave girl, Mimi. I am very proud of you. I intend to make it up to you, give you the family you have had to grow up without. If you only knew how relieved I am to see how well you have done here, how happy you are. The friends you have made. What that means to me. I couldn't bear it if you had been unhappy, deprived of your comfort."

A silence. Each of them lost in thoughts that lasted for some considerable time. Mimi burying forever in the recesses of her mind the miserable life she had been made to live from the time she left her father until her arrival at Beechtrees. She would tell him as little as possible of those years and dress them up. She had always known he would suffer if he knew the truth, and she could not bear that. That silence sealed forever the past and what war had done to them and their relationship in the name of survival. In that Karel was certain they would be no different from millions of other victims of the Second World War. They would both, father and daughter, live in the present with a love of life for themselves and each other. To ignore, as much as might be possible, Mimi's lost years. They sat in darkness hugging each other and watching New York all aglitter.

It was difficult for Karel and Mimi to admit to, and so they never did, but they were strangers. The long years of separation had done that to them. But they were strangers only in the sense that they had come a long way for a long time without each other. Nothing could change that. But because they loved each other it was easy to begin again, to take each other at face value, and let themselves unfold to each other the way they were now.

Eventually he broke the silence. "It's a magical city, isn't it, angel?"

"Yes, Poppa. Were you here much before the war?"

"No, not much. I hardly know this city."

Mimi knelt beside him and leaned close. Straining to see his face in the dark, she told him enthusiastically, "Oh, I do, Poppa, I could show you New York. It's a wonderful city."

"Good. Then you shall be my guide. Starting tomorrow."

Sophia, on entering the room, chastised Mimi for letting her father sit in the dark. She flipped a switch and the light from several attractive lamps brought warmth and considerable charm to the room. Karel thought he must, at the very least, send flowers to Kate Peabody for her care in the decoration of the apartment. Something more generous later on.

He had already heard, at length, about the Peabodys, and Barbara Dunmellyn, and someone called Jack, an FBI man, and Ching Lee. Even a man across the hall who made hats for her and Sophia and was teaching them how to make their own. He had hardly had time to think why Barbara had not said anything to him about knowing Mimi. But every time he looked across the room and saw her smiling in a glamorous black and white head-shot from its silver frame, he had no doubts. Whatever the reason, she had probably been right not to. He put the question, for the time being, out of his mind.

Sophia produced a tray with glasses and a bottle of Krug in an ice bucket. Two glasses. "Will this do, sir?" she asked.

"My dear Sophia, you are a treasure. Yes, very nicely, thank you. But another glass, please, for yourself."

Clearly both Mimi and Sophia were pleased. Mimi hopped off the sofa and said, "You sit down, Sophia. I'll get it."

"Sophia, I am greatly indebted to you for taking such care of Mimi. We will talk about that further, you and I."

"I love Mimi, Count Stefanik. Caring for her has turned out to be one of the joys of my life. I will miss her."

"You need not miss her. If you would consider it, you have

a place in our family for the rest of your life. I would not think of parting you from Mimi."

She had been crossing the room when she heard her father. She rushed into Sophia's arms after handing the woman the glass, hugged her and said, "Didn't I tell you he is the nicest, kindest, most handsome poppa in the world? You will say you will stay with us, Sophia? My poppa will give us the most wonderful life."

"We'll see."

"No we'll see. You want to, don't you?" badgered Mimi.

"Sophia," suggested Karel, as a soft-sounding pop of the cork he pulled and a slim stream of vapor escaped the bottle, "you're family, and you stay with us for as long as you like. Shall we leave it at that for now, and another day you and I will sit down and talk about it?" He poured the wine and the three watched the bubbles rise in the glasses.

They each made a toast before they drank. Sophia's was, "To Joe Pauley, for bringing Mimi to me and changing her life and mine." Then they drank.

In the week that followed the reunion, Karel was to learn from Sophia who Joe Pauley was and about Mimi's first appearance at Beechtrees, but precious little else. He had no doubt that the cook had been censored by Mimi. He had also heard about the deaths of Mashinka and Tatayana, and Mashinka's brother. The tears in Mimi's eyes and his own despair at her being orphaned by their deaths prevented any further questions about their deaths or where they were interred. He was never to question Mimi again.

Chapter 15

Every day for nearly a week they arrived, long-stemmed white roses. A different species to mark each day. With them his calling card inscribed with a line of sensuous poetry and nothing more.

Barbara was sitting cross-legged on the floor at one end of the studio, studying an enormous canvas, the first of her Storm Warnings series. She had captured something quite wonderful in the thin washes of an elephantine gray over mauve, and below that another wash of violet. Horizontal streaks of shiny black oil paint undulated mysteriously through the layers of pigment. At the far end of the studio she could hear the tap-tapping of a hammer. Her studio assistant, Henry Ho, a distant cousin of Lee, was stretching new canvas over a large frame. It was ten o'clock in the morning. The sun streamed through the skylight. Barbara was wearing a long loose shirt over blue jeans, around her hair a soft silk scarf tied with a bow that had slipped to one side.

Lee arrived carrying a silver tray with coffee, bacon and scrambled eggs, toast and apricot jam. On the tray yet another small white card. She recognized it at once. Lee placed the tray on the floor in front of her.

"More white roses?" she asked him.

"The loveliest yet, large, full-blown, with an extraordinary scent. Don't let your food get cold."

She left the card on the tray and poured a cup of strong black coffee. It was very hot, nearly burned her lip. She flinched from the heat and some of the liquid spilled into the saucer. Barbara placed the cup and saucer down on the tray. Tissues from the breast pocket of her shirt went under the cup. A flutter of cards, his calling cards, fell on to the tray. She ignored them and raised the gold-rimmed porcelain plate. With a silver fork, she ate ravenously while still studying her work in progress. Lee returned with a Lalique vase and the white roses. He set them on the floor where she could see them, in front of the canvas she had labeled Storm Warnings No. 1.

Lee sat down, cross-legged like his mistress, buttered a piece of toast for her and placed it on her plate.

"I'll go and help the boys."

"Yes. These eggs are perfect, Lee."

She had been staring into her painting. He had been with her for years. He knew how distracted she became when she worried and assumed it was this that was absorbing her. He was only partially right. She put the plate down next to her on the polished wooden floor and more cautiously drank the hot coffee. It felt good, the taste, the shot of caffeine. She stared down at the neat little pile of cards assembled distractedly by Lee, the latest one placed squarely on the top. She glanced at the white flowers, so pure in their voluptuousness, so vibrant and sexual against her painting.

She placed the cup and saucer on the tray and opened the small white envelope. She read the card, closed her eyes and let herself drift into lusty thoughts of sex with him. She set the small white card alongside the others. Roses every day and exquisite, provocative words to excite her fantasies, to remind her of the sexual hold they had upon each other. Words that caused her to think of her own erotic needs. He was her devil in bed and that was what satisfied her. With him she liked that sensation of feeling like a cat in heat, that yearning for cock, a trip into sexual madness. Sexual love with him surged in and out of her consciousness. She suspected the sexual love she felt for him had already become a factor in her life. Barbara knew in her heart she would always be ready for him. What made that more exciting was her sense that he would always be ready for her.

She refilled her now empty cup with hot coffee. While it cooled she dealt the small white calling cards as if from a deck, and spread them out in front of her. She re-read his love notes, savoring every word. Barbara rose from the floor, and with her fingers took the last rasher of bacon on the plate. She ate it between sips of coffee, and walked to the far end of the studio to see how the boys were getting on. She was excited by the progress she had made in her work that morning. Her yearnings for Karel and sex were something separate from the rest of her life and work. She was intelligent enough to understand and respect her own fearlessness in both work and sexual passion. She knew instinctively that she would deny neither of them, not ever, no matter what. She was enslaved to both at her own will. Both of them would take her where she wanted to go and, although at first it seemed reckless to give herself up so totally to Karel Stefanik, to sex and the desire to experience everything sexual that they demanded of each other, she now reveled in the prospect of going even further into erotic oblivion with him. If there was a puzzlement of any kind about their passion for each other, it was that they should feel so safe, so at one with each other. Theirs was an Eros till death us do part.

She watched the men working on the stretcher for several minutes, but her mind drifted away from them toward Karel. When would he return? Indeed, would they ever be together again? Strangely she had no anxiety about that. She was resolved that with him it would only be—when it would be. Barbara Dunmellyn had been a realist about her relationship with Count Karel Stefanik from their beginnings. Desire would not impair that. There would be other lovers, but none would be a substitute for him. What they had together was irreplaceable. But there would be other men, she was resigned to that. And there was Brandon, too, to be considered, although not to be mixed up in this very private, secret world of sex with Karel.

She had to smile to herself as she remembered Brandon's words two nights before. "I don't know who is sending these flowers, but whoever he is, he's very good for our sex life." Not bad of him to understand and ask no questions, make no demands but just enjoy her even more, and have the elan to acknowledge it.

Barbara felt happy, lucky, she would have them both. One thing was for certain: she and Karel would never dissolve their relationship. It worked naturally for them. Brandon? For as long as they loved each other and could make it work. About that she had no more illusions than he did.

Two hours later one assistant was priming the now stretched canvas; the other, at the far end of the studio, was cleaning brushes, taking stock of her paints, making lists for the art supplies store. Barbara, working diligently on Storm Warnings No. 1, was interrupted by Lee. She had no idea how long he had been standing there, quietly, patiently, waiting for her to look away from the canvas and to see him. "You want me?"

"Count Karel Stefanik is downstairs in the drawing room."

She looked at her watch. Barbara used a table—a white marble slab on a bank of shallow drawers set on large rubber wheels—as surface for her palette of paints and for old crocks to hold her brushes. She laid her brushes on the table and rolled the unit several feet back from the canvas she was working on, turning around to get a better perspective on her work. Crossing her arms across her breasts she viewed her efforts in silence, Lee standing near her.

"Well, what do you think, Lee?"

"Very powerful, Miss Barbara, also very sensitive."

"Yes, it may be sensitive." The moment she said the words she knew these paintings were much more than that. They had an erotic quality about them that none of her other works had ever expressed. A deep and abiding sexuality that made them enormously powerful. They were provocative paintings for all their sensitivity, they were as realistic, as figurative as hell, only painted in an abstract, expressionistic manner. They were the more mind- and emotion-expanding for it. This series of paintings was what she was waiting for. The breakthrough she had been working towards for years. These paintings would make her one of the finest painters in the New York school of art. She needed no critic, no dealer or museum director to tell her that. Now she was ready to take her place in the art world. These paintings would comprise her first solo show. Once she saw that, she understood and could accept the critical acclaim tentatively attached to her work for years.

Barbara pulled the table close to the ten-foot-long canvas once again. She squeezed out a long worm of cadmium white oil paint and worked quickly, mixing it with linseed oil and turpentine. She applied it with several brushes of various sizes in a misty wash. From there she built up a thicker layer of white pigment. On top of that, with the finest of brushes, she applied the slim ribbons, more a trickle, of an even glossier shade of white. Now she painted swiftly in broad strokes with a dry brush. It worked: the white emerged from the depths of the dark storm of paint and then slid behind the color, only to emerge again with even more power. It dived in and out several times. Some was rich, an erotic stream of come that shot an unbelievably sensuous light into the painting. It oozed sexuality, proclaimed its ecstasy. As she painted she called out over her shoulder to Lee, "Ask Count Stefanik to give me fifteen minutes. Offer him a drink in the library and then bring him up here to the studio."

She worked feverishly, perfectly. The work took possession of her. With that one, relatively small section of the canvas completed, the painting was transformed. She slapped the brushes down on the table, walked away from the painting, went back to it, once, twice, and then withdrew to where she could see it whole and entire. Then, with a deep sigh, she spun around. Hands on hips, feet set apart, she took a stance, and gave her work her most objective, critical gaze.

"Yes," almost in a whisper, then louder, "oh, yes, yes."

Finally she threw her hands, now clenched in closed fists, up into the air several times. With outstretched arms she punched toward the skylight as if wanting to break it and knock on heaven's door. She shouted it out again: "Yes, yes, yes, yes."

The two assistants on the far side of the studio left their work and went to stand behind her. It was the finest painting, the most important she had ever created. There was a wholeness about it, a sensuality, a vibrancy hitherto missing from her work. She was painting with a new inspiration, a new kind of freedom wrenched from her old self. Only she knew that Karel Stefanik had, maybe not everything, but certainly a great deal to do with it. She saw in the two young men's faces long before they were able to express it that they had just witnessed that moment of truth in a work of art that all creative artists strive for. Then there were pats on the back, the shaking of hands. After years of struggle, there it was.

She began to laugh, and it was then that Karel walked through the rear door. Was it always going to be like that? Her heart very nearly skipped a beat at the sight of him. Was she always going to have such a strong physical attraction to him? Would he always to able to draw her to him with that magnetic charm, that outrageous sexuality? She asked herself, already knowing the answer.

One of the young men handed her a cloth. She wiped her hands as she walked toward Karel, still laughing. Her laughter was infectious, and he smiled. She saw his gaze rest for a brief moment on the roses protruding from their glass vase in front of the canvas. She could see in his face how pleased he was that they were placed there.

"I was laughing because I had just had a monumental breakthrough in my work. A moment of awareness, and I was suddenly there. It had happened when I least expected it. And I was reminded of the Zen Buddhist monk's lesson to a disciple about awareness. It made me laugh, because having experienced something I had been seeking for so long I now understood what that Zen teacher meant. The Buddhist monk told his disciples, 'Awareness can come at any time, and in any number of ways.' I am paraphrasing, he actually said it much better. One of the dimmer of his disciples reckoned that wasn't much of a lesson. He kept asking, 'How will I know awareness?' The Zen master slapped the disciple as hard as he could across his face, and walked away. The white roses in front of my painting?" She laughed again, light laughter like the tinkle of tiny bells. She took him by the hand. "Come and see."

His arm was around her shoulders. Together they walked to stand in front of the canvas. They stayed in the studio, sitting in old wooden chairs before the canvas, drinking champagne with her assistants and Lee. And then quite suddenly she had had enough. Her assistants and Lee sensed it and vanished almost abruptly from the studio.

Barbara and Karel sat in silence, viewing the painting. The studio was very quiet. There was about the space a kind of purity, an ethereal atmosphere. It felt almost church-like. Finally he asked her to go to him.

She did. He remained seated, took her hand and held it above his head. He directed her around behind him, to stand at his side, finally to seat herself on his lap. That way nothing, not even Barbara, blocked his view of the painting. "You are a fine painter, Barbara. That . . ." and he raised his arm in an extravagant gesture ". . . I think might possibly be a very important painting. The roses may or may not have been your slap of awareness. For my own vain reasons I would like to think so. But this painting will be, for some, your Buddhist monk's slap in the face, their moment of awareness of something beyond what the eye sees. For others it might mean a humbling experience. For me, it's a most carnal painting, and I doubt that many people will miss that. To be crude, it is as if you had painted it with your cunt."

Before she could answer, he placed his lips to hers. They kissed each other hungrily. He opened her blue jeans and slipped his hand in to caress her. She felt his fingers parting her cunt lips. She sat with her head resting on his shoulder, feeling blissful and sighed. "I want this with you," he told her, "but first we have to talk." He removed his hand, put his lips on her mound of curly blonde hair to kiss it with great tenderness, then closed her blue jeans.

There was no note of sadness in his voice. She felt no separation looming between them. Those were the things she had felt with her other lovers. With men who had been besotted with her and with whom she had immensely enjoyed her love affairs, until the last moment when they had run their course. But nothing like that existed between Karel and Barbara. There was a sureness, a sense of the eternal, about their feelings for one another. A foreverness, if you like, was implicit in their sexual comings together. She had always felt, and still did, that everything they were, the past, the present, the future, was always wrapped up in the moment of being together. There would be for them nothing more, nothing less.

He had been right all those years ago. For them there would never be a beginning, a middle or an end to their love story. It would just be. Everything they would ever have together would only work in a wholly selfish sexual world for them. That was the power of their attraction. It was what gave them continuity, just being together, in flagrant sexual bliss. It was there they created their world, there that they would live free in wild sexual abandon. It was enough for them that they were there. Enough that destiny had slapped them in the face.

They kissed several times as they walked arm in arm from the studio, down the stairs and into the library. She ordered smoked salmon sandwiches and quails' eggs for lunch for them in the library room, a bottle of Pouilly Fuissé, and hot black coffee.

One of the revelations about their relationship was they never had to talk about it, nor did they talk very much about anything else. The outside world simply didn't enter their life. And so they were both easy about whatever it was he had to say to Barbara. It could change nothing for them. It was a luxury a woman rarely has with a man, a luxury two lovers rarely have. Neither of them was blasé about that, nor unappreciative.

He stood by the window, looking out on Fifth Avenue, then turned to face her. "You can imagine my surprise when I went with Mimi to the flat on Central Park West and saw your photographs in several silver frames dotted around the living room."

"Yes, I can."

"She describes you as her best friend, the person she would most like to emulate when she grows up. Barbara, Mimi loves you."

"Yes, I know, but as a friend. Mimi and I are the best of friends. We have taken care, very great care, not to strain our friendship by taking liberties with it. Mimi has remarkable qualities, that's what draws me to her."

"Yes, she is an admirable child. She always was. Even as an infant she had a self-contained, silent quality about her. She was a very good baby. Once I was over the emotional impact of our reunion, we picked up as if there had been no separation at all. It's as if those years apart never existed."

They were gazing directly at one another. She sensed that he wasn't going to ask her about Mimi, and that somehow made her feel uncomfortable. She volunteered, "Yes, I did know she was your daughter right from the moment I met her. It was an extraordinary coincidence that brought us together. And no, I never told her I knew you. It wasn't possible. It was a matter of loyalties. I think you can appreciate that. Loyalties, and an understanding of your predicament: having to do what you thought best for Mimi, even though she might not think so herself, gambling that the choices you made for her were the right ones.

"When you appeared several days ago, well, it seemed somehow awkward, not at all the right moment to tell you about my friendship with Mimi. I don't think you or she know how the lies you have had to live with to survive have affected you, or the people who have become involved with you. You and Mimi have built a wall of silence and secrecy which I doubt will ever be penetrated. I felt compromised by my loyalties in that room in the Plaza, but then I was able to see clearly my position in your lives. I have, you see, been true to all of us, you and Mimi and myself. And that, Karel, will not change. I intend my relationship with Mimi to remain as it is. Best friends. I see no reason for that to change."

A discreet knock at the door. She crossed the room to open it for Lee. There were smoked salmon sandwiches, small squares of brown bread, thick butter and succulent slices of Scottish salmon, with a lick of lemon juice and lots of freshly-milled black pepper. Barbara took a porcelain plate and placed several small sandwiches on it while Karel poured the wine. She went to sit on the arm of a leather wing chair. The chilled wine was dry, with just the right hint of fruitiness. Its taste seemed perfect. Karel sat in the same chair and took one of the sandwiches she offered him. Very cautiously—no need to spill a good wine—he pulled her off the arm of the chair into his lap. For some time they sat there savoring their sandwiches and wine. She was able to reach for the bottle to refill their glasses without disturbing them. He raised her hand and kissed it. Then, gazing into her eyes, he told her, "Her name is Lydia. It was a marriage of convenience arranged by our parents. We were both very spoiled, frivolous and young, with no interest in settling down to marriage. She was amazingly beautiful, selfish and capricious. Manipulative as hell. There was in her a basic dishonesty. She had no sense of loyalty, could never really understand right from wrong. She was amoral. But very beautiful and flirtatious. We disliked each other, except for the sex. We knew that two days after the engagement. The sex worked for us, but we had no illusions. We saw it as a saving grace to the marriage, nothing more. We were in an unworkable situation. Neither of us wanted to marry, and most certainly not to each other. But we would not go against our families, even though the more I came to know her, the more I considered talking to my father, at least making an attempt to get out of it. I was spared that. Lydia and I made an agreement, we had to. She became pregnant with our son. It was more a pact. Since it was to be a marriage of convenience that neither of us wanted, we would allow ourselves the freedom to go our separate ways, as long as we kept up a façade and were discreet. We ignored each other's lovers, our promiscuity. Lydia resented her pregnancy, giving me a son, and laid claim to him as if she'd produced him by virgin birth. But that didn't stop her from abandoning him when it suited her. Mimi was conceived during a yachting trip around the Greek Islands, a family affair where we had to put on a good show for both sets of parents. Lydia's second pregnancy was easy and she was happy. Those nine months were the best we ever had together. But once Mimi was born, neither of us was able to settle. Fact is, we were incompatible. Oh, there were times when she was great with the children, but she was never with them for very long. She was always traveling.

"In Paris she met and fell in love with the painter Auroyo. She took our son with her, and left Mimi to me. She was famous before the war for being his mistress, and then as his model, my son was painted, too. Auroyo disliked the name Lydia, he called her Marianne. She was obsessively in love with him. On rare occasions, when she was jealous of the other women, or of his fame, she would desert him and come home to us. He would come after her. That was the pattern of their lives and, to be honest, I didn't care one way or the other about her or the life she had chosen to live. I had Mimi, the women I wanted, my estates and money. I lived as I pleased, went where I wanted to go. Mimi was happy, a bright, loving child. When she did see her mother, she thought her a beautiful princess from some fairy tale. Her wet-nurse, Mashinka, and Tatyana, her nanny-cum-tutor, were her real mother-figures. And she had me, an adoring father, who took her with me most everywhere I went. Ours was a bad, worse than bad, a rotten marriage. But we never dissolved it. Finally Lydia abandoned us for good."

Barbara was amazed by the story. Paintings of Marianne were adorning every great modern museum in the world. Barbara had spent innumerable hours studying the Auroyo paintings of her. They were works of twentieth-century genius. The model's reputation was legendary. Karel was being generous about her compared to the stories that circulated in the art world. Her tantrums were notorious.

"Auroyo fell in love with an eighteen-year-old beauty, a would-be painter called Clementine. He brought her into their villa in the south of France and used her for his model. His relationship with Lydia was finished but she clung on, until she manipulated the girl out of the house and herself back into Auroyo's favor.

"Once I was out of Czechoslovakia I went to her in Paris and warned her of what I thought was coming. I begged her and Auroyo to leave France. I even suggested that she should come with or without Auroyo—to England with us and then on to America, if it could be managed. I would do what I could for them. I wanted her to care for the children, I had a war to wage, a country and a heritage to fight for, as well as my family.

"She was appalled at the idea of leaving Paris or Auroyo. We parted for the first time on very bad terms. Auroyo did his best for them during the occupation, even though he was finished with her. He saved my son, but she, by her own vanity and selfishness, ended up in Belsen. There were four American passports delivered by Mr. Bensen the other night. They were for my son and Lydia, as well as Mimi and myself. I found her, you see. She had only just survived Belsen concentration camp. She has been ill for a very long time, and would not travel until her looks and her health were restored. She and my son arrive in a week's time."

He eased himself out from under Barbara and kissed her on the forehead before removing the empty plate from her hands.

He placed several more sandwiches on it. He filled their glasses, sat on the arm of her chair, and ate one of the sandwiches and drank from his glass.

"I don't know what I am meant to say to all this."

"Nothing, there is nothing to say. It doesn't call for comment. What it's telling you is that I'm trying to put a family of sorts together for Mimi and Laslo, no matter how complex, how fragmented to may be, because we all of us need the support of a family to get on with our lives. Where my marriage failed, our family will not. Neither Lydia nor I have any illusions about our marriage. It didn't work before the war, nor will it now. But we need each other. Lydia intends to do her best for the children, but we are talking of a wrecked woman trying to put a severely damaged mind and body together again. I'm telling you all this because I want you to understand that when I walked in here several days ago, I had not planned for us to happen again, although I had hoped it might. Now that it has, not to tell you would have been to deceive you, and that I could not do."

"And if, when you came here the other day . . ."

He interrupted her, guessing correctly what she was going to ask. "I would have told you nothing. I would have handed you the flowers, then taken you to lunch and said thank you for a great wartime frolic. But, the way it is between us, you had to know that my first priority has to be the family, as least until the children are grown and have made lives for themselves."

Any other woman would have read that in half a dozen different ways, all promising a future. Barbara had no need to play that game with herself. She had seen too many women make that mistake and pay for it with broken hearts and bitter recriminations for perfectly good lovers. Instead she asked the only thing that seemed relevant to Karel's story. "How much of this does Mimi know?" Rising from the chair to walk to the desk, she sat on its edge, next to where Karel was now standing.

"Mimi seems to be fourteen going on forty. I've told her everything, more or less as I've told it to you. I thought the truth about us, our limitations and human frailties, was better to be shown and accepted by Mimi than pretending Lydia and

I are something we can never be. Rightly or wrongly, it's better for us all to start to live together as we mean to go on. You see, something had to be said. Mimi had never been given an explanation for Lydia's disappearance, nor her brother's. I think in her mind she assumed they were dead, although I had always told her they were away and maybe one day might come back."

He paused. The room was very quiet, Barbara and Karel gazing into each other's eyes, studying each other's faces, feeling once again the beat of their hearts. The outside world and all the complexities that go with it receded, as if swept away by an imperceptible, warm breeze. Barbara opened the buttons on her shirt. Karel observed her with admiring eyes. She slipped her arms seductively from the sleeves and the shirt dropped on the desk.

She caressed her breasts, took her nipples between her fingers and teased them, and closed her eyes for a few seconds, savoring the excitement she felt in showing him her erotic needs. He removed her hands, turned them up and kissed the palms, licked them with the point of his tongue. He wrapped her arms around his waist and kissed her. Her lips parted and they felt the inside of each other's mouths, the taste of each other. Karel picked up her shirt and helped her on with it. He held her close and told her, "Mimi has a long-time engagement with her schoolmates to go on a class outing to Washington, D.C., an educational tour of the Capitol. I wouldn't allow her to cancel it. I want her to carry on with her normal routine. Her life is about to change so radically when we start living *en famille,* I thought the trauma might be easier if we took it slowly. She has suffered enough of being abruptly uprooted. Is there somewhere we can go away for a few days, in the country, preferably by the sea? Just you and I and the sea, where we can be alone, lovers together, indulging ourselves in an orgy of sex. I have five days for us, if you are free."

There could be but one answer to that.

New York
London
Patmos

1964

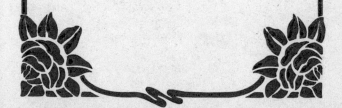

Chapter 16

Jay Steindler reached out in a half sleep for his wife. That was the way he liked to wake up, with the warmth of his wife's body against his, to feel her enfolded in his arms. He loved Mimi's body, the long slender back, her long limbs, the full, rounded breasts with their enticing, overly large, pale-peach nimbus, the narrow waist, the seductive curves of hip and bottom. He adored the feel of Mimi in his hands, her skin so soft and smooth, so sensual to the touch. He liked the feel of her flesh beneath him. He always imagined it as being sweet, rich and succulent. He often teased her about being his epicurean delight. But one thing he never did was to take for granted her being there. He sensed, although she had never done anything to suggest it, that Mimi was like a ball of quicksilver in the palm of the hand, mercurial, and with the least jolt capable of changing form, slipping through his fingers. Every morning of their ten-year marriage, when not away on business, he kissed her awake, and made love to her. And if he should awake and she was for some reason not there next to him, the day never seemed right.

Jay pulled himself up among the pillows and lit a cigarette. Dawn was just breaking the night sky. The light was sufficient to see her in the shadows, a silhouette lying on the chaise near the fireplace.

"How long have you been lying there?"

"Oh, not very long."

"Are you all right?"

"Fine, just fine."

She rose from the chaise and walked back to the bed. He reached out to switch on the bedside lamp. She plucked the cigarette from his fingers, crushed it in the ashtray next to the stacks of books on the eighteenth-century black lacquer table next to the bed.

"You smoke too much. You promised to cut down."

"I'm addicted, and I break promises. You seemed very pensive, a million miles away, over there on the chaise, in the dark."

"I was thinking about Barbara, what a good friend she's been, the most constant influence, except for Poppa, in my life. The best and most important friend I have."

"And what about me?"

"Oh." She smiled, embarrassed. "You're different, in a category all your own."

"Is that good or bad?"

"Not good, not bad, just special," she answered. "Remember we are giving a supper party for her this evening after the Museum of Modern Art exhibition."

He raised the covers of the bed. Mimi slipped out of a long, luxurious, black silk kimono with amazingly wide, seductive sleeves, lined with a rich, plum-colored taffeta that rustled with every move she made. She lay down next to him. He made love to her. Unfortunately for Mimi, the least exciting thing about their marriage was their sex life, but she went to great lengths so Jay need not know that. It was just one of those marriages where sex was good, good enough for her to reach orgasm, on rare occasions very good, but never sex that was exciting and adventurous, stimulating to their lives. Not the way their work and social life were. They were cosmopolitan New Yorkers. They lived their lives through achievement, a life intermittently in the public eye, without the kind of time in the bedroom that great sex needs.

Mimi loved Jay and her marriage, they were good. It was the kind of marriage that allowed them their freedom and their secrets. Jay was the right husband for her because she never fully revealed herself. Mimi always held back. That suited Jay, as long as Mimi revealed enough of herself for him to love. Some said that was part of her charm, her vivacity, the self that always remained hidden. Men and women alike were attracted to her as they always had been since she was a child. She was not a woman it was easy to say no to.

She seemed always to hold all the cards when she played games of seduction and charm.

Mimi Steindler lived in several worlds simultaneously. First the world her father had created for her and his family, one of culture and comfort, with a degree of old-world elegance. It was a geopolitical world of exiles and refugees still looking for freedom, still wanting to return home one day. She didn't much like the people who populated her father's world, because they lived only for the future and on dreams of what might be. It had always seemed strange to her that her father, who lived fully in the immediate present, should surround himself with such people. He had his hopes and dreams of a future, of a return to his estates and his homeland for himself and his children, but he was too much of a realist to lose the life he had in the hope of a new tomorrow. That tomorrow, he knew, might not come in his lifetime. So Mimi lived in his world, but never took seriously the hopes and dreams of the lost souls who sought him out. She was happy loving her father and having a family, even though her relationship with her mother, Lydia, was only mildly affectionate, and with her brother little more than that. No matter how complex the Stefanik family, it was Mimi's, and she was grateful and proud of being a member of it.

She preferred her husband's world. Like her father, he was a powerful charismatic man, clever, brilliant in business, a force in the publishing world who overshadowed his rivals. He had real power, enough for him and Mimi to be reluctant celebrities living a closed, very private life when they chose to. Some said Jay and his publishing house controlled the New York literary world. Mimi didn't know if that was true or an over-simplification of publishing gossip. She never bothered to ask Jay, since it didn't interest her one way or the other. She could only think it might be true because her husband was a controlling sort of man. For all his liberal thinking, his Mr. Nice Guy, he relished his power.

And then there was Mimi's world. First and foremost she was a femme fatale with men, who, for the most part, made dizzy fools of themselves over her. After watching Barbara Dunmellyn for years, Mimi had learned what celebrated, interesting and vital men look for in a woman. She liked hav-

ing them around her. She enjoyed the female power she
derived from their carnal lust for her. Men wanted Mimi, she
held a challenge for them. None had managed to achieve it.
Jay came less close to it than he thought. Like Barbara, Mimi
had the looks, the sexual hunger for men that attracts. But,
unlike Barbara, she was neither particularly creative nor a
considerable intellect. Although she could hold her own with
academics, artists, the literary establishment, she hadn't the
inclination to exploit those resources in herself. Her assets—
looks, charm, a certain entrepreneurial flair—came to her
naturally. She used these resources to promote herself with
the men of her choice and in business.

That was what Mimi had been thinking about sitting in the
dark while Jay slept. Men. How much they meant to her. Her
father, and then in her teens the horny young men who stirred
her own sexual awakenings. Prodded her ego because they so
desperately wanted her. The hopes and the promises of sexual
delights that would come if she "went all the way." Oh, how
serious they all were, and oh, what a drastic step it would be
when she finally did. Or so every physical education teacher
told her, every girlfriend insisted. She had never felt that way.
For her it was a natural instinct to give herself up body and
soul to Greg Slater. He had been twenty-seven and she had
been seventeen, a mature, sexually hungry seventeen.

It was her freshman year in college. He was her art history
teacher and the moment she saw him she fell in love. He was
handsome, classically handsome. He had a head not unlike a
marble bust of some ancient Roman god. Dark, short, curly
hair, a long straight Roman nose, the sexiest eyes she had
ever seen. Eyes that were set on her from the moment she
walked into his class. He had a sexual scent about him. He
was strong and haughty, and he stalked her with his eyes as
he moved seductively between the desks while he delivered
his first lecture. Bu the end of class most every girl in the
room had a crush on him. He stood at the door as the girls
left and looked them over more closely as they passed by
him. His eyes lingered that little bit longer on Mimi. She hesitated, only for a second, and gave him her most seductive
smile. The way he smiled back made her tremble and she had
hurried on. He was the first man she ever wanted sexually.

She knew it was only a matter of time before she would have him.

That night in bed she caressed her own body, teased her nipples, fondled the soft inner lips of her cunt. Pretending, always pretending, it was Greg Slater making love to her. A teenager's sexual frustration, a libido growing stronger with maturity. Desire to be with an older, sophisticated, very sexual man, to have him take her, was something real now, not just a fantasy to gossip with her girlfriends about.

It was a week before she took his class again. She dressed for it, made herself up as prettily as possible. But she was subtle. She knew her long blonde curly hair and stunningly beautiful violet eyes were her best asset, along with full, almost heavy, high firm breasts and an amazingly narrow waist. She wore a tiny green-and-black-checked shirtwaist dress with long sleeves pushed up. It was cinched by a wide black patent leather belt, and had a full skirt. On her feet, flat black ballet-type shoes. Mimi was aware of how very sexy she looked. She had turned enough male heads on the way from her house to the college to confirm her self-assurance. She entered the class and took her seat. She flirted with Greg Slater. He ignored her.

Mimi felt crushed as she left the college. She had been so certain he had wanted her. The pain of unrequited love, her first experience of it, was dreadful for her. She had never dreamed it could happen to her. She fled home where love was a certainty, where there was warmth and never rejection. Not even from Lydia, who, though unable to develop a strong mother-daughter bond with Mimi, was a least a good friend.

The following day with her sense of rejection under only slightly better control, Mimi attended her classes relieved that she would not have to see Greg Slater again for a whole week. But that did not stop her from daydreaming about him on and off during the day. Just to think of him was to set some sort of sexual yearning in motion. And that was the state she was in when, as she turned the corner away from the school, he walked up next to her and suggested, "Let me take you for a coffee. I know a place where they have great cherry cheesecake. Put me out of my misery and say yes. I've been thinking about you ever since I saw you that first day in class." Mimi fell helplessly in love.

Three days later he invited her to lunch, in a small dark steak-house. They were all the rage at the time. Sirloin or fi-let mignon grilled over charcoal, with green salad, was the extent of the menu. There was always a great bar, and a fancy dessert cart. This place had wooden booths and sawdust on the floor. It was across the street from Hattie Carnegie's. Mimi knew the exclusive ladies' dress salon well. That was where her mother shopped. They sat next to each other and Greg was impressive. Erudite one moment talking up to her, and the next telling her, "I wish we were alone. So I could take you in my arms. Feel you close to me. Wouldn't you like that?" As he stroked her thigh under the table, caressed the side of her cheek, stole a quick kiss.

"Yes," she answered breathlessly, struggling to keep herself under control.

He opened two more buttons of her blouse so he clearly could see the swell of her breasts. Mimi felt very grown-up and sophisticated, daring even, because she wore no bra. She tried to close the buttons again. They were after all in public. He told her, "Surely you are not going to play teasing games with me?"

But she did. He lived above the steak-house in a handsome duplex whose windows overlooked the street. There he opened her blouse and kissed her breasts. He laid her down and fondled her, but she managed to get away from him several times just before the main event. Mimi wanted him to be as much in love with her as she was with him. For several weeks she was in heaven, lost on a cloud of love. They teased her at home about the state she was in, but never probed as to just how serious her latest flirtation was, nor who the lucky boy was. They were more amused and pleased for her. They respected her right to be a teenager in love.

Then there came the night when he took her to a concert, Vivaldi, and afterward to his flat. For Greg Slater, it had been a long seduction. Mimi had managed to dangle him longer than most students. But he would have her this night or would never see her again. She sensed it. She was frightened, she was in love and so very hungry for sex with him, but she had never done it, gone all the way. She insisted he put out the lights. He was a magnificent lover. When Greg kissed Mimi he devoured her, and she slipped away into another world. He knew how to excite her. He sucked on her breasts until she squirmed with pleasure. He teased and taunted her nipples with his fingers, nibbled at them none too gently with his teeth. He bit into her flesh passionately. He licked her body, shocked her with his tongue between the cleft of her buttocks, and the way he used it on her clitoris. Mimi had him out of control with lust for her, and she enjoyed every minute of the state she had him in. She was reluctant when he wrapped her fingers around his penis, frightened to think he was going to push what seemed to her to be a massive throbbing organ into her. She wanted it inside her, but was afraid of the pain. She begged him to stop. But he would have none of that. He reassured her she could take him, that he could give her what she yearned for. Several times she pleaded with him to stop, but finally gave in to him. He was relentless in his fucking. She had to bite into her hand to quell the pain. Mimi was too ashamed to call out, and then later too shocked at her own passion for sexual intercourse to let him know the excitement she felt during the multiple orgasms he brought her to. Greg came copiously inside her and Mimi thought a man's come a most wonderful sensation. To have the warmth of his sperm caressing her was sheer bliss.

After he withdrew he collapsed on her and stayed that way for some time. Then he slid off her and, taking her into his arms, turned on the light. He was shocked at the tears he saw on her face. The spots of blood on the white sheet. He sat up. "You should have said. I had no idea you were a virgin. Why didn't you say?"

"I thought you knew?"

"You silly girl. How would I have known? You were so hot. You wanted it so much. I had no idea."

"Does it matter?" Mimi asked, sensing there was something wrong, tears welling up in her eyes.

He was about to tell her that it did. But he didn't have the heart. He was panicked because he realized that she loved him and that was why she had given herself to him. He did in some strange way love her, but he knew that was sexually and nothing more. He kissed her and told her, "This is sex, Mimi, not love, on my part anyway. Don't get lost in this. If you do I will hurt you and I don't want to do that."

But he did. In three weeks he was bored with her. If life had been unkind to Mimi, then certainly people had not been. Until now, she had known incredible kindness and caring from strangers, and here was a man she loved as deeply as she loved her father, the only man she ever wanted, to whom she hoped to be woman, lover and friend for the rest of her life. That was what she felt. It was what she told him.

He was appalled. It put him off her instantly. He told her, "We're not having sex anymore. You're a baby in bed. The passion is there, so is the desire for sex, cock. And you do like your orgasms, kid. But you don't know how to have fun with sex. You take it, this little fling, too seriously. And, Mimi, you make me think you did me the greatest favor in the world when you handed me your virginity. It isn't a big deal, Mimi. Not what I was after. I like women who know their way around in bed. You give off that sensual perfume as if you do. You're a great cock teaser, and when you grow up you'll be a great lay. And another reason we won't have sex again, Mimi—you equate sex with husband. Go find somebody who wants to play serious sex instead of fun and games."

Mimi did what most girls her age do when in love with love, have had a taste of great sex, and want more of it with the wrong lover. She called him incessantly. She chased after Greg Slater and made herself miserable. She stopped only when she had a phone call from his best friend Bill who said, "Greg gave me your phone number. He says he's not seeing you anymore and he doesn't mind if you and I pick up where he left off. He says you've got a hungry cunt. Mimi, come to my place. I'll feed it, I'll make us some supper, and you can eat me for dessert." A chuckle suggested he relished his own wit.

She felt humiliated, slammed the telephone down on him and rushed to her bathroom. There she was sick, and ended up on the floor next to the toilet, weeping. How could Greg hand her over to another man? He had talked about her sexuality! Her own most private and personal thing. She had meant it to be for him alone. Such betrayal. She fell out of love instantly. But the damage had been done. She remained flirtatious, indulged herself in heavy petting with her dates, but was celibate for years. Until a Yale boy came along when she was twenty-one. Then that fizzled out, and she met Jay.

Mimi had been thinking about Greg Slater, and that first time she had had sexual intercourse. What a great lover he was. Often, even after all these years, she tended to think about the sex with him—more of that than what a shit he had been to a young, impressionable girl. She imagined that most women never forget their first sexual experience. Mimi seemed unable ever to erase important points in the past out of her life.

There was another thing Mimi was never quite able to put behind her: the poverty-stricken years in Chicopee Falls, having been a displaced child fending for herself, the lies she had had to live in order to survive. Those aspects of her life she hid as best she could from the outside world. But within they gnawed at her. To some extent they governed everything she did, everything she was, even now as an adult.

There was something deep-rooted in her: a fear of having to live again those dreadful years in the Blocks. It drove her to work in some little way, every day. Even when, long ago, she and Sophia arrived in New York, and money was made available to them from the bank, Mimi could never quite believe that it would continue. It and her experience of working as a scullery maid instilled in her some sort of a work ethic, and a desire for money, a sense of commerce. "Just in case."

Mimi took to commerce, and sometimes thought of the fruit peddler. He had been her first exposure to commerce at work. As a child she had been fascinated by it. She got a lift, a charge of excitement, from making a deal for a Paul Klee or Henry Moore for a collector, a John Marin for a small museum in some midwest city. Ridiculously, but with great pride, she compared herself to Joe Pauley selling six boxes of corn to Ida Hall in Otis on the day he had taken her to Beechtrees. For Mimi he would always be her savior, her hero.

Now, in the sixties, as an adult and a married woman, she had the enviable reputation of being a chic and successful lady in business.

The family could not understand where Mimi got her sense of commerce. While still a child she learned to appreciate art through Kurt Valentine, an old friend of her father before the war, and a remarkable dealer in modern art, and through Barbara and her husband Brandon. When, in the early fifties, the death of Kurt Valentine left a space for the special sort of dealer that he was, it entered her mind to emulate him in some small way by dealing in certain works by appointment only. Years passed before that was to happen, but finally it did and she made inroads into the art world. She sold works of art from a small suite of offices on the tenth floor of a building on East Fifty-seventh Street, between Madison and Park Avenue. Unpretentious, not at all glamorous. Just a name, "M. Stefanik, Limited," in black letters on a frosted glass door.

She was the only one of the family who loved the hustle and the bustle of commerce that keeps New York running. Her second venture happened when she was out of college, but it too had begun in her childhood, with Mr. Spider. He was an aged, sick, fey in the extreme hat maker, whose fame had died out in the twenties, killed off by alcoholism. When he first saw Mimi there had been something about her that revived him, at least his spirit, enough to make her a hat, and afterward another, and then one for Sophia. He was the neighbor across the hall in the building on Central Park West. One of her first friends when she knew hardly anyone in the city. He taught her to make hats. And then, in the 1960s, people like Barbara Vreeland, the fashion guru, said, "Mimi has the best hat-sense in Manhattan." Mimi's atelier was the most exclusive for ladies' headwear in the city. She had working for her a rather amazing collection of elegant and for the most part chic Hungarian and Czech middle-aged, once wealthy refugees who now lived in genteel poverty and produced hats for the New York and Paris couture houses.

This then was Mimi's life, or one might say the many lives that, rolled up, made Mimi Steindler. She knew better than anyone who she was and what she was. That she was a happy lady, living a great Manhattan existence. But she often had to ask herself why she had a distinct feeling that her life had not yet begun?

It felt so good, it always felt so good, sex in the early morning with her husband. That was one of the things about Jay: he made women feel good. He didn't even have to fuck them. Just "Hello" and they felt good. He had about him all the qualities a woman looks for in a man. He was big in mind and body, and had that certain kind of New York Jewish handsomeness that Harvard had polished and Brooks Brothers had dressed. Jay had the basic Jewish New York intellectual aplomb that women love. He had that Jewish self-confidence that comes from mother-love, family support, higher education, creative thinking and a solid home. Women looked at Jay and saw a handsome, sensual man of intelligence, wealth, success, who knew how to make them feel good. That was the thing about Jay—no matter whom he spoke to, whom he bedded, whom he made a deal with, they always felt he had come down from a plinth just to make them feel good.

And what was so remarkable about him was that it was true. He was way above most people, he was like a rabbi who wasn't religious, a professor who didn't teach, a male chauvinist who conceded women's rights. He knew how to give people what they wanted, how to make them feel whole and successful, but most important satisfied with themselves. He supplied people with what they needed to reap benefits. He was not a greedy man.

Jay divorced his second wife to marry Mimi. It had been a friendly divorce. Most people stayed friendly with Jay. This ex-wife, tipsy once at a dinner party, had taken Mimi to one side and said, "In time you'll learn that you're marrying the best man you could wish for. Jay is lovely, you can almost forgive him anything. But remember, young thing, with him it's always the same—everyone always comes out a winner. He wouldn't have it any other way. With Jay, you can always be sure of having an orgasm, but by that time he's already had two, one above in his head, and one down below. That's the thing about the nicest bastard in New York City: Jay always gets twice as much as he gives, and you never know about it."

Mimi was, for some strange reason, remembering ex-wife number two's words this morning, with his kisses, his hands caressing her body. They lay jackknifed, she on her side, as slowly and methodically he fucked her. Jay had technique and stamina, the love of cunt. It felt so good the way he used his penis inside her. He knew how to find her more sensitive erotic places, and had an uncanny sense of knowing when he had hit the spot that gave her the most pleasure. Jay knew how to taunt her with his prowess, pulling out slowly and entering with long, luxurious fucks that drew from her whispers of pleasure, commands for more. He knew how to pace himself, quickening his rhythm always at just the right moment so they could come together.

Mimi's orgasms with her husband were always long and languorous. It was like sliding into submission by going down an easy slope. She closed her eyes and dozed while lying in his arms. Sex was never over with Jay, never finished, it just sort of dissipated. One minute he was still there inside her, even though no longer erect, next he had just slipped away. Then the soft white paper tissues. Married for ten years, and for ten years of orgasms, she had always meant to tell him how much she resented his use of Kleenex, but somehow she couldn't. It was such a little thing, the Kleenex and orgasm, but it did niggle away at their sexual life together.

Jay brought Mimi a cup of tea. They always had morning tea together, but never breakfast. Mimi had breakfast every morning with Sophia and her father in the family town house around the corner. Jay was a creature of habit, not unlike herself. After tea in bed with his wife, the next stop was always the wing chair near the fireplace, where he would read for an hour, then dress and dash for his first meeting over breakfast at the Pierre.

Sophia and Mimi's habit of rising at five in the morning and having breakfast together had not been broken. Jay used to tease Mimi by telling people they had been married ten years but she had never left home.

Chapter 17

It had been years, yet there was hardly a time when Mimi approached the Stefanik house just off Fifth Avenue as she did this morning that she didn't feel her life was something like a fairy tale. Was it all real? One pinch and she might wake up.

She had been very much in love with Jay when she married him. There was just one drawback: she had to leave home and the family. Looking at the house today, for some reason, she was feeling more strongly than usual the urge to have remained in her father's house. Mimi was very happy and comfortable in the home Jay and she had put together, but it was something apart. She looked over the black iron railings down into the stairwell to the lower level. The lights were on and Sophia was at the stove. These two hours, from seven to nine every morning, were usually the happiest of Mimi's day. They were the foundations on which she built. She looked up at the limestone-faced New York town house.

They had all come a long way since the first day Mimi had seen the house. During those early days after the reunion with her father at the skating rink, she had taken him to the Central Park West flat. She remembered the look on his face as she proudly showed him the luxury in which she was living with Sophia: not so much appalled as upset, though he tried to hide it. "Yes, it would have been perfect if there were only to be the two of us," he had explained. Then he had told her about her mother and brother and that they were all to be a family again. They needed a larger place, something more luxurious, with a garden and more privacy than a flat in a building could offer, if they were to make it work. Together they looked for a new home.

She remembered, when she had first seen the house, how extravagant she thought it was for them to live in it. Mimi had been born into luxury and wealth and then overnight been cast into poverty at too young an age for it not to have marked her for life. Her father had escaped that, so had Lydia and her brother. In Lydia and Laslo's case, they had suffered something else: loss of wealth, beautiful objects, properties, security and their freedom. In addition Lydia had almost lost her sanity: she had personally experienced man's inhumanity to man. They were marked by the war and how it had dealt with them. As a result they had their own idiosyncrasies.

Though it had been strange for all of them at the beginning, they did become a family, and took to the house off Fifth Avenue as if it had been theirs for always. The Stefaniks lived a conservative life, they watched how they spent their money, their time, but they did live elegantly, with style. They lived together, enjoyed each other and the luxury of being a united family. The one thing none of them did was to talk to each other about their lives during the war. They were as close as they could be, considering the differences between the four of them. Differences that had to do with wartime lies lived and deprivations endured in the name of survival.

Each of them in their own way had led furtive and necessarily deceitful existences. And it had affected their psyche. How? To what degree? Those questions were ignored. Life was easier without looking back. Mimi could only guess that they felt at least somewhat the way she did. Different on the inside from the person she presented to the world. Beneath the polished surface of their lives lurked their psychic scars. Father, mother and brother shared a black view of human nature that eluded Mimi. She had found comfort in strangers; human nature for her was an infinitely more hopeful prospect.

Only recently, with her mother's death, had she been able to look at Lydia with some objectivity. Beauty, as the proverb puts it, is skin deep. Lydia had such beauty. She was set apart from the hard-as-nails, more glamorous New York women with a dash of flash by her serene, timorous presence. Her face was commonly termed "enigmatic," but more often than not that look was merely a vapid expression. Emotion or spirituality seemed in Lydia to have been made null and void. Physically she was reticent, almost spinster-like, introverted. It was in fact a super-selfishness, not wanting to give anything away, wanting always to keep her divine self for herself.

With her platinum blonde hair and amazing green eyes, her slinky body, she had a nearly supernatural loveliness. To see her, to know her, was to understand why, when they were together, Auroyo had painted her incessantly. There had been an unearthliness about her, and yet she was like a rare exotic flower, an orchid maybe, that needed a close and clammy hothouse to bloom in. Everyone thought that her years in the bosom of her family had been that hothouse because she had bloomed, she had been happy. But they had been wrong. Her happiness was superficial, a showpiece that she wanted to believe in. But the loss of Auroyo, and then the horrors of Belsen, her past deeds and inability to hold on to an international playboy prince she had finally left the family for, caught up with her, and drove her finally and all too literally over the edge of sanity and into the Pacific Ocean. She left her robe on the beach in Malibu near where she lived in a house that the prince had built for her. A farewell message to Auroyo and the prince, nothing to Karel or the children. Then she walked naked into the sea.

There had been a will in favor of Laslo, nothing for Mimi. The justification given: she had the love of her father. After her death Karel found boxes of small diaries where she had recorded her years at Belsen, atrocity after atrocity, with profiles of her tormentors. The brutality and sadistic treatment of her by the officers who had used her as a prostitute, treating her fractionally less badly because she was not a Jew, and then, bored, thrown her out. The horror of the text was the greater for its being written in the present tense and dated "New York" with successive days, months and years. The first entry was made several weeks after they moved into the house off Fifth Avenue. And never, not once, had she spoken to her husband or her children about those years. Was she too ashamed? Or was she too busy reliving them? No one would ever know, but the family guessed that in the end Belsen had killed her. She had been faking life ever since. Karel had the diaries cremated with her.

Since Lydia's death, memories of things that happened to her as a child before she met Barbara sometimes troubled Mimi's mind. She neither understood nor respected that American trait of telling everything to anyone who would listen. All memories, all experiences, easily hashed over, discussed with any stranger who would listen. All that openness, intimate feelings and relationships laid bare over the dinner table or inside a bus, from a strap in the subway, during intervals at the opera, concert or ballet, over a martini in the crush of a cocktail party: it was not only embarrassing but boring. Who, after all, wants to know another man's bleeding heart, or his happy heart for that matter? It was the natural state of the Stefanik family to remain silent about their personal affairs, past or present. So, living with Jay and listening to his close-knit Jewish family spilling their guts out to each other at the least provocation, always confounded Mimi.

Before her father's house she took another look at the beautiful white limestone façade, the frieze of carved stone, the impressive architrave. The double front doors of iron fretwork in deep culicues and stunningly executed Longe lilies over clear glass. Her father often reminded her of when they had been taken for the first time through the interior of the house, and returned to the street to look at the façade again. He had asked, "What do you think, Mimi?"

"About what, Poppa?"

"About our living in this house."

"How many of us?"

"Four of us, and Sophia, if she wants to stay with us."

"Oh, I don't know. I think that's a lot of people to live on one floor."

He had laughed and said, "No, the whole house. We don't have to share a building anymore. Now what do you think of it? I mean, compared to the other houses."

She had answered, "It's a house and a half wide instead of a house wide, like the Peabodys', Poppa. Since we're going to be a different kind of family than most, I suppose we'd better have a different kind of house than most. I think we'll take this one."

He often told her, when he reminded her of that, "I didn't know quite what to say. I wanted us to be a family like any other, but I knew it wasn't possible. We'd better enjoy our differences."

What he had said to each of them on their first night together was: "These are our new beginnings as a family. This is our new home. Each of us has an obligation to the other, but mostly to himself, because of what we've all been through, and what the world has been through. This will be a happy home until one day we return to Prague. We'll give it and each other the best we've got. But if any of us is unhappy—let's out with it, solve it and move on."

And it had been a very happy house. It still was.

Mimi put her key in the basement door while bending to look in at the window and wave to Sophia.

This was her domain, and unless you were made known visually through the window, whether family or delivery man, you might have an airborne frying pan to deal with. In Sophia's kitchen, all strangers were burglars.

The two women kissed. Mimi loved that kitchen; so did Karel and Sophia. The house itself, with the exception of the lower-level kitchens, was architecturally quite magnificent and in good order. Karel considered it extravagant but a good investment, so he took his time and spent his money carefully in furnishing it. Now, after almost twenty years in New York, the Goodrich House, as it was named, after the original owners who had commissioned it at the turn of the century, was considered one of the finest in the city, a beautifully furnished house. It was known for its quiet dinners, with Trumans and Rockefellers and Harrimans as guests. A place where dissident hopefuls from the Eastern bloc, and all the Czechoslovakian or Hungarian intelligentsia, were wined and dined.

Mimi looked around the kitchen and reacted as she always did when she was there. This was where her heart was, no matter where she lived. Here in this kitchen, with Sophia and her father, she was at her happiest. Karel had been so clever and so generous about the kitchen. Though he never quite fathomed why it was so important to the two women, he had nevertheless created this place for them. He had gutted most of the basement until the kitchen was one vast area terminating in a series of French doors that opened on to a large garden.

Across the back of the house there were two terraces, one on the ground floor off the dining room and the second from the first-floor drawing room, a room the size of one full floor of the house. From the drawing room terrace, a graceful curved stone staircase led down to the garden.

It was a minor Manhattan palace. Its kitchen was handsome, grand even, but functional. Sections of it were just plain homely, with its log-burning fireplace, its sofas and wing chairs, rustic tables, and elegant Chien Lung Chinese Imari lamps. The walls were dotted with eighteenth-century walnut provincial armoires that were used as kitchen cupboards. Butcher's tables, old-fashioned wooden carpenter's benches, marble-topped iron tables used to roll out pastry, large pine tables scrubbed white with salt, had down their center glass preserve jars stuffed with peaches, plums, cherries, pickled lemons and oranges, green and black olives, turnips and radishes—every sort of culinary delight. Bowls of fruit and nuts glistened in the light. Jars of candied violets and carnations, chocolate-covered orange peel, silver-coated almonds. Lovely old cookie tins filled with delicious tidbits were standing everywhere. Above the main table a rack held copper skillets and pans of all shapes and sizes, hanging from black iron hooks. Between them bunches of dried herbs tied with colored ribbons. There were braids of large red Spanish onions and fresh white garlic. Eighteen inches below the ceiling, a frieze of copper fish kettles, antique apothecary jars, pottery bowls and mortar pestles stood on a walnut shelf which ran round each side of the room. Between the armoires and the French baker's racks, set against the walls, hung a collection of eighteenth-century Japanese prints by Utamaro and Hokusai in flat gilded frames. Sophia cooked on an eight-burner, four-oven black French iron stove, glistening with brass trim.

Karel loved his garden and his flowers. In the kitchen he saw to it that the women always had fresh flowers. Large, white daisies with big, yellow centers like fried eggs. Sun-

flowers when in season, and in season fresh tulips, his favorite flower, bowls of them. In terracotta pots, all the year
round, they grew for the kitchen rosemary and basil, marjo-
ram, chives, sage, dill. This room was Sophia's home, her sitting room, her place of work, most of her life. Just off it was
her bedroom, an average-size room where she slept but otherwise never retreated to. All her living was done in the
Stefanik kitchen or with the family.

Mimi's father arrived in the kitchen from the small green
house in the garden he kept specifically for raising orchids.
He was bearing a pot of white moth orchids. They were in
peak condition. He went to Mimi and kissed her. "Good
morning." Then he placed the pot on the breakfast table and
from his pocket removed a small silver knife and severed one
of the flowers from the plant's stem. He removed a pin from
the inside of his lapel, went to Mimi and pinned it in the perfect place high up on her shoulder. "Like a butterfly," he told
her. And kissed her on the cheek again. Then he sat down to
breakfast with his daughter.

"How was Paris, Poppa?"

"Still the grande dame of all cities. Met quite a few people
who had recently arrived from Prague."

"The usual dissidents and exiles longing to go home?"

"That more or less sums it up. Except for one young man,
just majoring in literature at the Sorbonne. I've taken rather
a liking to him, and so will you, I think."

It was her father's interest in the young man more than his
youth and maleness that sparked her own. "Why?"

"I suppose because he reminds me of myself as a young
man. Hungry for life, with a fierce love of his homeland—
where, by the way, he still lives. He's interesting and vital,
this young man. He will make something big out of his life
if his courage doesn't get him killed. His most recent esca-
pade was to organize the removal of the entire collection of
rare books from the Prague library. On Friday they closed the
library as usual. Monday morning, the director comes to open
up again for the readers—there's not a book left on the rari-
ties shelves. All gone. Enterprising, eh?"

"So they would not end up in Moscow? He does sound a
bit like you, Poppa."

"He says it was his own personal protest. Sort of an academic petrol bomb. His flower pushed down the barrel of a gun. I knew his father. I wonder if the boy is a womanizer like him?"

"You mean like you, you old devil," she teased.

"Yes, maybe."

There was something, a certain look in her father's eye. Clearly, for him, this ingenious young rebel was somehow different from the others who hounded him for one reason or another.

"You really do like him. He must be special."

"I trust him. And if you ever meet him, so will you. Oh, by the way, his name is Alexander—Alexander Janacek."

From breakfast with Sophia and her father, Mimi went to the office on Fifty-seventh Street where she had an appointment with someone to look at several Kurt Schwitters and Paul Klees. From there she went to have a coffee with Betty Parsons at her gallery. At two o'clock she was in the arms of her lover in his studio on Fourteenth Street.

Mimi had lovers. She had not expected to have them and had at first turned down plenty of men who had tried to fill that role. But then came the sixties, the Beatles and Flower Power, the hippies and the sexual revolution. He was young and fresh and a free spirit. It was like having love all the time, frivolity, fun, peace, dropping out of survival to play. Play therapy before the Jungians practiced it, a decade of movements for peace without power, sex without power, When had there been a time when people marched against the establishment to music, and gathered for love-ins? It was like the childhood Mimi had never had. She fell for it, admired it and liked it. And it liberated her sexually.

In her teens, when her libido stirred, sexual yearnings became part of her life. Boys and sex, new experiences to be dealt with, all handled within the morals of the times, and held respectably in check. She had had her fun and her pleasures, but promiscuity had not been part of them. Love was the operative word, and sex followed. When Jay Steindler offered those things and marriage, she happily took them on.

Promiscuity was fast becoming a new toy for Mimi, in this new liberated world of the sixties. It gave her a naughtiness, a frivolity she had missed in her childhood. She was amused by it, enjoying immensely the crazy irresponsibility it claimed brought peace and not war, love and not hate. It triggered the imagination and naughtiness in her, a new kind of sexual gratification that had nothing to do with security and belonging, success and survival of the fittest, those very things that Jay Steindler preserved for her so well.

This new phase of having a lover was one of her best kept secrets, at least from Jay Steindler. She was not so sure her father didn't sense what was going on in her life. Had Barbara too guessed Mimi's first important lover had appeared on the scene?

Rick Walters opened the door and leaned against the jamb, blocking her entrance. "Aren't you going to let me in?" she asked. A smile appeared on his lips, the happiness showed in his face.

"You're staring at me."

"Yeah, I know. You look awfully good. Every time I see you, I just think, 'Jesus, she's a good-looking woman.' "

"Well, are you going to let me in?"

He moved aside. She stepped into the flat, relaxed into his arms for a hug. Reluctantly, she pulled away from him to walk further into the small entrance hall.

"Hello, Mimi." They kissed and she felt instantly the warmth of his body. Then he closed the door behind him and stood with his back against it. She turned around to face him. He walked toward her and placed his arms around her shoulders and kissed her on the cheek.

"It's nice you're here."

"It certainly is for me."

"Have you had lunch?"

"No."

"Do you want something?"

"Just you."

That brought a smile to his face. "Say it again."

"Just you."

"You don't know how much I like to hear that, Mimi."

"And what about me? How do you think I feel? I always think it's a miracle that you should want me, that we should want each other."

Mimi felt a sensuous excitement. How she loved the tone of his voice, his youthfulness, that special kind of male beauty that she found difficult to keep her hands off. She put her arms around his neck, drew herself close into his arms and hugged him as hard as she could.

"About the other day . . ." he began.

She loosened her grip on him and he stepped back, just enough to tilt up her chin. Distracted by her beauty he forgot what he meant to say to her, and instead told her, "Those violet eyes, they've bewitched me. God, you're beautiful." He placed his lips on hers and they kissed. She loved touching him. Her hands roamed freely over his body. She found the buttons on his Levi's, her fingers fumbled with them. She felt a pounding in her heart and even greater sexual excitement, wild yearning, real hunger for this handsome young man. He was undoing the black silk, wrap-around dress she was wearing. Mimi bit into his lip. She had a passionate hunger for him, a voracious appetite that she could not control when it came to Rick.

"Mimi, the other night you were magnificent. You're always magnificent."

She put her fingers through his long blond hair and pulled tight on it. "You make me crazy. I do things with you I never dreamed of. The other night . . . I haven't stopped thinking about it. It was wonderful, you were wonderful. Why wasn't it obscene, debauched, depraved, for me to behave in such a manner? I asked myself. Why was it so good, so much fun, so exciting? Was it the dope or the wine? Rick, you make it so easy, the sex. Why does everything seem so natural with you? So uncomplicated."

"Because it is. Because we are."

There were naked now. He picked her up and put her in the deep armchair near the window. He draped her legs over the chair arms, dropping on to his knees between them. She watched him; she adored watching him lick her cunt, suck on its succulent fleshy inner lips. He was incredibly beautiful, the way he enjoyed her, the first man to perform cunnilingus on her. She had never known lovemaking like Rick's. Sex for nothing more than its own sake, for nothing more than mutual sexual pleasure. It had nothing to do with possession, belonging, a future. Sexual freedom without violence or preconceived ideas of what it should be like, what was expected, what was acceptable. It was she not he who was really under a spell. Mimi, ten years his senior, was seduced by him, and by promiscuity, free love. She watched the sun playing on his light brown hair, streaked a golden blond from years of surfing on the California coast. Even his hair seemed carefree and young. She touched her breasts. Her whole body yearned for his hands, for his tongue and mouth. She began to squirm under his assault and told him in a voice husky with passion, "What bliss, how divine." She felt rigid tension in her body, a flash of pleasure, then her orgasm. So did he, and sought out that special elixir with his tongue.

Rick pulled on her legs while he was still kissing her cunt and she slid slowly from the chair on to the floor. She came again and again in a succession of orgasms. "The pillows." She reached out for some black and white pony-skin cushions lying on the floor and placed them under her shoulders, at the back of her neck. The kisses never stopped. He changed position. Moved on top of her, and, straddling her now, his knees pressing into the carpet, once more eased his face between her open legs. Rick's penis, rigid with readiness for her, was just above her face. It taunted her, grazing her lips. She opened her mouth and began to suck. With Rick it was never hurried or a necessity. His sex drive was enormously powerful and exciting, adventurous.

They came together on a wave of orgasm that seemed to go on forever. Spent, he slid off his knees to lie on top of her. Putting his arms beneath her, grabbing her bottom, he hugged her tight against him, his face still resting between her legs. Mimi licked the luscious salty taste of his sperm from her lips. Sex with Rick was always the beginning of real feelings, of wanting more. She lay there now, every pore of her skin tingling with excitement, ready for more.

Until she met Rick it had never been that way. She had never felt freedom or ease with sexual love. She had never learned to experience a deep abiding fondness for orgasm, for exchanging sexual lust with anyone. With him, she did. Sex was nothing to Rick, and everything. It was easy and fun. It was there to float out on with the mind as well as the body. That he had taught her, and so much more.

Before Rick, she hadn't known the pleasure of having a man's penis in her mouth. The need of some men to demand, lovelessly, oral sex had until now seemed a dirty and ugly act of sexual selfishness. She had rejected it, had even been frightened by the very idea of swallowing a man's come. Unthinkable!

She had been a married woman for ten years, sexually happy with her husband, and had never taken an active role in their sexual life. With Jay, she had always been the submissive partner. That had always been enough for her. Now, having an affair with Rick, she realized what real submission to a man was. The enormous pleasure of giving yourself wholly to a lover, and the delights to be felt as a result. To lie back and have a man use his cock, his mouth, his fingers, imaginatively for her sole pleasure, to teach her the real value of orgasm-bliss.

Rick turned around and crawled up next to her, pulled her on to her side. He was caressing her breasts, mouthing her nipples. He could feel her so pliable in his hands now. Always, when she first arrived in his flat, there was a kind of tension in her, holding back which he eased her out of. She was malleable, vulnerable. He took advantage of that, but not for himself alone: for her as well. Every sexual act, every orgasm, was heightened for her by the ease and casualness with which he devoured her. He taught her what it was to die that little death in every orgasm. That it was all right to expire in lust and come, and to feel so quickly the return to life. He knew it was delicious, the rebirth of oneself. And now she knew. He taught her to be fearless in sex and exploring her own desires and fantasies, how to enjoy them, luxuriate in them, yet not to make more of them than they were. He made her understand that they were sexual acts, life-enhancing, but not life in themselves.

It was a very warm spring afternoon and the sun played on their bodies. Mimi felt the warmth of it eating into her skin and flesh, the very marrow of her bones. She felt really happy in herself. He ran his hands over the skin of her arms, her stomach, her thighs. She touched him in return. He reached out to the coffee table. There was a joint already rolled. He fumbled with the matches, found them and lit up. He took several drags of the joint and watched her caressing her body, licking from her fingers the moisture gathered from her cunt. It excited him to watch Mimi love herself. She had come a long way since that first time they had sex together, a very long way.

He passed the joint to her. She took it between her fingers and put it to her lips, took a deep drag on it. He had even had to teach her that, how to inhale a joint of grass, a little Lebanese Gold.

Rick had a thing about her breasts. He adored them and had been surprised when he had first seen them. They were incredibly beautiful, large, high and full, as if bursting with mother's milk. It was the aureole, the bright cloud that, halo-like, ringed her nipples, that intrigued him. They were usually large and an elegant light peach color. He loved to caress them, kiss them, excite them into puckering, her nipples becoming erect before he sucked deeply on them, trying to gather all of the aureole as well into his mouth. Sometimes he would rouge them. That changed Mimi's looks. Then her breasts seemed extraordinarily lewd and provocative. She looked like a whore with an angelically beautiful face. That too excited them. They created fantasies about her, and those fantasies excited their sexual hunger for new experiences. He taught her to play the whore, he the john.

In the beginning, when they had seen each other in the city several times, she had accused him of playing with life, playing with her and with sex. He had disarmed her by telling her "That's true, I do. Why do you make it sound like a vice? Why shouldn't we play? Isn't life hard enough, dreadful enough, unfair enough? That's what this age of Aquarius is all about. Less of that, and more play, more love and peace in the world."

And now she had learned his vice, how to play with life, how to play with him and with sex. Only with Rick did the Mimi that she projected to the world disappear and the Mimi inside come to life and show herself. The child, Mimi Alexandra Stefanik, whose father was a count and mother a beautiful countess, who had been made to deny herself, to become a

wet-nurse's daughter, and who had lived her childhood in lies
to survive as Mimi Kowalski, showed herself to Rick. She
could, because with this young man there were no taboos.
They vanished, were absorbed into the kindness of his soul, his
own child-like approach to life and death.

"Let's do it once more," he suggested.

He rammed the stub of the joint in the ashtray, and
brought her to her feet and into his arms. He turned her
around. With her back to him he draped his arm over her
shoulder across her breasts, holding her tight to him. She
felt his erect penis between the cheeks of her bottom, her
back against his chest. His other hand he dropped low over
her mound of curly blonde hair. Searching fingers found her
clitoris. Mimi moved lazily, languorously, up and down
against his body, her hand caressing her own breasts. She
loved the feel of her body, her skin, especially while in contact with his. This was one of their favorite positions, and in
the warmth of the sun they reveled in their embrace. Mimi,
experiencing several orgasms, kept repeating, "Lovely."
Short, delectably light, almost tender orgasms grew stronger,
inspired him, as did her submission to lust. Her clitoral orgasms were in his hands, and he continued, wanting to bring
her to a fever pitch where she was no longer in control of
them. He inserted his fingers, fondling her inner cunt lips,
moist and slippery smooth with her many orgasms. So sensuous to feel those flesh cunt lips sliding between his fingers. He adored them and her cunt, and making erotic love
with her as they now were.

So many times she tried to find words to tell him how exquisite it felt to have sex that way. What it felt like for a
woman to come again and again, to have every nerve end in
her body tingle, dance. What it was to live in that moment of
private passion when your orgasm breaks and you want to
scream, so great is the release, giving up, submitting to uncontrolled sex and passion. But she never found the words.
He had taught her that she had no need to tell him, only to
show him, as she was doing at that moment. It was uncanny
how he knew just when she was ready for her strongest, most
violent orgasms. Rick always held back his own release until
he sensed the moment was there. He walked with her still in

their embrace, continuing with his fingers, his kisses on her neck, holding her across her breasts.

He bent her over the back of a chair, arranged her limbs so that he had an unobstructed view of his quarry. She looked lusciously lewd and provocative. He entered her. This, and on her side, were the two positions where she felt more intensely the pleasure of being fucked. Where fucking left nothing inside her untouched. She felt his penis prodding the very eye of her cervix and wished it would open so he could enter, to feel him even there, deep into her womb. This was fucking for the sake of fucking. Sex and passion, erotic, love, for however long it lasted. This was sexual freedom, consenting adult style. They came together in a strong, enormously long and luscious orgasm. She felt the heat of his sperm and her own come flowing from her. They flowed together, and she was nourished by the sensation. She wished not to lose a drop, but to absorb it into her body and take their orgasms into her soul, and keep it all there forever. This was a gift from Rick: learning to appreciate all things erotic, sexual lust set free, secret desires fulfilled.

They collapsed together on to the sofa, she, wrapped in his arms and crying with the joy of reaching such heights with another human being. She lay there in his arms, feeling the soft touch of his lips in gentle kisses on her face before he dozed off. She closed her eyes and felt herself drifting into a half sleep, grateful that she hadn't missed the taste of unfettered sex.

When she opened her eyes he was sleeping, breathing deeply, his breath warm against her naked flesh. She felt exquisite, warmed by him and the sun, the feel of orgasm lingering on her cunt lips and soft flesh of her inner thighs. Now she understood her resentment of that small square of white tissue Jay used to clean away such bliss. Jay loved the act, not the condition of orgasm. Yet how could she say anything to him?

Mimi was careful. She turned her head to get a better look at Rick. She liked watching him while he slept. This beautiful young man, this generous loving creature who gave so much, enjoyed life so fully, this intelligent, uncomplicated human being who healed her when she never even knew she'd been hurt, who set her free when she had never known she'd been in prison. He moved, sighed, gave a little moan, the kind men give when they come out of a deep, delicious sleep. Unable to resist it, she bent forward and placed her lips gently on his to kiss him awake.

"Hi."

"Hmm," he grunted, "you're absolutely wonderful. Mimi?"

"Yes, darling."

"Allan wants to make love with us again. Would you like that? He wanted to be with us today, but I put him off. I had to know whether you enjoyed it, whether it was something you wanted to do again. It was exciting, wasn't it?"

"You know it was. It was incredibly exciting for me."

"Good. He wants to take us to lunch, can you make it? Romeo Salta's, tomorrow at one. After lunch we'll go somewhere to be together."

"Rick, I think you're my sexual devil."

"Well, we know all about sexual devils—only they can satisfy ladies like you." He kissed her neck.

She bit him playfully on his earlobe, "I wonder if that's true?"

"About tomorrow?"

"Yes. Well, I'll be there for lunch, anyway," she told him teasingly.

"If you will dine with us, dear Mimi, you most surely will not pass up the dessert?" He too could tease. He kissed her.

"Rick?"

"Yes."

"I'm not interested in him, you know. Only what we do together. I'd never have sex with two men if you weren't one of them. It's lovely, a fantasy come true, but it has to do with being governed by the right people, the right man. The right man is you, not Allan. Two men and me has to do with sex between you and me. You do understand that, don't you?"

"You didn't have to say it, Mimi. Even Allan is aware of that. He's a free spirit in bed like us. He wants it again because it was great, it was fun. There are no complications rising from it. You mustn't worry about Allan, he's good people like us. Can you take the afternoon and evening off tomorrow?"

"I'll fix it." She kissed him, feeling excited again. Rick looked at her. He always wanted her every time he saw her. Each time she gave herself to him he wanted her more. They did things for each other sexually that few women and men get to do. He knew that he was in love with Mimi but it was a temporary sensual love that didn't interfere with their lives. It was quite possible that was why he loved her. Because he knew he would leave her and move on, he never told her that he loved her, he didn't want to complicate her life.

He wanted her again now, she knew it, she sensed it, the way he looked at her. He eased himself out from her arms, stepped over her and stood up. Then he pulled her by the hands and she stood next to him. He had only to touch his penis, cup his balls in his hands and he was erect. He sat down on the sofa again and, taking her by the hand, pulled her toward him. She straddled him, he held her tight around the waist. With her hands she opened her cunt lips. He impaled her with one sharp push down on him. Exquisite pleasure prompted her to let out a cry. He withdrew, then again a thrust and was inside her, right up against her womb, his balls touching her bottom. He had only to touch her clitoris several times and she came. That was all he needed. He clasped her around her voluptuous bottom and lifted her to ride him up and down. Slowly, exquisitely, she came twice more. He released her to lie on his back and enjoy her moving up and down, unaided by him. Rick took her breasts in his hands and devoured them with a hungry mouth until the nipples he sucked became rigid. She squirmed with the pain and the pleasure of his lust for her. When he came, he placed his hands on her shoulders and pulled down hard. He was still savoring her breasts when he filled her again with his seed.

They collapsed into each other's arms and stayed quite still, wanting to sustain as long as possible such erotic splendor. He was cautious when he placed his legs together, keeping her prone on top of him, still experiencing the delight of her cunt-caresses. When he whispered in a voice thickened with lust of how he adored her erotic nature, how pleased he was that she should at last allow it to rise to the surface of her life, she wanted to weep with joy.

Mimi never bathed when she and Rick parted from a sexual rendezvous. She liked the scent of his body on her. She found it terribly raunchy to walk down the street while his seed was still inside her. It was a way of not letting him go. Only at home, in her own bath, did she wash him away. Only then did she accept that it was over, until the next time.

He dressed in a pair of jeans and a clean white shirt to see her down the stairs and into the street to find her a taxi to take her home.

An impulse made her tell the taxi-driver to stop. She leaned out of the window. Rick ran up beside the window and they kissed. He smiled, his handsome California smile, all teeth, blond hair, classic chin and cheekbones. "I'm giving a dinner tonight. For Barbara Dunmellyn, my best friend."

"The painter?"

"Yes, at my house. There'll be lots of people. Will you come?"

"I'd like that."

"Good. Only you will understand . . ."

He placed a finger over her lips to suggest that she stop speaking. "You don't have to say it. Of course I'll be discreet."

"I wasn't going to say that."

"I think it's what you meant to say."

They both laughed. "Well, yes, maybe," she admitted. "Would you like to bring someone?"

"I'll bring Zoe, if she can come. Do I have to let you know?"

"No, just come. I'll be so happy to see you there and have you in my house. It's going to be a good party. And, after all, I'm always going to yours."

Chapter 18

The sound of a harpsichord and eighteenth-century French music greeted Barbara as she entered Mimi's flat. As the guest of honor, she was one of the last people to arrive. The show at the Museum of Modern Art had been entitled "Four Americans," and she had been one of the four honored by the exhibition. The reception had been well attended. Pundits of the international art world were there in force. So were the top collectors of American abstract expressionist art. It was both a social and an artistic occasion. Now here she was arriving with Brandon, Frank Stella and Rothko, her staunch friends.

She felt really happy. Success had been hers for years, accolades from everywhere. Barbara Dunmellyn was hailed as one of America's greatest female abstract expressionist painters. But, tonight, this exhibition was extra special. The first of three that she was committed to at the Museum of Modern Art; the second was scheduled for three years' time, a retrospective of the life's work of Barbara Dunmellyn. An honor few artists, living or dead, were given.

Mimi was giving Barbara this party, in celebration of the evening. Just for close friends, and a few of Barbara's fellow painters. Sophia and Ching Lee, under Mimi's direction, had prepared the sit-down dinner for her forty guests. Barbara was looking forward to the evening. She knew well how good Mimi and Jay's dinner parties were. Interesting people, delicious food, impeccable wines. People who liked talking to each other, no gate-crashers. Jay was the perfect host, Mimi always a great delegator, supervised it all. Then by the time the first guest arrived, she had nothing to do but enjoy her own party. The sign of the perfect hostess. One look at Mimi was usually enough for everyone else to leap into a party mood. This night was no exception.

The flat looked handsome, comfortable and elegant, with books piled on tables everywhere, easy chairs covered in silver and gray Fortuny fabrics. Paintings and drawings, collected over the years, hanging on the walls, from skirting-board to ceiling. The room was bathed in soft lamplight. A partner's desk, eighteenth century and English, was at the far end of the large, square room. It was a homely house, inviting and relaxing. Its oriental carpets were of great age, its cushions covered in seventeenth-century French tapestries, each a work of art.

Barbara saw Jay coming toward her. She had always liked Jay Steindler. He made her feel good. She hadn't been surprised when Mimi married him, few girls would have turned him down. He kissed her. "A triumph, many congratulations." Then he kissed her again. He turned to greet David Rockefeller, who had arrived an elevator ride before Barbara. The two men shook hands, and the group all walked in together to mingle with the other guests who swarmed around Barbara. She felt happy in the bosom of her friends—and friends they were, not mere acquaintances.

Then she saw him, several women standing around him, looking at her across the crowd. He had not lost any of his sensual charisma. The years had been good to him. She reacted as she always had, for more than twenty years, wanting him. He smiled at her and gave her a jaunty salute. She lowered her eyes and smiled back and was swept away by the people congratulating her on her success.

Wall-size, plate-glass sliding doors led on to a vast terrace that overlooked the East River and Queens beyond. People were wandering back and forth from the living room to the terrace. The night was warm, there was no wind. Barbara felt an arm around her shoulder. She turned away from Barnet Newman and Betty Parsons to see who was standing behind her. He walked her on to the terrace and drank his whisky straight down.

"They were good years, weren't they?"

"The best while they lasted, Brandon. Thank God we both

knew when it was over. Otherwise I couldn't be as fond of you as I am now."

"This affection we have for each other drives the present Mrs. Wells round the bent."

Barbara began to laugh.

"You don't like her much, do you?"

"No, not much Brandon."

"But you still like me?"

"Very much."

Brandon Wells looked pleased with that. "Jesus, I don't know what I'd have done if we couldn't have remained close friends, if we had fucked it up in the end. I still love you, you know."

"I know."

"I still fancy you like hell. But you know that already, don't you?"

"Yes."

"And?"

"And it's not a good idea. We have too much to lose. We left that phase of our life in a courtroom, remember."

"That thought provokes another drink."

She watched him walk away. He was drunk but still holding his liquor well enough to get through the evening. She had had ten years of Brandon's heavy drinking, long enough to recognize the signs. He stopped a few paces from her, then turned and walked back to put an arm around her and whisper in her ear, "I always wanted to ask you . . ."

She removed his arm from her shoulder and slipped her arm through his. "Anything."

"Why did you give him up?" He looked around the room. "No one can hear me. I've always kept your secret, our secret."

"You mean you didn't know?"

"No."

"I gave him up for you. Because I married you, Brandon. Because I wanted our marriage to work. And he gave me up to raise a family, to try to make his already disastrous marriage work. I can't believe you never understood that."

"It's hard to tell. Sometimes I did." He walked away, but

after a few steps turned back. "One more question. Grant me one more question?"

He didn't have to ask it.

"Yes. When his wife left him and we were both free."

"Then why didn't you marry him?"

"We didn't have to, we had everything without marriage."

"Then why the secrecy?"

"For Mimi's sake."

"Ah, one more . . ." She stopped him. "No, Brandon, no more questions. And I don't know what prompted you to speak about this tonight, but please put it out of your mind. I trust you to keep your own counsel on this one."

"You have my word."

"And so I should."

"I love you and your work. I may even be a little sorry about those things that interfered with our marriage. Forgiven?"

"Long ago."

"Good. And now I need that drink."

She watched him walk away. She often thought about the good times they had together during those ten years of marriage. They had been the darlings of the art world, the art couple of the century. The booze, their success, his inability to say no to adoring young students, put an end to those good years, as did something else—domesticity. They played with that for as long as either of them could. Then it got to be too much of a commitment, too much boredom, banalities like a scream of pain in the night. Being married detracted too much from their work and their passions. How wonderful neither of them had any regrets.

Barbara saw his fourth wife enter the room, the very last to arrive, always having to make an entrance. Untalented, a jealous, mean-hearted little beauty. She was possessive of him, fed his weaknesses, took control of his life. Why shouldn't Barbara dislike her? She wasn't good enough for him.

Mimi was a clever hostess. She always injected into her parties, whether organized by Jay or by herself, some sparkling, beautiful young people to add a frisson. There was always someone with these qualifications. It added a buzz, an unexpected twist to the evening. Without her realizing it,

Mimi's invitations had become sought-after. She and Jay had become urbane New Yorkers, a social couple with a reputation for being intellectual power-brokers with a host of friends and a very private life. Not flash, just nice, chic liberal democrats.

For the most part the men were in black tie and smart dinner jackets but there were some who had not been invited to the black tie champagne reception at the Museum of Modern Art. They were dressed in tweeds, blue jeans or gray flannel, cream-colored corduroys, the occasional navy blue blazer from Chips. It had only been when people had begun arriving that Mimi realized she had forgotten to tell Rick the dress code for the evening. It therefore came as a tremendous surprise to her when he entered the room dressed immaculately in a well-cut dinner suit and black silk bow-tie. The girl with him was nearly six foot with waist-length, chestnut-colored hair, a face that was all bone structure and a California smile. Her body was slender and seductive, more feline than female. She wore a two inches above the knee, A-shaped dress covered in black bugle beads. Mimi could hardly conceal her surprise, which amused Rick. "Did you think we would come in hippy gear, a headband round my forehead? Zoe barefoot, a feather in her hair?" He couldn't help but tease her.

"I was so worried I'd forgotten to tell you, tie if possible. How did you know?"

He put an arm round Zoe's shoulders. By now she had the eyes of most of the men in the room on her, a few side-glances from the women. "We were at the Museum of Modern Art reception."

"That surprises me. It's so establishment," she teased. Hoping to get back at him just a little.

"And I'm so radical?"

"Well, yes, you know very well you are."

"Ah, then the question in your mind is 'Why did he go? How was it he got an invitation?' That's simple. My father owns more Clifford Stills than any private collector in the world, or any museum for that matter. By the way, you remember Zoe?"

"Yes, of course. Zoe, I'm sorry. You look absolutely gorgeous. Welcome." She slipped her arms between theirs and the trio walked into the room. She introduced them to some of her guests, but not before whispering to Rick, "And so do you." He squeezed her arm with his own. She didn't dare look at him. Instead she gave her attention to Zoe, wishing he had brought someone less sensational-looking and certainly a lot older. Zoe was one of those girls in their early twenties who still look sixteen.

Jay put out his hand. He and Rick greeted each other.

"Hi, I'm Jay Steindler."

"Rick Walters."

"California?"

"Quite right, Mr. Steindler."

"Jay. And Miss . . . ?"

"Zoe. Zoe Marsh, Nebraska."

He began to laugh. "I guess I deserve that. A bad habit of mine, always identifying people with the place they come from. I suppose its only a cut above that nasty habit we all have of greeting people with: 'What sort of work do you do?' I'll make amends. Come with me."

The young couple made an impression. It didn't take long for Zoe to gather a cluster of men around her.

The men found Rick more attractive than the women. He was definitely not New York lunching ladies type. Mimi tried to see her lover through their eyes: too young, a sixties drop-out, too beautiful, too West Coast empty-headed. She kept an eye, a very discreet eye, upon him. Several times she wondered what had possessed her to ask him to the party. Rick had a certain kind of charisma, an attraction that drew people to him. People like the men she saw talking to him now, Norman Mailer and George Plimpton. She saw Mark Rothko on the fringes of their conversation. When she joined them, George Plimpton was saying, "Is it true you guys are so addicted to surfing you will go anywhere for the perfect wave?"

"Anywhere. I am going anywhere, leaving next week, hitting the hippy trail with my surfboard."

Was he teasing Plimpton or was it true? There was an unmistakable twinkle in his eye. No, he would have told her. Then, on second thought, she knew he wouldn't have thought he had to tell her.

They were all filing into the dining room in small groups.

Four tables had been set up to accommodate the guests, ten to a table. The baroque clavichord music was exchanged for Mozart violin pieces. The room was aglow with many dozens of fat, ivory-colored candles, crisp white damask, silver, fine white porcelain. The scent was sublime, candle wax and mimosa. Only the paintings on the walls had electric lights, tiny spots recessed in the ceiling, focused to fit within the frame of each work of art. There were only four paintings, four very large paintings, one on each wall. A Brandon Wells, a Dunmellyn, a Rothko and a de Kooning. It was a spell-bindingly beautiful room. For a few moments the atmosphere in that room created a powerful presence that took over the guests. It silenced them, and then the hum of admiration resumed. People milled around and sat where they chose, next to whom they wanted to talk to. Mimi was quick to see that Rick sat next to Barbara.

There were courses of cold cherry soup, ravioli stuffed with lobster and dusted with finely-grated Romano cheese, roast breast of duck with white peaches, a salad of endive and watercress dressed in a raspberry vinaigrette, a dessert of white chocolate mousse, served with a hot dark chocolate and Grand Marnier sauce. Jay and Mimi wandered from table to table. The wines in the Steindler household were always perfection, their guests prodigious drinkers. They changed places between courses. It was the norm at a Steindler dinner party such as this, when almost all present were close friends. It was particularly nice for Rick and Zoe to be there this evening because they were swept up in the hospitality and made to feel as if they too were old friends.

The Steindlers did not smoke dope, it was not offered in their house. Yet, with people sitting on the floor, in the chairs, on chair arms, drinking coffee after dinner, three quarters of them were stoned. Where or how they came by grass and Lebanese Gold, no one asked and no one cared. The scent of sweet smoke in the guest bathroom pointed to an answer. All of them were riding a wave of good company, stunningly fine food, great wine and exquisite music.

Mimi went to sit on the arm of her father's chair. She saw him looking across the room at Barbara, who was engrossed in conversation with Brandon and de Kooning. Rothko, sitting on a cushion at her feet, looked pensive.

"She's remarkable, don't you think, Poppa? And looking as beautiful as ever tonight."

"Yes. My God, she's done well."

He held his daughter's hand and squeezed it, but his eyes never left Barbara. He loved the way she looked tonight. Because of him she always kept her hair the way he liked it, long and loose on her shoulders. She was dressed in a long dress of gloveskin leather, the color of dark, rich honey, sleeveless and cut Chinese style with a long slit on either side to almost above the knee. A Pierre Cardin dress few other women could wear. Around her neck she wore an Aztec necklace of soft twenty-two-karat gold that time had burnished. A magnificent work of art that Karel had bought for her from the best dealer in the world in pre-Columbian art. A gift for the more than twenty years they had been lovers. On her arms she wore pre-Columbian golden bangles.

"You've done her proud with this party, Mimi."

"I love her. Whatever I do for her will never be enough." She smiled and kissed her father on the forehead. It flashed through her mind as she left him how incredible it was that, in all the years since he had found her, he had hardly changed or aged at all. He was still as handsome, flirtatious, charismatic as ever. There was still hardly a woman in New York who would not have been pleased to be chosen by him. It was strange, she knew, for a daughter to feel pride that her father was still such an attractive man, a lover of women, and very discreet about it. But she had never blinded herself to Karel's womanizing, no matter how discreet he had been. Just one person, Barbara, had escaped her scrutiny. Mimi still had no idea about the intimate relationship between Barbara and her father.

"You've done it again." Jay interrupted her thoughts.

He took her hand and she stood up. He placed an arm around her and told her, "A wonderful party, and you're wonderful too. Among all the beauties in this room, you are still the one I choose. Nobody does it better, Mimi, getting an intimate mix of cultured people in this city together without affection and superficial chitchat. No one does it better."

There he was, Jay making a woman feel good again. Nobody does it better than Jay, she thought.

"I like your friend Rick. He looks more like a lifeguard than a surgeon. Young enough to be one. Wrong age, maybe, for the other. And his girlfriend, Zoe . . ." He was interrupted when several of the guests approached.

Mimi managed to get away from her husband a few minutes later. Together she and Barbara went out into the now chilly night. On the terrace they could hear muffled sounds of the city far below, the mournful sound of a ship's horn from somewhere on the East River. They watched the lights of several barges, one trailing after the other, chugging their way to Staten Island.

"Mimi, you've gone to an awful lot of trouble for me."

"Nothing I do for you is trouble, Barbara. Are you having a good time? That's all that matters."

"The best time. It's a lovely party. I like Rick."

"I somehow thought you might."

"Oh, to be young like that again! I admire what he's doing, dropping out for a while to see what life is really all about. I somehow suspect he already knows. He's a very interesting young man."

From the terrace, the two women watched him and the people clustered around him. There was little warmth left in the night air. Barbara and Mimi walked back into the living room. Rick was standing some distance from them, but not so far that they couldn't hear bits of his conversation with one of the guests, the middle-aged Cary Klaus, a nervous, introverted, bird-like woman, a sculptress in stone. She always wore glasses with very dark lenses, and chain smoked. Someone in the circle of people asked, "Feeling better, Cary?"

"Marginally," she answered. "It's always a matter of degree, the pain is always there. For months now I just haven't been able to get rid of it."

"The pain?" Mimi heard Rick ask.

"Yes, honestly, nothing to fuss about. I just have this headache that never goes away, hence the glasses."

"May I?" he asked. Without waiting for an answer he gently removed the glasses.

She objected. "No! Please don't. I can't do without my

glasses." An unmistakable note of anxiety crept into her voice.

"Yes, you can," he told her in a gentle, caring, but firm voice. She squinted, but stood quite still in front of him. He tilted up her chin and turned her head at a slight angle, so he could better see her eyes in the light of a nearby lamp.

"Are you a doctor?" she asked, a note of sarcasm in her voice.

"I could claim to be one." He turned her head back from the light and told her, "I'm going to take your headache away." The group around them stopped talking and watched with partygoers' curiosity. Rick removed the cigarette from Cary's fingers and stubbed it in an ashtray close at hand.

He saw her clench her fingers. Her hands became fists. "Relax," he told her. "Trust me. I'm going to take the pain away."

The people around them remained quiet, all eyes on Rick and the sculptress. He took Cary's clenched fists in his hands for a few moments. They gazed steadily into each other's eyes, Cary still squinting and evidently uncomfortable. Then he released the still tightly-clenched fists. Quite slowly her fingers relaxed.

Rick smiled at her, "Good. Trust me, I am going to take the pain away. It's never going to come back," he told her. His voice was clear and steady, calm and caressing.

Tears filled her eyes, but she remained where she was. Now he placed his hands on her shoulders and began to chant a mantra. "Omm, Omm." No one in their immediate circle moved. Something strange was happening, sensed by everyone in the room. Conversation stopped. Nothing but the sound of Rick's voice could be heard. The chant of the mantra seemed to fill the room, to bounce off the walls, the ceiling. Rick removed his hands from Cary's shoulders. Tears were trickling down her cheeks now. The steady chant continued. All eyes were on Cary. They saw her shoulders drop, the tension in her face slowly disappear, as he continued to chant. He placed the open palm of one hand lightly on top of her head, the other under her short, cropped hair at the base of her skull. She was crying openly. It was painful to watch.

Mimi saw Jay across the room. He was upset. He took a

step forward and Mimi sensed he was going to stop Rick and release Cary. Something told her that was a dangerous thing to do. She raised her hand and caught his attention. A shake of her head indicated that he was to do nothing. He stopped. Mimi could see it was against his better judgment, but he did stop. His attention reverted to Rick and the woman. The mantra continued. Still everyone in the room was riveted, unable to detach themselves from the scene being played out in front of them.

The crying petered out, the tears dried on Cary's cheeks. The squint was gone. Her eyes opened wide and became clear. She took a deep breath, and let out a great sigh. A sigh that sounded as if her very soul was expelling all the pain she had ever experienced in her life. Color, a lovely glow, came into her usually pasty face, and then, miraculously, a smile appeared at the corners of her mouth. She began to laugh. Deep rich laughter welled up from her. She seemed to be shedding the years like an old skin. Before their eyes she changed, to look like a young woman, a girl even. Now she laughed louder, more uproariously. It wasn't a laugh of hysteria but of pure joy, bliss. She couldn't stop laughing.

Rick removed his hands, first from the base of her skull and then, a few minutes later, from her forehead. Gently he replaced his hands on her shoulders. Her laughter tapered off, but then rose again. Uncontrollable, sweet happiness, the laughter of a child. He removed his hands from her shoulders. He smiled at her, and then stepped slowly a few paces back from her. Her laughter subsided, and she stood there, relaxed and smiling. She blinked her eyes several times and remained standing in front of Rick, very calm and quiet.

"How do you feel?" he asked.

"Wonderful. It's gone. The pain in my head has gone."

"It won't come back."

"I don't understand. It's wonderful, amazing, extraordinary! I haven't laughed like that since I was a child. I was five years old again. I was a child in Iowa watching a clown who was laughing. I haven't laughed like that in forty-five years."

She touched the palm of her hand against her forehead and moved it back and forth several times. She told Rick, "It's gone." She placed her fingers gently over closed eyelids. When she removed them and reopened her eyes she seemed astonished. "It's gone . . ."

Rick interrupted her. "That dull pain at the back of your eyeballs?"

"Yes, it's just not there, it's gone. I can see everything clearly. It seems as if everything is sharper with more of an edge to it."

"Yes," he said.

"That's amazing. How do you do that?" asked someone standing close to them.

No one was more impressed than Jay. Mimi had never seen her husband genuinely astonished.

"Where did you learn that?" he asked Rick. "I doubt it was at Harvard Medical School."

Rick laughed good-naturedly. "You would be quite right. No, in India."

"Can you explain it?"

"You saw what happened. Think about what you saw and heard, it's self-explanatory. The brain is a complex and extraordinary organ, it can react to all sorts of treatment. You just saw an alternative one to the scalpel. We know so little about the true working of the brain."

"You said you were a surgeon."

"That's true, a brain surgeon."

"Yes, so young. But not practicing. I completed my residency at Johns Hopkins. But for the last two years I've been Dr. Michael Quinn's assistant."

There were several raised eyebrows at that information. Michael Quinn was supposedly one of the finest, if not the top man in the world, in his field of surgery.

"And now?"

"Now I've dropped out for a while."

"But you will practice, not give up all those years of work?"

"I'm a surgeon. Of course I'll practice. At least that's what I think now. But we'll see how I feel about it when I drop back into the world again." A smile on his lips, a twinkle in his eye. No one was quite sure whether to believe him or not. Most did.

"Good men like you are needed. What about your career?"

"That's what I'm doing it for—to further my career, further my life. To enhance the lives of the people I hope to treat. There are all sorts of things that are not in school to be learned. I've gone as far as I can there, and with Dr. Quinn. I want to learn more. This is an age of mind-expanding drugs and experiences, broader views, eastern philosophies come west to add to our lives. I'm interested in those things, and in peace, and the love of my fellow man. I'm a man of our times. My surfboard is as important to me as my scalpel."

Mimi sensed he was setting them up, teasing them because he recognized how trapped they all were in their own lives. She was amused. She could afford to be; she felt neither trapped in her life nor dissatisfied with it, any more than she felt dissatisfied with her marriage or her husband. She felt neither confusion nor anxiety about having an affair with Rick. It seemed not at all relevant to her marriage or Jay.

Having a lover had to do with a need to expand herself which she neither questioned nor analyzed. Had it been a different kind of man than Rick, one not steeped in freedom of the mind, body and soul, not interested in humanity, peace and love, it might have been different. Love did not come into it, nor the sort of love that concerns a man and woman in possession of each other, marriage. What she had with Jay. No, she felt no guilt at having Rick for a lover.

Through him she was learning about a greater kind of love. Something that circumvented those things. Before the age of new music and dance, Flower Power and the new consciousness that was sweeping the country, the world in fact, what had people to look forward to? War and violence? Well, Mimi knew at first hand what that did to people. This outrageous quest for happiness and fun in all things—food, clothing, sex, freedom for all—and this embracing of eastern philosophies and western change appealed to her. The question was: would it only be the dream of the few? No, claimed the hippies. Love and peace were for everyone. Mimi was taken by that idea. Millions of people around the world were. It triggered the same thing in her as it did in everyone else. Glorious hope.

Mimi was listening, learning, trying it out. She was not

blinkered enough to ignore it, to see this new age as nothing more than a generation gap she couldn't leap, something she couldn't understand or be a part of. That was not because it was there and sweeping the world, but because of Rick. He made it so easy for her. But then he made it easy for everyone else as well.

Mimi had met, through Rick, several of his Harvard friends, professors and doctors who had dropped out in the various ways because they saw a bigger beyond and that it was the age to move in on it. Mimi loved that child-like quality, innocence, frivolity, and most of all youth and energy harnessed by this generation on the hippy trail in search of they knew not what. Better than war, better than bullets, better than slavery, there were a lot of better thans, and a lot of bandwagons to climb on to.

The musicians, all of them students from the Juilliard School of Music, had joined the party for coffee. They had been as impressed with Rick's mantra and powers of healing as everyone else in the room. A slender reed of a young man with haunting, pale blue eyes had listened possibly closer than anyone else to his exchange with Jay.

When the two men's conversation had come to its natural end, the musician picked up his flute and played a haunting tune. Softly at first, almost imperceptibly, people felt it more than they heard it, sensed it as in a dream. Like a modern-day Pied Piper, he tamed forty-odd guests into silence and attention and they drifted on the young man's fantasy. The sound of the flute tapered off. For several seconds, sweet, ethereal, it hung in the air. The cellist on the far side of the room took up her bow and played something equally haunting. When she stopped, the flautist picked up again. This time he enchanted the guests with the exquisite notes of Rimsky-Koraskov's *Scheherazade*.

Chapter 19

Mimi arrived at Romeo Salta's on time. Neither Rick nor his friend had arrived. It was crowded with people dining or waiting for tables, drinking Negronis at the small bar.

Mouthwatering Italian food in an uptown restaurant frequented by successful uptown businessmen: it seemed hardly the place two California surfing dropouts would choose. Somewhere was found for her to sit. She ordered a very dry martini with a twist of lemon.

The maître d' smoothly, but somewhat confusingly asked, "Are you dining with us today, Mrs. Steindler?"

"Why, yes," she answered. It seemed an odd question. But when she remembered the table would not have been booked in her name or Jay's, Carlo's question did not seem so strange. "No, you wouldn't have it under my name, Carlo, or Mr. Steindler's. I'm a guest."

"Ah." He looked relieved. "You see, we are in fact overbooked. I would not have wanted to disappoint you. The name?" He looked at his list. He had neither of the men's names down for a reservation. She was neither surprised nor annoyed, but rather amused.

"How bad of them not to make a reservation. Can you do something for us?"

He looked even more concerned, frown lines appearing on his forehead. She half expected dots of nervous perspiration to appear on his upper lip. Finally, after some pencil-scratching and a good deal of tongue-clicking, "Yes, I'll manage something."

Mimi took another sip of the perfectly chilled martini. It

felt good, the bite of the gin on her tongue. No reservation, and they were late. All very typical and just what she should have expected, she told herself.

An hour later, when the rush was over and the tables were filled, the scent of sizzling scampi in garlic and butter tormented her. The aroma perfumed the room. Mimi smiled to herself. Once, when dining there with Jay and a friend, Ronny, their guest had said of that scent, "Italian Chanel No. 5."

Mimi was fast getting bored with those games women play with themselves so as not to walk out of a restaurant in a huff when kept waiting for too long by a lover they want *right now*. I'll count to ten. If they don't come in by then, I'm going. A count to ten, then another. Eventually more than ten counts of ten, slow counts. Still they had not appeared. It was almost a relief when it was so late the restaurant door was hardly opened. But Italian Chanel No. 5 had done its work, she was famished.

A sizzling platter arrived with lovely large fresh scampi and a plate of Italian bread. Distracted by the food, its perfume, and her own hunger, she pronged one of the scampi.

"God, they look good." Rick reached over her shoulder, took the fork from her hand when it was halfway to her mouth.

"Oh, no!" she exclaimed. But by the time she turned round to face him, she was smiling. Rick handed back the empty fork and kissed her on the cheek. So did his friend Allan as he took the empty fork from her hand, pronged another shrimp and offered it to her. How could she be angry at being kept waiting by two handsome young men who found time irrelevant, unimportant, and something never to get hung up about?

"I'm starved."

"I'm famished."

"I thought you'd forgotten me." She couldn't just let it drop. Something had to be said.

"We did." Even that didn't upset her. "We got caught up in red tape at the Air India office."

The maître d' approached with a scowl. Rick held up his hand. "No problem." From their pockets two tweed-jacketed young men produced clip-on bow-ties that brought a look of gratitude to the maître d's face.

"I suppose you were busy booking seats for your surf-boards?"

"Spot on." Only she among them thought of this as sarcastic. "Do you think it's easy, traveling with a surfboard?" Rick asked Mimi.

"It should be," answered Allan.

"It isn't," Rick offered.

Mimi looked at the still sizzling, empty, oval metal dish on the wooden platter in front of her. They had made short shrift of that. She looked at the maître d'. "I'd like some scampi, please. I think we all would, while we decide what else to order."

He showed them to a table. The two men sat on the banquette on either side of her, still talking about the logistics of locating their first perfect wave in India. She listened and bit the side of her lip. Less from anxiety than the need to distract herself from a fit of the giggles. How could two grown men with an education and background such as theirs see that as, for the moment, the most important event of their lives?

Rick ordered a bottle of Valpolicella, Allan pulled out a rolled joint from his pocket and placed it between his lips. He was just about to strike a match when he saw the look on Mimi's face. "Oh, shit, I forgot where I am." He stuffed it back in his pocket. Mimi smiled and said, "You thought you were already in India."

"You're right. I was seeing a magnificent long beach fringed with palm trees."

"And that's the place of your long wave?"

"No, I don't think so, not a surfer's paradise there, but it's a paradise for other things. Why don't you drop all this, Mimi, and come with us? It's going to be great."

Again she had to suppress a smile. The last thing she wanted was for them to think she was laughing at them. She wasn't. It was a kind of indulgent admiration of their ability to play with their lives. She was enjoying it, even being on the fringe was fun. She wanted to tease them with, "What happened to brown rice and vegetarianism, Zen food?" when they were ordering escalope of veal marsala, osso buco, veal and peppers.

"You look happy," said Allan, bending to kiss her on the cheek, "and beautiful."

"I am happy and beautiful, and a little tipsy. Two martinis, all that garlic and half a bottle of wine. It was irresistible," she told them, "I can hardly believe you fellows have abandoned vegetarian cutlets for the likes of this."

"Old habits die hard. Another thing I can blame on Benton and Bowles. Do you think being an advertising executive dropout is easy? It takes time," said Allan. She liked that about Rick and Allan: they laughed at themselves.

The risotto arrived, and they talked non-stop about Rome, food and India. And the men tried to explain to her the unimaginable excitement and beauty of the perfect wave, of what it was like to ride in the pipeline, that hollow place where the great wave rises, curves over and rolls. How, if you have been surfing as they had been since they were children, it's part of living. To give it up would be to miss the great adrenaline high of all time.

When the main courses arrived, accompanied by a heaped dish of sauted spinach in garlic and oil with yet another bottle of Valpolicella, she was amused again by the way the two handsome young men flummoxed the waiter. Unsure of who was to get what, he asked, "Who gets the osso buco?" and was answered, "Does it matter?" Of course it didn't matter to them. They were eating out of each other's plates, sharing everything on the table, but that wasn't exactly the norm at Romeo Salta's. It was part of their new wave charm, sharing everything naturally, from the heart. But Mimi sometimes wondered about all that universal sharing. How natural could it be when so much was made of it? The sixties people were so insistent upon it, on not being selfish. Did they not protest too much sometimes?

One thing was for certain: Rick's crowd opened their arms to anyone who wanted to walk into them. Mimi had been made to feel included, very much family. That was how his crowd was: one big extended family. Things that had been considered taboo and which she had missed in her life now seemed to be the norm with this age of Aquarius. She knew she didn't really belong in it, but it was nice, really great, to be a guest there, to see her own inhibitions slip away. The luxury of what's mine is yours, what's yours is mine, took some getting used to, and it made life so easy. But there lurked a cynic in Mimi who kept asking herself how long would this Flower Power last? How long would it be before it ran its course? Still, while it was here, it was, to quote Zoe, "A trip and a half."

A pretty woman all dressed in white with a small white hat and a veil of ivory just covering her eyes, stopped at their table. "Mimi." She touched her shoulder.

"Nancy."

The woman ignored the two handsome young men. As they began to rise she held out her hand. "Please don't bother, carry on with your meal. This is just to say hello and my best to Jay."

Mimi knew Nancy. It would never occur to the woman that these young men could be so important in Mimi's life. As for Jay, he could easily have been dining at Romeo Salta's, could have seen her with them and would actually have joined them, been amused, showed enthusiasm for their travel plans. It would never have entered his mind that she might be sexually interested in them.

The three of them left the restaurant. They took a taxi to the marina on the West Side where Allan kept his boat. When he had quit Benton and Bowles, and had sold his Upper East Side flat, he had bought a cabin cruiser. That was where he now lived when in New York. It was anchored on the Hudson River, several hundred yards off the dock. The marina attendant took them out to Allan's boat in a small speedboat. Allan placed an arm around Mimi's shoulder and kissed her cheek. The three were standing in the speedboat, hanging on to a safety bar. Allan shouted above the roar of the motors: "One year living on my houseboat in Kashmir did it for me. I love living like this, it's so civilized and private. Come to Kashmir. You can stay with me on the *Khukavar*—that's my houseboat." He kissed her cheek again and she knew he meant it, wanting her to share the experience of the Kashmiri lakes and living on a houseboat with him.

Once aboard, Mimi understood what he meant. Anchored

just off the city, a few hundred yards away from the marina's dock, with the peace and tranquility of the river, Allan and his floating home were set apart from the other vessels. He had lit his joint in the taxi, and the three of them had shared another in the speedboat. They were replete with wine, dope, good food, and crashed in the stateroom of *Madison Avenue Mouse*. It was a large bedroom with a king-size bed in the center of the room, a four-poster constructed from narwhal tusks with a canopy of transparent white silk. Curtains of the same material were tied back. The cover on the bed was black fox and reached luxuriously down to the floor of polished cherrywood. Large featherdown pillows in white cotton edged in embroidered flowers, black daisies with bright yellow centers, lay plumply on the fox fur. There were three portholes on either side of the room. The sun poured in to make it cheerful and bright. Wing chairs covered in white raw silk, and small inlaid mother-of-pearl tables casually dotted around the room. Madison Avenue chic did die hard.

Rick put on some Mozart. They all collapsed on the bed, Mimi between the two men. They lay quietly listening to the music. She felt wonderful, lying there with them both. Safe, as if she belonged with them. She drifted with the marijuana. It was all so easy, so sweet to give herself up to them. It took no effort at all. It just happened. They undressed her and themselves and together they held her in their arms and kissed and fondled her. They took her in slow and easy stages, and the three of them had sex. It was exciting, but it was also beautiful to have first one man kiss you, make love to you in his own special way, and then to feel immediately the passion of another. To see two men sucking on your breasts, enjoying you, adoring you. To see their flagrant rampant erections, hold them, make love to two phalluses at the same time, and have these strapping, beautiful young men take turns fucking you. To be held in the arms of one, with his kisses and his fondling of your breasts, while the other takes possession of you in a long and luscious, steady fucking.

This was erotic beyond Mimi's imagination, a reality she had never expected to partake of or derive such exquisite pleasure from. They knew how to pace her and themselves, to wring from her and themselves the ultimate in orgasms. How, for the three of them, to ride out all at the same time into sexual oblivion as they came together inside her. To lie in their arms replete with lust, to kiss them with affection and love for this shared experience, filled her heart with gratitude for having been enriched by them. And to see them caress each other, as they caressed her, not out of homosexual lust but with affection, humbly: it opened her eyes to the fact that men could and did love men. That was their first coupling that afternoon, and one she would remember forever.

For the remainder of the day until early evening the *ménage à trois* was continually imaginative, exciting, adventurous with each other and with sex. Mimi would come so many times, she was to feel faint. They held her while she dozed, and fed her tea sweetened with honey. She drifted back to the real world the richer and happier for her experience. She had been in an erotic world where sex, affection and love had taken over and exercised their special magic on her. It was a foreign land she knew she could only visit with the right man, that one special lover of a lifetime.

Sobered now into the old Mimi, she realized how much more complete she felt, more whole as a human being for having given herself so completely. It humbled her. She felt a new confidence in herself for having had the courage to go where she wanted to with Rick and Allan. As those beautiful young girls who frequented Rick's world said, all too frequently, "The trip of a lifetime." "Tripping out" was an expression she had never understood before her sexual escapades with Rick and Allan. There was always the opportunity of another trip in the hippy world. To fuck, get stoned, eat ice cream, ride a wave, be a stockbroker, gambler, a baker, a candlestick-maker. The trips were endless.

This was the sixties thinking, the chatter of the age of Aquarius. Mimi, a woman born in the early thirties, felt as if she were born again, were adding a new life to the one she had. As if there were more lives coming her way. She had just had a taste of real honey. That was exciting. But who in her intimate circle would understand this new feeling, how much these Flower Power people were contributing to her life? Her father? Yes, maybe he would understand. She could, of course, never talk to him about it, anymore than she could have talked to him about her lost childhood, her identity lost because of a war and his will to fight for freedom. Laslo, her brother? They were friends, they loved each other, but this was nothing one could discuss with a brother who was conservative and withdrawn at the best of times. She couldn't share with him what she shared with these two young men, affection (never mind the sex), the loving without possessiveness, not her past—family history made that impossible. Sophia would think she was mad. Her friends, the Peabody girls, would never understand this. In her mind she went through a list of friends, even distant ones such as Pierre, Max and Juliet. Max was King now, Pierre a Minister of State, Juliet a royal princess with five children. They were kind and wonderful to her, much as they had always been as children, but in adulthood were staid and conservative, just as she had imagined she would remain. How could she explain to them, when she could hardly explain to herself, her affiliation with the revolution of the young?

Before they dressed to leave the boat they bathed together, the three of them, in an overly-large bath filled with hot water scented with oils of sandalwood and jasmine. They washed her, held her in their arms and fondled her breasts. They knew every inch of her body and were generous in their praise of it. She was touched by their words of love and admiration for her as a woman. And then she realized the only two people in the world who might understand her lusty sexual relationship with these two men: Brandon and Barbara. Brandon for certain would have appreciated this mini-orgy of theirs, probably would have liked to join them. Barbara would have understood it, and loved Mimi all the more for having taken advantage of it.

They dressed, quite sober now. Allan lit another joint, Mimi and Rick declined it. It was over. There was nothing awkward about that or their being together. Then Rick did a very odd thing. He lined them up together in front of the fulllength mirrored wall, arms around each other's shoulders. They looked so young and handsome . . . no, more beautiful than handsome. That was how the three of them seemed to Mimi.

They viewed themselves in the mirror. And Mimi could understand what they were all about, what she had missed in her life. Being a child, having carefree child-like qualities, the innocence that eliminates evil, was there in the two young adults and the woman in her early middle age reflected in the mirror. Would that they never had to grow up and face the truth of the ways of the world. They had such hope, such enthusiasm for a better time. She was neither educated nor a forward thinker, nor as intelligent and courageous as the two men standing either side of her. But with them she found for a few moments such things in herself. It was a step forward, this new discovery of Mimi. It showed in her face. She had no need to tell them or even herself what happiness she felt. Their hope for a better world had rubbed off on her.

The fortitude she had exerted as a child had burned her out. Years of security, her father, a family, a husband, and now these two young men, most especially Rick, lit the flame in her again. The world was hers. Time didn't matter, nor age, she would go out and grab it with a new kind of enthusiasm. She was like the fairy-tale princess awoken by a kiss.

She took stock of Mimi in the mirror. How had she missed it before, not recognized what others had seen in her, what enticed men? The charisma of Karel was in her too. A seductive beauty with blonde curly hair and violet eyes, a body that was sensuous and provocative, announcing her sexuality. Dressed in the classic chic of a seductive shift of black crêpe-de-chine, bone-colored stockings and high-heeled, elegant shoes. The cover-up, hiding a hungry heart. Her glance caught Rick's and for a few seconds they were locked in something deep and abiding. She knew that what she saw in the gaze that passed between them was to be hers forever. He had, for a few seconds, a glimpse of eternity in her violet eyes. And then it was gone. When Mimi's eyes met those of Allan there was something there too, but it was different. Friendship between those who shared a brief encounter.

Up on deck it was still warm, one of those unusual, overly warm springtimes in New York when the tulips and daffodils are in full bloom though the calendar has declared them premature. Above them the sky was black but bright with stars.

Chapter 20

Even after so many years, there was that sense of delight on seeing Barbara. It never waned, any more than her beauty and elegance had. Beechtrees and Mimi's first sight of Barbara seemed as vivid to her as if it had all happened yesterday, not more than twenty years ago.

Barbara was stepping from the plum-colored Rolls. Every head on the street turned her way: she still had sensational looks. A special charisma that women ignored and men adored. As children, Mimi and Max, Juliet and Pierre, had been dazzled by her. Mimi couldn't help smiling that Barbara could still do that to her. Easy to understand why men made fools of themselves over her. Famous and powerful men were putty in her hands, even now, when she was no longer a young woman. If anything, her success and the tempestuous, at times notorious, private life she led seemed only to add to that charisma.

Barbara had the best of all worlds. With an international reputation as one of the finest painters in the world, she had paintings in every museum in every capital city in Europe and America. She had what most great artists craved: fame in work and privacy in life. In intellectual and artistic circles of both continents her private life was the subject of constant speculation. Mimi had watched it at close range. She could honestly say that the occasional scandals arose only because Barbara was true to herself.

Mimi was aware of the air-taxi pilot standing next to her, staring with obvious admiration at Barbara, who was looking radiant in a pair of baggy Levi's, a white cotton shirt with a dropped shoulder and huge balloon-shaped sleeves that fitted tight around her wrists. Reminiscent of an eighteenth-century English gentleman's shirt, it bloused over a rich, coral-colored, braided-leather belt with a large buckle of silver and semi-precious stones: garnets and citrines, beryl and topaz. Her hair was tied back with a large soft bow of coral chiffon. She wore no jewelry except a pair of large, square-cut yellow diamond earrings.

Barbara still had looks reminiscent of Rita Hayworth and the glamorous forties. Anyone who knew her could understand why the Greek poet Stratikatou dedicated to her one of the great love-lyrics of the century. In literary and artistic circles, his mad passion for her had been well known and well recorded. Many blamed her when, finally spurned by her, he put a gun to his temple and pulled the trigger.

Mimi had always taken in stride rumors about Barbara's lovelife. Her often volatile ten-year marriage to Brandon had not daunted other men. They still pursued her. Mimi had watched her toy with them, never let them go, but never, while married to Brandon, accept them as lovers. There was much to admire in Barbara, not least her creative and independent spirit. For all her fame, success and self-interest, she was still not just able, but only too pleased, to set all that aside to stand behind any man she loved. She had no need to be in the forefront of a relationship. Many times Mimi had seen her in the shadows of a concert-hall stage, applauding with enthusiasm a famous conductor, her lover. Or sitting quietly at a rally for a Senator with his eye on the White House. She actually liked being in the shadow of her own fame. In that, Mimi was not unlike her. Maybe she'd even learned it from Barbara.

She watched her friend unloading the Rolls with Ching Lee. Barbara saw Mimi, raised a hand, waved and smiled. Then Mimi and the air-taxi pilot went to help them carry the luggage to the plane. Barbara was going to open her studio in East Hampton, to stay and work there for a while in seclusion. Ching Lee was accompanying her, as always. Mimi was going for the ride, to return at sunset with the pilot.

It had been two weeks since the party. They had spoken several times since then, Barbara had mentioned Rick. Several times Mimi had thought to tell Barbara about her relationship with him, but the right opening in their conversations hadn't occurred.

Rick was gone now. Two days gone. She had seen him off at Kennedy Airport, him and Allan, on this trip in search of the perfect wave. She recalled his last words: "If you need me, you'll find me."

What kind of cryptic directions were those? she had asked herself as she had walked away from him. Yet she knew exactly what he meant. Driving back from the airport, she kept thinking about the postcards that could come from Katmandu, Delhi, the African coast, the Great Barrier Reef, Fiji, Samoa, God knew where. The search for the perfect wave? A better philosophy to live by? How many head-trips, LSD and Est trips? How long, she wondered, will this self-absorbed journey last? How long will it take to overcome whatever dysfunction handsome, intelligent young men like Allan and Rick suffer in trying to reclaim the inner child in themselves? Only then had she realized that that might be what she was doing in this affair with Rick. It hadn't been just sex, she had known that all along. But if she was reclaiming the inner child in her own self, a question had to be faced: Why was that need so great? That question opened too many old wounds, so she shelved it. No doubt it would recur some time. Not a happy thought. In the taxi on the way back to the city, she saw the skyline of Manhattan on the other side of the East River and relaxed into thinking to herself, a wave is a wave is a wave. She began to laugh. It had been such fun, and very sexy.

They climbed on board. The motors spluttered to life, and the pilot revved them until the small plane shimmied and shook. Then slowly he taxied away from the dock and on to the river for his choppy take-off. On the river a tugboat, pulling two long barges piled high with rubbish beneath a cloud of fat, squawking seagulls that swooped all over this moveable feast, crossed their path, sounding its horn. The pilot gave a signal-sound of his own. They bumped along against the current until the pilot turned the plane, gave it all the power he could. Mimi braced herself. The plane shot forward at a terrific speed. Spray billowed up from the pontoons and blinkered their view. It was thrilling and scary. In moments they were off the water, airborne at a steep angle and leaving Manhattan behind. Mimi liked the danger and excitement of taking off from the river. She and Jay used it frequently to go to Long Island, Fire Island, or to their weather-worn Cape Cod house on Martha's Vineyard.

They circled the shoreline of East Hampton several times, and buzzed Barbara's studio for the caretaker. He waved and hopped into the Mercedes station wagon. He would be there waiting for them by the time they landed. Landing was as thrilling as taking off, but too thrilling if tried on the ocean in front of Barbara's studio. That might have been thrilling to death.

The two women left it to Ching Lee and the pilot to un-load first the plane, then the station wagon, and open the house. The sun was high in the cloudless sky. It felt good, the sun after winter, the smell of the ocean after the aroma of city life. Barbara and Mimi abandoned the house and chores to sit on deck chairs by the water's edge. Lee would organize lunch. Shoes were discarded and blouses opened, breasts bared to the sun. A private beach shared by Barbara and neighbors who hadn't opened their houses yet. For more than an hour the two women dozed silently in the sun. It warmed their skin, they could feel it penetrate their flesh. It made them lazy, speechless. It eased out city-life ten-sions. The ocean was calm. Small waves broke and glided smoothly on to the shore, creating a mesmerizing sym-phony. The muffled sound of the pull and push, the roll of the cold Atlantic Ocean, today little more than the steady lapping of waves on the sand.

For nearly an hour then neither moved nor spoke, barely even strung thoughts together.

"Barbara?"

"Mmmm."

"This is heaven."

"Mmmm."

The sun was coloring their faces, burning the tender nip-ples of their breasts, tanning their skin. Barbara stretched, moved her feet and toes. She sighed as if to say, "delicious."

"Barbara?"

"Mmmm."

"Have you ever slept with two men at the same time?"

A long pause. Then Barbara said, "That's quite a question, Mimi."

"Yes, I guess it is."

"Can I think about whether or not I want to answer that?"

"Does it take thinking about?"

"Yes. Or care how I answer that."

"I can understand that."

"Rick?"

"How did you know, Barbara?"

"I didn't know, it was a good guess."

"Was I so obvious?"

"Not at all. But there were little things he said during dinner. Strange because they were not even specific to you. I recognized them as what a man says when infatuated with a woman. We were, after all, dinner companions at my party. I found him an interesting young man. We talked about Clifford Still and his work and reclusive behavior, about Rick's father, his collection. I felt curious about Rick when he worked his magic on Cary."

"I've never talked to him about his father or his father's collection."

"Well, I daresay not. When he's with you I doubt that he needs small talk. But at least this young man makes interesting small talk. That was the giveaway for me, all that dinner-party chatter and no mention of the hostess. I didn't realize then that there might be something between you. Yet I felt him actually pull himself up, stiffen even, when someone mentioned your name. But no one else would have guessed there might be something between you."

"Had been, had been! I saw him off yesterday at Kennedy Airport. He's hit the hippy trail or something like that, in search of the endless summer and the perfect wave. Can you believe this, a young man like that?"

"Do I hear wind hurtling down the generation gap?"

"I hope not. No, this has to do with young people looking for an endless summer to play in. When I first met him I thought how ridiculous. Now I'm not so sure. The Beat Generation of the fifties was more interesting, but these sixties people are a lot more fun."

There was a pause. Both women turned their heads to look at each other and began to laugh. They turned their faces back into the sun and remained quiet, listening to the sound of the waves on the shore. Mimi felt the sun deliciously warm on her face. The sun is not nearly as hot as it was on the Greek island of Patmos that last day in August, she thought. She closed her eyes. Mimi could hear her own voice as if disembodied from herself telling Barbara her story. She liked the sound of it.

"It happened on Patmos last summer, yet it all really began at Martha's Vineyard. You know how we always pick up sticks, Jay and I, and spend July and August in our house in Martha's Vineyard. How we love that house and the island. Everything was running in its usual pattern last summer. Jay working in July from the Vineyard house. Flying into New York for emergency meetings. His associates flying out to us when necessary. Sailing, swimming, having a great summer. It's the only time we really have all four of his children together, and they're great. They were coming and going as usual with a host of friends. The best part of seeing them on the island is that we don't have any interference from the two distraught ex-wives. It's my fun time with them. They are at that age, the youngest is now seventeen, when we can enjoy each other's company.

"I should have guessed, there were so many whispers, something was afoot. And then the five of them sprang it on me. Jay had rented a house in Greece for the month of August. For ten years we had spent August in Martha's Vineyard. Now the children and he decided to take me on a holiday, a reward, they said, for being stalwart for all those summers. It was a surprise, and I did like the idea, and it's great to travel with Jay. He likes his comforts when he travels, and he's adventurous and knows everybody everywhere. It was bound to be fun. In fact it was great fun. The house was large and white with lots of levels, rambling along a cove, a barren dry landscape with the sea practically at your door. It was a forty-five-minute walk into the port. It was perfect. Owned by a Greek millionare, one of those Anglophile Greek families with real taste. It was furnished simply but with great charm. The housekeeper, Greek, was used to entertaining on a lavish scale for an international jet-set. She'd got Greek cooking down to a fine art, and as we all know, that takes some doing.

"Anyway, Jay and the children gave me a great month. Nothing to do but swim and sail together, take long walks over the island, go into port and up to Hora. It's a magical place, the village and monastery high above the port, looking out across the Aegean. I found it full of mystery, and very ethereal. It's no wonder that St. John wrote the Book of the Apocalypse there. That was always hovering in the mind. I found it a power-place, one that played on the emotions, even those buried deep in my subconscious. Several times I felt a deep, deep sadness, without reason, such unhappiness, such utter despair. One night sitting in the port at a table close to the water having dinner with Jay, I suddenly burst into tears, weeping as I have never wept before. Poor Jay. He hardly knew what to do for me. It passed, and I was all right again, but shaken by the experience.

"But I digress. Our month was up. Although the owners said we could stay on, we decided it was time to leave. We were all packed. We had had the best time as a family any of us had remembered. I love Jay's boys. I loved them as my own because they belonged to Jay and were terrific kids, but I'd never been as close to them as I was in those weeks at Patmos.

"I don't know how or why it happened, but the night before we were all to take the ferry back to Athens, two of the boys and I, with the wholehearted approval of Jay, decided to stay on for another week. Ostensibly to make a couple of excursions to the mainland. The next morning we saw Jay and the other two boys off at the boat returning to Athens.

"The following day the two boys and I walked into town to have supper. I had seen several times a group of ten people sitting at a long table in the port near the water's edge. They lived even further out than we did in an island house overlooking the sea. Our boys had been up there and had spent some time with them. Jay and I saw them as too young for us, and so had little to do with them. That night, at the table, I saw Rick for the first time. He stood out among the others. He had a bronze tan and his hair was bleached almost white from the sun. He looked so young, like a boy of eighteen. He had a French girl with him. I assumed they were in love. All the laughter in the world seemed to be at that table. They were an international set: English, French and Italian, several Greeks, a couple of Americans, Rick being one of them. We were distracted by them, unable to make headway with our own plans. Our ideas, once adventurous and interesting, now seemed dull. They were overshadowed by the laughter and amusing anecdotes that drifted into our hearing.

"Before long they had swept us into their orbit and we too were laughing. Unable to stagger home across the island on foot, we went back by the light of a hissing gas lantern in a fisherman's wooden rowboat, singing horribly out of tune all the way.

"The next morning I got wonderful reviews from Jay's boys. 'You were great. Mimi, they loved you.' They were so happy and bubbling with excitement, I only managed to get half of what they were telling me. I tried to put it together, but it actually had to be spelled out to me. A change of plans—we were joining the others. A French boy was sailing in from Simi that morning in a reconditioned caique and we were going to island-hop for a week, winding up somewhere on the Mediterranean coast of Turkey. From there we would be going overland, exploring ancient Greek monuments.

"I was so tempted, but I felt so ridiculous; I was old enough to be their mother. It had been great fun that night with them all, but they were so very young. Appealing as they were, I convinced Larry and Sam they were not letting me down if they went off without me. In fact. I insisted upon it. Larry was twenty years old, Sam twenty-two. The last thing they needed was a chaperone, and a stepmother chaperone at that.

"I sent them off with my blessing. The cook was already gone, the housekeeper leaving the following day. I would be alone. You know how I enjoy my own company, being alone is not a problem for me. I was quite happy to swim naked in the sea, to lie on the beach and listen to good music. I took my time looking at maps, deciding what excursions to take on my own. I felt no need to rush away. Being alone was wonderful, especially being alone in Patmos. It is an out-of-this-world place, and something strange was happening to me. I know it was all in the mind, but it was happening. I felt happy, a kind of happiness that I don't think I had experienced before. It was a kind of selfish, self-contained happiness that had nothing to do with family or friends, just me. I felt quite elated by it, extraordinarily brave.

"I said goodbye to the housekeeper who assured me she would be back in a week, and told me who to call if I needed anything. The following day I lazed about and swam, and then I took the footpath over the island and decided to stay in town for lunch.

"The people at the restaurant where we usually ate greeted me with their usual enthusiasm. I went into the kitchen and peered into the pots, chose what I wanted. They placed a table at the far end of the quay next to the sea. It was particularly quiet that day. I was late, that was probably it. People were on their way home for the siesta. I had an ouzo, unusually for me at midday. Then they brought me a bottle of retsina. There was nothing left but octopodi grilled over charcoal and barbounia, a kind of red mullet, I think. Not my favorite fish, but I was hungry. I had nothing on under my long cotton skirt and large, loose cotton T-shirt. Just Greek sandals on my feet, no make up. I felt such a tourist, and liked the feeling. There was something transient and exciting about being there that way. No Jay, no kids. I ate ravenously, and every morsel tasted better than any food I'd ever eaten.

"Everything about that day seemed to be heightened. Then, quite suddenly, he was standing at my table.

" 'Hello again. Do you mind if I sit down?' "

"I pulled out a chair for him. 'I thought you had gone with my stepsons.' "

" 'Ah, so that's the relationship.' "

"I held out the plate of octopodi. He took a piece between his fingers and chewed on it. I saw the waiter coming and I asked him, 'Will you join me for some food?' He nodded his head. I asked for another plate and a glass.

"I don't even much remember what we talked about. He was pleasant and we lingered over the food. There was hardly a soul left in the port. We were going in the same direction so why not together, taking the footpath that edged along the sea? I had a basket containing bread, a piece of cheese, an aubergine, a few eggs and an onion. The heat was really oppressive. When we came to the fork in the road where my way was down the path that ran parallel to the sea and his went up over the hill further on, he said, 'Not a good idea, this walk in the midday sun, without a hat,' and insisted on seeing me home.

"There was a small cove with a perfect little beach about fifteen minutes from the house. We often swam there. There was a flat rock, cantilevered by nature to hang over the sand. Jay called it God's Umbrella. Rick suggested we get out of the sun and under it, to cool down. Not a bad suggestion. It really was hot. We scrambled down the rocks. It took some care to get to the beach without gashing a hand or a foot, but we made it. He touched me on the shoulder and pointed to God's Umbrella.

" 'Oh, yes,' I remember saying to him. 'I could use that.' "

"I removed my shoes, pulled my skirt up to rest on my thighs, and sat next to him in the shade. If felt good to get out of that relentless sun. I cooled down quite quickly. We didn't say much, just listened to the lapping of the sapphire blue, crystal clear water, watching it roll on to the beach. Like the waves rolling in here now. The water sparkled like the sun reflected off a mirror. We looked at each other. I could see he fancied a swim.

" 'No suit,' I told him, 'you go ahead.' "

"Don't be ridiculous," he said, and lifted my T-shirt over my head. He took me quite by surprise. There was a look of sheer pleasure in his eyes at the sight of my bare breasts. I wasn't going to protest at his audacity. My skirt had a row of bone buttons going down the front, he was opening them one by one. His smile silenced me. It was neither smug nor smutty. He made it easy for me, and I was so hot, and the water so seductively inviting. He was naked himself before he held a hand out to pull me up from the sand. We ran into the sea.

"I was stunned with admiration for his young, handsome body, the narrow hips, wide shoulders and broad chest, sexy rounded muscular bottom, massively strong thighs, a beautiful large and thick circumcised penis. Such young flesh, so tanned and healthy. I was too busy enjoying his body to think about my own running naked into the sea on a Greek island with a stranger. I felt immediately revived in the water. It felt good, that cool clear water, with the surface warmed by the hot sun. We swam together. We were good swimmers on and under water. We dived down deep and frolicked like dolphins.

"On shore we were dried by the heat in minutes. We dressed and walked the rest of the way home, talking more now about the sea and the island. He stayed for supper, there was a full moon, thousands of stars. At one o'clock in the morning he walked in the glow of the moon over the barren rocks back to his home.

"I couldn't sleep at all that night, I kept thinking about him. I had no idea how much I wanted him until he appeared the next morning.

" 'Hello,' he said. I was enormously happy to see him. 'I am going to do some sightseeing. Care to come with me?' "

"I heard myself saying yes. Not where, when, for how long? Just yes. There seemed no reason to say no. I was free, Jay knew I was traveling, and expected to see me when he saw me. The boys weren't returning to the island. It was only a matter of closing up the house, leaving the key at the coffeehouse with Phillippos."

Mimi rose from the deck chair and walked the few yards to the water's edge. Barbara opened her eyes and watched her walk along the shore. Then she slumped back against her chair and closed her eyes again. Several minutes went by and she heard Mimi climb back into the creaking deck chair. Barbara was not surprised when she picked up her narrative where she had left off.

"Funny, the little things you remember. We had the use of a boat, quite a good size. I had only a small case, a change of clothes, my handbag, a large, beat-up, old straw hat. He had nothing but a scruffy soft leather briefcase. He flung it in the boat, and we stood there looking at each other for several minutes before we pushed it into the water. I was out of character, wanting him and his body. I was acutely aware of thinking of him as an object of desire, the man I'd never had, the one I really wanted, way down deep somewhere in my sexual soul. I simply could not stop thinking of sex."

" 'Well, I guess that's it, let's go.' "

"I climbed into the boat. I was feeling terribly dull, not being able to think of something to say. I wanted to be clever, but instead dutifully did as he told me, just climbed into the boat. He pushed it out, and after several tries the motor snapped into life with a high-pitched sound in the silence of that beautiful place.

"I thought we were making for the ferry to take us away from the island. But no, we boarded instead a large working caique with a crew of three. They made us comfortable, pitched a makeshift sunshade for me in the bow of the boat, gave us a watermelon, and then retreated to the other end of the boat. It was so romantic on that caique with him—a cloudless sky, the heat intense but seemingly not so, with a light breeze coming off the water. 'This is madness,' I told him."

"He looked genuinely surprised. 'Madness?' "

" 'I want you.' "

"He laughed and I became angry. 'Are you laughing at me?' "

" 'Yes.' "

"I jumped to my feet. He grabbed me by the wrist and pulled me back down on to the deck, under the blanket stretched with ropes, my awning.

" 'Why am I laughing at you? Because I'm yours and you don't even know it.' "

"Then he left me and went to talk to the crew. I felt so happy. He wanted me as much as I wanted him. It was a kind of love-madness, and it felt so good. And when he returned to me he smiled at me with an intimacy I had rarely felt with another human being. We both knew we were on a quest. He is a remarkable young man. You see, he knew it was sexual love. I had thought it was love. He wasted no time in making me understand the difference. Not with words, or denying me what I felt. It was by his actions that I understood.

"That first night the caique sailed into Ikaria. The port was quiet, it was early morning and everyone was asleep. We walked along a road that ran parallel to the shore to the edge of town. There the road stopped, and by moonlight we climbed down some rocks and around a small cove, up a

steep flight of stairs carved from the rocks and on to a prom-
ontory. There, looming grandly in the moonlight, was a large
Neo-classical Greek island house, surrounded on three sides
by the sea.

"It was dark, but he found a key for the front door under
a pot. Inside, a note on the table. His friends were traveling,
no date for their return. The walk had been long and we were
tired. We took the largest bedroom overlooking the sea. It
was on the first floor, over the entrance of the house. We undressed and fell into each other's arms on the bed. And sound
asleep, you may be surprised to learn.

"But, starting the next day, it was a sexual orgy for two.
He is an extraordinary lover, Barbara. He taught me the real
meaning of erotic pleasure. Every sexual inhibition I ever had
dissolved. The touch of his skin, the . . . oh, I don't have to
go into all that, I am sure you know well the way it was. He
tapped into the sexual side of my nature. He taught me how
to make love to a man in ways I never dreamed would give
so much pleasure, and he made love to me. Our demands on
each other drove us further, always further, into an erotic
land, foreign to me till then.

"His friends returned. They were amusing, and charming.
Very young, very open, free, and in love with themselves and
their drug-taking. High on everybody doing their thing, whatever it was. Acceptance was the name of their game. There
was music, and gaiety, and laughter, and I felt as much a part
of it as I could possibly feel. By the end of those few days
spent with them nothing surprised me. I, too, found it all acceptable. The orgy for two had now become an orgy for
seven. It was down to the sexual nitty-gritty. Changes of partners, genders. I knew I was mesmerized by it all but he had
triggered something in me. Mimi, the kid, wanted to experience it all, at least once."

She paused. "Are you shocked, Barbara?"

She opened her eyes. Until that moment, she had thought
it best not to look at Mimi. They were friends, she wasn't a
critic. Mimi did not need her approval. That was the basis of
this long-lasting friendship. It was a rare relationship, especially so because of the difference in ages between the two
women. Barbara closed the buttons of her blouse and pulled

herself up in the deck chair. The two women turned in their chairs. Sitting on the edge of them they faced each other, their knees nearly touching. Mimi held up her hand as if to stop Barbara speaking.

Barbara smiled. "That's a very stupid question."

"I know you. You love me more for it. For having the courage to slake my thirst and get on with adding to my life."

The two women leaned forward. It was an emotional moment. They flung their arms around each other and hugged, tears in their eyes, because they loved each other. Barbara, because this had once been the lost, isolated child with more emotional scars than she had ever seen in a child. And this was Karel's daughter, a part of him, the daughter they never had together, a shrewd and beautiful woman with the courage always to take that next step forward to enrich her life. This was her friend, a woman now, who at last was a free spirit about to do everything she wanted because she understood her hunger. She could accept that the heart is a lonely hunter.

For the first time Barbara regretted the way they had deceived Mimi all these years about their relationship. Surely Mimi could be trusted to understand it now? Even though that might be true, there still was Karel to deal with, and her loyalty to him. She would still have to keep her secret. Barbara had always known that Karel could never face the truth. While Mimi had suffered in loneliness and considerable despair, he had been close, oh so close, yet had not made even a phone call. No matter the danger, there had been any number of ways he could have made contact. Could have eased the stress his child was living through. They were still trapped, the three of them, in lies told in the name of love and survival.

The two women slipped out of their hug of affection, love and respect. Barbara told her, "Yes, Mimi, I have slept with two men at the same time, and it was madly sexual and exciting. And still is, on the rare occasions I do it now. I have a long-time erotic relationship, and a special kind of love, with a man. It is based on a kind of mutual sexual madness that enhances our lives. Some people call that kind of madness being in love. We are sexually in love with each other, have been for decades, always will be. Like you, we feel no guilt for our actions, our hungry hearts. I imagine you too will understand, as we did, right from when we first met, that this sexual need we feel for each other doesn't impinge on the rest of our lives. That's why it's still young and fresh for us. It's my secret love, his too. And I'll never tell you who he is, or when I see him. That's my own personal, private domain. But, yes, I have and do sleep occasionally with two men at a time. There, that's the answer to your question. No more now, please, till we've put away some lunch."

The two women rose from the chairs. Arm in arm they walked from the beach over the dunes to the studio. The laughter of young girls was in their hearts.

Barbara waved the seaplane off, Mimi at the window, all smiles, waving back at her. She stood at the water's edge and watched the plane soar into the sky. Was "cherish" too dramatic a word to characterize her friendship with Mimi? Well, maybe not. Mimi was as remarkable a woman as she had been a child and young girl. It was always a joy to see her and hear her news, for they lived such different lives.

The small seaplane banked sharply and headed back toward Barbara. She smiled as they zoomed in low over her head, buzzed her, and both pilot and Mimi gave a final wave, before they flew away, heading for the city.

In the car going back to the studio, she thought about Mimi and their close friendship. It had surmounted many hurdles that it might have broken on: Barbara's secret love for Karel; Lydia, for whom Mimi might have abandoned her; younger friends, lovers, a husband.

Jay. Why did Barbara sense that there might be hairline cracks appearing in Mimi's marriage? She had said nothing to make Barbara believe that there might be trouble there. Silly. How many times had she heard it from both Mimi and Jay: that they were grateful to whichever gods had gotten them to the altar. They had a happy and glittering marriage that worked for both of them. They knew it, and New Yorkers who knew them could only admire it.

Ten years. Where had the time gone? Barbara recalled that first day Mimi and Jay met. She and Mimi had gone to a publishing party, something neither of them did often. Simply not their scene. But this was for the launch of Brandon's book

The Surrealist Painters before the Second World War. Mimi was twenty-three years old, and uncertain what she wanted to do with her life. She was dabbling with hats, designing and making them with Mr. Spider. It filled her time. Having majored in art history at college, she had no burning desire to do more with that—unless, perhaps, it was to become a dealer in art, an agent rather than a gallery owner. She was a great beauty, with a seductive charm that drew men to her. She liked that as much as she liked anything. Mimi was not ambitious. Well, not till she saw Jay Steindler standing off to one side with a bevy of women around him. It only took a second glance. Barbara remembered her words: "Look, over then. Now there's a man! I would like to marry a man like that, handsome, experienced, and very sexy. There is a man I could build a life with. Just looking at him makes me feel good. I feel drawn to him, as if he could keep me happy and safe *and* make love to me. He has a powerful presence, like Poppa, don't you think?"

Barbara didn't know Jay Steindler, but she could see what Mimi meant. He was a power-broker. You could sense it coming, like invisible waves rolling across the room. The power, the intelligence, niceness, charm. The deal. They found Brandon in the crush of people and Mimi pointed to Jay Steindler. He laughed. "Great choice, Mimi. He's a terrific guy." He hesitated just long enough to tease her. "And the word is he's one of the best fucks in the city." He took her hand and making his way through the crowd, delivered her into Jay's hands.

Mimi never settled down with any of her admirers or lovers. Barbara, in that instant when Jay and Mimi met, understood why. Including her present lover, the intense Yale graduate student, they were boys, and she wanted a man. Mimi married Jay Steindler because he fitted the bill. He answered all her needs at that time in her life.

If it had been instantly her ambition to marry him, it had been instantly his desire to snatch into his bed what he considered to be one of the great young flirtatious beauties of New York. There was a certain mysterious and very silent quality about Mimi that seduced Jay Steindler. That and an incredibly sensual fire in her he wanted to scorch his wings on.

Barbara wanted to whisper in her ear, "Mimi, he's great but he's a mere shadow of your father, if that's what you're looking for, a father-figure as a husband." But by the time she got around to saying that to Mimi, it no longer mattered. Barbara had been present: she had read the sign. For Mimi and Jay Steindler it was love at first sight. They fell head over heels in love with each other. He took her from the book launch party to dinner, and then booked them into a room at the Pierre. There he made love to her. Brandon had been right: Jay Steindler was brilliant with his cock. And he had stamina such as the relatively inexperienced Mimi had not hoped to encounter in a man. He was romantic, kind, and generous. He loved her and promised to marry her, which he did five months later. And it had been a happy union. Still was, so far as Barbara knew.

But, she wondered, why do I feel Mimi is at a crossroads in her life? Is she outgrowing her marriage? Well, if she was, Barbara knew one thing for certain: she and Jay loved being married to each other, loved the life they had created for themselves. They would find a way, no matter what it took to keep it together. They, unlike herself and Karel, needed marriage and all it entailed.

Chapter 21

When Mimi married Jay Steindler he was twenty years older than she was. He had had four children and wanted no more. That suited her very well. She had no desire to bear children. Jay's boys would be her children. Not once during their marriage had she regretted her decision.

Mimi's life was rich, full and absorbing. For nearly two years after her affair with Rick, there had been no other lovers. She didn't know why, because there was no doubt that she missed—too much—not having a young lover. But what with life with Jay, her work, and her father, she seemed too busy to take on a lover.

How well she understood the older man who finds something unique in a young girl. It's not only young flesh that excited the sexual drive, but a young spirit. How blind she would have remained to all that, had she not met Rick on Patmos. Always he and their affair hovered over her marriage. That was one more reason to understand her father's lust for young, beautiful women. Even Jay's attraction to every beautiful and talented young woman who crossed his path. It was unthinkable that he would have an affair with any of them. He adored Mimi. He had in her everything he ever wanted in a woman. Part of his attraction to her was that she was amazingly sexy and so much younger than he was. Even after all their years of marriage, she remained an enigma to him, both sexually and as a woman. He had her, but he never possessed her. He never got from Mimi that extra dividend he so subtly demanded and received from any other deal, any other relationship. What held her to him so devotedly was that he seemed always on the brink of getting that extra dividend with every fuck he gave her. In that, the sexual aspect of their marriage, he had yet to collect the extra bonus he sought. In all else in the marriage Mimi had delivered.

Then one day she found some time for a young admirer. Mimi added to her life sexual affairs with young, handsome men. She was discreet, but not discreet enough for her father to miss what was going on. However, no matter how liberal, or in this case libertine, a father is, discussing a daughter's infidelities creates awkwardness. And so he kept his knowledge to himself. The paternal antennae were tactfully lowered.

It always amused Karel when he traveled with Mimi to see how men desired her. How well she charmed and flirted with a flock of admirers trying to attach themselves to her. Mimi and Karel were on a week's holiday in Paris staying at the Ritz when a book he had been angling after for years was made suddenly available. Needing to leave Mimi in Paris for the night, he called his young friend Alexander and suggested that he call on Mimi. Then he flew off to Athens to secure the coveted volume.

Alexander duly made the call to Mimi. He had never met her, had heard little about her except that she was Karel's only daughter and married and had developed an aversion to politics, particularly the European brand. Karel attributed it to her having been torn away from Prague by the Second World War and unfortunately lost to him for years.

Alexander's interest was stirred when Mimi consented to drinks and dinner with him. There had been so much generosity toward him from Karel: here at least was an agreeable way to start repaying his mentor.

Alexander had no idea what he had expected. Certainly not the woman who answered the door of the suite at the Ritz. Nor to fall in love the moment their eyes met. Paris offered the most chic and beautiful women. He had willingly responded to its offer. So the last thing he had expected was to be bowled over by Karel Stefanik's daughter.

He took her to the Cafe Lippe. On the way over in the taxi they made polite talk. But all the while he was absorbing everything about Mimi. Rarely had he seen such magnificent violet eyes, hair like spun sugar. He could hardly keep his eyes from her long shapely legs encased in their ivory stockings, her slender feet shod in red high-heeled sandals.

Her red chiffon skirt, cut on the bias to fall seductively close on her hips and flare out to just above her knees, disturbed this new admirer. She could feel it. When their eyes met, all doubt vanished from his mind that a sexual attraction was sparking between them. She seemed surprised. She was about to say something to him but changed her mind. He was moved when she placed a hand on his cheek and said, "If only I were younger." Then she smiled and laughed away her attraction for him. He hardly knew what to say. Alexander was ravenous for her and knew he would be for the rest of his life. He was temporarily saved by their arrival. He watched her swing out of the taxi. Slipping his arm through hers he escorted her into the Cafe Lippe. Every eye was upon them. They took a table and he ordered Pernod.

She sat opposite. Mimi's jacket was white, a fine flannel, beautifully tailored to show off her narrow waist and large, voluptuous breasts. It had a sailor collar with gold bands and a star in each corner. She was much to be admired. He told her, "You look half-child, half-seductress, in your sailor suit."

"We've only just met. And how well you know me already."

These early words to him were nearly the last she spoke. At that moment a taxi pulled up. From it Jay's brother emerged. How completely she had forgotten her promise to go to the opera with him and a party of friends. She had left her whereabouts at the hotel in case her father were to call. And now here was Sammy. There was nothing for it but to leave Alexander with profuse apologies. They were shaking hands when an impulse made her bend forward and kiss him on the cheek. "Neither sailor nor siren. Just two ships passing in the night. How sad for me."

He held tight to her hand and replied, "For us. Another time, another place." And he surprised her, this young man, when he raised her hand and kissed it. She gave him her most flirtatious smile and was gone. Alexander thought he would never forget the flick of that red chiffon skirt as she snapped it into the taxi just before the door slammed shut. She did not look back. The impression she had made on him was indelible.

When rumors surfaced about Mimi's penchant for young men, Jay was deaf to them. He was certain they could not be true. And, in some perverse way, he was amused by the rumors, flattered even that to other men, and young men at that, his Mimi's charms were irresistible. How could those rumors be true? Not once since they had married had she rejected him sexually, not once had she quit their bed sexually unsatisfied. Jay Steindler was a great lover, all the New York literary world would attest that. And that was their marriage, that was the way it was and would always be. Or so they both thought.

But all that changed with a phone call from Rick. The postcards had arrived, two, three, maybe as many as five in nearly two years. She had at first been pathetic about them. Reading them over again and again, trying to get close to him through a postcard. Behaving like a silly teenager. They arrived at the office from which she dealt in works of art, and there she had kept them, under her desk blotter. And now suddenly his voice was on the telephone. Of course she went to meet him. Not merely went, she rushed, absolutely rushed to meet him. All the way over to the address he gave her on Sutton Place, she marveled at how she could have missed him so much and not realized it until she heard his voice. The magic was still there. She forgot who and what she was. She became the young Mimi all over again.

The taxi pulled up at an address that she had written on a piece of paper. A pretty New York town house in this most exclusive of city squares. She was just opening the door of the taxi when he came rushing out of the house to sweep her up into his arms. She had a shock. He looked even younger than she had remembered. In no way less handsome, less sensual. They were hardly inside the house when he told her, "Those eyes, your violet eyes. They have haunted me all around the world." He kissed one eyelid and then the other. "And those lips . . . those oh-so-sexy lips!" And he placed his lips upon hers and kissed them, nibbling at them. Hers parted. The kiss was deep and passionate now. He was undressing her. A trail of her clothes marked their progress up the staircase to the first floor and the back bedroom overlooking a charming town garden. The room was large, elegantly furnished in conservative style, far from the hippy world he was living in. She had a million questions for him. Where was she? Whose house was it? Was he going to stay? None was uttered.

Undressed, he walked with her to stand in front of a full-length mirror where, with arms around each other's shoulders, they studied themselves. He turned her away from the mirror to face him. "Remember the last time? I carried that image of us, that wonderful afternoon. I never let it go. It never ceased to turn me on. I never ceased to want you."

Then he stood back two paces and studied her, particularly the breasts, those gorgeous breasts. He cupped them in his hands. He caressed them, adoring their roundness. He was filled with tenderness for her. He bent forward and gently kissed the nipples, licked the large nimbus, that pale aureole that made breasts look lewd, even more seductive. He adored that. It excited imaginings of things to do with her.

The way he touched her sent shivers through her body. He caressed her waist, clenched it between his large hands and squeezed it, then gently ran his hands over her hips, round her full and firm, high and provocative buttocks. He was adoring her, and she was reacting to his adoration by peeling away layers of Mimi she offered to the world. Anxious only to show him her real, most private, most intimate self. He picked her up in his arms, held her against him. She encircled him in her arms and squeezed herself close into him, as hard as she could. Oh, the feel of him, his naked flesh, his very skin. That sensuous male scent of his body drove her a bit crazy to be fucked, to be rent open and pummeled by his rampant penis. She yearned for the taste of his sperm, to feel her own orgasms.

He laid her on the bed, then climbed on to it next to her. They lay on their sides against each other. He raised her leg and placed it on his shoulder. And then, as if jackknifed, he slid his legs between hers and with her help was guided into that place he was so desperate to be.

Who can explain sexual lust, how it can make the heart sing? She felt him more intensely than ever before. She felt sex, orgasm, crescendos of exquisite joy with every nerve end exposed, as if her skin had been flayed from her body. He was relentless with his thrusts. They were deep and powerful, with a rhythm that excited her passion for more, always more. His lust was all but overpowering, tempered only by his desire to give her pleasure, to excite her into floods of orgasm, enough to make her swoon with exhaustion. He felt her submitting, always submitting to the power of his fucking, his demands. She lost all inhibitions, called out obscenities that drove him on, and when he came, he too was down with her in the sexual dirt where they loved to wallow together. So intense was his orgasm that he couldn't hold back. He screamed, his heart pounded, he bit into her flesh, breaking the skin in a trickle of blood around the nimbus of her breast. They collapsed in each other's arms and wept, both of them, from sheer release of the sexual pressure they had carried within themselves being apart for so long.

They took cat-naps in each other's arms or talked of their erotic love for each other. They had sex twice more that afternoon. It became dark. He turned on the lights. "Will you be missed at home?"

She pulled herself up against the pillows and was about to speak, but he was quicker. "Oh God," he said and she followed his eyes to her breast.

"No," she answered, touching his cheek with the back of her hand. "No, don't worry, I cherish every mark."

He smiled. "And Jay?"

"He's away, he left this afternoon. He won't be back for a week. Paris, Lisbon, Rome ... meetings, conferences."

"I can't believe my luck."

"Neither can I. Nor the timing."

"Leave him, come away with me. I want us to make babies, beautiful girls with blond, curly hair and violet eyes. I want them to look exactly like you. I want to see them nurse at your breast. I want this sexual passion we have for each other to create something alive and wonderful, something unique just to us, a child we can love. A child to celebrate us, what we have together."

"That's very romantic."

"Of course it is. I am a romantic."

A child. It had never entered her mind. Not with him or Jay or any man. But suddenly, with Rick saying it, it seemed so natural, so right. How hadn't she felt it before? To have a baby. The very thought of it suddenly sobered her. She looked at her lover. He was ten years younger than she was, a grown man looking for the perfect wave. Madness even to think of having his baby. Once she had thought that, she had to wonder whether she was right. Rick fathering a baby with her . . . suddenly it didn't seem quite so mad.

She thought it best to change the subject. "Whose home is this?"

"Dr. Quinn. I returned because of him."

"Oh?"

"He was in an automobile accident. He had severe head injuries. They called me to come to relieve the pressure on the brain. He wouldn't let anyone else touch him. I owed him that much. He was wonderful to me during the two years I assisted him."

"How long have you been here?"

"A week. He's fine now, in great shape actually, making a good recovery. Mimi, you've got a week. Come to the West Coast with me, come to Malibu. I'll be flying back to Ceylon across the Pacific. We'll have a good time, just hang out and maybe make a baby."

"What is this business about a baby? Why are you suddenly thinking you and I have to make a baby?"

"It's for you, a gift from me. Mimi, maybe one day you'll want babies and it'll be too late. The old biological clock is ticking away. I love you, in my own strange and drifting way. I care about you, and I like Jay and his kids."

"This is madness. One of us is going mad. You want us to have a baby for me, and Jay is just going to take all this, be happy with it?"

"If he isn't, leave him."

"Walk out on my marriage? I have no reason to leave Jay. I've got a good marriage."

"Then stay with him, and if you're not going to have my child, have his."

"Maybe I don't want children."

"Obviously you don't want children, but think about it. Maybe till now you had a lot of reasons not to have children, but that's changed."

"How do you know that? What do you know about me?"

Rick felt her anger. It had never been his intention to upset Mimi. He knew he was some sort of catalyst for her, and that he evoked in her the child that had never been. She could play with him as she had never played as a child, but she could also be a woman, one with a sexual hunger that she was not afraid to reveal to him. Rick was able to trigger something in Mimi that allowed her to enjoy sex as she rarely had as a young woman or even as an adult. It seemed to him a natural progression for her now to want to understand the miracle of giving birth, of creating an image of herself and her lover or Jay in another human being. To see a child enter the world, the flesh and bones of two other human beings. How could he make her understand how sad it would be if there was not going to be another generation of Mimi's? That she had hardly contemplated it came as no surprise to him, but this was not the same Mimi as the woman he had watched for a few weeks on the island of Patmos three years before. He had changed her life, and he was not at all ashamed of having added something to it. He had done it because he loved her, first from afar, and even more so once he had had her.

"Mimi," he told her, "this is a different age from the one you were brought up in, the world of your teens and early twenties. An age when love and passion are as valid as the bonds of marriage. Where illegitimate children no longer exist, just one-parent children, or couples who live together, unmarried, with a child born of free love. Mimi, you have choices you never thought existed. Why should you be deprived of enjoying a child unless it's because of some fear from the past that need no longer exist? Just think about it, Mimi. Talk to Jay."

"You've managed to confuse me. When I talk to you, I forget who I am, I forget the ten-year difference between us. My life, every day in my life, is full and rich and rewarding. To have children? A purely selfish act, unless you are prepared to make a child the first priority in your life. I suffered from not being the priority of two terrific, exciting parents. I wouldn't want to do that to a child." She was stunned to hear those words come out of her mouth. Had she been carrying that belief all her life? She must have been. It quite shocked her. Yet, having voiced it she felt some sort of relief, as if she had been carrying a large boulder around forever and had now dropped it. Rick might be her lover, but she thought of Cary that night at her house when she had seen him as some kind of miracle-worker, a healer. Was he her healer, too, the only person to recognize she was ill? She never had.

"Mimi, don't talk about this now. You're going to talk it to death. You've analyzed it, talked about it in your head. Maybe it's been in your psyche for years and you killed it long ago. I'm offering you something new and fresh, a new life, a child to love and play with, someone to add to your life and share it with."

"Don't go on."

"OK, I've said all I have to say." He did not mention it again.

They spent the night together, not leaving that lovely bedroom in the pretty house in Sutton Place. They lay in bed and Mimi listened to him talk about his adventures. It was all much more than the perfect wave, more than the surfer who was a brain surgeon. He was a true original and a rolling stone. She wanted him and what he represented, but she wanted the stability, the security, of Jay. Rick's way of life was marvelous, child's play, but her marriage gave her something as desirable.

She was starved of passion, hungry for uninhibited sexual ecstasy, things that she had with Rick. But she was of another generation, of another time when values were different. No matter how much she could change, there was a history of thinking and maturity developed in the hard realities of an ugly world. Blond boys, beach bums from Malibu, with all their East Coast education and skills, were players who knew only how to roll the dice in favor of fun. Their time to grow up would come. Mimi would be old when they came into their prime, long past her own.

He was licking her fingers, running his tongue over her hand. He was almost eating her flesh. His eyes declared her succulent. Then she took his testicles in her mouth, licked them and rolled them around with her tongue. Cupping his penis in her hands, she caressed it, hand over hand. She could think of no pleasure greater than to have a love-child created from extreme sexual ardor with Rick. That made sense to her now. What had blinded her from seeing that before? She sucked her lover deep, and thought about her husband's sons. What a joy they were to Jay and her, what pleasure she derived from the company of his boys. Why hadn't she thought of it herself? A child created in a moment of passion, in an excess of lust. What better way? And he had been right, her rolling stone. She could deal with being a mother only when she became a mother. She could for the first time see a whole part of life she would miss if she were to abandon the idea. Her life, Mimi's life. Her life with Jay, and how her having children would add to their marriage. It was not a possible life with Rick she was thinking about, because she knew instinctively there would be no life for them, not a permanent one, the way there was with Jay.

Rick came in a long copious orgasm, and she swallowed and sucked and swallowed, knew how much she loved her young lover and that he was right.

In the morning they awoke in each other's arms, ravenous. Mimi was surprised by the smell of cooking. They bathed together, dressed and went down to the kitchen where the doctor's houseman was cooking breakfast. Smoked bacon and cheese souffles, tiny sausages, black coffee, followed by bowls of ripe strawberries with powdered sugar and fresh cream. They were almost embarrassed at having devoured all of that and remaining hungry. They asked for toasted brioche with butter and honey, and more black coffee.

She went with Rick to the hospital. After his examination of Dr. Quinn, he brought her in and introduced her to the eminent surgeon. "Talk some sense into him, I'm prepared to become his assistant anytime he asks," said the doctor, barely above a whisper.

There was a look of astonishment on Rick's face, a sense of pride that she had never seen before. She realized what a sacrifice it was for him to follow the sun, to seek the perfect wave. She understood then what great strength Rick had, and that, when he did find it, he'd be home and would indeed step into this man's shoes. Rick seemed to her now extraordinarily intelligent and humane, truly a life-saver. She felt proud that he should have sought her out and made a great romantic love affair for her. Of course she must have a son. He had seen her, she had revealed herself to him. He had divined what they both wanted, even if she hadn't known it.

She heard herself addressing Dr. Quinn. "Talk some sense

into him? I think he has talked some sense into me, maybe even to us, only you haven't heard him yet. He'll come home. This is not a man who toys with his life. It only appears that way to us, because we've forgotten how to play with life and learn from it at the same time. He'll come home when he's found his wave, and the answers he needs to go forward, take his next step." She patted the doctor's hand, left teacher and pupil together and went to wait for Rick in the hospital corridor.

Before they left the hospital floor, she whispered something in his ear. He smiled, and she bit her lower lip. He could see the happiness in her eyes. He knew better than to speak about it. Instead they walked together down the corridors to the elevator. Rick was still dressed in blue jeans, a clean blue-and-white-striped, well-tailored shirt tucked into them, cowboy boots that had seen better days. Yet even without the trappings of the well-turned-out doctor, he commanded respect among doctors and nurses they passed. Rick took on the mantle of authority without being pompous or arrogant. He held her hand while the gynecologist removed the contraceptive. He kissed her, at first on the hand and then lightly on the lips.

Rick canceled his trip to California. Mimi called Barbara and borrowed Beechtrees for a week. It was the beginning of June, a perfect time to be there, before people descended to open houses, or music-lovers from all over the world came to listen in the grass fields or in the concert hall at Tanglewood. Then the countryside would change. The life and style of those quiet New England towns, Stockbridge, Tanglewood, Lenox, the area for thirty miles around, would become busy and exciting. But, for the moment it was old faces and a slow pace. Only the Boston Symphony Orchestra was in residence, just a few great houses were open for the summer.

It had been an inspired idea. Beechtrees was opened and made ready for Mimi. Once there, she gave the staff a week's holiday. They wanted to be alone, just the two of them, so they could have sex when and where they pleased. Where they could bring to fruition their excesses of passion and their erotic fantasies.

Mimi had returned to Beechtrees many times since the day she was brought through the gate by Joe Pauley. Yet she had never felt as she felt now, being there with Rick. It wasn't just the sex and passion, or talking about the world and themselves. There were picnics on the small island, long walks in the parkland. Dinners and lunches held for several people that they met at their favorite drinking place, Avaloch, a great old rambling white mansion made into a country house hotel, with a wonderful bar. Crazy, amusing people of Rick's age, a few even her age. Mostly clever young professional New Yorkers, masters of the one-liner, hard players, music-lovers. It was always amazing to Mimi how improbably detached she was from everything else in her life when she was with Rick. He swept her into this frivolous, carefree existence of fun and sex, a little dope, drink, and drifting, that wonderful feeling of drifting, in and out of the experiences of the moment. Reading poetry, listening to music, this was the whole world; laughing and playing, this was the whole world.

Then one day, when they were driving through the tall, rusting ornamental ironwork gates into Beechtrees, Mimi put a hand on Rick's arm. "Stop," she told him, and got out of the car. It was a very hot day. She stood at first quietly next to the car, then took several steps away from it. The soft top of the car was down. Rick could see quite plainly that something was wrong. Mimi was wearing a blue-and-white-checked cotton shirt, open at the collar and tucked into a pair of wide, white flannel trousers. He watched her place her hand inside the collar, pull it away from her neck and move her head from side to side, taking deep breaths as if she were suffocating. She looked past him, eyes wide, filled not so much with fear as curiosity, apprehension.

He very quietly opened the door and slipped out of the car. He stood across from her, watching. Anxious not to disturb her, he moved slowly, making his way round the front of the car toward her. She seemed unaware of his presence until, standing only inches away from her, quite gently, he placed a hand on her arm. She looked at him and sighed.

"Oooh," she said, "it was as if someone walked over my grave." It was all right, she was all right. She wiped her brow, then placed her hands over her face. They were trembling.

"Who did you see?"

"Quite extraordinary. Let's walk a little and I'll tell you

about it. I don't know what happened. My head . . . Suddenly
the years rolled back, and it was that first time when I rode
through those gates in a Mac truck. Just imagine, after all
these years, I remember being in a Mac truck. Green, I think.
I was so unhappy, utterly unlike the way I feel here with you
at Beechtrees now."

She gave him a wan smile. "I had been living in a nightmare for years. My only friend, other than the two women I
lived with, was this fruit peddler. He was a big man, strong,
like the strong men in a circus. He was tough, a hard man, but
soft inside. He befriended us. Oh, it's too upsetting to tell. We
lived in such dire poverty. The two women in whose care I
was could never cope. They sort of went to pieces. One went
slightly mad and died while still a young woman. Of what I
was never quite sure. The other, who was like a mother to me,
whom I'd loved since I was born, became an alcoholic. Oh
God, why am I thinking about it now? I don't want to talk
about it anymore. Joe Pauley, the peddler, saved me. I was
about to be orphaned. I'll never forget the kindness of that
stranger. But for him, who knows what might have happened
to me? He brought me here to Beechtrees, to be a companion
to a little girl, and a scullery maid in the kitchen. That, compared to my previous life, was a huge step forward. It was
only about sixty miles away from here, that horrible place
where I lived, the Blocks in Chicopee Falls. Oh, my God, I've
been through this gate a hundred times since that day and
hardly thought about it. I've never told Barbara, never told
my father, not a living soul, how lonely and miserable I was.
Only now can I see it and tell you about it. Maybe because it
doesn't matter anymore."

"Maybe because you're ready to let it go. You mean you
never went back to bury the ghost?"

"Never."

"You never saw Joe Pauley again?"

"Yes, many times during that first summer he came to sell
his fruit. But not after the family went off to England and I
went to New York. He only came out to this area because of
the family who lived here. Joe Pauley," she reminisced, "used
to read me stories from a Jewish newspaper called *The Forward*. He loved the writer Isaac Bashevis Singer. He was

reading him in Yiddish long before he became famous in English translation. Joe Pauley used to translate from Yiddish to Polish for us. He would read to us for a half hour, no more, no less. He was a man who like to keep to a schedule. Joe was a different man when he was in the house with Mashinka and me. House—it was more a hovel. He seemed at home there, quite relaxed. I think we did something for him. He certainly did a lot for us.

"I'd always wondered about his family, and then one day he came with his very beautiful, spoiled daughter, who hated the Blocks as much as I did, and the truck and the peddling of fruit even more. I'm sure she left home as soon as she was able to. He was kind to her, though but loving. I think I felt his love more than she did. As a child I thought what he showed me was love. Now I know it was affection. That's it, he showed her no affection. She saw me, and resented me on sight. I only saw her twice. We became friends the second time we met, when she saw me as no threat to her. Then she vanished. She was my first friend after her father, and then they both went out of my life. This is morbid."

"No, not morbid. I think it's wonderful that it no longer bothers you."

"Oh, yes it does. It's just out in the open."

"Don't you have any curiosity, don't you want to see the Blocks again?"

"You're leading me into something, Rick, and I don't think I'm ready for it."

"Go on. Take a ride down there. I'll get out a map. We'll find your Chicopee Falls, take a look at it, see it again, so it will vanish forever from your life."

"You make it sound like an evil place. How did you know?"

"No, not an evil place, just a transient hell you had to go through. Just remember there is no going back, no going home. You can't go home. This is only a viewing, just having a good old last look."

"Good God, Rick, who would want to go back home to the Blocks? Viewing will be enough, thank you. And I'm not even certain I want to do that."

"We don't have to go, Mimi."

She hesitated for only a second, "No, we'll go. It's Wednesday. I chose today because Wednesday is the day Joe Pauley always went to the Blocks."

"OK, then, let's take a look at your Blocks," he told her, "and then we'll go to a great restaurant on the Connecticut River I once went to, if I can find the place on the map. You'll love it. The food is great, the place and the people."

"Rick, I want to go by way of Otis. I'll show you Ida Hall's General Store."

"When's the last time you were there?"

"Probably the day you were born." She began to laugh. "I can't believe we are doing this."

It was quite remarkable to Mimi. Nothing looked very changed. There it was, the kerosene pump in the courtyard of Ida Hall's Store. She couldn't equate it with being here as an adult. It was like some banal Norman Rockwell painting, the cover of *The Saturday Evening Post*. Too perfect, too picture-postcard, too untouched. She adored it. Memories of the day she stopped here as a child were so vivid, and somehow seemed more real than sitting in the car as an adult with Rick, her young lover, at her side.

"Don't pull in, let's keep going."

"You're not afraid, are you?"

"No, not afraid. But I suddenly remember how hungry I was. We had fresh hot doughnuts. The daughter understood how starved I was. Ida Hall's was where I made my first girlfriend. It was only for a few hours that we were friends but they were the most important few hours of my life to date."

They drove through the leafy green forests of the Berkshires, followed the map to Springfield and then to Chicopee Falls.

"Do you recognize anything?" he kept asking her.

"I wouldn't recognize anything. You don't seem to understand. I lived with two paranoid caretakers who hardly let me out of the house. The furthest we ever went was to Chicopee, and that was only once or twice. Maybe once to Springfield. No, I recognize nothing. You've no idea how awful a life it was, Rick. I don't actually know what we're doing here, but funnily I'm less upset than I thought I would be."

They had to ask several people the way. Then finally, in a

chrome and red plastic diner where they had a cup of coffee and huge wedges of coconut cream pie, Mimi asked the short-order cook, who was grilling hamburgers, if he knew where the Blocks were. He gave them directions and made no other comment. Who was this Mimi Steindler sitting with a young lover in a diner in Chicopee Falls, Massachusetts? What madness was she dragging back into her life? She suddenly began to laugh. She looked at her lover and kissed him on the cheek. He smiled.

"You've turned me into an adventuress, frightened of nothing, looking for my perfect wave. A child again." They both began to laugh, and left the diner.

"You see how easy it is to live and to love? Don't mess it up, don't make complications. Life can be sweet."

"My God, you're an innocent."

"No, not an innocent, a hopeful. Mimi, you don't know what misery and poverty really are. You haven't been to Calcutta or Bombay."

"And you haven't been a displaced child living in an alien world on the Blocks."

The directions given at the diner were perfect. Ten minutes later they turned a corner and down a narrow street, and there they were. The place was exactly as she remembered it. It looked no different to her from the day she left in a peddler's truck during a relentless heat wave. It was not as hot today as it had been when she left Mashinka there to die, and was sent out into the world alone to find a place for herself. But not a blade of grass had grown in all those years, not a tree had been planted, nor a house been painted. The Blocks were more dilapidated than ever. The long flights of wooden stairs baking in the sun seemed more rickety. The children looked the same as the children of her day: dirty, disheveled, wild.

Rick parked the car and they got out. They stepped off the granite curb stone and walked down the barren road between the buildings. A breeze ruffled dust from the hard-packed earth. Mimi felt grit in the back of her throat.

That generation of immigrants fled to America at the turn of the century. Till before the Second World War they clung to the old world, resisted learning English, still wanted to be European with American citizenship. Now they seemed to be dying out on the Blocks. They were there still, but were rapidly being replaced by their Americanized children, who were prettier, more slender, wore rollers in their hair, were possibly a little less poor, a little more educated, but still living with a ghetto mentality, factory workers and wives as they had always been. And Mimi noted the same ability to scream, pinch, and smack their unruly children hard.

She looked away from them. As the adult Mimi, Mimi Steindler of the Upper East Side, New York, she could stand aside, as Rick had suggested, and consider this place, these people, with an objectivity she never had as a girl. She could no longer feel the pain of that little girl. It could have been someone else. How could she have carried it so long? Now, miraculously, it was gone. With no pang of nostalgia or unhappiness, she was so free of it, she felt a kind of elation. About to tell this to Rick, she looked up at him and stopped herself. She saw the look on his face, and understood. He recognized the Blocks for what they were: ugliness, survival accommodation and nothing more. Nothing had changed. New generations didn't mean a thing to the place. It had not suddenly become a beautiful housing development.

"I had no idea. I simply had no idea that places like this still existed. Christ, it's like the concentration camps. The Nazis might have modeled them on this place. Mimi, I . . ."

"It's OK. I'm an onlooker now, seeing it the same way you are. It really doesn't hurt anymore."

"Which one did you live in?"

She couldn't tell him. They all looked the same to her. She did try to remember. Mimi even imagined herself inside one of the ground-level flats, looking out of a window. What would she have seen that might pinpoint the location of those survival years on the Blocks? The views would be the same whichever window she looked through. It was of no help, she could not locate the exact flat.

They walked down the center road. People looked at them. She did see the occasional old woman who surely had been there in her time. The same peasant stock in thin loose-fitting printed cotton dresses over fleshy, aged bodies seated on old wooden chairs. The language was Polish. Still the reek of raw onions and stale bodies. They wouldn't know her. She could pin no name on any of them. Mimi and Rick were almost in the center of the Blocks when she saw two women, old, fat and wobbly in their cotton dresses, visibly without bras, old-timers who would know about Joe Pauley. She put her arm through Rick's, approached them and spoke to them in Polish.

"Excuse me," she asked, "a long time ago a fruit peddler used to come here. He was called Joe Pauley."

One of them answered. "The fruit peddler. He comes still, once a week, today. He doesn't come in winter anymore, only in summer. In winter he goes to Florida. He makes so much money, he goes to Florida. What do you want with Joe?" But before Mimi could answer, she heard the rattle of the truck jumping the granite curb stone, and then the horn. It honked three times.

"That's him," she told Rick.

She turned around just as one of the women confirmed, "There he is, there's the peddler."

She watched the truck—no longer a Mac but a Ford, no longer green but red—kick up dust as it rolled down the road. The screen doors of the houses opened, children ran out and women followed. Slovenly women with curlers in their hair. The dismal femininity of the Blocks steamed out of their dark houses into the sun, gravitating toward the peddler's truck. Mimi could hardly believe she was watching this scene. As the truck rumbled slowly down the road toward them, she placed her hands over her face, trying to isolate herself for a minute, to regain her ebbing composure. Rick looked nonplussed.

"What now?" he asked.

"I don't know. Let's see."

They walked toward the Ford truck. She saw him clearly as the cab doors swung open and he stepped out on to the running board of the cab. He removed a cap and placed it on the seat, then lumbered down from the cab slowly and, she could see, painfully. He had a slight limp. Mimi and Rick stood with the others and watched the peddler drop the tailgate and hang the galvanized scale. He looked old, worn, much shorter than she remembered. He seemed to have shrunk in size and stature. He was thinner. He still had all his hair, but it was gray. And his eyes looked sad, tired. He wore silver-rimmed glasses. The shirt was the same lumberjack plaid, blue and white, and the trousers heavy-duty cotton. He saw her but didn't recognize her. She drew his attention because she was different, not belonging in the Blocks. He greeted his customers, a tired old man, his assistant doing the hawking, taking care of the younger women. Joe attended to his old cronies and spoke to them in Polish, teased them and gossiped with them, and filled paper bags with fruit and vegetables for them.

Finally he turned to Mimi and asked her, "Did you want something? You don't have to wait, they'll understand. You want something? Plums, maybe. Got first class, sweet, like sugar. Grapes? The peaches are a little hard, but a few days and they'll be perfect. Better than you'll find in the supermarket."

"Plums," she said in Polish, "I was always partial to plums, Mr. Joe."

"You know me?"

"Yes. When I was a little girl, you were very kind to me." All this she told him in Polish. "I lived here in the Blocks with Mashinka and Tatayana. I'm Mimi. You knew me as Mimi Kowalski."

She had to bite her lip to hold back the tears that brimmed in her eyes. Quickly, she put on her sunglasses.

"How long ago was that?"

He didn't remember. That took her aback. He had been the kindest man in the world to her and he didn't remember.

She swallowed hard, and gathered strength. "A very long time ago, more than twenty years. It was during the war. You were very kind and helpful to us. You were my only friend, and you read me *The Jewish Daily Forward,* Mr. Singer's stories. You would come to our house, take a snack with us. We were so poor you used to supply little extras for us, and Mashinka used to make something special for you, some Polish speciality. You found us doctors and lawyers, and helped us all you could, because we were strangers unable to cope once Mashinka's brother died. I don't know how we would have survived without your weekly visits."

"Kowalski . . . the drunk. A bum and a liar. Yes, now I remember. Mashinka, a good woman. Little Mimi, you never belonged here. Such a pretty little girl."

"You took me to Beechtrees, to the exiled royal family, remember?"

"Sure I remember. That's a long time ago. Well, you turned out a pretty woman like you were a pretty child. Ah, well, it's nice to see you." He took her hand, shook it and said, "You'll excuse me? I've got to make a little business here."

Mimi could hardly believe it. That was it with the man who saved her life. This man, who was the kindest of strangers, and that was *it*. She didn't know what she had expected. She had, after all, made no contact with him for years. She looked up at Rick. He shook his head as if he understood. "Let's go." And they turned to walk back to their car.

"Are you upset?"

"Yes, I think I am. He seemed so uninterested."

"He's an old man now and not well."

"How do you know that?"

"His eyes, the way he holds his head."

"Should we do something?"

"I'm sure his family knows and takes care of him."

"Should he be working?"

Rick was touched by the concern in her voice. "Yes, probably. It won't be for long."

"I feel terribly sad. He was such a giant of a man, so strong. He loved his work, and his truck. I used to think him such a powerful presence, and now he seems almost frail."

"Miss, miss," someone was shouting. They turned to see Joe's young assistant running towards them. He caught up with them. "Here. Joe says he remembers you like bananas, a little on the green side. And he's put in some grapes. He says you were always partial to black grapes."

"Please wait a minute," she begged.

"I've got to get back."

"Just one moment, please." She opened her handbag, pulled out a notepad and wrote quickly on it: "My Dear Joe, Always taking care of me. I have never forgotten you and I never will, Mimi." She pushed it into the young man's hand and watched him run back toward the truck where Joe was engulfed by women intent upon cheap vegetables, the insatiable in pursuit of the affordable. His back was turned to Mimi.

Chapter 22

"Remember, Poste Restante, Columbo. For the next month they'll have a forwarding address. No regrets?"

"No, no regrets."

"Good. If it's positive you'll cable me. And if you want to join me, you'll cable me. Give it a week for me to get my post. If I'm on a longer trip, don't panic. I'll get back to you."

They were at the Pan Am building at Kennedy Airport. A stewardess was running down the narrow corridor leading to the plane. "Dr. Walters, Dr. Walters! Please, we'll lose our place in the line for take-off. Now, Dr. Walters, we won't hold the plane any longer."

Without another word he grabbed Mimi in his arms. "Be happy, Mimi." He kissed her deeply, and she kissed him with the same hunger she always had for him. And then he turned on his heel and ran with the stewardess down the funnel-like entrance that led to the open door of the plane. He turned once more to wave goodbye to her, and then he was gone and the airplane door slammed shut.

Mimi walked quickly down the ramps round the terminal towards the exit. Suddenly, just when she thought she had their parting under control, she had to sit down. At first she felt as if she were going to be sick, and then she felt quite weak-kneed. She found a chair and from her bag took a handkerchief to cover her mouth. Instead, there were involuntary floods of tears, sobs as if her heart would break. The sickness passed, and the tears and the sadness slowly ebbed. How many women, she wondered, had seen their lovers off as bravely as she had, only to succumb in the aftermath of parting? Millions, just millions. She didn't have time to analyze why she should feel that way.

Two stewardesses and a security man came to her rescue. "Is there something wrong? Are you all right?" Still the tears trickled. But choked up as she was she managed, "No, I'm not all right, but I will be. I'm sorry, there isn't a problem. I'm not ill, just an emotional wreck."

"Oh, that's it." One of the stewardesses sat next to her and, putting an arm around her, said, "We know about that. We've all been there." Those kind words from a stranger, a beautiful, kind young woman trained to serve in-flight tea and sympathy, a ministering angel of the air. Rarely would she appreciate a stewardess more than this grounded angel.

"I'm all right." Mimi smiled. "I'm actually not even unhappy."

"Just emotional," said the security guard.

"Yes." She smiled up at him. "Just emotional."

"Partings are never easy, especially for the one not on board. I'm sure it would have been different if he'd left by ship. It makes things more acute, the airplane, the flying away. I often think about that. I know you'd feel a lot less bad if you'd seen him off on a Greyhound bus."

"Even worse," said the other stewardess, "if it was Pennsylvania Station or Grand Central. Nothing like a railway station for bringing out the tears." It was kindly meant.

"Grand Central," said the security guard. "It's more dramatic there, lovers parting under the clock and all that."

What a bunch of romantics, thought Mimi. It had worked. She was laughing. They smiled. "I feel quite foolish."

"And we got quite carried away on your emotions."

The stewardess stood up. "You all right now?"

"Just fine."

"It's usually more than just the parting of a loved one," said the philosopher security guard, "all those emotions running riot. The one you're leaving most times has hardly anything to do with it."

Yet another psychiatrist, thought Mimi. She shook his hand, amused by the disinterested concern of these strangers. How extraordinary, she thought as she walked away, I'm still amazed at the kindness of strangers who are always saving my life: Joe Pauley, Barbara, Rick. These people I'll never see again, helpful in a moment of need, replacing the comfort of family. Is it my function always to elicit the kindness of strangers? How pure and real that can be. Something to do with no strings attached. A case in point, Joe Pauley. Had she, she wondered, all her life been confusing love with kindness? Well, it no longer mattered. Even if she had, it had saved her emotionally enough times for her to distinguish now between love and the kindness of strangers.

Driving back into Manhattan, Mimi had a good deal of sorting out to do in her mind. Yet, when she tried to unravel what had happened to her in the last week, it had been, as Rick had predicted, less complicated.

She was ready for the next step in her life. Now the idea of having a child, either Rick's or Jay's, of being a real mother instead of the surrogate she had been to Jay's boys, seemed natural, as it never had before. Until her affair with Rick, it had seemed an unnatural act for her to have a child; now it seemed right, exciting, a natural progression in her life. For a moment she thought of going home, not the home she shared with Jay but her family home, to her father and Sophia in the town house off Fifth Avenue. But just as she was about to make the turn into the street she changed her mind and drove to her own home, hers and Jay's. First and foremost this was to be between them.

The following afternoon she found herself yet again at Kennedy Airport, this time at the terminal where Alitalia came in. She was waiting for Jay, something she rarely did, meeting him at the airport. As many times as she had offered, he had rejected the idea. "It's too much trouble, not at all necessary."

And she, not fond of public places like airports and railway stations, had been happy to oblige. So Jay's secretary was surprised when she asked for his arrival time and flight number. She even tried to discourage Mimi from going to the airport. In a moment of wavering Mimi agreed with Debbie: it was a hassle, she wouldn't go. But here she was, having changed her mind again, and glad of it. The sooner she saw Jay and they went home to talk through the changes she wanted to make in their lives, the better for both.

The flight arrival was announced over the public address system. It echoed through the terminal. Mimi felt a shiver of excitement. She joined the crowd waiting for the passengers to exit from the customs hall. It was not overly crowded, no holiday-weekend stampede. But the people were standing four-deep, waiting for lovers, friends, business associates. She marveled at how differently she perceived the airport today from yesterday, how different a sense of herself she had had there with Rick from her sense of Mimi there today awaiting her husband. How important it now felt that she had come to Kennedy to meet Jay. She was aware of her feelings of happiness, love for Jay, for the life they had built together, for the marriage that had worked so well and for so long for them both. Those feelings quite overwhelmed her. She felt strong and determined that this path she wanted to take with Jay was the right one. She could only hope that he would feel the same. Her determination that it should work out for them, that he would understand, gave her strength.

The waiting seemed interminable. She distracted herself by people-watching. They were not a particularly interesting crowd, standing there impatiently, nor notably attractive. More drab than gruesome, except a few young people garishly dressed.

Unmanageable children, bored and mischievous, ruffled their elders. A group of chanting, orange-robed, shaven-headed Hare Krishna people limply tapped their tambourines. Mimi predicted loud and enthusiastic performance once their friends came through customs. It would provide a few minutes' distraction. She spotted at twenty yards from where she was standing a woman with a baby. Not an enchanting baby. Curly dark hair, a pinched, half-appealing face. But he was good. He laughed and giggled and played patty-cake with his hands while in the arms of his nanny, a young woman in gray. Mimi knew nothing about babies but thought this one must be about a year old, possibly eighteen months. He kept chattering baby-talk, a dialogue of one. "Yum, yum, nana, baby, mummy, dada." A babel comprehensible to God alone. She liked the way he was dressed. How comfortably old-fashioned-looking he was, with a white cotton shirt trimmed with broderie anglaise, and a pair of pants with buttons at the waist, attached to suspenders that went over his little shoulders. They were puffy, bloomer-like trousers, like a little Dutch boy's costume, in a navy blue corduroy. She watched the child for several minutes and became enchanted by him. She began to see he was quick and had a clever look. She detected sweetness, affection in the way he occasionally pulled his nanny's collar to make her bend her head. He would give her a kiss, then giggle. Mimi, rarely drawn to babies, saw this little boy in a different light. She began to hope that, against the odds, she and Rick had been lucky, that she might already be carrying an embryo within her womb.

She was distracted from the child by a rush of people through customs. She looked for Jay among the crowd. Not there. Her attention was caught for a moment: a squeal of pleasure from the child in the nanny's arms. She watched as he reached out, excited by the nanny telling him, "Here's Mama, here's Dada."

"Mama, Dada."

Mimi turned her attention to the arrivals. There was Jay, briefcase in one hand, a girl in the other, passing by her without a glance. He hadn't seen her, perhaps. So many people. Mimi was only a few feet away. She raised her hand, and was about to call to him. She saw him stop and talk to the beautiful young girl with him, kiss her. She was a classic, Bennington College, bright-young-thing type, with long blonde hair and dark blue eyes. A very American, Mayflower, WASP kind of face. Slender limbs. Wearing a smart pink cotton shirtdress with sleeves pushed up, ivory bangles on her wrists. Still Mimi could have called out, he was that close. But he was having words with the girl, and had on one of his very serious faces. At last the Bennington miss nodded. A look of relief came over Jay's face. He placed his briefcase on the floor, took the young girl in his arms and told her something that seemed to appease her. He picked up his briefcase again and was about to walk on. Mimi was surprised rather than stunned at what she was seeing. She had lost neither her composure nor her determination to confront what was going on.

She pushed her way past the people between Jay and herself. "Jay, Jay!" She waved. The look on the young girl's face said it all. It was relief rather than anxiety at Mimi's appearance. For the first time since she had known her husband, he said the wrong word at the wrong time.

"But you never come to the airport."

"That's true. Clearly I'm not meant to."

The girl did not move, said never a word. One hand was still gripping Jay's, the other was clenched in a tight fist. He tried to slip his hand from hers. "This is awkward," he said with his usual suave charm. Just a little embarrassment at finding no words equal to the situation. No guilt. But he needn't have worried about Mimi catching him with the girl. Worse was to come.

"Dada, Mama." The curly-haired baby and its Swiss nanny had pushed their way toward Jay and his blonde. "Dada, Mama." Hands outstretched, gurgles of laughter. Jay blenched.

"Well, I guess that about says it all, Jay."

The Bennington girl took her baby in her arms, kissed it and then shoved it upon Jay, obliging him to exchange baby for briefcase. Kisses and cuddles from the baby. A kind word for it from Jay, and he passed it back to the Bennington girl.

"The car's outside. You take it. I'll call you," he told her.

Mimi could see he was angry, less with her than with the girl. He picked up his briefcase. Then taking Mimi by the arm over the barrier that was still between them, walked her swiftly from the hall.

"Did you come by car or taxi?"

"Actually I came with my father's car and driver. Yours and your driver were unavailable. Or so your secretary said."

"Are you all right, Mimi? I didn't want this to happen. I wanted you never to know."

"The irony is too much, Jay."

"Irony? That's a bit subtle."

"Oh, but it is. You don't think so because you don't know why it's ironic."

"Mimi, we have to talk."

"Let me tell you why it is ironic. I came here because I could hardly wait, wanting to talk to you. To tell you I want to have a baby."

"Don't be ridiculous. At this stage in our life, have a baby?"

"Ironic, I told you." He flushed red with embarrassment. "Didn't I just see a baby? It was your child I saw. Or am I wrong?"

"I didn't want it. Look, we have to talk about this."

"You may not want it. But it was still a child I saw. And I saw that upmarket bimbo you're playing Dadas and Mamas with."

"Mimi, please!"

She held up her hand. "No wearisome explanations, please. And spare me the love saga."

"It is not a love saga. You and I are that, for me."

"Oh!"

"You're not going to dispute that, are you?" Jay was shaping a defense.

"No, actually I'm not, because I know it's true."

The look of relief on his face was immense. They were at Karel's car now, a 1948 Rolls in a deep, rich maroon color with a thin black coachline. He shook hands with Karel's chauffeur, then looked at Mimi. She was already seated comfortably in the back of the car. He slipped in next to her. "We can't talk, not here."

"Of course we can." And she pushed a button. The magic of hydraulics raised a glass partition between the driver and the rear compartment.

"Mimi, about Claire and the baby . . ."

"Do you want to leave me? Do you want to marry her?"

"No, I don't want to leave you, ever, I adore you. I like you being my wife, and our marriage. That is not what this is about."

"So what is it about?"

"A brief infatuation, an unwanted child—unwanted by me."

"A brief affair, an unwanted child? That child looks to me to be more than a year old. The mother a traveling companion, a brief encounter? I hardly think so. Listen, this is the moment of truth for us. Do you want to leave me and marry this young woman? If you do, speak up now, Jay."

"Absolutely not, it's out of the question."

"You merely want to have two families, one with her and another with me?"

"No, I don't even want that."

"What do you want, Jay? Or let me rephrase that: What do you have, Jay?"

"Are you sure you're up to this, Mimi?"

"Oh, yes, I'm very sure I'm up to this."

"I know you're angry."

"Mmmm, yes, I think I am angry. But not because you've deceived me. If you think that, you had better know you've got it wrong. You felt something lacking in your life. Maybe whatever it was had nothing to do with me or our marriage. I'm sure enough about us and our relationship to bank on that. For whatever reason, you had an affair with Claire, and an unwanted baby. Is that how it is?"

"Well, not exactly."

"Oh. Well, how was it—exactly?"

"Well, to be honest, I didn't like her all that much. But she was bright and amusing. I wanted her, so I took her. That's all. It's hard for me to explain it. I promise it has nothing to do with us, you are quite right about that. It was a fling. She got pregnant. Intentionally, I think. A child was out of the question, I thought. Then she said she wanted to have the baby, and I realized my boys were grown up, practically men now. All that family business of babies and raising children was over for me. You and I were not into all that, we had made the decision never to have children, and here I'd gone and made one."

Jay frowned. "Though I didn't like the idea, I couldn't just ignore it. Another piece of me entering the world, that sort of thing. She wanted it, I agreed. I support the child, not her. I would have, you should know that, but she's wealthy in her own right. She is jealous of my marriage with you. She knows you have a hold on me, and that I love and respect you as I never could her. That I will never divorce you for her. But she's the mother of my child, and occasionally I go away with her. She tries to play your role in my life, but not very well. It's not even sordid, it's rather pathetic.

"His name is Barney, by the way. When he was born, much as I resisted the idea of playing father again, he made

me feel great. There really is no more to say about this. I'm
not even going to ask for forgiveness. I am asking you to stay
with me. Don't leave me because of this. I love you more
than anyone else in the world. My children come second."

"Your Bennington deb?"

"She's the mother of my child. I feel about her the same
as I feel about the other mothers of my children. I'll never
see her again."

"Don't be ridiculous, of course you will. She's the mother
of your son. You're going to want to see him."

"Mimi, you won't leave me, will you?"

"I don't know, it all depends. I want children."

"Mimi, you never wanted children. We agreed no more
children for me."

"So you went ahead and had one! You've broken that
agreement, Jay."

"Once. A mistake. I wanted a marriage without children.
We agreed."

"Suppose *I* want to change the agreement?"

"Mimi, I consented to Barney because he was already a
living thing, flesh and blood. I also consented because he was
coming to me without diapers, sleepless nights and colic,
whooping cough, chicken pox, scraped knees and screams. I
can't go through that again. With Barney, she had it all. I
don't. I've got the son, she takes care of the mess and trouble,
and that's OK. You don't know what you have to give up to
have children. The responsibility. How it changes your life.
You've never had children, never even wanted children till
now."

"If this marriage is going to work, it's going to have to be
with me having children and us acknowledging Barney in our
lives, with or without his mother."

"I'll never go away with her again."

"I didn't ask you to do that. I'm not asking you to do anything about this affair of yours. That's up to you. Barney's
welcome in our house, he's your son. I have cared for and
loved your other sons. Would I do less for an illegitimate
one?"

Tears came into his eyes. They were genuine. "I can't believe you're not going to leave me over this."

"I am going to leave you, but not over this. I am going to leave you if you don't consent to our having children. I don't want to play true confessions here, but I have had the occasional lapse in my marital vows. I can understand you only because I understand myself and my own needs." She had slipped it in.

"Then the rumors were true?"

"You never believed them?"

"No, never. That you had lovers? Never. That you toyed with them and played with them was obvious. I know fifty men who would bed you in a minute. You are, after all, a very sexy lady. Like Karel, a natural flirt, a charmer and seducer. It's part of that Czech charm of yours. But that you actually took young lovers? No, that was not an adventure I thought you would go for."

"Do you feel cheated?"

"Yes, I do, as a matter of fact."

"None of my admirers meant anything to me, except for one. The only one you ever met. He has been an important lover in my life. Not just for sex, but because he was an extraordinary young man. He has made me grow up in many ways where I have been kept a child by you. You feel cheated because you're the marrying kind. Would you want me to divorce you for him, and then divorce him because he wasn't the right man? No, Jay, I've always known being married to you was the best marriage I would ever make. Anything outside our marriage has to be something else. And, actually, I think you have just proved that point."

"It's that young doctor, Rick, isn't it?"

"Yes."

"Mimi, I don't want lose you to Rick, not to anyone. But consider me. I enjoy our marriage just the way it is. I don't want it disrupted by bringing up another family. I'm not a young man anymore, I don't pretend to be. You know that. Twenty years was bound to make a difference as I grew older. We had no illusions about that."

"Jay, I shall leave you, little as I may want to. I promise you I will, unless you agree to have children with me."

"Well, let's not make any rash decisions, let's think about it. And Rick?"

"He's a rolling stone. He rolls in and out of my life and doesn't gather me to him. He lets nothing cling to him. Not for any length of time. And I am too old for him, anyway."

"But you love him?"

"Oh, yes, I love him, but not in the way you think. Not the way I love you. He understands that, and assumes you will."

"You've talked to him about me?"

"Of course. He's my young lover, just as that girl is your young lover. I don't know that that says much for us, but it may say a lot for our marriage if it can cope with this situation. It's because of him that I want to have children. He taught me how much fun being a child can be, something I had forgotten. My own childhood and fun were cut short. He made me understand that I should have no fear of raising children of my own. I could enjoy them and play with them and learn with them about love and innocence, those things I lost as a child."

"Am I such a bad lover that you needed to find other men?"

"Oh, Jay, that's not worthy of you. I might ask you the same thing. We can go on this way, but it won't get us anywhere. Whatever we've done is because something in ourselves needs to go outside marriage. I can accept that, that it happened to you as well as me. I don't intend us to hash this over, or talk about it ever again. You know my terms: children."

"What if we have these children and you decide it wasn't such a good idea? What then? We would have to move house, change our lives. You're asking a lot. I love my life with you the way it is now."

"You'll like it better, I promise."

"And if I don't?"

"I'll have Rick's children."

"And marry him?"

"No, I'll never marry him. But he wants to give me babies, wants to create another kind of life with me outside marriage."

"Jesus Christ!"

"What?"

"It's all that hippy talk. All that love and Flower Power

and mother earth. Well, maybe you should make a baby with him."

"I may have. That's something else you should know. I would like to have a baby of his, and so we tried."

"I don't believe this. You have the nerve to . . ."

"To what, Jay? Face it. At best we've got an extended family already. Four sons you've fathered, two ex-wives, who have always drifted in and out of our lives, a mistress, and now Barney. I can accept him as I have accepted and loved all your children. Would you throw me out because I might be having a baby with Rick? That's OK, Jay, that's a chance I took. I won't like it, but I'll accept it. Although I would have thought that you were a bigger man than that. You don't want me or children with me? I'll go back home to my father and raise my babies there."

"I feel trapped."

"That's disgusting. Trapped by what? I told you, I'm ready to leave unless you give me what I want. And I'll do it quietly, no fuss, no bother."

"That's what has trapped me. You know I've never been able to resist you. There was always something about you, a special kind of femininity that excites me, a charm you use on me, on all men, as no other woman I have known can. It grabs me and holds me. I could no sooner lose you than my life, and you know it."

"You're angry."

"Yes, and you'd goddam well better know I am!"

"Angry, why?"

"Because I love you and I'll never let you go. And our marriage is too important, too solid to break. Now please, let this rest for a while. We'll talk more about it later." That was his last word for the moment and Mimi knew it. She knew Jay was telling her the truth. She respected that. She would let the matter rest.

That evening they dined with Karel. It was informal, a delicious meal down in the kitchen with Sophia cooking and serving. Mimi marveled at how unperturbed she was at the day's events. At the strength she had to stand up and fight for her marriage, for her unborn babies, and for the right to have a child with Rick. Jay, himself the consummate charmer in his own literary world, the most humane, intelligent, uncomplicated of men, was besotted with her. She had always known that, but had never until now taken advantage of it. Mimi knew that she could charm without any effort of will. It was one of her greatest assets. Since a child, both men and women had been besotted by her. Finally it was that inborn charm that allowed her to seek out her destiny, to stave off that hungry heart of hers.

Jay was charming, amusing. Karel had liked him from the first. On grounds of religious and age difference, he had had doubts. Would a marriage between them work? But he had not stood in Mimi's way. Now he was happy about that. Jay and her father liked each other's company. There was always stimulating conversation between them. And this evening was no exception. Jay was relaxed and happy, enjoying himself as if no problem existed between them. He was pleased to be married into the Stefanik family. It suited him. Would he, she wondered, choose to lose all this? She wanted to stay with him, but she would go if Jay would not give her what she desired.

They had coffee in the garden. Mimi sat back and listened to her father and her husband. She looked at Karel and Jay, and saw, still, at their age, two of the most attractive men in the city, so different in character but similar in many ways. Charismatic figures, highly intelligent, interesting, articulate. They were powerful men, heroic figures, men who in their lifetimes had taken great leaps. Adventurous men in their thinking. She was in awe of that, respected them for it. She had always given them what they wanted for as long as she had known them. Now, in this one thing, it was their turn. She would not waver.

Mimi and Jay had walked to Karel's house, so they walked back home.

"Mimi?"

"Yes."

"You're being wonderful about Barney and his mother. Surely you must be angry?"

"Oh, I think I am angry. But only because, if it was so unimportant, why did you have to deceive me for so long about it?"

"I don't think of myself as a deceitful man."

Mimi began to laugh. It was a sarcastic laugh. "But you are, Jay, selfish and greedy, only you've got a great cover-up, more than most. You are a very nice man, and you do care about people. That's one of your many saving graces."

They had reached a corner and the light was against them. They waited for it to change. He took her by the arm.

"I don't want you to leave me. But you will, won't you? You'll walk out on this marriage, and me, and you won't even think about my feelings, unless you get your way?"

"No, that's not true. I'll walk out on you unless we go down a new path together. And that includes finding a way to live with our extended families."

He took her by the arm and they crossed the street. Safe on the other side, he pulled her toward him and kissed her roughly. That kiss was filled with passion and anxiety and a kind of truthfulness new to them. Arm in arm they walked home.

In bed he took her in his arms and kissed her. He turned upon his wife the virile and exciting Jay Steindler charm. He was at his most sexually seductive. He was her new lover. This was not the husband who fucked her every morning of their marriage. He had reverted to the lover she had fallen for before he set the ground rules of their sex life and marriage years earlier.

"I like you too much to trick you," Mimi whispered in his ear, "so I have to remind you, I am no longer baby-proof."

"Jesus, Mimi, you do pick your moments. Shut up." He sealed her lips with a passionate kiss. She felt him enter her, and he accompanied his continual thrusts with whispered confessions of adoration and love.

The following morning Jay Steindler woke as usual by stretching out to feel the warmth of his wife's body next to him. He fucked her. Jay had his morning fuck just as they always had every morning of their married life if they were together. Their morning routine proceeded as normal.

He took her to lunch in the Russian Tea Room. That was unusual, they rarely lunched together. Between the smoked salmon and the main course and the stopping of numerous persons at their table—most of the literary world lunched there—he presented her with a long, slim, black-velvet jewelry box. "Is this a bribe?" she asked, amused because this was so out of character for Jay. Their jewelry buying was always done together. She opened it. Inside was a magnificent two-inch-wide Art Deco diamond and emerald bracelet. It was an extravagance unheard of for Jay. "Oh!" she exclaimed, her breath quite taken away. "This *is* a bribe." She raised it in her fingers to watch the light play on the diamonds, the emeralds glow, the pattern dazzle the eye. He reached across the table and clapped it on her wrist.

"It's a bribe only if it works. If it doesn't work, it's just a beautiful bracelet because I love you, much more than I thought."

Another publisher and agent came to the table to greet them. Jay stood up, and the agent lifted Mimi's hand to admire the gift. "Wow, is this a bribe? Jay's way of getting what he wants?" he said. The tease had more bite to it than the man realized.

She began to laugh. "It's a bracelet trying to be a bribe."

"Mimi, if he's been naughty, you leave him. I've always wanted to snatch you away from him." They all laughed. The three men shook hands, one patted Mimi on the shoulder, the other kissed her on the cheek and whispered in her ear, but loud enough for all to hear, "I mean it." The pair then left them to finish their lunch.

That evening she wore her new bracelet and a smart, short, black silk dress together with a tiny hat, a small tricorn of black silk set fetchingly to one side with an enticing black veil that just covered the eyes. It was sheer, with an intricate design along the bottom. One of those little hats that women buy because they are fetchingly seductive, and tease men.

With her blonde curly hair, violet eyes and voluptuous figure, and that teasing charm of hers, Mimi seemed impossibly sexy and young, with a newly carefree attitude that Jay found provoking. He couldn't blame several men who made a play for her at the cocktail party. If she hadn't been his wife, he would be doing the same thing, and that was what he loved about her. Even as a young girl, when he had picked her up and subsequently married her, it was that kind of seductive romanticism about her, mixed with a certain reserve, a mysterious remoteness which still didn't exclude flirtatiousness, that had kept him. Even now, it intrigued him. But a mother? More children, the disruption of their lives, the years of commitment it would take to raise children—could he do it for her? He would do anything to keep her. But that?

The following morning he made love to her. The sex was great, the way it always was for them. Not nearly as exciting as when they did it two nights ago, but great like always. When he felt her come, and was holding her, all warm and female, and they were momentarily slipping out of their routine lives and into a world of bliss all their own, he was certain she would drop this fantasy. He kissed her and left her in bed.

He brought Mimi her breakfast. Their housekeeper had prepared it, but it was he who brought it into the room. He placed it over her lap and climbed in carefully next to her. They ate off the same tray: fresh pineapple and Scottish raspberries, black coffee, toasted wholemeal bread with butter and honey. They usually ate sparingly at that hour in the morning. It was just tea for them, followed by breakfast meetings at some grand hotel for Jay. She had her breakfast later with her father and Sophia. He was being so obvious now, it was easy to be on to him.

"This is a bribe, like the bracelet." She smiled at him.

"I'm not going to give in on this, Mimi. Much as I love you and don't want to lose you, I am not going to give in to this whim of yours. It's all too complicated. We would have to leave here, give up our lovely home, create another. Look, you've been wonderful about Barney. Be wonderful one more time about this."

"It was easy being wonderful, as you put it, about Barney. He doesn't affect out lives. I'm only taking in another one of your children. As for Miss Bennington, I saw the look in her eyes. She thinks I'll leave you. She's right, I will, but not because of her. Only because you won't give me what I want."

"Look, let's give this time. No rash decisions."

"Fine. Time you need? Time you'll have."

Mimi was remarkably calm. She chose a plump piece of pineapple, took it delicately between her fingers and offered it to Jay. He opened his mouth and she fed it to him. She smiled, and slid naked from between the sheets to walk across the room, slipping into a dressing gown to vanish into the bathroom. He felt uneasy when she returned to the bedroom. He watched her moving several dresses from the armoire to lay them over the chaise.

"What's all that about?" he asked. "Are you leaving me? Is that what *you're* bribing me with, a divorce?"

"It never entered my mind, Jay. Divorce, that is. I'm leaving you only temporarily, I hope. I'm going to father's, I think you need some space to think this out."

"And you don't?"

"No, I don't."

"Don't be silly. Stay here. We'll take some time thinking about it."

"No, I think not. It's not unusual for me to stay there for a few days. I don't intend to say anything to Dad or anyone else about this matter. You'll find me there when you want me."

Jay was at the Stefanik house for dinner that night. Mimi was terribly tired and went to bed early. He stayed up talking to Karel until the early hours of the morning, and then, rather than going home, slept with her in her bedroom in her father's house. Nothing there for anyone in the house to get suspicious about: they often stayed over.

In the morning he woke and made love to her, fucked her as if nothing threatened their relationship. She seemed to Jay exceptionally responsive to his lust for possession of her. He was tying his tie, looking at her in the mirror.

"Shall I see you home tonight, or will you come with me now? I have to get some papers I left there."

"I'm living here now, remember?"

Jay turned. "What are you talking about?"

"I'm not going home until I get what I want."

"Are you saying this marriage is over?"

"No, I'm not. It's you who's going to have to say that."

"I won't come round tonight. You need time to think about this."

Three weeks later Mimi flew to Bali to spend a week with Rick. She was pregnant. Whether with Rick's child or Jay's didn't matter to either of them. They were happy. If it ever mattered to Rick or to Jay the paternity of the child could be decided by tests after it was born.

"And Jay?" a delighted Rick had asked her when she told him the news.

"He doesn't know. He's busy trying to decide what to do about what he calls this whim of mine. He knows about us."

"And?"

"There is no 'and.' He just knows about us."

It was an idyllic week of sex on the Balinese beaches, and in a secluded house with a lush, romantic tropical garden. He was divine, but she felt the difference in their age and their lifestyles more acutely than ever in that tropical paradise. He seemed to her younger, more carefree than ever, directionless, and loving every minute of it, making the most of just hanging out. Although they took a house by themselves, he was very much in Bali with his friends, who roamed in and out of their lives as if they too belonged in their affair. All that communal living, all that youthful belief in universal love, it was great for them, for Rick, but seemed more wrong than ever for her. Mimi put those feelings aside for another week: the sex was too good to leave, the bond between them so strong it took more time to adjust to leaving him and their tropical paradise.

At the airport it was not easy for them to let each other go, but they needed no words to know that's what they were doing.

"And the baby?" he asked.

"I'll send you a cable."

"And what about Jay?"

"He'll come round. He loves me and our marriage too much to let either of us go." She boarded the plane for the first lap of her long journey back to New York.

Chapter 23

Mimi and Jay saw each other. They were husband and wife with a marriage still very intact but a bizarre arrangement of living in separate houses. At least, that was the way New York tongue-waggers voiced it, and more or less how it was. And that was what Karel and Sophia knew to be the case. Only they knew the facts, what had driven the couple to a separation.

Several days after Mimi's return from Ceylon she went to her father. Karel was in the library, absorbed in a book. Mimi watched him for several minutes. He was still handsome, charismatic. There emanated from him still that special male quality of strength and courage and sexual libertinism that, as his daughter, and once she had understood it, she had always been able to look at objectively.

The room seemed so very quiet, the library a world of its own. How she loved this room, this house, her father. Long ago, when he returned from the war and made this home and a family of sorts for herself, her mother and brother, he had never pretended that theirs would be a normal household, nor even a normal family. He made certain his children understood the state of his and their mother's relationship. They were all together under one roof because the war had torn their lives apart. In so doing, it had made him appreciate that, no matter what their individual flaws, they needed to be together as a family to reassemble their lives. It had been Karel who had taught her that all families have their own bizarre arrangements. As long as there was security and comfort in being together, that was about all one could ask for. Except love. In most families that came in its own peculiar fashion.

Mimi had no doubt that Karel more than anyone else would understand what she was doing. But she felt she had to be cautious in explaining her position and the unusual family she herself intended to create. She was ever sensitive that Karel and she could not, even after all these years, bring themselves to talk to each other about her childhood during the war. Mimi had come to terms with it when after his return to her, and over many years, the true picture emerged of Count Karel Stefanik's heroic flight with her from Prague, and his choice to fight as hero rather than be exiled as a mere father. That he loved his country more than his daughter was a thought that never entered her head. Neither of them could allow that. But still it niggled at them both in the recesses of their minds. Mimi talked freely to Karel about everything she wanted to. That was the way he brought her up. And so it was not difficult for her to go to him.

Very quietly, she walked over and gently placed a hand on his shoulder. "Poppa."

He looked up from his book. Ever the ladies' man, ever sensitive to a beautiful woman. He smiled. "You look particularly pretty today, Mimi. I always like you in that dress. White suits you."

His compliments always made her feel like the most beautiful woman in the world. She laughed. "Poppa, you're such a flirt."

"That's true."

"But I love it."

"That's why men do it, because women love it and because, when a woman is beautiful, it gives such pleasure to a man. Well, this man anyway." He raised her hand and lowered his lips to place a kiss on it. "Did you want something, Mimi?"

"A talk. I know I am interrupting you, but do you mind?"

He left his book open on the reading table and rising from his chair went to sit on the sofa. He patted the cushion next to him, an invitation for her to sit beside him. "Important?" he asked.

"Yes."

"And exciting. I can see that in your face."

"Yes, very, Poppa. This odd way I am living with Jay. It's my doing, Poppa. I'd like to tell you about it."

Karel removed a strand of hair from Mimi's cheek, then took her hand in his and nodded. It was as if he was saying: "What a good idea."

"I have had a very successful and happy marriage with Jay, Poppa. We like being married to each other, that hasn't changed, but what has is me. A few years ago I met a young man, I mean really young, ten years younger than myself. I think you can guess that it was a sexual thing. But it turned out to be more. Not love the way I love you or Jay, but a carefree, hippy kind of irresponsible love. Fun-love and sex that I missed in my youth. He's a man with a free spirit, who knows how to play with life. A quite remarkable young man, a doctor, surgeon, most accomplished and respected, but outside the operating theater still a child who plays with life. There is something frivolous about Rick that stops him from being the great love of my life or my even contemplating the breakup of my marriage. It's quite strange and difficult to explain but I grew up both sexually and spiritually with Rick. He's a healing and teaching human being. That's his life. Not marriage and a family. But he did recognize those instincts in me."

"I think I met this young man once. A party you gave for Barbara?"

"That's right, Poppa. Shortly after that party, he went away for a couple of years. Then recently he returned. And when he did I realized that there was a bond between us. A closeness, an understanding, and it's that not the sex or the affection we feel for each other that keeps adding to my life. He finds a way deep into my innermost feelings and brings them to light.

"As you well know, when I married Jay we agreed not to have children. Neither of us wanted them. Each of us for our own reasons. It's quite simple, Poppa. Knowing Rick, growing up with him, has changed all that. I feel secure enough in myself now to have children, and almost too late I have decided to have them. Jay is furious, he says no, he likes our marriage just the way it is. I have told him it's to be children for me, in or out of our marriage. He has yet to make up his mind. I'm three months pregnant."

"His or Rick's?"

"I don't know.

"And Jay knows that?"

"Yes."

"And accepts it?"

"He has little choice if we are to stay together. You see, by chance I discovered he has a baby out of wedlock that he acknowledges but keeps a deep dark secret so as to save our marriage. And, unbelievably, he still wants to deny me children. Still he claims he wants no babies to interfere with our life. I have put it to him that this time we do what I want or I leave him. We have this child, bring it up together, and open our family to include Barney, his baby, and the mother of the child, and Rick, as we have always accepted his ex-wives and his children in our life, and we live with our extended family openly. I promised to add those things to our life. They won't diminish the marriage we have had all these years, only add to it."

"And what about your old dad? What is expected of him? That he becomes the patriarch of this horde you are creating? The grandfather of this dynasty you are set on establishing for us all? What am I expected to say to all this?" he asked, not quite sternly, but certainly seriously. Until a smile broke slowly at the corners of his mouth. "Well, I'll tell you what I say, my Mimi. Jay would be a fool to lose you. But Jay is no fool, far from it. He will make a fine patriarch and I will be honored to be the Grand Patriarch of the family. What an adventure for me! To have a chance to love your children as I love you. They will keep us young and gay in our old age, Mimi."

"Oh, Poppa." She flung her arms around her father's neck. Tears began trickling from the corners of her eyes. "It will be a big, wonderful, crazy kind of family. But I know we'll make it work."

"Of course we will, Mimi, that's what all families are, one way or another. You have only to look at your own family to see that. Now I think this calls for a grand lunch, anywhere of your choosing, in celebration of new life."

If Mimi had had any doubt about what she was doing, it vanished with Karel's delight in her news. She knew that he was looking at her as both daughter and a woman of substance. That he was relating to her more as that woman than as his child. He loved beautiful, adventurous, seductive women who took on life with both hands. It suddenly occurred to Mimi that this was the first time she had showed him that side of her.

When Mimi was three months pregnant, Jay had quite adjusted to the idea that she was going to have a child. He still couldn't be sure whose. Then one morning it no longer matter whose it was. He couldn't give her up. They went shopping for a new house, and they found one at 13 East Sixty-third Street, between Fifth and Madison Avenue, just across the street from the Hammersteins and Jolie Gabor, mother of Zsa Zsa—the estate agent was proud to announce. A beautiful town house, converted for the moment into two flats. Once they had agreed to buy it, Mimi flung her arms around Jay's neck, kissed him and whispered in his ear, "You'll never regret this. You'll be happy, I promise you, you'll be happy." She would make certain that he would be, Mimi vowed to herself. She did, after all, love him and want to make him happy. A moment after she had said it, she looked at his passive face and felt a pang of guilt, but it soon vanished when a smile broke across his face. He picked her up by the waist, swung her round and put her down.

"I am, I'm already happy about it. I've come to terms with this idea of us being one large extended family. I'm quite looking forward to fixing up this house. But I hope you know what you're taking on because I have the feeling we're going to have an interesting, but unconventional marriage from here on in."

"You're sure about this, Jay?"

"Sure about it? No. But you are, and that's enough for me. It has to be, doesn't it, because I can't take the alternative."

The worst problem they had during her pregnancy and the moving from the apartment to the new house, the momentous changes in their lives, was the girl Mimi called Miss Bennington—Claire. When Jay told her that Mimi and he were going to have a baby, and wanted to make a family where Claire and Barney were free to come and go openly in their lives, she resisted all thought of it. She was furious that Mimi had accepted the situation. But in time, Barney's mother, like Jay's two ex-wives, came round to the reality that Jay was always the winner. He got what he wanted, peace among his women and children. Not always an easy peace.

Mimi had one of those pregnancies that women dream about. Except for the first few weeks, when all she wanted to do was sleep, she felt just fine. Her energy was up, she was buoyant and happy. She carried her pregnancy beautifully, hardly showing until her eighth month. But she'd been clever about the way she dressed. Chic, and no maternity clothes for her. She got no pleasure from playing the pregnant role, the mother-to-be, as some women do. She simply got on with her life. No fuss, no bother, no classes. She planned to deal with the birth as best she could, once she was in the throes of it, and that would be that.

No one appreciated her attitude more than Jay. Together they renovated the house at 13 East Sixty-third Street. Mimi was as good as her word to him. Their lifestyle did not change, only their residence. Her determination that having a child was going to add to Jay's life never wavered. She happily worked hard on their marriage to ensure that that would be the case. Mimi and Jay's relationship took on a new kind of intimacy during the months of pregnancy. They both accepted that Claire, as the mother of Barney, would always be part of his life, that Rick as the putative father of Mimi's child would always be a part of hers.

These were tough decisions to take within a marriage, but they had to agree that, if they wanted to stay together, this extended family was the way for them to live. They were more excited by the prospect of an extended family than either of them had expected to be. And what if it didn't work? If they could not cope with what they were doing, if they should lose the marriage that bound them together so tightly—what then? They would part. It would be as simple as that. They believed they were creating an open marriage because they were strong enough to sustain it.

As Mimi's time drew near, it seemed increasingly important to her that Rick should be there. She really wanted him to see her baby born. Especially since Jay, larding it with many apologies, told her he could not bear to be involved in the birth of the baby. He had not been present for his other five children. He would not be for Mimi's. Too raw, too messy, too intimate, and altogether physical for Jay. He hoped that she understood. She did, and it did not pose a problem for them. She wanted to tell him how much she wished Rick to be there, but somehow she couldn't bring herself to do so.

But Jay was a remarkable man: he did know how to make people happy. It was an instinctive thing with him, giving people what they wanted, no matter how much he benefited. He was still an original, a good man, a generous person. He derived great pleasure from being the giver, more than most people understood. It was out of a deep love and respect, gratitude even to Mimi for not imposing her pregnancy on him. Her having said barely a word to him about the child to come, omitted to talk of hospital or doctors, or any of the stress of being pregnant or giving birth. His obsession to love and possess her motivated him to do what he did. Because, finally, Jay only ever did what suited Jay, what gave him what he wanted. Jay had his own brand of enlightened cunning. It was he who found and asked Rick to come back for the birth of the baby. Mimi knew nothing about it until he appeared. Shrewd and very wise, Jay knew Rick was no threat to his possession of Mimi or his marriage, he knew what Rick represented that both attracted and repelled Mimi. And he could understand that and live with it.

Mimi had a long and difficult labor, but finally gave birth to twins, a boy and a girl. She named the boy Milos and the girl Angelica. And only after they were born and she held them in her arms, nursed them at her breasts, did she fully appreciate what she might have missed had Rick never entered her life. She was happy discovering new kinds of love through her babies. New kinds of caring. But already a mature, middle-aged woman when she had her children, Mimi was able to put the birth of her children into perspective and slot them into the rest of her life. They became her prime concern, her most important loves, but they did not absorb her so much that she lost sight of the rest of her life.

Eighteen months later she gave birth to a son. Jay's son. Fortunately the Steindlers had the money to maintain a large staff to keep their lives ticking, which removed the mundane chores of motherhood and fatherhood. Mimi was happier than she had ever been. She had the children she wanted and her extended family and a husband who adored her more than ever. Her father and Sophia. Predictably, Sophia adored Mimi's babies. But if there was one thing that surprised and disappointed, although Mimi kept it very much to herself, it was that, though Karel behaved like a doting grandparent when he saw the children, away from them it was as if they hardly existed at all. After several months Mimi realized that, when she was with her father, unless the children were present, she rarely spoke about them. It was a shock at first to see how Karel could just cut them out of his life while he got on with his own. It niggled at first, until she could accept that that was what he had also done with her.

For the first three months after the twins and Robert were born she stayed at home, away from the hat salon and art dealership. But, when she returned to her work, it was with a new kind of interest and vigor that did not go unnoticed. It seemed that success brought success. The media took her up and made much of Mimi Steindler, her work and her famous husband, her large family, and fabulous lifestyle. Mimi maintained her fascination as she grew older. Her life flourished and there was, more so every year, a stronger sensual freedom about her that made her, not unlike Karel, amazingly attractive. There was no doubt that Mimi, like her father and her still good friend Barbara, had that special sensual seductiveness that is irresistible to the opposite sex. Mimi had matured into something special, and there was hardly anyone who could resist her charm.

From birth to five years, before school and lessons, the endless after-school activities that fill children's lives, and parties—never a birthday without a party—Mimi took her children with her everywhere she possibly could. She left them with Jay and the nannies and the rest of the family only occasionally in those five years—to take a holiday with her father. When the children were old enough, they too were included on those journeys to fascinating places.

The extended family worked. They were an unusual family, solid and lovely and together. And Milos and Angelica and Robert under the influence of Jay whom they adored as they did Mimi, and Rick whom they experienced as he drifted in and out of their lives as their frivolous godfather, were happy, bright and charming children. They were close with Barney, and the four much older sons of Jay's, who spoiled them and spend as much time with them in the Steindler house on East Sixty-third Street as they could.

One day when Mimi's three children, who were eight and six years old, were sitting with her in the kitchen of the Stefanik house having lunch, Milos asked, "Mommy, do you remember my friend Jimmy?"

"A blond boy with big sad eyes?"

"I don't know about sad. They're just eyes. He was at my party."

"He sat next to me," interjected Angelica.

Mimi did remember him. "Oh, yes. What about him?"

Mimi could not miss the looks that passed between the three children. They were in cahoots about something, that was for certain. There were very close, told each other everything. Sophia, hovering around the table refilling plates, suddenly sat down, a platter in her hand. Now Mimi knew something was really on. Her children adored Sophia and confided everything in her. She was in on whatever they were about to spring on her.

"Can he come and live with us?" It was left to Milos to pop the question, but Mimi could see it posed in the eyes of all the children.

"What's this about, Milos?" she asked.

"He likes it at our house. He lives with a cousin. He's got no mother or father or sisters or brothers like we do. Nobody really to play with and take care of him."

"What about his cousin?"

"She's very neurotic. She forgets about him most of the time," said Angelica.

"Who said she's neurotic?"

"I heard my teacher at school tell that to the principal," said Milos.

"Do you know what neurotic means?" asked Mimi.

"No," all three chimed in at the same time.

"But it can't be good," announced Robert.

"Why do you say that, Robby?"

"Because if it was, he wouldn't want to come and live with us." All three were looking at their mother as if she as really rather stupid.

Mimi turned to Sophia, feeling somewhat outsmarted by her children. "What do you know about this?"

"Only that every time I see that child he reminds me of you that first day you were brought to me at Beechtrees. He has the same lost, alone look in his eyes."

Mimi had come such a long way since that day, her fortunes had changed so drastically, that such memories, though still there, were difficult to square with her life now. But her children—so sweet and innocent, secure in themselves and with their family, pleading for a little friend—and Sophia's words made her feel pain for a child she hardly knew. She thought of the kindness of all the strangers who had come to her aid. Then she thought of Barbara, who had befriended her and given her the greatest and most consistent support.

She called her children to her side. Mimi kissed Angelica. She was such a beautiful, calm and clever child, with a seductive charm that by now Mimi could recognize as a Stefanik trait. No one could resist Angelica, any more than they had been able to resist Mimi when she had been a child. She kissed her daughter, who leaned in against her mother. Robert pulled his chair close to Mimi's and the two boys sat on it. Milos on the seat, Robert balanced on the back. "What will happen if Jimmy doesn't come to live with us?"

"He'll be sent to boarding school next term."

"And he doesn't want to go?"

"No."

"And what if he comes to live with us, and then one day something should happen and we're unable to keep him? Think how desperate he would feel to be left behind."

"But that wouldn't happen. You wouldn't let it happen, Mom." That was Milos.

"Well, you're right about that. I won't let that happen. That's why he cannot come to live with us."

"You won't help him? But we told him you would help. And Dad would too," a dejected-looking Angelica told Mimi.

"I didn't say I wouldn't help, Angelica. I said he couldn't come and live with us."

"OK, Mom. How?"

"Well, first of all, why don't I go and see the neurotic cousin?" They all began to giggle at that idea.

"Why?" asked Sophia.

"To ask her if we may invite Jimmy to come and stay with us for the summer in the house in Martha's Vineyard." Mimi saw just a vestige of approval in the faces sitting around her. "What do you think of that idea?" Grudging nods of assent.

"That's nice, Mom, but it doesn't much solve the problem of school and sleeping over at our house."

"Well, it might if I was to suggest to his cousin that we would be pleased to have Jimmy at our house any time that it's convenient for his cousin. Weekends as well, during the school year. And, you guys, if that's not a good solution for all concerned, then we'll rethink Jimmy's problem."

"Why is that better than just living with us?"

"Because he will have the best friends and a second home to come to, and he won't feel left out. More a welcome visitor, with a home and family of his own. Trust me on this. I know what I'm talking about."

Sophia rose from the far end of the table and went to Mimi. She took her face in her hands. There were tears in her eyes when she kissed Mimi on the forehead. Sophia understood in her the deep emotional sources of such reasoning. The children read that as a seal of approval. The boys jumped off the chair with a clatter and dramatically shook each other's hands.

"Tomorrow?" Robert demanded.

"As soon as the cousin can see me."

"That'll do," declared Milos.

"But!"

"Oh, there's always a but." Angelica looked very annoyed. Buts didn't suit her temperament.

"Dad has to approve."

"No problem," said Milos. The children knew that Mimi would have no problem with Jay about Jimmy. They had learned that it is the woman who decides what happens at home. Each of them in turn declared Mimi a wonderful mother, and begged to be taken to tea at Rumpelmayer's.

What made this large family work was their devotion to a family life. The successful careers of both Mimi and Jay financed it. Jay's fascinating work in publishing, the power he held in that mercurial world, furnished the entire family with interesting people and events. Life felt expansive. Their house was filled with people, love and good times. The wide range in the ages of the children ensured a constant stream of young adults. The youngest children, with all their friends and trends, their projects and interests, made a hectic fiesta of their lives. The ex-wives and the ex-lovers, Rick and Claire, wove themselves into the fabric of Mimi and Jay's life, as friends, leaving their intimate relationships to rest in peace in the past.

Rick did pick up the mantle that Dr. Quinn threw down and worked his practice out of California, but never altered his lifestyle. His reputation in the States was that of "finest brain surgeon," but "an eccentric man." To the Third World he was "the eminent Dr. Walters, surgeon, healer, guru." He remained the same free spirit. The surfer seeking the perfect wave. The handsome, suntanned charmer. Young beauties came and went from his life. Everyone in the family loved him for the same reasons Mimi did. She, of course, though they rarely got together, still loved him sexually.

After the birth of the twins they remained sexually apart. Although neither of them ever discussed the subject, that was they way it evolved. But after many years, one day when he was in New York, they were having lunch together at his favorite Japanese restaurant. The conversation took a turn where neither of them could ignore the inevitable. They had been talking about a family dinner at the house the night before. It was a spectacular event with all the children and adults and Barbara and Karel and Sophia. A very amusing occasion. Now, having hashed over the events of the evening, Rick was saying, "You're even more beautiful and happy than that first time I saw you in Patmos. You and Jay have made a wonder-family. Almost a dynasty, actually. I can understand, I always did, why you like being married to him. He makes you feel good."

Mimi smiled. "That's true. Jay knows how to consistently make you feel good. The only thing is, he never makes you feel great. Now you, on the other hand, make me feel great. Oops, Freudian slip. What I meant was, people—you make people feel great."

She was smiling. It was one of Mimi's more seductive and sensual smiles that he had not picked up on for years. He made no comment, simply called for the bill. And then, it was there in his eyes, an understanding of her sexual hunger, her desire for sexual oblivion, greatness rather than good.

"This is a frivolous thing to do."

"If that's the way you want to think of it, fine."

In bed at the Plaza, Rick was overwhelmed by her passion, her hunger for all things erotic between them. He was moved by the many times she told him how much he was missed sexually, the bliss she experienced because he set her free. Later, after they had dressed and were having a glass of champagne in the sitting room of his suite, it prompted him to say, "Mimi, I assumed you had with Jay what we have just had. I never asked you. I don't actually feel I should now, but I need to know that you are happy with him and in your marriage. Because if . . ."

"Stop. You have to know I am very happy. I passed up great sex feeding my libido for good sex. If you call having an orgasm every time your husband fucks you, and he fucks you every day, good sex. That's what I chose because I wanted a great marriage and the family I have more. I have no regrets. Please don't say anything. I wouldn't have missed the experience of my marriage and family for anything. And especially the twins and Robert and your being a part of my life. I have a household with a buzz. It keeps Jay and me young in heart and spirit. It's our life. Now let's go home to Jay and the children, they'll be waiting for us."

Gossip wove envious tales around the Steindlers and their lifestyle. Mimi's life looked set: husband, children, success, the American dream in New York City.

Chapter 24

It was not a difficult decision to make. This, the opulent eighties, was a time when the Western world had gone mad with extravagance. There were more millionaires and billionaires than avarice could have imagined. Karel went first to the bank and drew out of the safe-deposit box the red leather envelope. He had not looked inside it for more than thirty years. He placed it in a brown envelope, tucked it under his arm and set out for Christie's, the auction house.

Mimi was now Karel's only surviving child. A road accident in France had killed Laslo, his only son. Much as he loved Mimi's three children they didn't seem to come into it anymore than Mimi did. She was a wealthy woman in her own right, and Jay was a very wealthy man. They had no need of the contents of the red leather envelope. When Karel died, Mimi and her children would inherit a tidy sum, more than sufficient. Selfish to rob her of the vast wealth these gems would bring? Maybe so. He gave it hardly a thought. He ruled his life, his family, he always had. He saw no need to ask Mimi, or in fact even to tell her what he was doing. The estimate was in excess of ten million dollars. Christie's needed three months for cataloguing and hyping. The contents of the case would go into their most prestigious Jewelry and Gems sale of the year in Geneva. Karel never thought twice about it, but assigned the jewels to the sale.

Several months later he went to Paris with the proceeds of the Christie's sale. They were into a savings account.

Astonishingly he had received twenty-four million dollars. With lawyers and two Czech dissidents, intellectuals who made more political sense than he had heard in the last thirty years, documents were drawn up releasing the funds as soon as the country had extricated itself from Soviet puppet rule. They were to be used specifically for a free Czechoslovakia, unencumbered by any foreign power. On one condition: everything there that was legally his should be returned to his daughter, the Countess Mimi Alexandra Stefanik. That all other private property confiscated since the Second World War should be returned to its rightful owners.

Then he flew home to his house and his books, to New York that he now loved as he once loved Prague, to the women who could satisfy his lust, and to Barbara, the enchantress who still held him as no other woman had. This was his world now. With this final gift he felt that he had done all that he could for his country.

Mimi sensed a subtle change in Karel. She knew nothing about the sale in Geneva or the account opened in Paris. She simply sensed a change, a lightheartedness (not that he had ever been exactly heavyhearted). It was an extra lift of spirits in him. The most outward sign of change was his reluctance to see any of the Czech exiles and refugees to whom his door had always been open since his arrival in New York. He seemed to have less patience with the endless political talk that had been so much a part of their lives and that Mimi had rebelled against for the last twenty years. She felt great relief: his loyalty and passion for his country had burned itself out at last. Mimi had her father all to herself. His real mistress, the one who had stolen him from her—his country and its politics—had at last been ousted. Why, she wondered, had it taken so long?

She sat on the end of the bed watching her father pack. "I wish you would let me take you to the airport, Poppa."

"Not necessary, angel."

"How long will you be away, Poppa?"

"I'm leaving it open-ended. But I think about a month."

Mimi never questioned too closely her father's travel plans, but she was certain he was not traveling alone. And if she were wrong, and he was, then most likely there would be a lovely young thing waiting at an airport somewhere for him. Karel remained, even as he grew older, the same charismatic figure that women had always been drawn to.

His houseman-chauffeur arrived for Karel's traveling bag,

bearing a silver ice bucket. Buried up to its neck in shaved ice was a bottle of vintage Bollinger, with two champagne flutes.

"Here or downstairs?" Karel asked her.

"Here, I think. I do so love this room. I think it's the handsomest and most interesting in the house. Except for the library, of course. This bedroom could never belong to anyone but you, Poppa. It's such a perfect reflection of you."

"You always did like it, ever since the first day we moved into this house. Remember how you used to climb into bed with me and we would have breakfast together? And now the twins, whenever they're here in the house staying over, do exactly the same."

They were served their flutes of champagne and together sat on the end of the four-poster bed and drank. They watched the chauffeur gather up the things: suitcase, coat over the arm, several books. Then he left the room, announcing, "Twenty minutes, Count."

"He still calls you 'Count,' even after all these years. He sees you as the hero-Count," Mimi teased.

"He will never change. He has worn me down, can call me whatever he likes. Remember, Mimi, if you need anything, he's here for you as he has always been for me."

"You make it sound as if you are going away forever."

"Well, I'm not." Father and daughter were gazing into each other's eyes. He reached out and touched her golden hair. "Mimi, I don't think I tell you often enough what a splendid woman you have turned out to be. I love you as a daughter, Mimi, but I think I love you even more as a woman. You have it all. No wonder Jay never let you go."

She was stunned. That was not like Karel. He had always been a flatterer, but never one to express his deeper feelings. In order to cover her own emotional response, she teased her father, "Are you saying, you wouldn't either?"

He hesitated for only a second, then drained his glass. Placing it on the occasional table in front of him, he turned back to face her. "Well, I haven't, have I, my Mimi?"

Then taking her face in his hands he kissed her gently on the lips. He took her hand and said, "Let's go, there's a plane

I have to catch." He touched the tip of her nose with the tip of his finger and added, "I'll bring you back a surprise."

Barbara Dunmellyn had the best kind of fame and fortune, the kind that allows you privacy. A condition where your work is more photographed than yourself, where gossip circulates only narrowly, among those involved in the art world and the private life of one of their stars. Where the work you create demands solitude, the luxury of spending great slices of the day alone in the world of your imagination. That marvelous, selfish place that confers complete control of what you do with it. Barbara understood why men found those aspects of her attractive. They added a frisson, a bonus, when you had the looks of an aging movie star, a provocative female sensuality, and a lust for men that drew them like bees to a flower. If men adored her, which they did, and she could still draw, as she did, men of all ages to her, who yearned only to be loved by her, she was bound to excite the curiosity of other women. Those men's women, the wives, girlfriends, lovers, were confounded by the power and control Barbara had over her suitors.

She had always enjoyed the company of men. She had never put them aside from her life, only from her work. And only during that long period of time while she was married to Brandon had she confined them to the fringes of her life. Marriage and painting had come first. Those years were crucial in the development of her work. Barbara had never fooled herself, even during that time, that men were as crucial to her life as her painting was.

No one was more surprised than she herself that her marriage to Brandon had lasted as long as it had. Their work, the demands of the New York art world, the busy creative minds working on overdrive, virtually precluded domesticity. The marriage demanded sacrifice. But sacrifice only works when it is offered naturally, when it is not an obligation. Intelligence and a mutual love and admiration for each other had kept the marriage together. Those same qualities sustained the friendship between Brandon and her even after their divorce.

Several times Barbara had come close to undertaking marriage again. There had been several men whom she knew could have added to her life; interesting, successful men, intelligent enough to know how they might make a marriage with her work. But always Barbara had stopped just short of the commitment. Finally, only one man interested her beyond all others: Count Karel Stefanik.

Even now, after all these years, he had only to appear across the room and she was his. He could still thrill her with the honeyed sound of his voice. She could still give herself up to him sexually as to no other man. Never, since that first day at the Stork Club, had she missed a shiver of delight at seeing him, or not felt immediate desire, wanting him. They had been lovers for a very long time. Sometimes they thought of themselves as tragic lovers, the playthings of fate that pre-dated their own first meeting. For several years now Barbara had realized that she would marry no one: she was emotionally pledged to Karel. Not once had she ever revealed that to him. It was her secret, for her alone to live with. She saw no reason to lay on him the burden of her commitment to him. They were happy enough the way they were. Nothing ever changed for them. When they were together, erotic desire overcame words, they were wholly together.

Barbara's special kind of fame was suited perfectly for a long-time affair with Karel. Except for their attachment to Mimi, they lived in worlds that never overlapped. That was a blessing for a secret love affair. It gave them the freedom to travel together unafraid of bumping into a friend or colleague. And Karel did like to take Barbara away to romantic places around the world least once a year. Only Ching Lee knew about the affair, because in New York it was conducted in Barbara's flat or in her studio.

She opened her eyes to the warmth of his breath on her shoulder, to the feel of his lips and their gentle kiss on the nape of her neck. She sighed and rolled over to face him.

"Is it morning already?"

"Not quite, that's why I woke you. Almost. It will be soon. I want us to see the dawn break over this mountain before we leave."

In the dark she couldn't make out his features, but she traced them with her fingers and kissed them with hungry lips. They were naked, on a large bed. It was hot, very hot, even at that hour, even in the darkness with the stars still visible. They were in a love-pavilion that he had created just for them, a place of stone and glass, little more than a great square room with a bed, and a glass roof that slid back. A love-pavilion on top of a small mountain of cypress, olive and pine trees running wild, left to nature for years, of scrubby bush and wild flowers that plunged all the way down the small rocky island into the Aegean Sea. He had built it for her, for them, and would take no other woman there. It was their special place in the world, a place where they made love, with extravagant, unbridled sexual ardor, where they could call in their ecstasy of sexual bliss upon the Greek gods, where assuredly no one else would hear the violence of their passion, shared only with the mountain. This was their private world where they indulged themselves in their passion for each other.

She felt his lips on her nipples, his hands caressing her breasts, the touch of his skin on her fingertips. The night was fading, the sky turning from black to gray. He pulled her into his arms and they lay on their sides together, hands caressing, lips making love, as they sensed the light break over the sea, over their island haven. A morning mist was lingering low all around them. It was a magical place he had found, as others before him had in ancient times. Once the sun burned away the mist, from their bed they could look down through the scrub and trees to see a near-perfect small Greek temple. Its roof was gone, but the marble columns and pediments stood intact after many hundreds of years. Further below it and off to the right, another smaller temple, round, of similar white marble, an aesthetically perfect jewel. In that light one could see no more than dark forms, and barely discern the water under a moon and stars not yet vanished from the sky. Karel had discovered this tiny island, so like a limb of heaven cast upon the sea by one of the mythical Greek gods. It was several miles from a larger island with villages and people, but a remote, not obviously alluring place, off the tourist maps. He had bought the drop in the sea, which is what he called it, with its one deep cove, its grotto and miniature temples. There he had built a modest house of several rooms, and there too lived a caretaker and cook. Nearby he kept a small boat. These people never ventured up the mountain when Karel was there with Barbara. They allowed them their private world.

A streak of light pierced what was left of the night. The dawn light and the heat of the sun began burning off the mist. It was like the dawn of creation, up there on their mountain. The sun, like a bright pink spotlight, illuminated the round temple and inched its way up from there, meeting the trees and at last the rectangular building of ancient columns. Light crept toward their own pavilion.

Barbara slipped from his arms and on to her knees, the better to look down the mountain. On his knees behind her he took his position and grasped her waist. He was stirred by the dawn of another day, and distracted by the sensuous, seductive movement of her bottom back and forth against him. His fingers opened a place for him, and he plunged in. She marveled that she could after all these years, after all the sex there had been between them, still feel as if he were taking her for the first time. They fucked, he withdrawing and plunging in slowly and deliberately, again and again taking possession of her cunt, making her his own. And Barbara used her cunt muscles to caress him, to entice him, to excite him with her own fuckings.

The sunlight was moving fast now across the stone floor, and poured over them from the open roof above. She pulled his hand away from her waist over her shoulder, until she was able to reach it, and bit hard into his flesh. She came, and called out. He loved it, to hear her voice echo with ecstasy in that deserted romantic island of the gods. And now he fucked her harder, with greater passion.

For hours they indulged themselves in sex and orgasms. They bathed in a sunken bath on a lower level of their love-pavilion. Then naked, under the now-bright sunshine, they lay on the mats on the stone terrace and ate fruit and bread, honey and butter, and drank hot black coffee brewed on a stove sunk into the stones of the terrace. Karel never seemed to get enough of Barbara during their sexual escapades. Even after the sex he lingered over her. He knew every inch of her body, could make it his own with just his tongue and his fingers.

They were to leave the island: it was a matter of only a few hours, but still he lingered over her. He licked her body, her breasts, the nipples, rubbed his face in her soft pubic hair, opened the lips of her cunt and licked her clitoris with pointed tongue, and then trailed it along her slit. He kissed her there and nibbled with a hungry mouth. Unperturbed, the birds were singing their early morning song, the cicadas were clicking their incessant tune, a soft breeze rustled the leaves in the trees, and the sun was baking her body. His tongue told her all she needed to hear of his feelings for her.

She stretched like a lazy, slinky cat, her very skin feeling so alive, every morsel of her being teeming with life. She came, he rolled her over on her side and hugged her to him. They kissed and he whispered, "We have to go."

In the pavilion, she slipped into her white cotton trousers and a white shirt, which she tied in a knot under her naked breasts. As he watched her, she sensed the strength of his desire for her. It seemed even greater than usual. The effect on him of this mountain, she thought, this piece of heaven fallen into the sea. The pressure of so much time past, of all those who had worshiped here, rowed out in boats and spent time on this tiny island to build a temple to their gods. He stepped into his white cotton trousers, rolled up the sleeves of his white shirt and left it hanging open, unbuttoned. They put on sandals and tidied the pavilion. Karel cranked back the roof and they closed the doors. They placed a stone lid over the camp burner, looked once more at their love-pavilion, then hand in hand walked away from it to take the narrow stone path cut through the bush down to the temples. There they stood in silence just looking out to sea.

Here they had a different vantage point on the mountain and the sea. One filled with mystery, echoes of another age, whispers on the breeze seemingly from the gods of this place. For them it was an Olympus, a spiritual home, as Olympus was home to the gods of the Greeks. But it was even more than that for Barbara and Karel, it was eternity. He recited to her quietly in the words of the Greek poet Seferis,

Since then I've seen many new landscapes: green plains intermingling soil and sky, man and seed, in an irresistible dampness; plane-trees and fir trees; lakes with wrinkled visions and swans immortal because they'd lost their voices—scenery unfolded by my willing companion, that strolling player, as he sounded the long horn that had ruined his lips and that destroyed with its shrill note whatever I managed to build, like the trumpet at Jericho. I saw an old picture in some low-ceiling room; a lot of people were admiring it. It showed the raising of Lazarus. I don't recall either the Christ in it or the Lazarus. Only in one corner, the disgust portrayed on someone's face as he gazed at the miracle as if he were smelling it. He was trying to protect his breathing with the huge cloth draped around his head. This "Renaissance" gentleman taught me not to expect much from the Second Coming . . .

and he touched her soul. In the little round temple they stood leaning against the pillars, silent once more, just listening to the sea, the sound of the birds, nature. She marveled at the sensitive soul Karel hid from the world so well, a soul that could seek out such a place as this, make it his own and save it for posterity, and then give it to her. Arms around each other's waist, they walked down from the round temple and walked through the wild bush, the olive trees and cypress to find the path leading to the steep stone steps Karel had had carved from the sea to the top of the mountain and their pavilion.

Before they descended he turned to have a last look at the small temples nestling in the trees, the sun beating down on the white, weather- and time-worn marble now. He turned away from them to look at her. He stroked Barbara's hair and touched her cheek with the back of his hand, kissed her lips with tenderness.

"No regrets?"

"Regrets?"

"I have to know."

"No regrets. About us?"

"Yes, about us."

"Regrets, Karel? Only passion, ecstasy, love, that's all I know with you."

"It's been the love of a lifetime for me too."

There were tears in their eyes. There were hardly any words to describe the magic of that moment. It was the island, the mountain, the temples. There was a magic there that suggested eternity, something greater than life itself. It was momentarily theirs, and they knew it. He gathered her hands in his, raised them to his lips and kissed them. Then, quite gracefully, he went down on his knees and asked her, "Marry me. Until this moment I hardly realized we have been one heart, one soul, ever since that first time I made love to you, that New Year's Eve during the war. Now there is so little time left, I want us to be together more, for the whole world to see us. I want everyone to know the place you have in my heart. Will you become my wife? Do me that honor."

There could be but one answer to that. Hand in hand they walked slowly down the mountain. Occasionally they would stop for a few seconds to drink in the beauty of the place, and then proceed. It was like a little Zen prayer, or a form of thanks to the gods for the gift of life.

Yorgos the caretaker and Marika the cook were as tearful as usual when they said goodbye. Barbara and Karel boarded the small boat and piloted it themselves back to the main island. There they only just caught the ferryboat going to Athens. Only when standing at the prow, among other travelers, watching the island recede to become a dot on the horizon, did Barbara realize what a momentous thing had happened. Marrying each other! It had been so important to them and so very private that they had not even announced it to the caretaker and his wife. Nor did they mention it to each other again, not on the *Narida,* en route to Piraeus, nor on the plane from Athens to New York.

In the taxi driving from Kennedy Airport the first sight of New York's skyline brought smiles to their faces.

They were still in their Greek island clothes. "I'm taking you home to change," he told her. "I'll pick you up for lunch. Wear something glamorous, wonderful. I'll call Mimi and Jay to see if they can join us. No." He changed his mind. "That can wait. You and I, just you and I for a celebratory lunch. Where would you like to have lunch?"

When the taxi pulled up to her apartment house on Fifth

Avenue, Karel stepped out. They greeted the doorman who took her luggage. He walked her to the elevator.

"Happy?"

"A kind of happiness I've never experienced before."

"Me too. New beginnings."

"It's always new beginnings when I'm with you, and it always will be. One o'clock. I'll be back for you at one o'clock. No, better still, would you mind meeting me?"

"No."

"Good, I've something to do. We'll meet at one o'clock, don't be late," he called over her shoulder.

She watched him, happier than she had ever known him. Barbara rushed into the flat and flung her arms round Lee. "You're the first to know, the *very* first to know—we're going to get married. We're going to grow old together, to begin again. A new life, all over again, just like the first time we met in 1943. I have to hurry, bathe and change. I want to look really glamorous. I've had the most wonderful time. I'm so happy, Lee."

The look on Ching Lee's face told her how pleased he was for her. He vanished, to return with a bottle of champagne and two glasses. The ever-faithful Lee and she drank together. Barbara had been away only ten days with Karel, but now, here in her home again, it seemed to her that she had been with him a lifetime on that mountain. And that, in some strange sense, they had brought their mountain home with them.

"No messages, no calls, no mail, nothing. Don't tell me anything, Lee. I want nothing outside my own selfish little world to touch me yet. I just have to dress and go to lunch, and then we'll do everything later. I don't want to keep him waiting, not one minute. And not a word, Lee, not a word to anyone, until we are ready to announce our news."

They had chosen the Oak Room at the Plaza for sentimental reasons, she thought. That's where they had dined when he had returned after the war. In the bath she could think of nothing but the morning when she had awakened in the pavilion on the mountain. The sun as it broke through the mist and burned it off. The views from the bed. The feel of him inside her, that moment of orgasm shared, all under the cool marble eye of the ancient Greek temple glistening white in the sun. His voice, the words of Seferis ringing in her ears, that moment when he had kissed her hand and dropped to his knees. Regrets? Not since that first day when she had seen him across the room at the Stork Club had she had one regret. Not in forty years of loving him. Not one regret about how they had handled their long-time affair. Regret? Only passion, love, bliss had she known with him.

She reached for the sponge floating in her warm scented bath of essence of almond, and plunged it in the water, squeezed it out over her body. She recalled their breakfast together, lying on mats under the sun. No plump, purple figs could ever taste so divine as those had tasted to her. Her very taste buds seemed to stir at the memory. She sponged her body and silky rivulets of warm water trickled over her shoulders and breasts, and she thought of him. The memories would keep returning, holding a vision of their life together in her mind's eye, with the intensity of a romantic motion picture. They had loved each other so much, and they had lived so well with their love. Here was a love affair to rival Abelard and Eloise, Romeo and Juliet, Tristan and Isolde. She began laughing at herself. Silly sentimentality, romanticism gone mad. "A woman your age, and you are dreaming like a fool!" she scolded herself.

Barbara chose a two-piece dress: a white skirt of raw silk, its top of tiny black and white checks in the same material that clung to the body. It was tight at the waist, with a short flare at the bottom of the jacket. The sleeves were cut to be narrow from the elbow down, puffed from the elbow up, and to sit on the shoulder. Tailoring at its best from Yves Saint Laurent. The buttons of the jacket were black jet, so she chose black, high-heeled, alligator sandals and a Hermès handbag of black alligator, the shoulder strap a gold chain. Barbara had been lucky all her life to be able to dress her own hair. She did it now in the way she had worn it the first night they had met.

She rang for Lee, who on her instructions had snipped some white camellias off the tree in the conservatory, and now helped her place them in her hair. Her makeup was perfection. She viewed herself in the mirror. Karel was going to adore the way she looked.

She was still standing there looking at herself, feeling his happiness as strongly as her own, when Lee knocked at the door. He entered her bedroom. "A messenger brought this."

A small package in silver wrapping and gold ribbon, with a card attached to it. She knew immediately who it was from.

She tore open the envelope and read the card: "Wear this for me, for us, forever. I love you, Karel." She tore off the paper, then the lid of the box. Inside was a smaller box, a gray-velvet ring box. She opened it. She could hardly have imagined he would do such a thing. A square-cut diamond of enormous size, a million-dollar gem. She was overwhelmed by the lavishness of his gesture. Karel was not an extravagant man in such things. Oh, yes, a rare book, a fine painting—but such extravagance as this? In all their years together he had never showered her with luxurious gifts. Wonderful holidays and building her the love-pavilion had been the limit of his extravagances. Perhaps the odd piece of costly jewelry. But a million-dollar gem? She lifted the ring from the box. It was extraordinary, two baguettes on either side. She slipped it on her finger: it was a near perfect fit. She was dazzled by it. She had fifteen minutes left to get to him.

On the way over to the Plaza in the cab she could think only of the moment she would see him again, of how she felt about him. She had always felt that knowing him, having him for a lover, made her one of the luckiest women in the world. She was greeted effusively by the maître d', who shook her hand and led her to their table. Karel had booked exactly the right table, next to the window overlooking the park, the table where they had dined before. It was his favorite table: he had loved the Oak Room since their first dinner together there.

She was surprised not to find him sitting there waiting for her. He was late. She ordered a martini, very dry, with a twist of lemon. Her gaze kept returning to her ring. It was more than being dazzled by it; it was the sheer beauty of the object, the perfection of it, the clarity, the light and fire, its purity. On her finger it appeared such an enormous symbol of his love for her, of their love for each other. She checked her watch. He was very late. She ordered a second martini.

By two o'clock she knew that something was wrong. He wasn't coming. She was so devastated, she didn't know what to do about it. Quite obviously something must have come up. She would wait for a message. She perked herself up, and ordered oysters, September oysters, the first of the season, and a bottle of Chablis. He would want her to start. He would have a good explanation. An old beau passed the table and stopped to greet her. She realized she was chattering on, wanting him not to leave. But he did, and she was alone again, exposed to a growing anxiety. She ordered lamb cutlets and mint sauce, baby potatoes roasted, and mange-tout. When a waiter came and removed the other place setting, she told him in a voice that was much too loud, strident with tension. "Don't touch that, he's just late, he'll be here." Her own words calmed her.

By three o'clock the room was nearly empty. Soon she was the last one sitting at a table. Still she hoped he would appear. At a quarter to four the maître d' asked her if he could do anything for her before he left. He would leave the lights on if she wanted to remain at the table.

At 4:10 Lee walked into the dining room. She was sitting rigidly at the table. He sat down opposite her.

"Miss Barbara." Tears came into her eyes. "You will have to come with me."

Tears moistened her cheeks. She bit her upper lip.

"He's calling for you."

"How bad is it?"

Lee could barely speak. He shook his head.

"Where is he? What's happened?"

"He's had a bad stroke. He was leaving his house. Just as he was walking down the stairs, he collapsed."

"Mimi?"

"She's with him. She's taken it very badly. Sophia called me. She and somebody on the street helped him into the house. I got there real fast and we put him to bed. I called his doctor. He came right over. By the time I found Mimi we knew our worst fears had been realized. It was confirmed, a massive stroke."

Barbara covered her eyes. Her hands were trembling.

"When Mimi arrived she had already called a specialist, that man Rick, her friend the brain surgeon. He's there now."

"Can he speak?"

"It's very difficult for him to form words, and then only in a whisper. Rick sent me here for you. The Count was able to say 'Barbara.' That was all, just 'Barbara.' The doctor understood and asked me where you were. I knew you were here. You must go to him."

"Are they taking him to the hospital?"

"The doctor says no, no use. He's more comfortable where he is."

"Is there no hope?"

"No, none. I'm so sorry, Miss Barbara."

She swallowed hard. She took out her compact and dabbed at her eyes. Tears stained her face. "I don't think I can stand upright without your help, Lee," she told him, a tremor in her voice.

He helped her from the chair and together, she leaning on his arm, they walked slowly from the Oak Room of the Plaza Hotel to the car awaiting them.

Chapter 25

Sophia was the first person Barbara saw on entering the house, but she was too distraught even to acknowledge her presence. Barbara was in control of herself, but it was a tenuous control. She entered Karel's room. Jay was there standing at the window looking down into the garden. It was a beautiful room, large, with plum-colored walls and draperies of plum and silver-gray fabric, tied back with huge gray tassels. Sheer white curtains covering the open windows were moving in the warm breeze. On the walls were drawings by Leonardo da Vinci, Raphael and Titian, in carved gilt frames. In the seventeenth-century four-poster bed of Venetian silver-gilt he lay, his head resting on ivory linen-covered pillows edged in ecru lace, a poignantly mortal man amid the more durable finery he had amassed. Sitting next to him in a chair was Mimi, holding his hand. Rick was standing close by. It was he who saw Barbara at the door. He took her outside into the hall and closed the door quietly behind him.

"Can you save him, Rick?"

"No. I think you've come only just in time. He's been asking for you. I'll get Mimi out of the room."

"Will he know me?"

"Yes."

"What about Mimi?"

"He's all that matters now."

"Yes, of course."

Rick brought Barbara into the room. Mimi looked up. Her tear-stained face was filled with misery.

"He's going to die. Oh, Barbara, he's going to die. I can't bear it."

"You have to be brave," said Rick. "Come with me, I'm going to give you a shot and let Barbara sit with him."

"No, I don't want to leave him."

"Let Barbara sit with him."

"Barbara, he's asked for you, but I don't know if he'll recognize you. I'm so glad you're here."

She drew on all the strength she had in her body. She entered the room, sat down in the chair and took Karel's hand in hers. She thought for a moment her heart would break. He looked fine, exactly the same as when she had left him hours before. Only now his skin, the flesh of his hand, was cold. She couldn't bear the coldness of his hand. She stroked it, trying to bring warmth back into it. She felt him squeeze her hand ever so slightly. Maybe there was hope. She stroked his face, his hair, she bent forward and kissed him on the lips. They were still warm. She kissed him again, grateful to feel some warmth still in his body. Jay saw her and tears filled his eyes. He tiptoed quietly out of the room, leaving them alone.

Rick returned. With a massive effort of will Karel opened his eyes and focused them on Barbara. She smiled at him as best she could and placed his hand over hers so that he could feel the ring, and then her other hand over his. She could feel a faint movement, acknowledging that he understood she was wearing it.

"Move closer, move the chair closer, up towards him," suggested Rick. They moved it together. Rick carefully placed another pillow under his head and turned Karel slightly so that he had a better view of Barbara. It was a tremendous struggle and took many moments, but Karel did managed to form the words "love you," in a whisper just loud enough for Rick and Barbara to hear it.

She stood up and leaned over her lover. She told him, "I know. I love you too, I've always loved you, and I'll never leave you." Tears formed at the corner of his eyes. This man, who only hours before had been an energetic, vital human being of extraordinary quality and charm, virile, her handsome lover, was dying by inches.

"I'd better get Mimi," Rick told her.

Barbara wanted to slip in between the sheets and gather him in her arms, for him to die there knowing the warmth of her body for one last time, how much she loved him. But she knew that was impossible, for Mimi's sake. Their relationship had been a secret they had both lived with for her sake at the beginning. It had continued thus for complex and emotionally volatile reasons. This seemed no time to change the pattern that had grown to be her and Karel's life together. If he had lived, they could have faced breaking the truth to Mimi, but now? She sat down again in the chair and continued caressing his hair. She felt his body giving out, slipping away into death.

Mimi appeared in the room. Barbara began to rise from the chair, still holding Karel's hand. Rick touched her shoulder and said, "No, stay there, Barbara. Mimi, why don't you hold him, he loves you so much?" She crawled on to the bed and Rick raised Karel enough for her to slip an arm behind him. She sat there holding him, with Barbara stroking his hand or his hair. He barely formed the words with his lips, no sound came out, but Barbara was able to read them. "Love you." Then he closed his eyes. His life had gone.

Mimi was not prepared for the death of her father. Her whole life, her entire existence, had hinged on him; he had always meant life for her. Even during those years of silence and separation, she had always known that he was alive and loved her. She couldn't imagine a world without her father in it. He had always been her tower of strength, and now, in a matter of moments, the strength that had sustained her was gone. The loss of her father was incalculable, her life was altered utterly. Those around her understood and gave their support. Mimi's love for her husband and her children, her extended family, was what gave her the strength to get on with her life. Not being prepared for the death of her father was one thing, but the aftermath of his death also was something she had been totally unprepared for.

Karel left his affairs in good order with explicit instructions that his body was to be returned to his family's estate, a hundred miles outside Prague. There his ancestors had been interred for the last five hundred years. Mimi had been so traumatized during the last hour of her father's life that, although she was there with him to the end, she simply had not comprehended his overwhelming love and devotion to Barbara. She did not understand the relationship between Barbara and her father, nor that his last words were for her. It was all Mimi could do to comprehend that he was dying. It had been impossible for her to understand anything else. Barbara Dunmellyn had been Mimi's friend for most of her life. She had been slipping in and out of the Stefanik household as a friend of Mimi's for years. The relationship between Karel and Barbara had always appeared to be one of cordiality, respect, a warm but distant kind of affection. Mimi had not considered it odd that Barbara should be present at her father's deathbed or holding his hand. The gesture had accorded with her own distress. Barbara was her best friend, who loved her father because he was first a remarkable man and second Mimi's father. Only the men, Rick and Jay, had understood immediately that a great secret love had existed between Karel and Barbara. Neither had discussed it with Mimi, sensing this was not the time or the place for her to assimilate a secret kept from her by two people who loved her as much as they had.

As for Barbara, she kept up a façade of controlled emotion. There was the right amount of sadness for the death of her close friend's father. In reality she was no less shattered by Karel's death than Mimi. He was the great love of her life, theirs had been a great love story. She felt his loss as she had never felt the loss of any other man who loved her. When Karel had asked her to marry him and they had acknowledged to each other how powerful their feelings were, how committed they were to each other, and had been for all those years, only then had she realized that always he had been and would be the only love of her life.

Should she now emerge from the shadows of their other lives to show the world their passionate relationship? It was something she had yearned for, but had never known. When Ching Lee had appeared in the Oak Room at the Plaza with the terrible news, her happiness had been blotting out all else. So only then had she thought of Mimi and how they would have explained their relationship to her. But none of that mattered now he was gone. What they had been to each other would die their secret. With his death a part of Barbara died too. Truths such as that could not be told. It was therefore extremely difficult for her, but a necessity, to ask Mimi to allow her to accompany Karel's body to Czechoslovakia with her. Mimi took it as a gesture of support and accepted. So the two women, with help from Barbara's uncle, obtained through the Soviet Embassy the necessary documents to allow them, quietly and without any fanfare, to transport the body of Count Karel Stefanik back to his homeland and bury it on the family estate.

Neither woman was prepared for the aftermath of Karel's death any more than for his sudden demise. He had long ago given up the Catholic faith. But, according to his wishes, a service was held for him in St. Patrick's Cathedral on Fifth Avenue. Two bishops and a cardinal, whom he had known for years, officiated at the service. Since he had become an American citizen, Karel had dropped his title, but during that service he was remembered as Count Karel Stefanik. Both women were much moved that hundreds of people attended the service and many more wrote letters of condolence from all around the world, people neither woman had ever heard of. He was a man who, after his courageous action for the people of his country, had kept a low profile for the rest of his life. But he had, too, lived a life of many secrets that neither woman knew anything about. Involved in it were some of the people that came to mourn him. Apart from the actual death of her father, what shattered Mimi most was that he had lived an enormously rich and varied life that she had never been a part of. She had only been a small portion of his life, whereas she had been made to feel that she was very nearly the whole of it. He had blocked her out of so much going on in his life, and she had never known it. That didn't diminish her love for him, only made her realize she had succumbed to his charm and the love he had for her. Yet it was only a crumb of what he could have given her.

When she read the obituaries in the London *Times,* the *New York Times,* and the other papers from around the world, she realized what real power he had maintained in several walks of life. That he was an existential man in every sense of the word. That he had never been tied down by anything, a free

spirit who never stopped fighting for the right of every man
to live that way. Every day fresh revelations as to who this
man had been, what this man had done with his life, came to
light. Mimi had had a giant of a father, and Barbara had had
a giant of a lover. Neither of them would ever fully replace
him in her heart.

Karel died on September 7th, 1987, and his body was returning to a homeland still under Soviet control after the invasion that had taken place years before. Mimi had left
Czechoslovakia as a child of five and had never returned, nor
had any desire to. She could barely understand why her father
should request this last ritual, knowing well that the country
was still under the influence of the Soviet Union.

She had long ago ceased to think about Czechoslovakia, it
had no relation to her or her life. Mimi was very American,
had embraced the American way of life since she was a child.
Her husband and children were American, she felt even less
European than the other members of her family. She felt no
connection with Czechoslovakia. So she hardly knew how to
handle the local details that needed her attention if she was to
bring her father home to rest. It was because of that she made
contact for the first time with distant cousins to announce her
imminent arrival and the purpose of her visit. "Keep it quiet
and we'll help" had come the answer. And so Barbara and
Mimi left with the coffin for Prague. Jay, denied permission
to accompany the cortège for reasons not revealed to them,
saw off the grieving women at Kennedy Airport.

Mimi was extremely nervous and could only think of getting in and out as fast as possible. From the moment the
wheels touched down at the airport on the fringes of Prague,
she felt disoriented. She watched her father's casket manhan-
dled from the plane to a waiting hearse. It was hot and extremely humid. She and Barbara were surrounded by a dozen
men, officials of various departments there with documents
and seemingly endless stamps and seals needed to process the
paperwork. Questions, escorts and demands were a nightmare
for the two women. The first half hour was a muddle which
Mimi could hardly cope with. The cousins, whom she had
never met, were as confused and indecisive about what to do
as Mimi herself. Finally it all wore her down. She lost her

temper and took over with an assertiveness and efficiency that stunned the men she was dealing with. For them this was unheard-of behavior. Fluent in Czech and Polish, and only slightly less so in Russian, she was quite capable of making herself understood. An hour and a half later they were out of customs and leaving the airport.

Some distance outside Prague, much to her surprise, having shaken off all the red tape and disposed of the government escorts, their convoy of a hearse and two cars was stopped on the road by a policeman who signaled them to pull over to the soft shoulder behind two black Citroens. The policeman vanished immediately, riding away from the cars on his motorcycle down a nearly deserted secondary motorway. Mimi's heart nearly stopped. She had no idea what to expect: least of all the several men who walked from the cars to greet her. They opened the doors. She stepped out when she recognized them as some of the dissidents who had known her father, men of whom Karel had been particularly fond.

For many years they had frequented his house and dined at his table in New York.

Mimi nearly burst into tears at the sight of their sad faces, that and relief that they were friends not foes. This was so hard for her, this return that she had never expected to make. She was wearing a deep purple linen dress bordered in black along the hem and cuffs. On her head she wore a black, wide-brimmed hat that shaded her eyes; she had black gloves and a matching handbag. As soon as she recognized the men she removed her hat. Her blonde hair shone in the sun. She handed it to Barbara who had followed her from the car. One by one the men greeted Mimi and kissed her hand. She was amazed that they should be there and insist on accompanying her to the crypt where Karel was to be interred.

Standing at the side of the road surrounded by them, Mimi felt extraordinarily strange—not ill but not all well either. She put it down to grief. It was as if she were only half there, as if someone else was in her shoes living through this ordeal. At one point she thought she might even faint. But she rallied herself, and suddenly she was really all there and very much aware of what was going on. She turned away from the men she was talking to because she was suddenly conscious of one particular man, the only man there she didn't know. She felt herself being drawn to him. He had a powerfully calming and yet exciting presence. He was a handsome young man with black hair, dark sensuous eyes that sparkled with life, a quiet man with dimples when he smiled and a bushy moustache. It was madness, utterly ridiculous, but she wished that he would hold her in his arms, not to comfort her but to instill in her some of himself. His passion for life, his quiescent sensuality, those things she felt she had lost since the day Karel died.

They gazed into each other's eyes. He felt something so strong for Mimi that without hesitation he made his way past the other men to stand in front of her. In all the excitement of this roadside reunion, introductions somehow escaped them. He raised her hand in both of his and held it for several seconds before he kissed it.

Mimi sensed destiny. There was no other way to explain her sense of belonging, of being some part of this stranger's life. She felt a shiver of excitement, and it was visible. She knew he understood. She could see it in his eyes. They spoke to her of sensual love, of new beginnings, and he knew she heard him. His first words to her were, "Have courage, soon you will be free . . ." He hesitated, suddenly aware that others were listening. Then he continued, ". . . to put your life together after this sad time." But Mimi knew that he meant much more than that. She could see in those seductive, intelligent eyes that he wanted to say more, but the time and place were against him.

"Your father was a remarkable man who impressed me very much. I may have liked his politics but I liked even more his self-possession, his will to live his life on his terms. He grabbed his destiny with both hands and made a life for himself with it. Everything changes. That's life, the changes. I am so happy to meet you, even if it has had to be under these sad circumstances."

What was he telling her? That destiny was placing a continental kiss on her hand on a soft verge in a Communist country she had hoped never to see again? Mimi tried to make light of what she was feeling for this young man and his words, but it was difficult because he spoke to her in English, a soft voice with an accent not unlike her father's, sensuous and filled with charm.

He smiled at her. It was one of those smiles conjured up to give reassurance, support, the message "I'm with you."

"Thank you. You seem very wise about my father, as if you knew him very well. Were you a frequent visitor to his house? I don't recall seeing you there."

"No, in Paris. I knew your father there." She didn't remember him. But that was the only hint he intended to give her.

Mimi's attention was drawn away from the young man by someone trying to organize the cortège, and before she realized it seating arrangements were reorganized and she and Barbara were riding with two of the dissidents rather than her cousins.

They were unaware of how or when it began, but as the convoy of cars approached the Stefanik Estate people came out of the houses and shops in the villages they passed through to hand flowers through the windows of the cars. Looking back, Mimi was amazed to see a tail of twenty or thirty cars now traveling behind them. She asked, "What's happening? I don't understand—how do they know? Isn't it dangerous? We're supposed to keep a low profile."

"Yes, you are, officially. But your father is still a hero to many in this country. We couldn't let him come home without showing him how we feel." It was Alexji who answered her; who, seeing tears of emotion fill her eyes, placed an arm around her shoulder and told her, "His death is a sad thing for many of us, too."

Mimi could accept being comforted by Alexji, she had known him and his story for years. He was one of her father's refugees who had been in and out of the Fifth Avenue house for many years. Alexji had been imprisoned four times between visits. Mimi knew him to be a fighter for the same things her father had once fought for and that she had thought he had ceased fighting for.

"I don't want any trouble, Alexji. My father is past all that now. We only want to bury him in the family crypt and leave this place."

"Don't you have any feeling for your country, Mimi?"

"I don't think I do."

"That's because you're grieving."

Mimi thought it best to leave it at that. She saw no point in making an issue of her indifference to something Alexji was still in the good fight for. Emotionally she felt on shaky ground. It was impossible for Mimi and Barbara not to be shocked by the sight of hundreds of people along the road, the cars filled with flowers, and not a policeman in sight, not a soldier to frighten them. It was all so totally unexpected. They had geared themselves to a sad and lonely cortège of one hearse, one car and a few cousins, and the misery of their loss which they could express in any way they liked since there would be no one there to put up a front for.

"I'm afraid of all this, Alexji. What if they appear, the police, the Army? Those dreadful Soviet officials we were stuck with at the airport?"

"They won't, and anyone who does will turn a blind eye. It'll be easier for them. It's near Prague that you have to worry. They would still like to know some of the Count's secrets. They might even want to question you but you will be gone before they figure that out. They are slower, less efficient and organized that you think."

The house was a fifty-room country palace, now pathetically derelict, set in more than a square mile of parkland, and still in the hands of some Communist union. Her heart sank as the cortège passed through the once magnificent gates. Parkland gone to ruin, uncared for. Fountains dry, broken. The family chapel, once a baroque gem, in disrepair, sad, unloved-looking, and as if God himself had abandoned it. When the cortège pulled up to it there were horse-drawn flat carts, three of them, piled high with flowers. Local people from the estate, villagers from a hundred miles around, were gathered there, waiting to pay their respects to Count Karel Stefanik. Possibly as many as three hundred old friends and compatriots, distant relatives and just plain admirers from a young generation Mimi was surprised had ever heard of him, were milling in front of the chapel. It was beyond her comprehension, this display of emotion for her father. The moment they saw Mimi with Alexji and the cousin, the crowd rushed toward her to grab her hand and kiss it. In Czech they told her, "Welcome home, Countess. Countess come home. Countess, he was never forgotten. This is your home now, Countess." One old peasant woman took the hem of Mimi's skirt in her hand and kissed it. "Countess," she wept, "the Count has come home."

Once she stepped out of the car she was caught in the crush of people. She and Barbara were swept up and moved with them in a wave of humanity toward the chapel, up the stairs, and through the chapel doors. No longer the place where she had known magnificent statues, paintings, nativity scenes, the risen Christ. Where were the gold chalices, gilt tables, tapestry cushions on which as a child she had knelt with her father to pray? The only remnants of those things were the once magnificent floors, now cracked and filthy, even in some places scorched by fire; frescoes neglected and peeling. The roof had enormously large holes in it, some covered with corrugated metal, others nailed inadequately with planks of wood. Mimi could only think how sad it was that Karel should be brought to this ruin as his last resting place above the ground. Alive he would have wept at what they had done to his family's tribute to God.

Someone had taken the time to repair what was left of the pews, to knock together rustic benches, find a few old wooden chairs. The people were scrambling for a seat, some clambering to get into the chapel. They were lining the walls and every available surface with flowers. The chapel became an arbor of blossoms more fit for royalty than a mere expatriate nobleman.

They all crammed into the chapel. Somehow Barbara and she settled in seats in front of what was left of the baroque altar. It was now a bower of flowers with a makeshift wooden table covered with lace cloth, waiting for the casket to be brought in by the pallbearers. Alexji and her cousin were the only men who did not relinquish their places as pallbearers. The other men did so in turn, allowing after a few minutes others to take their places, carrying Karel home for the last time. Mostly older men like himself, with whom he had worked during the resistance days of World War Two. It was such a moving tribute to her father, Mimi could only feel touched by the overwhelming love people had for him. The courage they had too, publicly to come and pay their last respects to Count Stefanik. It was in its own way a jab at the occupying Soviet regime to honor a hero like Count Stefanik, especially since only a few years ago they had come through a time of severe restrictions and repression at the hands of the Soviet regime. Mimi felt displaced yet again in her adult life, as she had as a child when she had been sent away from this place to survive. An outsider, who did not really understand all that was happening. The man she had known as a private person seemed here a stranger to her in his public persona.

There was something about the people and their love for this brave man that she found unreal. It all appeared so feudal, the gathering of people standing around waiting for something to happen now that he had returned. They were expecting something from her and she didn't know what. She felt a strange resentment at being called Countess Stefanik and kept answering, "My name is Mimi Steindler. Steindler. I am not a Countess, there is no Countess." In vain. No one listened.

She turned to Alexji and said, "Why do they do it? Keep going on like that. I am Mrs. Steindler and not the Countess Stefanik. Countess Stefanik is dead, that was my mother."

"And you are the Count's heir. Look, they heard of the death of your brother a couple of years ago. They consider you to be the rightful Countess Stefanik. It won't change anything, they will never see you as Mrs. Steindler."

"Let it go, Mimi," advised Barbara. "In twenty-four hours we'll be out of here and home. And your father would have liked it, been proud for you to carry his name, I'm sure of that. Let it be."

The service was a long one, considering how repressed religion was under the Communist state. After the funeral, the people filed out of the church and the priests blessed them. They walked from the chapel to the family plot and the crypt, whose bronze doors were open. Mimi watched as her father's coffin disappeared through them. Inside, someone had arranged dozens of candles. Mimi saw then twinkling in the darkness and found it impossible to follow the coffin in. She broke down and was swept up by a group of strangers, who tried to comfort her. It was Barbara who went inside the mausoleum and said her last farewell. On leaving, someone asked for the candles to be blown out and removed. Barbara stood framed in the open door, the candle flames flickering in the dark crypt behind her. She told Mimi, "Please tell them to leave the candles, let them burn down in their own time, leave your father in the light for as long as possible." Mimi gave the instructions. Only then did Barbara step aside to allow them to close the bronze doors and padlock them.

Many of the old-timers filed by Mimi to tell her who they were and how they had remembered her. But none of that made any sense to Mimi, she was too distraught. Finally he was gone, and she felt a sadness even deeper than she had at the time of death.

Mimi was swallowed up by the crush of people, separated from Barbara and the dissidents who had come to her aid on the road. And now she really did think she could no longer cope. She felt herself slipping, as if she were going to faint, when she felt his arm around her. He was supporting her as he pushed through the crowd. She felt him pull her hat from her head and it vanished into the crowds.

"My hat?"

"Fewer people will recognize you without it. Another face in the crowd, that sort of thing."

He pushed on until they were on the fringes of the crowd. Then, taking her around the back of the cemetery, he walked her very quickly toward the fields and high grass. Mimi was trembling.

"Are you all right?"

"No." She could barely manage to speak. She blurted out, "I think I'm out of control." And then came the sobs and tears.

They were alone now, walking through the high grass. He felt her slipping toward the ground and caught her in his arms and ran with her further into the field where there was a huge old oak tree. There he laid her down in the grass, leaning against the massive trunk.

"My name is Alexander Janacek," he told her.

She did not react. She was hysterical, he recognized that. The sobs would not stop. She could hardly catch her breath.

"Hold me, please, please," she begged, "I hate him. I hate my father, he's always leaving me. I can't love him anymore the way I did my whole life, making believe it didn't matter all those years he abandoned me when I was a child. And now he's dead, gone forever and I won't spend another lifetime loving him, trying to make up for what he did to me. I hate him! Maybe I have always hated him as much as I have loved him. That's it, I hate him. I can say it now. I hate him for all those years he forgot about me."

She spoke while beating with clenched fists on the ground and in between sobs. His heart went out to her. He could not bear her pain any longer. He knelt down in front of her and slapped her hard across the face several times. She beat him hard on the chest, went for his face with her fists, and slapped him with the flat of her hands until she wore herself out. The sobbing stopped enough for him to pull her into his arms. "It was the only way to stop you, the only way. You're free of your father now, Mimi. Now you can really love him."

And with that he roughly grabbed for her. Alexander felt a violent passion for this wildly erotic beauty so filled with love and hate, so full of pain, for this so hungry heart, for carnal and for real love, for one so female. Her power was overwhelming. All thought vanished from his mind. Everything that was lust in him took over. He hugged her hard and kissed her lips again and again, licking them. He had a voracious appetite for Mimi. He felt her ease into his kisses and open her lips. They kissed deeply until a wildness took her over. She bit into his lips, pulled at his hair, tears still streaming down her face. He could feel in their crazy lovemaking all Mimi was, all she would ever be, and he fell in love. With a wild urgency she tore at the buttons of her dress and fumbled with his coat and shirt. His hands were already exploring her naked flesh, caressing her bare bottom, fingers searching between the lips of her cunt. Now she was driving him into an erotic frenzy with her sexuality and desire for oblivion with him.

He was a magnificent lover. She came several times before they came together in an orgasm that seemed to go on forever. She had to put a hand over his mouth to silence his wails of pleasure. Exhausted, lying wrapped in each other's arms, with only the sound of a warm breeze rustling the tall grass, the leaves of the old oak, he whispered his sense of how divine an erotic find she was. Mimi felt she had never had sex before where she sensed such love and tenderness, mixed with violent passion. Alexander gloried in her body, and devoured it with a hunger for erotic pleasure at least as strong as hers. He had bitten into her flesh and sucked on it and left her with love bites and bruises, marks of the power of his adoration.

They helped each other dress. And then he asked her: "Stay with me, here in Prague. We could be happy together. We are each other's destiny, Mimi. Don't tell me you didn't sense that."

"I don't know. You must give me some time. I've never felt so close to anyone as I do now to you. But my head tells me that's madness, that we've known each other only a few hours. Give me time. Let me work out my grief, my freedom, to see where I go from here."

"They'll be looking for you, Mimi."

"Don't you want to talk about this?"

"No, it's all been said."

"Best we say goodbye here, Alexander. I couldn't bear to do that in front of all those people."

They kissed passionately, promising each other another beginning when the time was right.

In the car on the way back to Prague she told Barbara, "It gets worse, it doesn't get better. At first he was dying, and I thought that was the worst, but then there was the funeral and the service at St. Patrick's—and that was terrible because of all the tributes from the world he lived in that I knew nothing about. But even then he was still with me, so long as he was in the coffin and I knew that it was there and the final step hadn't been taken. Then I thought the worst was when his coffin was unloaded from the plane in Prague. After the service I felt him somehow swept away from me by all those people. There seemed nothing of him left for me. Now he's sealed in the crypt and he is more gone than I ever dreamed he could be. I somehow don't think I will ever recover from this loss."

"It will take a long time," Barbara told her, placing an arm around Mimi's shoulders and kissing her tearstained cheek.

The two women returned to New York and to their lives, lives that no longer included Count Karel Stefanik. When he had been alive and such an important factor in the women's lives he had had that certain way of relating to them in a manner that seemed wholly personal and private. He had never become involved in their other relationships. That made it easier for them to get on with their everyday living.

Barbara had been less overwhelmed in Czechoslovakia. It had all been beyond Mimi's comprehension, and that was precisely what revealed her lack of understanding of who and what Karel really had been. Suppose he had been a voyeur at his own funeral: he would have found the events natural, as Barbara had, despite knowing relatively little about his political life. But she did know the heart and inner soul of her long-time lover, her almost husband. It was evident to Barbara that Mimi's eyes had been opened as never before during this forty-eight hours in Czechoslovakia. A time both dreadful and extraordinarily wonderful: dreadful for their shared loss and the emotions that went with it, magnificent with the hope and love extended by all those strangers.

Barbara knew instinctively when they carried his body into the chapel that she, only she, had seen him and loved him totally, with all his faults and all his goodness, his selfishness, together with his libidinous nature, which had led him away from her. That, at the very end of his life, he loved her beyond all else, as she did him. That he had died with her name on his lips, and with his last breath reminded her how much he loved her, bound her to him for eternity. His death, therefore, was much harder on her than on Mimi.

Mimi's pain would go on for years now that her eyes were open. She would be forced to see what her father was not: the image she had created of him, believed and lived with until his death. The same image that had forced Karel and Barbara to keep their relationship a long dark secret, so as not to disillusion her. Mimi lost a father, a man she loved but didn't know or understand. No one wanted to make light of the loss that she had sustained, least of all Barbara. Possibly because Mimi had the relationship of love with her father that both father and daughter wanted. The love they had for each other suited them: it had covered up all the flaws in their relationship.

On her return from Prague, Barbara, alone at last, with the funeral behind her and Mimi back in the bosom of her family, was struck with grief. It began to sink in that Karel would never walk through the door again, that their lustful hearts would never be sated by each other again. Not even once more would their erotic souls flow together. She knew he was dead, buried, gone. Yet in her heart and her mind he was still with her—body and soul. His presence was right there with her, as strongly as if he were still alive. It was obvious to Barbara that neither of them had yet been able to render Karel into nothing more than a spirit that she could carry in her heart for all eternity while yet achieving a life without him.

They had yet to say a final goodbye, to set each other free. Death alone doesn't do that. There was but one place where she felt they could release each other to go their separate ways so that his spirit might be finally set to rest and hers emotionally freed from Karel.

Some weeks after they had left their island, she returned. She knew in her heart that this was where he would have wanted her to say her final farewell to him, in the privacy of their secret erotic world.

Jay had never felt that Karel's presence interfered with his marriage. He was a factor in Mimi's life, one that Jay accepted readily and respected. He understood her closeness with her father, and she had slotted her love for him into their relationship quite neatly. But now that he was gone, Jay recognized how private their love had been, still was. Mimi hardly talked about him. She neither dwelt upon his death nor used him, as some fixated, doting daughters do, as a paragon to be held in posthumous awe.

Jay sometimes thought that he grieved more over Karel's death than Mimi or their children. He watched and waited for some sign in her of how much she was repressing her grief, expecting it to issue in some sort of emotional breakdown. But this never happened. He found it very odd that they should not discuss her intentions about the house off Fifth Avenue, Karel's important library of rare books, his possessions, what she intended to do with the remnants of her father's life.

But Jay would find that odd: he came from a family who talked incessantly about themselves and their lives. Not so Mimi. Silence was one of her great charms, and the mysterious silence she hid behind, that still, after years of marriage, bound him to her. Mimi was never wrapped up in anything to the exclusion of all else. She had a facility for handling her life as it came along. Even among New York women, who need to be sharp, quick and clever, eager to experience all that the city has to offer, Mimi could seem unique.

Because of Mimi, Jay had the selfish marriage he wanted with her, and a family life rich in love and affection around him. She attracted his children as she had always lured man and women alike with her charm and vivacity, that same mysterious charisma Jay had married her for.

His older children, who were now grown-up adults living lives of their own, floated in and out of their home as if they still lived there. All the children, his ex-wives and Claire and Rick, made a large loving family that Jay adored and knew would never have existed but for Mimi. She had become the matriarch of Jay's household, this woman he had married as a young girl.

She had managed that in much the same way she had managed her role as a respected art agent and the hat atelier, one day at a time, step by step, grateful for every little reward. She and Jay were growing old together in their Manhattan life as well as their family life. It was as vibrant and exciting as the best of Manhattan lives can be. Each of them had their career, and they had a family to be proud of, and they carried on building, always constructing something, creating something. That act of creation in the city of New York, where the competition is the keenest in the world, kept them young in spirit, on their toes, and always involved with the living. The dead have very little place in a Manhattan existence. Either you live hot or die a slow, cold death.

Mimi did not sell the house off Fifth Avenue, nor did she change her schedule, even though her father was dead and gone. She went there every morning to breakfast with Sophia. The only change she made was to close her office on East

Fifty-seventh Street and to move her art agency to Karel's house. For a year she did nothing about the house or her father's things. Then she realized that, with her extended family, the best thing to do would be to keep it as an annex to her and Jay's home. The overflow of children and friends could stay there. Jay could use one of the rooms as his own small study. The house came alive with their family living in and out of it. Out of respect for Karel's exceptionally fine library Mimi hired a curator. Now it could be opened to the public by appointment. Reading areas were created for scholars. Collectors came from all over the world. Though it had not been her intention, she turned it into just the sort of place he would have appreciated.

The library was so successful that Mimi expanded her own small art dealership by putting on permanent exhibition her father's paintings and those she dealt in. Again, visits were by appointment only. It became a very special place, difficult of access, only for those interested in rare books and fine works of art. That rare combination of private family home and a private museum.

Strangely, after Count Karel Stefanik's death, Mimi seemed to grow more like her father with every year that passed. Sophia was getting old now, but she remained the constant companion and friend she had always been. Only now it was not just to Mimi but to her children as well, all of the children in fact, who drifted in and out of Sophia's culinary kingdom just off Fifth Avenue. They were a close-knit family and knew how to ride the everyday changes that come with family life, how to shift gears quickly, take up a new adventure.

Not long after Karel's death, Jay sensed that, like her father's, Mimi's libido would eventually demand that she add lovers to her already full life. That would remain always a suspicion, one he chose to banish to the back of his mind. He actually did not want to know whether it was true or not. There seemed no point: they had everything they wanted together in their marriage. It was as solid and unshakeable as any marriage could be. And so he kept his suspicions to himself.

But Mimi did not take on any lovers. She was busy trying to work out her life. And she was waiting for Alexander Janacek to substantiate his claim that they were each other's destiny.

Chapter 26

"I want you for myself. I want you for entirely selfish reasons. And that's the truth of it."

When the convoy of cars escorting Mimi and Barbara from the funeral service back to Prague had pulled off into a slip road on the outskirts of the city and stopped, those were the words Alexander had whispered in Mimi's ear. He had taken his place in line just as the others had, to embrace her, to place a kiss on each cheek, and to wish her Godspeed and farewell. But what he had wanted was to kidnap her, lock her away in his house in Prague and continue what had begun several hours before under that oak tree in the field. It had excited him to think that she was standing there still wet with his seed, that he had marked her for life with his lust. That their sexual encounter was but a beginning he had no doubt.

He had wanted to say those things to her at the Lippe in Paris when she had dazzled him with her presence, when the intrusion of *her* world snatched her away from him. How cruel love can be, how hurtful. He had remembered everything about her. She had remembered nothing of him.

He had been neither disturbed nor surprised. He had been young, too besotted with her and in awe of the Count to pursue the married, older and very chic Mimi.

For months after they had met that first time in Paris, he had considered seeking her out because he wanted her so badly and because she had been other things as well: so very young in spirit, flirtatious, sensual as hell, interested in him, seeking her out. He hadn't missed that fleeting moment that can happen between a man and a woman, striking an erotic spark. There had been that and more, that imperceptible something that can make a woman the grand passion of your life. The great love. It was no delusion. Alexander was not a man to delude himself, and most especially not about women.

They were each other's destiny, he knew it then, he knew it now. Back then it had been quite easy for him to place his passion for Mimi in a corner of his heart and not to suffer unrequited love. He considered love, in this instance, to be merely dormant, needing only the right time and the right place to awaken from its deep sleep.

The wait had been long, but it had been worth it because on the day he had held Mimi in his arms she had come alive to him. She had recognized something in him that she could give herself to, as possibly she had never done with any other human being. There would be no turning back from what they had found in each other that afternoon.

He suspected that she had been all her life a peripheral and mysterious figure to the men who loved her. As she had been to him until that day. With the death of her father and her return to Czechoslovakia, and while in Alexander's arms, she had faced her deepest feelings. He had no doubt that what Mimi had learned from the shattering experiences of her childhood was how to keep one's distance. Now that was over, made redundant in one embrace.

Alexander Janacek carried within him several deep-seated notions that he lived by and wrote about. Life was timing, destiny, history. Love was a complex emotion made so by the outside world interfering with erotic, sexual passion, every man and woman's libido. The rage to live, to be free, for politics and power, was combined in his life and work. Europe and England had for years appreciated his mastery of those elements in his books, and only recently in literary America he was fast becoming the rising star.

Mimi's sensuality, physical beauty, her hungry heart, those were the things that he had been instantly attracted to. But there had been more, that female essence that men who love women fall in love with and feel the need to possess. There was erotic passion between them, yes, but in time there would be more, love for each other being the most powerful thing that would bind them together, the thing that would govern their lives.

That last time he had seen her, she had pressed his hand
hard, caressed it briefly with her fingers, in acknowledgment
of his whisper. And her violet eyes had seemed almost to
smolder, so warm was her gaze when she mouthed, "Thank
you." Releasing his hand she had placed hers over her heart.
And then he had moved on. Having lost himself in lust with
her, he had sat in the back of the Citroen between two
friends, reliving what it was like fucking Mimi with such
wild abandon, while the car sped down the slip road away
from the woman he loved.

She had been on a night flight to Paris. It had not occurred
to either of them that she should change her plans. The timing had been wrong. Emotionally, politically. So anxious had
she been to leave Prague and not get caught up with the red
regime that still ruled the country, he doubted that she realized just how momentous their sexual encounter had been.
She would. When she was back home in New York in the
bosom of her family, where she felt safe. She would know it
then, and would act upon it. A smile had crossed Alexander's
lips. He had delighted in imagining Mimi's reliving their sexual extravagances and the pleasure she would yet again derive
from them. While he could understand that she might have
tears, he could understand more that they each of them had to
change their lives before they could come together, never to
part. And he had had no doubts that they would do just that.

That evening he dined with his friends at a small restaurant
on the river several miles from Prague. They were well
known there and had been expected. They drank a great deal
of wine and ate roast duck and red cabbage and potato dumplings as light as air. Each of the men spoke eloquently about
Karel Stefanik. They were the last to leave the cozy yet rustic
restaurant, a wooden building in a small wood. Very drunk
and full of love for Count Karel and all he represented, for
their country, and Alexander for the Count's daughter, to
travel to Prague was impossible. The men managed to
squeeze themselves into an old rowing boat and the restaurant's proprietor rowed them for ten minutes from the dock to
a small wooded island the size of two double tennis courts in
the middle of the river. It was there in Alexander's dilapidated three-hundred-year-old fishing lodge that the men spent

the night. By candlelight they talked politics and poetry and women until the sun was high in the sky and they all went to sleep.

That next afternoon Alexander rubbed the stubble on his chin as he walked through the courtyard to the eighteenth-century stables behind what had once been his family's town house. Now that it was occupied by the Embassy of the Soviet Union, he had long ago ceased to think of it as home. He climbed the iron staircase and walked across the balcony. Before he could place his key in the lock, the door was flung open. "You might have called?"

"Oh."

"Oh? Is that all you have to say?"

Claudine was not shouting. She wasn't even angry. Claudine never shouted, she was never angry. Or if she was, she was clever enough never to let him know about it. They understood each other. Any sign of unhappiness on her part and he would send her away. She had only tested him once, many years ago, and he *had* sent her away and she had found life without him unbearable.

"Are you upset with me, Claudine?"

It was the tone of his voice. She was frightened by it. But she dared not lie to him. "Yes, a little."

"Why?"

She hardly knew what to say. How many nights had he stayed away? Not just one but several at a time, sometimes for weeks and never called. She had for years accepted that he had his freedom and his women and that all that held them together was that he liked her best of any of the others who came and went in his life.

Alexander removed his jacket, never taking his gaze from Claudine. He loosened his tie, took down his suspenders. He went to her and placed an arm around her shoulders. He kissed her on the cheek and together they walked through the sitting room, through the bedroom, to the bath. Alexander sat down on the edge. He watched Claudine turn on the taps.

He had met her in Paris when she was nineteen and one of Dior's favorite models. She was wealthy and spoiled and pampered, the only daughter of a French industrialist. She played with her modeling and life in the same way she had played with her toys when she had been a child. Greedily, she grabbed the things she wanted and the moment she was bored with them abandoned them for something new. Alexander was the exception to her rule.

She had been, and was still, sought after by men because of her sensational good looks. A beauty with raven-colored hair and skin the color of cream, with dark sultry eyes and an aquiline nose, and an amazingly sensuous mouth whose upper lip looked as if it had been stung by a bee.

Alexander coveted her body, so slender and yet curvaceous. He liked fucking Claudine. When he had first met her she had been sexually frigid. But Alexander adored women and everything sexual about them. He had the ability to ruin women for other men because he was a courageous, adventurous, even dangerous lover who made enormous sexual demands on them. Women complied willingly because he was kind, generous, honest. He could even be selfless with them. Alexander was a virile sexy man, a sensitive artist and poet with them. What woman would not give everything to a man such as that? Certainly Claudine did. He was the man who taught her to enjoy sex. It was that which kept them together. Sex and love on her part, and the power she derived from running his day-to-day life. It was Claudine who kept the world at bay so he could work. No little thing for a dedicated writer. It was not an easy arrangement. What made it workable was that she lived in Paris and he lived in Prague. She was known as his on-again, off-again mistress, but liked to think of herself as his muse. But everyone knew his work was his wife. In order to keep the position Claudine had carved for herself in his life, she gave him his freedom and accepted the love affairs that he conducted openly. As the years passed and he became more successful she was less and less inclined to give him up. He had suggested she should many times. They finally agreed upon a close friendship that included sex and the acceptance that it would one day have to end. At the right time, in the right place, no matter the reason or the consequences, he would send her away and Claudine would not resist.

The bath was nearly full. She had been moving around the room, collecting bath towels for him and a sponge. She put fresh essence of pine in the water, laid out his terrycloth robe and slippers. He had been watching her, admiring her elegant good looks. She was wearing blue jeans and a white silk shirt with large voluminous long sleeves. He was watching her and wanting Mimi.

He rose from the edge of the tub, and taking her hand led Claudine from the bathroom into the bedroom. He sat down on the edge of the bed taking her with him. He reached for her hand and held it. He caressed it and told her, "Claudine, we are coming to the end of this love affair."

She went visibly pale. She saw it in his gaze. This time it was a fact, not an idea. "Are you certain about that?"

"Yes, very."

"But it's not over yet?"

"It should be, Claudine. It's only a matter of time."

"And how many years does this new woman have invested in your life? I have ten. Doesn't that count for something?" He rose from the bed and standing in front of her, told her, "I have no intention of having a scene about this. We promised that when the time came to leave each other there would be no unpleasantness."

"How long have you known?" she asked, quite calm now.

"Less than twenty-four hours."

"And when does she move into your life?"

"Not for a long time. She has a life to change, and I have things to do. It doesn't matter how long it takes, the point is she will be here, and you have to know that when that happens there will be no other women in my life. The last thing I want is this to come as a blow to you. That's why I am telling you now. So you can ease yourself out of my life. It was bound to happen, Claudine. We were never each other's destiny, and you know that as well as I do."

He sat down next to her and placed an arm around her. She leaned against him. They were silent for several minutes and then she spoke. "What about the book you're working on?"

"That's where all my energy is directed, not her. She will come to me when she can, and until then I have my work and many changes of my own to make. I want to be ready for her."

"Do me a favor, don't tell me about her."

"Fair enough."

"One question?"

"Go on then."

"Your other women, will they be told?"

"No, there's no need. They know I make no promises, there is no future, only the present and fun. I had to tell you because you have woven yourself into my life in spite of having known all these years that it would one day end for us. You mean a great deal to me, Claudine. As you have rightly said, in ten years we have a history."

And from that day on Alexander was swept away on a tide of creative writing such as he had never experienced before. He secluded himself as best he could from world recognition on a scale he had never dreamed possible. But not from the politics and world events that were affecting his country. It was all happening, a lifetime of dreams was coming true, and he was right there in the middle of it. The timing was right, destiny at work.

Czechoslovakia had its Velvet Revolution. For the first time since the Second World War the Communists were vanquished. And he knew as freedom swept through his country and the rest of Eastern Europe that it was time for him to do something about Mimi. Nearly two years, and so many vast changes in his life had given Alexander everything to bring her home to. Now they had a new world to build a life on. The one his mentor Count Karel Stefanik had believed in but never lived to see.

Chapter 27

This was Mimi's favorite night of the year, Christmas Eve, the night she and Jay gave their annual family party, the night when all their children and their extended family came from various parts of the world for Mimi's Christmas Eve. As the family grew ever larger, the venue of the party had to be changed. Christmas Eve for the last few years had been held in the Stefanik house just off Fifth Avenue. With Mimi and Jay's own house jammed to the rafters with children and house guests, as was the Stefanik house, Mimi and Jay had taken to sleeping there in what had been Karel's bedroom. It was one of the finest rooms Mimi would ever know. She loved that room, as she had ever since she was a child. It still retained the same plum-and-silver antique Fortuny draperies and the massive silver-gilt bed, the magnificent drawings on the wall. Mimi had made that room her own after her father's death. She and Jay shared this room when they stayed in the Stefanik house.

She was sitting on the end of the bed in an ivory-colored silk kimono embroidered with cranes in pure golden threads—a gift from Rick many years ago on his return from one of his extensive travels. She was watching Jay's reflection in the mirror. He was fussing with his already perfect black bow-tie. She was actually admiring her husband, still in his seventies handsome and fit, looking like a man of fifty. He caught her gaze and spoke into the mirror.

"Not bad for a man my age—I hope you're thinking."

For years Mimi had watched Jay with a certain admira-

tion for his vanity, but somehow this evening it came home
to her.

"My God, I don't think I ever realized just how vain you
are, Jay."

He turned around and smiled at her. "My dear, after all
these years, surely it doesn't come as a surprise to you?"

"God, Jay, are you really gone on your vanity!"

"Trouble is, I think I am. I've never hidden my admiration
for myself." He laughed, using the easy Steindler charm to
tease her back into some sort of admiration for him. It
worked to an extent. He went to her and put his hand gently
on her shoulder.

"I think you'd better get ready."

"I have only to slip into my dress."

She removed her kimono, and for a few minutes stood naked. Seeing her thus, in her high-heeled satin pumps, stockings that were held on her thighs by nothing more than lace
garters, Jay felt the same kind of vanity for his wife that he
felt for himself. She still had the figure of a young woman.
Mimi was voluptuous without clothes. She caught sight of
her husband looking at her nakedness and did not miss the
pleasure in his eyes. But it was the sort of pleasure one has
in possessing a pretty object, pleasure that is taken for
granted. She saw no passion, only hunger for her naked body,
for a still excitingly sexual woman. She was actually stunned
by the look Jay gave her. It was a look she had seen so many
times before for so many years of their marriage without it
occurring to her that there was something missing from that
look. The thing that she still hungered for, passionate erotic
love, he simply didn't have for her. Mimi tried to block it out
of her mind, but it was as if scales had fallen from her eyes.
She was seeing Jay in a different light tonight.

She bent over her dress lying on the bed, took it carefully
in her hands and stepped into it. The luscious color, violet
with rich midnight blue undertones, seemed black yet hardly
black at all. It complemented her violet eyes. The silk taffeta
rustled as she adjusted it on her body.

She tried to shrug off her feelings of discontent with Jay's
gaze, but still she felt cheated by it. She slipped the gown
over her shoulders and adjusted the bodice, then standing in

front of the mirror, asked Jay to do up the back for her. She
sensed that she was being foolish. She touched the puffed
sleeves, a miracle of draping and stitching. It was a romantic
Yves Saint Laurent festive gown. She had splurged on it. It
had been an extravagance that was irresistible to her. It was
cut low, almost to the waist in the back, while in the front the
neckline plunged down to show just enough cleavage, sensuous yet not vulgar. It seemed to be all puffed sleeves and tight
bodice. The skirt was cut on the bias and clung to her in all
the right places to flare out into a train just long enough both
to provoke and remain elegant. There was something particularly festive and exciting about the gown. She had had her
hair dressed for it, wearing the blonde tresses long and swept
off her face, held back by several small combs topped with a
sprig of roses set in diamonds and platinum that had once
been worn by her mother.

"I don't think I've ever seen you look more beautiful than
you do tonight, Mimi. You still look like the young girl I
married all those years ago."

She turned around to face her husband. "It's nice of you to
say so, Jay. It is a long time since I thought of myself as a
young girl."

He took her hands in his and stepped back, then twirled her
around with one hand. She caught his look of approval and
admiration.

"Mimi?" He hesitated.

"What is it, Jay?"

"Maybe this isn't the time."

"Maybe it is."

"Mimi, why don't you retire, get rid of the atelier? Saks
wants to buy it. You divide your time too much. Give up the art
agency. Look, you've had all the amusement you can get from
them. Surely you don't need the money? I have enough for the
rest of our days. They have been great amusement for you, successful even. That should be enough. You've had a good time
playing with them. Now, maybe it's time to move on."

"Played with these things, Jay?"

He sensed the edge on her voice and realized he had not
been diplomatic. "This isn't the time or the place, Mimi. Just
think about it. We'll talk about it another time."

"Sell everything for what? I mean, why? I don't understand."

"Or give it to some of the children to take over."

"They have their own lives to lead. And besides, they're not children anymore."

"Well, that's the point, isn't it? Get rid of everything."

"And do what?"

"Stay home and cultivate yourself."

"Stay home and cultivate myself? Do you find me an uncultivated woman?"

"No, of course not. Here, turn around, I'll finish the fastenings."

She obliged, and he continued closing her dress. "But let's face it, you could do a lot with your brain you haven't done. You've always had this little bit of a commercial thing, of having to see money come across the counter every day. It's all a bit vulgar, especially since you don't need it. You could stay home."

"We'll travel?" she said facetiously.

"Yes, that's what I said before. Become more cultured, more cultivated. There." He had finished the fastenings. Now he turned Mimi around to face him. "You are absolutely magnificent. Don't look like that, it was only an idea."

"I don't think I quite understand. You do appreciate how lucrative these businesses you have suddenly started calling mere toys have been? And that their success has brought me a reputation in several fields?"

"Oh, yes, you've done admirably with them. What I'm saying is that maybe it's time for a change."

"And while I'm cultivating myself, what about you?"

"We'll have more time for each other. Maybe go and live in the sun somewhere."

Mimi began to laugh. "Jay, we would be bored to death, hate each other in a week. You are a workaholic, need masses of people and power and deals just to get through one day. You love sharing yourself out, being Mr. Nice Guy in a ratfink business where you are the last of the great gentlemen publishers. I have spent a lifetime making do with the time you can spare me. And now you are telling me that's going to change if *I* give up my work, what interests me. What's brought this on?"

"I've been meaning to talk to you about it for ages. Just never got around to it. How many are we downstairs?"

"Forty-two."

"Forty-two for dinner. Forty-two of our family, my children, your children, our children. We've made a marvelous family out of them all. And it's been fun most of the time, although a lot of hard work—mostly for you. How you've done it I don't know, but it's given me a great life, just as you promised it would. But it's all gone now, except for Christmases. We don't have any children any more, they've all grown up. The businesses are the same, all grown up. You don't need those little projects to distract you from me."

"You mean, you've never seen the value in my work or my part in what we've done together?"

"Well, of course I have. I'm just saying they don't matter that much."

"They've been my life, and you tell me they don't matter that much?"

"Let's talk about this another time."

"Jay, I'm not going down those stairs with you until you tell me what this is all about."

"I promise it's not about anything. Now you've made your point, and I don't see any reason for you to go on with it."

"No, you're quite right, so we won't go on with it. We'll drop it here and now."

"Mimi, we're talking at cross purposes here. I think we'll forget this conversation until after Christmas. Merry Christmas, my darling. The fruits of all our labors and all our joy in loving each other are downstairs waiting. I love you, Mimi, and the life we've had together. I think you look young and beautiful, and every one of those people downstairs admires you and is grateful to you for the family you created for us."

He slipped his arm through hers and kissed her on the tip of her nose. Together they left the bedroom to walk down the stairs. Mimi forgot about Jay's suggestions; they vanished from her mind when, from the top of the stairs, she looked down and saw her whole family below, the men in black tie, the women in long dresses, the children in party dresses.

They were the fruits of her labor, that was true, a magnificent family, the children and adults who had given her the family life she had yearned for as a child, insisted upon as an adult. She felt their closeness, the warmth and energy of their love rising toward her. Turning to Jay to say something, she realized that only he didn't have that energy for her. He had energy all right, but he was always directing it elsewhere: to these people below, the man in the street, his colleagues, any fresh young face that drifted into the Jay Steindler orbit. But for her it just wasn't there. How had she not noticed that? She had spent very nearly her entire adult life married to Jay, believing she enjoyed a near-perfect marriage with this man, and with a sexual life that had been satisfying if not adventurous. So how had she not noticed that he loved her in the image he had created to suffice for himself, and that had been all? Passion, the lust he had for life—those things he had always kept to himself, except for the fraction he distributed like largesse. He had cleverly made Mimi think, as he had most people, that he gave those things away with a generous heart.

He slipped his hand through her arm and beamed down at her. "Merry Christmas, old girl," he intoned, and they walked together down the stairs. There butlers were filling glasses from magnums of Bollinger. It was in the hall that they drank their champagne around the twelve-foot Christmas tree glowing with colored lights and silver tinsel. Presents, beautifully wrapped in colored papers with extravagant silk ribbons in large, luscious bows, were piled high. The house smelled of roast goose and apple rings fried in butter and cinnamon, red cabbage and Christmas stuffing of crab and shrimp, and chestnuts roasted with sage, onion and cream.

Barbara was there with her new husband, looking ravishing in a short bolero jacket of crimson velvet over a see-through black chiffon blouse and a skirt of black silk taffeta, a wide sash of purple satin tied in a massive soft bow at the waist, tails hanging very nearly to the floor. Several of the women in the hall, adoring fans of her handsome, temperamental, husband (who had eyes only for her), surrounded him.

Barbara had married a very short time after Karel's death. Her world-famous conductor husband was no longer a young man, but still the same dashing, charismatic musical genius that women had always pursued. He had disillusioned many romantic hopefuls with his marriage to Barbara, who, he had announced at the time, he had loved and whose acceptance of him he had awaited for more than a decade. Barbara traveled extensively with him, having taken a sabbatical from her work that appeared to be becoming permanent. They were always at Mimi's Christmas Eve party, having become members of the Steindler extended family.

Rick was there too. Still so very young and handsome-looking while we all grow older, thought Mimi as their eyes met and he blew her a kiss. At forty-five he looked like a young man of thirty, his hair bleached by the sun. He had returned from Malaysia for Christmas to be with the twins, and Mimi and the rest of the Steindler family which he felt to be his family as well.

"Mommy, you look gorgeous, absolutely gorgeous." Angelica kissed her, and then all the children followed suit.

They were a handsome group of people, vital and exciting. This was Mimi's proudest moment. She had given them all everything she herself had missed as a child. Now they made up for her years of deprivation and separateness during childhood, those formative years she had struggled through at the hands of kind strangers.

The Steindler Christmas Eve party was something of a New York occasion. First Mimi had the family for drinks in the grand front hall, and then a full sit-down Christmas Eve dinner. It was customary for the entire party and household to attend midnight mass at St. Patrick's Cathedral. On their return they opened the house to any friends who wanted to come. The pattern of Christmas Eve never changed.

Everyone milled around the great hall, drank champagne and chatted to each other, gossiping and laughing. Mimi loved that hall with its giant tree, the staircase balustrade wound around with garlands of fresh green pine that filled the hall with a woodland scent. There were decorations of red ribbon, great silk bows of it, and fat white candles that added their own aroma of hot wax.

Eventually everyone paired off, instructed by Mimi and Jay, to file into the dining room and seat themselves at one long table covered in white damask, with snowy white napkins trimmed in lace. They drank from glasses of Baccarat crystal. The dinner plates and a baroque silver collection of tureens and ornamental pieces glistened in the candlelight. The cutlery was gold, the dinner service Limoges. Both had belonged to Karel. And the great candelabra of French baroque silver standing four feet high, incorporating naked nymphs and satyrs, were for this occasion wreathed in abundant twists of mistletoe and Christmas roses. Christmas Eve dinner was always one of the happiest occasions anyone who attended could think of. A jovial group, with Jay at the head of the table, Rick at the foot, Mimi sitting in the center, flanked on either side and opposite by all the wives, children and ex-lovers who had become one close-knit family, and by Barbara, and one or two close friends of Jay. There were always four plump geese to be carved, one presented to Rick, one to Jay, the other two to be carved by Jay's eldest sons, who traditionally sat one on Mimi's right, the other on Barbara's, directly across the table from Mimi. A little bit of table-theater: there were always bets on who would complete the task first.

Before the goose, Scottish smoked salmon was served with individual shrimp mousses, brown bread and butter, and chilled Montrachet. After that came pumpkin soup, served by the waiters with great silver ladles from whole scooped-out pumpkins. Hot pumpkin soup, with a large spoonful of whipped cream and snipped chives, was a gourmet's treat. It was one of Jay's favorite dishes and Mimi adored it. By now everyone shared their addiction.

Then came the goose, roasted to a shiny bronze and surrounded by sweet potatoes and stuffing, succulent and rich. The bread was crisp and buttery, the chestnuts firm and crunchy, while the mushrooms, crab and shrimp, the parsley, thyme, and sage and onion were rich, soft and creamy. Silver tureens proffered brussels sprouts, roasted parsnips, baby carrots and potato puffs. The wine was Chateau Margaux of impeccable vintage. For dessert, hot, steaming individual Christmas puddings the size of golf balls were served, surrounded by rum butter, ice cream and a sprig of holly. Chateau Yquem was the sweet dessert wine, followed by demitasses of strong black coffee with a curl of cinnamon on the top. There were always Christmas carols sung in the great hall as they drank their champagne. Jay and Mimi affected a grand entrance down the stairs.

During dinner a harpist sat in the corner playing Debussy. All through dinner entertainments varied with the courses. Everyone was allowed an after-dinner speech or party piece. Most were amusing. And later, the customary semiserious procession from dining table to hall for coats, and then into cars for church. This was for Mimi a sentimental time. Each Christmas made up for those when she had been deprived of her family.

Several times during the evening she found herself thinking of Jay. He was wonderful with everyone as he always was. He had passion for his family and friends. Mimi was certain she was not imagining it: there was no passion for her. Not that he was any different to her. She had realized for the first time that what he had for her was love, adoration even, but that was not the same thing. Had she perhaps known it all along but blocked it from her mind? The rewards of a good marriage had perhaps been worth that compromise. And did it matter now? Jay and Rick had become friends many years before. Even in that friendship, she thought, Jay showed more passion than he afforded her. Was she getting paranoid? she wondered, smiling to herself, and dropped the discomforting notion.

In the hall she was slipping into her full-length white ermine coat with a huge shawl collar, a twenties coat by the great designer Poiret, a collector's dream. Karel had bought it for Mimi's mother. She heard Jay tell Rick, "I'm the luckiest man alive to have a wife like her. And now the children are all grown, I want her to retire from those little businesses of hers, to do something serious or else nothing at all. Nothing would be just fine so far as I'm concerned. It'd give her some time to educate herself. Work on her, Rick. She listens to you."

Mimi's evening was not shattered by Jay's disloyalty, as disloyalty it was in her book. To talk about her behind her back demeaned such an evening. She was more surprised than disappointed by his having never regarded all her years of work as anything more than frivolity, mere playing with a career. Mimi had always known Jay to be an intellectual snob. His penchant for the Miss Benningtons of this world, for higher education—academic worth counted high with Jay—was something she had been aware of all their shared life. She had hardly considered herself uneducated, even if stumbling around on the lower rungs of Jay's ladder. The revelation had been that, even in her, this still counted with him.

She closed her coat and stepped in between the two men, slipping her arms through theirs. "Church." She almost suggested that Jay should not go. It was not his faith, but she knew how much he enjoyed the church service. It had atmosphere. Just being there felt good to him. For herself, she hoped she derived something more from church than a cozy benediction.

She dismissed all thought of what he had said to Rick until they returned home. Some friends had already arrived. The family began distributing the gifts from under the tree, while hot rum punch and mince pies, eggnog and whisky toddies, and Christmas cake with a rum-butter icing were being served. Some of Jay's family brought with them a beautiful, dark-haired Israeli girl no more than twenty years old. Two editorial assistants from his office arrived, young Miss Bennington types. For some time Mimi watched the look in Jay's eyes: affection, charm, intelligence—he shone in their presence as he no longer shone for her.

It suddenly occurred to her that her own passions had not dimmed in her long life with Jay, except for him. Rick had been proof of that, and now Alexander had rekindled in her the rage to live again. Though there had been no contact between him and Mimi since they kissed goodbye under that ancient oak, she had come to believe that he might be right. Perhaps they were each other's destiny. His silence had surprised her, and yet she was grateful for it. She needed to be free of more than her father before she could meet this head-on. As for Jay, his lack of passion toward her was troubling her less by the minute now. She was merely curious as to why she hadn't noticed it before, why it hadn't counted before as it did now.

Christmas Day was always a lazy day in the Steindler

household. Children and friends came in and out as they chose. Breakfast went on forever. Then an ongoing buffet down in the kitchen ran through the afternoon and evening. Everyone pretty much lazed around the house and did what they wanted, and so everyone stayed up until the early hours of the morning before. There was a whole day to recuperate. Nothing ever spoiled Christmas Eve for Mimi. The revelations about Jay certainly didn't. She had a wonderful time. Everyone did.

It was after three before she made her retreat. From excess of wine and laughter she fell into a deep sleep before Jay came to bed. She had no idea what time it was when she opened her eyes. It must have been late: a chink between the not-quite-closed curtains streamed bright with sunshine. She closed her eyes again. It hadn't been the light that had awakened her, just the warmth of Jay tight up against her back, his hands caressing her arms, round her waist and then up to her breasts. He rolled her on to her back and lifted her silk nightgown, deftly raised her in his arms, and pulled it up over her head to let it drop on the floor. Then he covered her naked body with his by sliding on top of her, kissing her lips, making all the right gestures, the same gestures he had been making all their married life, the same sexual awakening. Her legs opened wide and she felt his penis rubbing up and down her slit, teasing it open. With one thrust his ample cock was deep inside her. It felt good, it always felt good, in spite of the sleepiness and possibly not wanting to have sex half-awake all the time. But to have sex with Jay, to be awakened slowly in a steady rhythm of penetration, to come fully awake in orgasm: how well he did it, how cunningly he found the right erogenous places inside her cunt. She let herself enjoy him and enjoy herself. She came, a strong orgasm, satisfying, warm and luscious. Oh, he would be pleased. He was especially gratified when she was unable to hold back, and yielded a moan of pleasure.

She opened her eyes and watched him as he continued to fuck her. How much he enjoyed her, how much he enjoyed himself, taking possession of her. He was methodical, caring, loving even, just as he always was. Then, when he was ready, he came. He reached out to take from the dressing table a fine linen handkerchief and put it between the lips of her cunt to catch their come. He tucked it between her cunt lips, lay on his side and held her in his arms. He kissed her neck, her chin. A sigh, and then he closed his eyes.

Mimi slid from the bed to stand naked looking at him for a minute before she slipped into the silk kimono and went into the bathroom.

"You were wonderful, you're the best!" he called after her. She was just closing the door, but now she opened it, went back into the bedroom and leaned against the doorjamb.

How many times had he told her that? It had become a kind of incantation every morning after he fucked her. "Sorry, Jay, I didn't quite catch that. What did you say?"

He repeated the exact words, looking creditably surprised that she should demand an encore.

"Oh! How nice for you."

It was as if he had not heard her words. He continued, "Beautiful. You are so sexy and beautiful when you come, and I could tell you were satisfied. Was it wonderful for you?"

Nothing original. Inspiration had obviously eluded him. Saying more never meant saying different. It was always the same, every morning, every fuck. "Oh, it's always wonderful for me, Jay. You're a terrific lover. I know it and I have been grateful for that every morning of my life with you. We've had enough fucks together to prove that."

She closed her kimono walked toward the bed and gazed at him, this handsome, charming husband of hers, who had given her such a good life for so long. She sat down on the bed next to him, raised his hand and considered it. Such a large hand, masculine, yet elegant and refined. She replaced it on the bed. Smiling at him, she asked, "Jay, would you do something for me?"

"Yes, darling, anything."

"Good. Then, please, dear, don't ever fuck me like that again. If you do, I'll leave you."

Then she rose from the bed, kissed him lightly on the lips, went to the bathroom and closed the door. She leaned against it and felt the most incredible relief. Relief from a sexual tension she had never really realized she suffered with Jay. Oh, she knew resentment had infected the welcome she gave those morning fucks, a kind of deep-down resentment that she hadn't really admitted to. The rest of their life had been so good. Only now, with the relief she was feeling, did she understand how very deep she had buried a resentment that had now become untenable. She tried not to think of the stunned, hurt look on Jay's face as she had walked away from him to the bathroom.

Mimi drew her bath. She added oil of gardenia and honeysuckle. She felt suddenly lighthearted, very happy, as if she had broken invisible chains constraining her. She took a long and leisurely bath. When she emerged wrapped in a cream-colored terrycloth robe, piped with wide bands of coral silk moiré, she had almost forgotten that Jay would still be there. He was sitting on the end of the bed. Was it confusion or exasperation he was feeling?

"Do you want to talk about this?" he asked.

"No, I don't think so," she said cheerily.

"Well I do, godammit! What was that all about?"

"Nothing more nor less than it sounded. There's nothing to talk about, Jay. I don't want you ever again to wake me with a fuck. It's as simple as that."

"Oh? You prefer an alarm clock?"

She smiled at him. "You're making fun of me."

"Not just you. I think I'm making fun of both of us. You don't want me ever to fuck you again. Is that what this is all about?"

"No, I didn't say that. I said I don't ever want you to wake me up with one of your good-morning fucks, not ever again." Mimi surprised herself with her own emphatic tone. She continued, "The trouble is I've suddenly realized that you fuck me without passion. All the passionate things you are, Jay, all you have in your life, you share with someone else, not with me. There's no passion in your morning fucks. Not passion for me, anyway. It's all there, Jay, but reserved for you. I saw that for the first time this morning."

"That can't be true. After thirty-some years of marriage and so many fucks, you claim I've never fucked you with passion?"

"Almost never. You're a selfish pig, Jay. You fuck for you.

You give me pleasure because it does something for you, not for me. I have an orgasm, so you've made a conquest. It's just another notch on your success-belt. Never again. Work it out. We won't talk about it anymore."

"What's this all about? This isn't about a fuck in the morning, this is about my asking you to rise above what you are."

"Maybe it is, and maybe I have. Anyway, this is not going to ruin our Christmas. Figure it out, Jay. I've got some working out to do myself. Being the matriarch of this family, running two businesses and being your wife is all shifting gears, because time has changed things. You're right about that."

"You're angry."

"No, I'm not."

"Look, Mimi, you can do better than those chic hats. You could have a great gallery instead of being an exclusive art agent who sells only on rare occasions. These are the eighties, Mimi. Boom years like New York has never seen them before. But you never climbed on the bandwagon. Maybe that's to your credit; and then again, maybe you just couldn't expand with the times. All I say is, if you can't, then retire. The family's big and dispersing and, well, it's time for a change."

"I think you're right. Don't worry, Jay, we'll work it out."

"You do mean that, don't you?"

"Oh, yes, I mean that."

"Well, it isn't that there's anything wrong with our marriage. Everybody knows that you're Mrs. Steindler and how wonderful you are."

"Jay."

"Yes."

"Don't worry about it, it'll all be all right."

"And what about all this morning stuff?"

"You'll have to find another way to get your day going, Jay, but don't do anything hasty now. Don't say something you'll regret."

"Oh, I don't intend to."

"Good, come on. The children will be up and downstairs. It's a wonderful day." She kissed him on the cheek.

"You do love me?" he asked. A man less vain might have begun to doubt it.

"I've always loved you, Jay. I just kept forgetting what a selfish pig you are, that's all."

They both laughed. "How could you forget that? The whole world knows it. And I would have thought my ex-wives had drilled that into you by now."

That was one of his endearing features, he could face up to himself. But to think that it meant he was about to change would have been a triumph of hope over experience. Pigs would fly? Not this one.

Chapter 28

About three in the afternoon, Rick turned up and a group assembled to undertake a long walk in the park. It was crisp and cold out. The kind of weather that wanted to snow but was too cold to do it. Mimi felt terribly happy: Rick noticed that at once. There were about eight of them meandering in pairs over a stone bridge. Rick, with one arm around Mimi's shoulder, steered them away from the others to lean against the side of the bridge. For some moments they stood together, viewing the park in its cold winter splendor, the fringe of buildings and skyscrapers in the distance, one of the best of New York City's landscapes.

"You seem different from yesterday," he told her.

"Something has happened."

"Good or bad?"

"Oh, good. Very good."

Rick smiled, feeling a tremendous surge of affection for her, and bent down and kissed her with an intensity that he had not displayed for some time. They gazed into each other's eyes. It was a long, searching look that passed between them.

"I'm having a moment of déjà vu," he told her, a sexual huskiness in his voice.

"Oh? You think we've lived this moment before?"

"I know we've lived this moment before. It was on a Greek island called Patmos, when we first met. I felt your hunger then, I feel it now."

"Hunger for what?" she asked, rather coyly, he thought.

"Something to still your heart."

That disarmed her. "You can be very perceptive about me, Rick."

"Ah, if only I had been clever, too." He gave her a cryptic look. "You were like a starved child who didn't know how to come out and play with life then. I was your first sexual playmate. I sense now you might be ready to come out and play again."

"I think you may be right. But that was a long time ago. I have to ask myself, what about a woman now in mid-life, restless, with the heart of a young woman, still with some of the innocence of a child? I've become restless, Rick, with my children, my marriage, my work. It's all moved on, it's all changing. But it's my life, and I think I have to go out and add to it. Or die. I found out something: no one else does it for you, adds to your life, no matter how much you think they do. That's an illusion. You do it all yourself."

They were lingering too long. The children had walked further ahead of them and were calling for Rick and Mimi to catch up. Hand in hand they resumed their walk. "The things you do in the name of survival," she said.

"Are you trying to tell me something?"

"Merely that I've become a mistress of compromise in the name of survival, only to find out at my age that survival isn't everything. Sometimes you can pay too high a price for it. My mother did, in a concentration camp in Poland, and it haunted her for the remainder of her life. Finally she committed suicide. I read something recently about survivors, the Jews of the Holocaust, and how many of them in their old age commit suicide as they come closer to facing death once more. Maybe they made too many compromises for their survival. You . . ." She hesitated, as if she wasn't quite sure she should go on, but at last she smiled at him and continued, "It was you who taught me to play with life, a lesson I haven't forgotten."

She kissed him on the cheek, then put her arm through his and treated him to that enchanting Mimi smile. They continued walking.

"Has Christmas triggered all this?" he asked her, not at all unhappy with what she was telling him.

"No, not Christmas. Jay, actually. World events, maybe. The sheer passing of time. It could simply be that. Or else facing my own mortality. Who knows? But maybe a combination of all those things has made me restless, wanting to begin all over again. Perhaps this time without survival so much in mind. After all, I have done all that. Maybe I am a woman with many lives to live. This time around I might try one with less compromise and more passion in it." She began to laugh.

"Have I missed something?" he asked.

"Yes, actually you have. Only this morning I accused Jay of having no passion for me. All the passion he has in his life is for himself. What he doles out is the leftovers. He has been cheating me of real passion all our married life."

"Don't be hard on him, he's been a great husband and a good father."

"A selfish bastard, a male chauvinist pig," she added.

"Still a great guy." They both began to laugh.

"He is, isn't he? No, I won't be hard on him. He did after all give me what I wanted, only not everything I wanted."

The air seemed raw, a chill to it that would gnaw you to the bone. By the time the group was returning to the house they felt it badly. They rang the front doorbell several times before Ben, one of Jay's sons from his first marriage, opened the door and greeted Mimi with a kiss.

"You look like you could use a whisky."

"I'm frozen."

"We're all downstairs in the kitchen where it's warm. There's a good big fire going," he told her.

"You're not going to believe this but I'm hungry again." That was Rick.

Robert, Mimi's youngest, announced, "I'm going to try and hold off for another hour before I pig out again."

There was a rush to shed mufflers and fur hats, jackets and coats, and fur-lined boots. Mimi loved all that, the coming and going of people, the house filled with children, friends, family. She watched the brood as they dispersed, some up the stairs to the drawing room, others down to the kitchen, some to the library. She lined up the wet boots, shook out several scarves.

She felt happy, satisfied with her lot, the more so for understanding that a change was upon them. She smiled, content but a realist about the future. She ran her fingers through her hair and looked at herself in the hall mirror. Rick came up behind her. He stroked her hair and put his cheek next to hers. They gazed at their reflections.

"What's happening, Mimi?"

"Destiny at work."

He took her hand in his, clasped it and put the palm to his lips to kiss it. "Then I'll say goodbye."

"Why goodbye?" she asked, surprised and somewhat disturbed.

"Because I have always known that I was never your destiny, any more than Jay is." There was emotion in his words, yet she saw affection and joy in his eyes for her. Abruptly he left her standing in the hall and joined the others in the kitchen.

Mimi trembled with emotion. Her present life was quite swiftly slipping into the past. Briefly she remembered their sexual passion for each other. Three times during the years since the twins were born they had had brief sexual encounters: a passionate, uncontrollably sensual few days in his house in Malibu, another in Mexico, and at the Plaza in New York. She had to close her eyes to calm her heart which was racing.

She started down the stairs. She could hear Jay talking. "Gorbachev's *glasnost* and *perestroika* have a certain logic, but we're talking here of a despotic empire, multi-ethnic, all at very different levels of civilization. How do you liberalize that? I think it takes another kind of logic. But Gorbachev's grand design, whatever happens to it, we have to face. The power structure in the world is changing. It's inevitable with what's happening there and in the Third World, and it's going to gather momentum faster than you think. Just look at what's happened already. More elbow room was available and we've seen spontaneous action from those lost Communist-dominated countries outside the USSR. When the opportunity was there they grabbed it—first the Poles and the Hungarians. That spirit of defiance was like a tonic for Eastern Europe. It broke out in East Germany, and then in my wife's own country, Czechoslovakia, and to a lesser degree maybe in little Bulgaria."

Jay was laying down the law about the effect of Gorbachev's attempts to liberalize the Soviet Union. An avid

TV-watcher, he had gathered opinions as well as seeing the events. He could pronounce authoritatively on trends in Eastern Europe and particularly on what he termed "my wife's own country." He meant Czechoslovakia. He made it sound more significant than "little Bulgaria," which he allowed to have had its share of upheaval too.

"I don't think we in the West appreciate what's really happening." Mimi recognized the voice of a friend of theirs, a delegate from Great Britain to the United Nations.

She heard her son, "I'm not so sure we don't appreciate what's happening, maybe take a charge of excitement from it ourselves. I was there with my Dad in Berlin on November 10th. Then I was told it had been one of the great moments in history, when they broke through the Berlin Wall. Its coming down has changed the world. Maybe it's the speed of it all that we don't appreciate here, the swiftness of change. Having to respond and not knowing how because the changes are so enormous. Everywhere you look countries are being transformed. Even that's a new kind of revolution. It begins to look more like a game of chess."

"They still shoot people who demonstrate on the streets." That was Jay again. "Only Romania," he continued, "insisted on a real bloody revolution. Karel, Mimi's father, would have loved to have been here, to have seen this day. The end of the Marxist-Leninist-Stalinist, totalitarian structure of power in Europe. Finished forever, one hopes."

Mimi stopped on the stair and flattened herself against the wall, listening to Jay talk about her father.

"He predicted all this, Karel did. Thirty years ago he was prophesying all this. Well, which of them wasn't, those old patriots? It was all that kept them alive. They had to believe it. No one else would. He would have loved to have returned to his Czechoslovakia, to see it for the first time able to shape the lives of its people without foreign interference. I wish Karel, or at least his daughter, had been in Prague in that exhilarating week in November. He would have said that it is our children, his grandchildren, who brought us freedom. It's true. It was the intervention of those admirably disciplined young people that created the Velvet Revolution."

"You are quite right, Mr. Steindler. It is all happening so

quickly, and with so little violence that it seems more like a miracle than the active will of the people. I have no doubts that my friend Vaclav Havel will be elected President of our country. This is a new world."

Mimi recognized the voice. It was full of hope and vigor. He spoke perfect English, but with an accent and tone reminiscent of her father's. She felt quite shaken, touched to her very soul to hear it again.

She took a deep breath and descended the remaining stairs into the kitchen. Alexander was standing at the fireplace, glass in hand, and addressing her family and friends.

"I'm full of hope and gratitude and belief that we can rise above the demoralizing effects of the hammer and sickle."

"But what a hard and long road," offered Mimi at the foot of the stairs. Everyone turned to face her. "But exciting."

She went to stand next to Angelica. "Thanks, Jay."

"For what?"

"For appreciating my father." She left it at that and quickly stepped forward to shake Alexander's hand.

"It was very presumptuous of me to call on you like this, especially on Christmas Day. I would have phoned but I didn't have a telephone number. I never use the telephone unless I must. Not my favorite instrument. You don't remember me?" Alexander felt compelled to say that: she seemed to him so aloof while he was so excited at seeing her again.

"Yes, I do. I don't remember much of that dreadful forty-eight hours in Prague, but I do remember you."

"Oh, good." He smiled, and a light came into his eyes. Mimi felt his warmth, his passion, and smiled back at him and suggested they find a more private place to talk, since he had taken the trouble to seek her out.

They were alone at last in the library. It seemed to Mimi an eternity from kitchen to the book-lined retreat. Alexander seemed somehow more handsome than she remembered. In his early forties, and still the sensualist, he was the man for whom she yearned in the quiet of the night.

He wasn't particularly tall, nor was his a movie-star handsomeness, but there was about him a macho manliness that was exciting and engaging, and only intensified by the stillness and calm he projected. His chunky physique was

matched by an intense sensitivity. Such contrasts enhanced
the interest of him. Yes, she felt physically attracted to him.
Possibly even more so free of stress of that day they met near
Prague, or the hysterics that preceded their wild passionate
fucking. She had never, not for one day, forgotten what it was
like to have his cock taming her cunt. Alexander carrying her
away from the pain of mourning into sexual ecstasy.

It was a small thing but it stuck in her mind: he had shaved
off his moustache. He was better dressed than the last time
she had seen him and well tailored, the salt-and-pepper tweed
jacket, the blue shirt with button-down collar, the wool tie in
a striking rust color, and gray flannel trousers with cuffs. He
had seemed shabbier at her father's funeral. He had a seductive charm, a natural sensuality that she found extremely attractive when alone with him in the seclusion of the library.
That had not changed.

Alexander felt a surge of desire for Mimi. He had not forgotten her, nor her grief, nor their sexual rutting in the tall
grass in the field. Did that sound crass? It wasn't meant to,
but they had been like two crazed animals whose intent was
to couple to the death. She had held for him an immediate
sensual attraction. A *coup de foudre*, not utterly unlike one
featured in a novel he wrote soon after meeting her. His heart
had been touched by the sight of Mimi Steindler, the daughter
of Count Karel Stefanik. She had not become an obsession
but a secret love, an unattainable goddess. Thus she had remained in the back of his mind as he got on with his life.
Destiny cannot be rushed, only obeyed.

Alexander smiled at her, he couldn't help it. He thought
himself such a fool, a fool in love.

She went directly to him and raised his hands and kissed
them, first one then the other, several times. He touched her
hair, ran his fingers through it. He closed his eyes and tried
to still his heart. He placed an arm around her shoulders and
they studied each other's faces. Just enjoying the scent of
each other, the warmth, their pleasure at seeing each other
again. "You're so changed without your moustache. If I had
seen a photo of you I might have not known you."

"But in the flesh?" he asked, teasing her.

She had the good grace to blush. Then she said, "Photo. I

don't believe this!" Removing his arm from her shoulder, she walked quickly to a worn, leather-covered wing chair. From the table next to it she searched a pile of books and withdrew one. She returned to him and placed it on the desk where he was standing. His face looked up at them from the dust jacket.

"Alexander Janacek! I must be mad. You've never left my heart and yet I never made the connection that you could possibly be this Alexander Janacek."

"Oh." That was all he could manage to say. He was too overjoyed. She had declared herself. She had been carrying him in her heart.

Mimi turned the book over and studied the photograph of him on the back. A black-and-white close-up of his attractive and intelligent face with sexy eyes that twinkled back at her. She looked from the photograph into those eyes. Mimi smiled. "I've not read it. I only just received it for Christmas. It's had rave reviews. My husband is in publishing."

"Oh."

"He tried to buy your book. It seems everyone tried to buy your book. I don't understand, Jay must know who you are, I can't believe he didn't trap you into a literary conversation."

"I never gave him my name."

Mimi began to laugh. "Whyever not?"

"He didn't ask me."

"Alexander, I think I'm confused. He invited you into the house, but never asked your name?"

He sat on the edge of the desk. "May I smoke? It's a dreadful habit but it's one I don't intend to break. I enjoy my cigarettes too much. But I can resist, if you'd prefer I didn't smoke in this room."

"Smoke if you must," she told him.

He drew a Gauloise from a packet in his pocket and placed it between his lips. From another pocket he pulled out a tiny box of matches. He lowered his eyes as he struck the match. His lashes were long and thick, his movements lazy, laid-back. There was something fiercely sensual in them.

"I arrived at your door on an impulse. I am not normally an impulsive man. I agonized these last ten days in New York about coming. But I had to. You see, I still believe we are destined to be together. In a few days' time we will have a new man at the helm in Czechoslovakia. Come back with me, stand with us during this momentous election. We can't lose. We have the taste of freedom again. There are new beginnings. Come home Mimi.

"That's why I came to your door, to ask you just that. One of your sons let me in. I said I was looking for you, your father had been a friend to us, and that I had met you in Prague. He asked me to wait and led me down to the kitchen where I was introduced to your husband as a man from Prague, a friend of the family. I began to protest, but somehow between my protestations and your husband's hospitality, introductions were lost."

Mimi began to laugh. "Jay will be furious. If he had known your name, he would have signed you by now to a two-book deal at the very least. You have taken literary New York by storm with this book. How have you managed to slip into the city for ten days and escape my husband and the book-hounds?"

"Quite simple. Only my agent knew I was here and we held most of our meetings in my room at the Algonquin."

"Some people think it the most sensitive and beautiful erotic novel ever written. Literary erotica is almost unheard of. My husband says, one day, with a body of work behind you you will win the Nobel Prize for Literature."

"He flatters me. And he underestimates Swedish prudery. Will you come to Prague with me for these next momentous days in our history?"

They stared into each other's eyes. Alexander could only guess how long they remained that way, facing each other, locked in a gaze that transfixed their emotions. Things were happening to him. It was seeing her again after such a long time. Loving her, as he had done from afar since their few hours together at the funeral, was one thing. But loving her where he could reach out and touch her was another. She had that fatal feminine charm over which chivalrous men in times past had dueled at dawn. Everything physical about her—her hair, her eyes, the smiling, sensuous lips, the slim body with large breasts, the way she moved with a hungry sensual fire kept in check, her elegance, the tone of her skin, and her hands with long tapering fingers—was perfect. He closed his eyes for a moment. Was he hoping that she would vanish, having seen her once again? Had the apparition of love he had conjured up gone?

Slowly he opened his eyes. She was still there. He ground out his cigarette in a glass ashtray and took the few steps that separated them. He slipped one arm around her, the other over her shoulder. He gently clasped the back of her head and drew her slowly, sensually, into his arms.

He told her, "You are the most dangerous woman I have ever met." Then he placed his lips lightly on hers. He felt the flesh of those lips he had dreamed about, so soft and succulent, and pressed his kiss harder. He felt her lips tremble. He could feel her breasts against his chest, the warmth of her body against his. He pressed more strongly, until her lips parted ever so slightly. With pointed tongue he licked the underside of her upper lip, then sucked it lightly, sweetly, and then the lower one. Once more he kissed her. He felt her give way, trembling in his arms. He realized he too was trembling. He knew she was his. But he knew also that he was an intruder in her house. That she was not free, and until she was, would not return to Prague with him. He could not bear her to reject him. He knew instinctively what he must do.

Mimi thought she would swoon, so exciting was his kiss, so strong his yearning for her. One moment he was there and nothing else in the world mattered. The next, before she realized what was happening, he was gone. He had gathered up his hat, coat and scarf, and was gone from the room before she could recover herself.

When she did regain her equilibrium she went after him. She ran from the library into the hall, resplendent with Christmas decorations, to see the entrance hall door of glass and ironwork close, a silhouette descending the steps and disappearing against the background of falling snow. Mimi nearly ran after him. She had her hand on the large, decorative bronze and wrought-iron handle of the door, but her feet didn't move. She was too overwhelmed to do anything. She felt pressured as never before. No kiss in her entire life had inspired in her the feeling of love evoked by his. It was as if the sun broke through a great cloud that had been her life. It

warmed her as almost no other love had. It was an erotic kiss,
which reached down into her soul. She felt something for this
man, this near stranger, that she had rarely felt for any other
human being. It was all the love she had felt for her father
when a child before the war, all the love and passion she
shared with Rick. All this, yet more.

Mimi's hand was flat against the cold glass of the door.
She watched the snow. She felt beyond life again. He loved
her. This sensitive intellectual, who had recently swept the literary world with his genius, loved her, had chosen her.

She felt a hand on her shoulder.

"Mimi?"

Jay's voice was drawing her back, away from the warmth
of that special romantic love that moved her so deeply. She
resisted him for as long as she could, trying to retain Alexander's kiss, his passionate desire for her. Jay turned her around
to face him. He took her hands in his.

"You're ice cold." He went through the motions of rubbing
warmth back into them.

"A nice guy. I presume he's gone?"

"Yes."

Jay did not miss the faraway look in her eyes.

"Another conquest, Mimi? Another admirer?"

She could not at that moment cope with his teasing. Reluctantly she told him, "Yes, I do believe he is."

"I could tell the moment you walked down the stairs into
the kitchen. He was lost to your charms."

"Jay, don't be a prick!"

He began to laugh. "Just teasing."

"No, you weren't."

"You know, Mimi, the older you get, the more like Karel
you become. Women swarmed around him even in his old
age. Men cluster around you, it seems, the more so as you get
older. That fatal Stefanik charm. Men are enslaved by you.
You're like a siren. One look and they're castaways for life."

She began to laugh. "You do exaggerate. You don't look
like a castaway to me, Jay."

"Oh, but I am, beached on your stony heart. But I don't
suppose he came here on Christmas Day to confess his undy-
ing love. At least, not yet."

Mimi smiled at his sheer wrongness, took it that she was amused and was flattered.

"Jay, you're going to hate yourself when I tell you who that man was."

"Oh?"

"That was Alexander Janacek."

"Don't be ridiculous." He began to laugh. "It's impossible. If Alexander Janacek were in New York, I can tell you I would have known it. So would anyone who counts in publishing. I would have recognized him, for a start."

"Then why didn't you?" What she wanted to say was, "Jay, that was Alexander Janacek and he loves me, he has a passion for me. You don't recognize anything."

"Mimi, you're not serious. You're just doing this to tease me, to annoy me because we lost him to another publishing house in the auction for his book. You are teasing me?"

"Whyever didn't you ask him his name, Jay?"

"I just thought he was another of those Czech dissidents your father gave haven to. Tell me it wasn't Janacek. Tell me it wasn't."

"It was, Jay."

"Where is he staying?"

"I don't know."

"How long is he here for?"

"He's leaving tomorrow."

"What did he want with you? You've got to get him back."

"If I talk to him . . ."

Jay, taking off on a tangent, interrupted her: "I'm sure I'd be able to make some deal with him for the future. I must talk to him, Mimi. We might have a Nobel Prize winner here. I want him for my firm." He stopped. Composing himself, he asked her yet again, "It's not true, is it?" And began to laugh. "You got me there for a while. Whatever made you make that up? Now who is he really?"

"One of the new Czech breed who thought I might like to be in Prague for the elections in a few days' time."

"God, what a relief. You would have ruined my Christmas Day. I swear, if I thought Janacek was in New York, I would search every hotel until I found him."

She began to laugh again.

"You're a cruel woman, Mimi." He put his arms around her. "A terrible tease. Come on downstairs. We're playing Christmas charades."

"I'll follow you. I need a few minutes in the library. I won't be long."

She returned to the library. It still held the aroma of strong French tobacco. She sat down in the chair and thought about this startling man. Is it true, she wondered, that it can take only a minute, not even a minute, a moment, to fall in love? She felt happy, so very happy. Was this really happening to her, and in middle age? Romantic love was for the movies, for other people, for those possessed by fantasy. He wouldn't be there yet, she would call him later at the Algonquin—at least she knew where he was staying. To say what? She had no clear idea. Just to hear his voice at least once more seemed all important to Mimi. That was it. She wanted that.

But she did not call the Algonquin. Hesitation, interruptions by the children, then charades took over. Too much mirth, an excess of champagne ... When she finally found time, and all hesitation had vanished, it was much too late. The moment had passed. She knew that and pacified herself by rationalizing: time enough to call him in the morning. She went to bed and fell into a deep, comfortable sleep.

Jay was gone when she awakened. There was a note pinned on his pillow.

Good morning, my dear. Something is missing from my life. This is getting boring, I am not a happy man. How about we change the game?

Love,
Jay

Mimi smiled. She sat up in bed, her head full of Alexander's love, his sexuality, the delights of erotic intercourse. She could hardly put out of her mind his sensual kiss, his tongue teasing between her lips, his hands caressing her. A shiver of delight passed through her body. She felt electrified at the thought of a sensuous life with Alexander. She reached for the telephone and called the Algonquin. They claimed he wasn't there. She insisted he was, until they admitted that he had been there but had checked out an hour before.

Mimi could hardly believe it; she had been so sure she would hear his voice, that there was something real and special in store for them. Her disappointment hurt. "Well, that's that," she said aloud. She left the warmth of her bed, opened the curtains and looked down into the garden. It was cold and she wanted it to be fresh, with green leaves and flowers everywhere. Fate had stepped in, the timing was off, this wasn't meant to be. With such thoughts she strove to put him firmly out of her mind. In spite of her disillusion, he had instilled in Mimi such optimism, such a renewed alertness to the sensual, she could hardly allow herself to wallow in self-pity. He had left her feeling marvelous: she was not going to turn her back on what he had given her. There were things to be done. But this time differently.

All her life Mimi had slipped into doing things for her survival. It was the pattern of her life, a blueprint first laid down by her father: she had learned well how to follow it. After her father there had always been strangers who, out of kindness toward a displaced child, indicated a path for her to follow. She had learned to accommodate herself to the demands of survival, to enjoy each day with the best of what she had been given. As Mimi had lived her entire life that way, she assumed everyone else did. Only with maturity and seeing her own children and Jay's grow up did she realize that sometimes you leap chasms, take chances, plump for adventure, live spontaneously without survival in mind. Risk itself may be a pleasurable experience.

Alexander Janacek and his declaration of love came to mind. Why hadn't she rushed out into the snow after him? She felt something for him, something very special. Why was she so slow to react? Why had he run away? What did he mean, that she was a dangerous woman? Why had she waited so long that morning to call his hotel? All those questions one intended to answer.

Chapter 29

Several times during Mimi's busy day she felt a tremendous surge of aloneness. It was a strange and somewhat frightening feeling. She had not experienced loneliness since she was a young girl and Karel returned to claim her. She had mixed feelings about Alexander's having left New York without a word. She blamed him for her present unease. He had appeared to ignite in her a flame guttered in his flight from her. There could be no happiness without him. But the changes in her life that would have to be made to be with him? Monumental. She had to ask herself whether life with him would be worth it.

Lights were ablaze all over the house as the taxi pulled up. Home and family. She savored the comfort, the safety. It felt good. She placed her key in the lock and walked into the hall. It looked festive, with its Christmas decorations and twinkling lights. Laughter was coming from the library. The twins were there reading something that evidently amused them. They were extremely close, even if they had been separated by university and college, Milos at Yale, and Angelica at Vassar. Handsome children, he unmistakably the son of Rick, though many of his mannerisms resembled Jay's. He had been brought up more by Jay than his own father. Angelica was almost the image of Mimi at her age.

She called out, "I'm home."

"Your latest admirer sent flowers, Mom," Angelica told her.

"Where have you hidden them?"

"They've been put upstairs in your bedroom. A note in an

envelope came with them. No card. It's on the silver tray in the hall." Then they forgot about her. The book seemed to offer more immediate entertainment.

"Where's Jay?" she called over her shoulder.

"Not home yet."

She found the envelope on the tray, picked it up and, after dispensing with her coat and hat, went up to the bedroom. Three dozen long-stemmed tea roses confronted her, the loveliest color, the heavenliest scent. They were partially open, dramatically beautiful. Only then did she think they might be from Alexander. It had not occurred to her that he might send flowers. She had thought the children were teasing her when they had talked of an admirer. Flowers might be anticipated from any number of people who had been at the house over Christmas. But, having seen the roses, she looked excitedly at the envelope in her hand. She liked the way he wrote her name. With a firmness and determination. She walked to the desk and picked up the ivory letter-opener. Slipping it under the flap she slit open the envelope, careful not to tear the paper.

Dear Mimi,

The heart is indeed a lonely hunter. I walked the streets of New York last night thinking of you and my silly, stupid performance. Now I have declared myself, no matter how badly, at least I have done that.

There were so many things I wanted to say to you before I blurted out my feelings. It was a vain hope to think that you might return to Prague with me, even in the coming months. Yet, there is no one in this world I'd rather have at my side to share the momentous changes happening in our country, the country you left so long ago.

I wanted to give it back to you, fresh and new, as I want to give myself to you. You have been a magnificent obsession ever since the first day we met at that sad time in your life. I loved you, Mimi. My dreams are erotic, exciting, and always filled with you. And in my waking hours you drift in and out of my life, an apparition, a lovely creature I yearn for.

To roll back the years and return to the beginning is

to see all other loves, other happinesses, evaporate into the past. Mimi, I told you, you are a dangerous woman. How many other men have loved you, wanted you and become obsessed with having you? Many, I am sure, have tried; some like myself from afar, others like your husband, from closer. How many have you given yourself to? That's what makes you dangerous, Mimi. You draw men to you like a siren. But how many are you drawn to? How many have you loved, how many have you given yourself up to as you gave yourself up to me?

Mimi, you were born to be loved magnificently. Few men can resist a challenge such as that. I know I can't. I did want you to come back to Prague with me, I did want you to stand by my side for our new beginnings. That was selfish, a selfish dream, part of the fantasy I have that you will love me one day as I love you. But where would we be without our dreams, without our fantasies? What have we to look forward to unless we reach down into our sleepy, lazy hearts, our cold souls, and pump warm rich love into them? To live in our dreams, Mimi, live in our fantasies, make them realities—that's what makes us rich, you and I. I don't know your dreams, your fantasies, I know you've lived in them all your life and made most of them come true, and I love you for that. Mimi, we are lovers bound together by our lust, but we are more, much more than that, too. I could write you erotic love letters and share my dreams, open my soul to you, give you my heart. But instead I send you tea roses because they suit you, because their scent is sweet, their blossom voluptuous, rich, special, as you are to me.

I lay down my pen and will write no more to you until we have had each other as we did in the tall grass on that late summer's day, till we can be what we should be to each other, until you come to Prague and find me.

Yours,
Alexander

Mimi was overwhelmed. Here was proof. It hadn't been a mere foolish hope. This man had declared his love. He had loved her for years and kept his counsel, given her time, lived in his fantasies. She had sensed that masculine, sensitive Czech charm that her father had. His declaration of love stood apart from those of her former devotees. It was true, everything he wrote about her. They had hardly said a word to each other but he knew her so well. He had arrived in her life at just the right moment, the timing was perfect. But he had also been right to run away. There were momentous changes happening to Mimi, in her own little world as well as in the world outside. There was something about this man that was different from any other she had known. The closest she had come to feeling as she did for him was the love she had felt for her father, and for Rick.

Time, she needed time. Mimi would not go to him, unless she was sure of herself, of her feelings for him. She was astute enough to know that, if she gave herself to Alexander as she had given herself to Rick, it would not be the same thing. Alexander was no rolling stone, he was as dangerous as she was. To have a relationship with him that was erotic and nothing more would be impossible. Here she sensed was real passion, committed love. They would be well matched in their lust for each other, and their love of life. Neither age nor other people nor places would affect their love for each other.

She touched the roses, bathed her face in their scent. If she were to go to him, it would not be because he flattered her, or for her own survival, or so that she could get on with her life. No, she would not go to him, ever, unless she felt ready to give herself up to him solely because they loved each other beyond all else in life. With Alexander it would be a matter of sharing themselves with each other. Nothing less would do.

She folded the letter and placed it in the envelope. She had had love letters before from admirers. Usually unworthy of serious consideration, there had always been something not quite genuine about them. This was her first real love letter. Mimi consigned it to the drawer where she kept her jewelry. She slipped out of her dress into a black satin nightdress, its bodice of black lace with thin black satin shoestring cords which she passed over the shoulders. She was no sooner in her bed than she slid into a deep, dark, dreamless sleep. One of those real undisturbed sleeps which neither sounds nor people can easily penetrate. For several hours she unconsciously wallowed in the warmth and softness, the luscious comfort of nothingness.

Mimi ran one foot against the other, trying to come alive out of her sleep. The feel of her own skin, the warmth of her body lured her back, down into the depths where she might succumb once more to warm sensuous sleep. In its depths this time she sensed the libidinous Mimi. They were good feelings. She struggled once more to free herself from sleep. Impossible. That lovely velvet world beckoned still. In a half-dreaming state her skin was like satin to her own touch, to his touch, the feel of a man's hands waking her body. She gave in to those hands caressing her skin, her hair, the feel of a kiss at the back of the neck, the warmth of a man up against her back, holding her tight in to him. In his nakedness he stirred her erotic soul and she felt her sexual yearnings, aroused, hot even, and liked the feeling, squirmed obediently to the sensation, trying halfheartedly to wake herself. She felt her legs being spread to accommodate him, the black satin gown being raised, caressing of her thighs. His hands were everywhere, working magic over her skin. She sighed, felt the stirrings of desire for penis and intercourse and orgasm. She tried to fight her way out of this dream, this sleep.

A twilight of wakening? Mimi felt herself raised off the bed, the gown being pulled higher, and then over her head. She slipped back against the pillows. Her body could resist no longer. She gave in, began moving, tiny rocking pelvic motions. Now she was caressing her own body, squeezing her cunt muscles with strong spasms, and the muscles in her bottom. She luxuriated in her own hunger for intercourse. Her breasts were free of black lace now, and in her half-sleep she caressed them and felt herself wildly sexual, getting closer to orgasm. This was sleep sexualized. She dived back into that deep sleep, taking desire with her. She imagined the warmth of his body, so masculine. Men, sex, delicious. She felt the tip of a penis touching, probing, her now moist labia. Her excitement mounted. And then an admirable cock, with a single, hard thrust, was inside her tight up, against the cervix. The violence of that man, that cock, broke the dream.

She placed a hand over her eyes, and opened them. She

was awake. Jay was on top of her, fucking her. Her cunt was alive and reacting to every penetration, drawing him in. It was that intercourse that had awakened her from her deep dreamless sleep. It had not been a dream, he had fucked her in her sleep. Taken her when she had been dead to the world. Mimi was shocked. She had required of him only one thing: never to do that again. This was his gross way of imposing yet another of his morning fucks on her.

The room was dark, as it always was in the early hours of the morning, their usual rising time. Just a soft light from the lamp set on the table next to his side of the bed. The light he normally reached out to when fucking her and switched on when he judged she was ready to come. He liked seeing her face when she came.

Mimi moved her hands from her eyes and looked at her husband. A look of utter delight was on his face when he said, "Give this up? You could no more abandon this morning fuck than I can. You like it too much, Mimi. We're too good together. It was an idea you had, and a bad one, my never fucking you like this again. Listen to your cunt, Mimi, not your head. It makes more sense."

She was appalled. This was so unlike Jay. "Cunt" was not a word in his vocabulary, nor was the anger she sensed familiar. In their entire married life Jay had never been more rude, never ridden so roughshod over her feelings. She recognized an extra forcefulness in every thrust of his cock, an angry edge to his way of fucking her. She bit her hand and stared into his eyes. Wild with anger herself, she concentrated on restraining her own orgasm. She knew he would not want to come inside her until she had been satisfied. It was part of his pride, part of his possession of her, what turned him on.

Finally she told him even as he moved in and out of her, "Get off me, Jay. Now." As if he would! He saw the anger in her eyes, heard it in her voice. But it made no difference. He pulled her tight against him, fucked her harder and with a faster pace.

"Don't fight me on this, Mimi. You're on the edge and you want to come. Don't pretend you're not enjoying this."

"I warned you, Jay, but you never took it seriously."

"Not for one moment."

She tried to push him off her. She was angry now and began to fight. She felt as if she were being raped, violated. There was no consent. They were two people, husband and wife, behaving utterly out of character. This was not the Jay she had known and loved, had a family with. The moment seemed to transform her too.

They were both shocked. She raised her hand and it descended to crack him hard across the face. He withdrew immediately from her body, then left the bedroom.

Mimi lay among the pillows on the bed, her eyes closed, moist with tears, one hand covering them. She was distressed, not just for herself but for both of them. When Jay came out of the bathroom with a towel wrapped around his waist, having shaved and showered, he walked around the room, putting on the lamps, dressing. Mimi watched him. The anger was gone. Something like sadness seemed to be taking them over. She seemed mesmerized by his movements, unable to take her eyes off him. She wanted to cry, but she couldn't, nor could she speak. Neither could he.

He finished knotting the black silk tie with the tiny white dots on it. A gray pin-striped waistcoat went on over a white button-down shirt. He turned toward her. He was looking down at his fingers deftly buttoning the form-fitting waistcoat. He walked to the bed and stood over Mimi. She watched him as she had watched him a hundred times snappily adjusting the waistcoat so that it fitted smoothly.

"Mimi, I make no apologies for what just happened, nor do I want you to. I have never behaved so badly to you or any woman as I have this morning. You're dangerous, Mimi. I honestly think it is you who have driven me to behave as I have, and I don't appreciate it, not at all. I'm moving, going back to our house. If you come home, it had better be . . ."

She interrupted, "Don't say any more, Jay. You don't have to spell it out for me, nor do you have to issue ultimatums."

"So long as you understand."

"And if I don't?"

"Well, then, we'll have to come to some amicable arrangement, won't we?"

Mimi had rarely seen him so cold and angry, but rarely had

she so trampled on his pride. She watched him turn, put on his jacket and button it up.

"Jay," she called out.

He turned around. "Yes, Mimi."

She could see in his eyes that he expected her to apologize. In a moment of weakness, from fear of losing him, she very nearly did. Instead she asked, "Would you pass me my robe?" unable even to stand naked in front of him. He handed it to her. Once more she was about to say something to soothe his anger, but then she saw her black lace nightdress lying on the floor where he had thrown it. He had taken her while she was still unconscious in sleep. That was the reality. Mimi knew she had blinded herself to it long enough. She would never apologize. Nor would she ever go back to him.

She slipped on the silk kimono. With him still watching her, she rose from the bed. He seemed to be waiting for that apology or at the very least an explanation.

"I did ask you never to fuck me like that again. I won't be coming back home, I think I'd like to stay here. I think we should live separately for a while."

"Just like that?"

"No, Jay, not just like that. Because this marriage is over. What happened this morning should not have happened to two people who have had a good long run in marriage with lots of rewards in it. Ours still had, a few days ago."

He sat down on the bed and gently took her by the arm. "There is someone else?"

"This had only to do with us, you and I. Our marriage has been the best there could be, but it's had its run."

"Because you don't want to change?"

"No, Jay, because I *do* want to change, but not the way you want me to."

"The family?"

"I'm not deserting you or the family. I'm quitting a marriage that no longer works. You should admit that. It can't work if I'm not happy, and I can't change to suit you."

"What's all this about, Mimi, suddenly not being happy?" Then he surprised her. "No, don't bother to answer that. I don't really want to know. You want some space, a separation. You try it. But, Mimi, I hope you know what you're getting into. From being a happily married woman in New York for your entire life to being just another chic divorcée ... you think that's going to bring you happiness? You just think that way, and wait and see. What a rude awakening you are going to get, my dear. You've had a terrific marriage, it's opened all doors. Sex just about every day of your married life, and no husband could have been more devoted to giving you pleasure in that. You've been spoiled all your life. Dump me, dear, and your father's gone, and while Rick is a great guy, he'll never give you the stability or the life I have. Divorce, living alone in New York, that's a different ball game, and it's tough.

"You're not as easy to love and live with as you think, Mimi. You're private, closed up in many ways. I called you dangerous before, and you are, because you held me prisoner with sex, your charm and aloofness, your Slovak coquetry. You've held me all these years by those things. I saw them as a challenge to get through in order to take possession of you. It never occurred to me that I might never possess you. After all these years I see that you never gave yourself wholly to me as I wanted you to. I never possessed you totally, brought you to heel as I did my other wives and lovers. Instead you took me over, possessed me. Maybe we've both had enough, only I wouldn't give in whereas you did."

Mimi looked genuinely shocked. He smiled. "You think I'm being cruel because you're leaving me? It's not true. I'm not a cruel man. Selfish, yes. I have two other wives who will attest to that, and several lovers. But not cruel. Maybe honest, blunt even, because I'm hurt, because I feel cheated that I never did possess you." He fell silent. Mimi could think of nothing to say. They looked at each other, and it was more embarrassing and sad than anything else. Finally he cleared his throat and told her, "I think it's all been said now."

He stood up. "Let's keep it amicable." He reached out for her hand and she gave it to him. That old Jay Steindler charm was in play. He pulled her up by the hand, clasped her in his arms, stroked her hair and said, "Let's keep it quiet, the divorce, as quiet as possible. Reno, Nevada, I think. Call your lawyer."

Again the feeling of shock. She stepped back. "I hadn't

even thought about divorce. Nor about being a woman alone without a husband in New York. A cruel dig, Jay."

"Yes, maybe. I left both my other wives. This way round maybe you have to allow me a little cruelty. I've never been walked out on before. But I don't like sounding cruel, or being thought cruel, so we won't give that away, will we?"

"You don't like getting less than you bargained for."

"That's true." He smiled.

"And you always bargain to get twice as much as you give, Jay."

"Yes, that's true too, Mimi. Who will tell the children?"

"We will tell the children," she said. "But let's for the moment get rid of the anger we both have before we tell anyone."

She was surprised, even relieved, to see tears come into Jay's eyes. They were genuine. She hadn't lived with him for more than a quarter of a century not to know that. She bit her lip to hold back her own tears. She saw him visibly brace himself, gather all his strength to restrain those tears.

"You'll be staying here?"

"Yes."

"Why don't we both come and go as we like? As you said, you're not leaving the family. It's only me you're leaving." He cleared his throat. "We have a dinner engagement tonight, let's keep it."

"I think not, Jay."

He kissed her on the forehead. A cold kiss that said he was gone from her life. She hadn't fully realized during all their years together how really selfish he was. How quickly he would dispose of things that no longer gave him what he wanted. She was grateful for that selfishness.

Chapter 30

A spin-off of leading a separate life was the amount of leisure time. Mimi marveled at how many more things she could fit in a day merely by not being married to Jay.

A few days after their break-up she went to their house and arranged to remove her personal things. When she had brought them to the Stefanik house, Mimi really felt as if she were beginning her life all over again, although she was still living pretty much as she had when she had been married to Jay, the difference being that there was more time. So much more time.

How could she not miss Jay? He had been such a mainstay of her existence for more than half her life. What she didn't miss was living with his selfishness, his underlying disrespect for her as a woman, an independent human being. He had tried to mold her to fit his needs, his complex desires. That Mimi had lived with that for so long and had ignored it for everything that was good about him and their marriage was the hardest thing to take about their split up.

The children had been shocked. They loved Mimi and Jay, the family, but reluctantly respected their parents' decision. The extended family, though less supportive at first, eventually rallied, especially when Jay made it clear that Mimi, whether he lived with her or without her, would always be its matriarch. It was only she who was not so sure of that. Mimi was not so certain of anything. The changes were too swift and left her reeling, reassembling, re-evaluating her life and what she wanted. Sophia was loyal and supportive as ever. Her only comment, "My Gott." And then she baked a mocha cream cake, Mimi's favorite.

Those first days after she left Jay, Mimi contemplated calling Alexander in Prague. He was not always in her thoughts, but certainly at the back of her mind. Often she would remove his letter from her drawer. Long after the roses were gone, she thought about them, wondered what he was doing, what his life was like, and half-expected he might replace them. But he never had.

Mimi knew in her heart she would one day go to Prague to seek him out. That conviction grew stronger every day, but she would not move in haste. She wanted to get her own house in order before she took such a momentous step. Nearly every day of the months of silence since he had appeared at the house, she sat down and wrote him a letter which she never posted. She tied them with a yellow satin ribbon and placed them in a drawer. One day she would give them to him.

Since her father's death, Mimi had hardly disturbed Karel's papers. There had always been tomorrow to do that in. Now it seemed tomorrow had come. Mimi divided her time between that fascinating labor and working with some of the women at the atelier, only to find that she had lost interest in that business. She thought of re-designing her department at Saks, but the moment she started discussions at the Fifth Avenue shop she was bored. The notion faded. Only dealing in contemporary paintings mildly held her interest. If she could find anything to dislike Jay for—apart, of course, from selfishness and manipulation of her during their years of marriage—it was that he had destroyed for her those slender lifelines that had ensured her survival. Before long Mimi's greatest interest, her utter fascination, was getting to know Karel through his papers. She fell in love with him all over again, but this time more as a man than as a father. Slowly she began to understand his passion for his country. Czechoslovakia began once again to be her country. The remarkable events that took place the day of his interment on the family estate were now seen quite differently. And always with her investigation into her father's life and that sad day when he was sealed forever in the family crypt, her thoughts drifted toward Alexander. She relived their first meeting, their sexual possession of each other. The memory could still excite her.

Their attraction for each other, that kiss in this very house. There was much to contemplate.

Her decision came suddenly. At the first opportunity of assembling Angelica, Milos and Robert for supper she set their minds at rest about what she was going to do. She hoped it might ease their concern about her. Though she loved them dearly, she could not bear their constant phone calls, their idea that she was lonely and unable to create a life for herself beyond being their mother, the wife of Jay Steindler, chic hat designer, private art dealer.

A dinner was held in the kitchen of the Stefanik house: Sophia, Mimi, and her three children attended. Each had made an effort to be there. It was a happy dinner and delicious, with Sophia cooking all the things the children loved. And after dinner, when Mimi told them that she had become caught up in her father's papers, his life and his country, and that they had opened new interests for her. They seemed pleased, encouraging her to take time to rediscover her heritage. Then she told them, "Guys, leaving your father was the beginning of many changes for me. I want a new life. That's not to say that I want to abandon all of my old one, just to move away from some of it. I hope you can understand that."

There had been endless questions, to which she could give very few answers. But when Angelica asked, "What about the hat business?" she answered without hesitation.

"I'm selling that company off."

"And the art dealing?" asked Robert, who with Milos had been keen on that since they were children when Mimi and Barbara had taken them around exhibitions and museums.

"All dealing suspended for the time being."

"You're dropping out of your life," suggested Angelica.

"And beginning all over again. How exciting. Mom, you're the greatest."

"You can travel, go around the world," offered Milos.

"Just don't let yourself get picked up by some gigolo. You're a stunner, Mummy, and you have money. Alone, out in society . . . you know, all that sort of stuff. It happened to my friend Jessie's mom," warned Angelica.

"But Jessie's mom is pretty dumb and was sort of desperate for a man. That's not our mom, Ange," said Robert, a note of annoyance in his voice.

"Sorry, Mom, Robby's right. A stupid thought. Travel sounds great, bumming around the world without a care in the world. You deserve at least that, Mummy."

"Well, I might return to Czechoslovakia." Mimi hadn't realized until that moment that that was really what she wanted to do.

"Return to your roots and all that."

"Something like that." *And the man I have fallen in love with,* she mentally footnoted her statement.

Mimi was quite taken aback by their loyalty, their affection for her, their enthusiasm for a new life for their mother. Not one day more did she hesitate. Lawyers were galvanized into preparing the sale of her businesses, the first of a series of events that coincided to persuade Mimi to take a leap into the unknown. For the first time since she had left her father's house to live with Jay, Mimi had time to review her father's life. He seemed to occupy much of her thoughts now she was once more living in the house he had left her. His things represented a world that had been snatched from her as a child. Those same things which, in the years when they had come together as a family, she had tolerated but had in her heart rejected, now suddenly took on a new importance for her. She realized how very cosmopolitan the house was. Alone there with Sophia, it was like being in an island, a European island, in the middle of Manhattan. She had ceased to think of herself as a Czech, a non-American, after she had arrived with Sophia in New York. It was not a matter of denial. That would have been impossible once her father had returned to find her and she had lived with her family in this very house. It was more that she had assimilated with New York, America. They represented safety, success, excitement, life, love and happiness. Everything that might have lost its significance, but hadn't.

Mimi had assumed that Karel had become like her. On the surface, he had. She read his papers and diaries, she searched out documents, records of the possessions he still held in Czechoslovakia, which had many years before been made over to the Countess Mimi Alexandra Stefanik. Recovering from the surprise of her father's gifts, and his silence about them in his lifetime, Mimi began to understand that, although he had left his country behind him, he had neither abandoned nor driven it from his heart. His homeland remained the center of his life until his death. He had chosen to love two countries, America and the country of his birth. One was like a secret lover, a mistress that he kept hidden, the other was his life, where he flourished and chose to display his love openly. Or so she had once thought. The years since his death had always held surprises concerning Karel, whom she had come to understand but had never really known. The man she knew was the man of her dreams. She had recognized only what he had been in her dreams, in her fantasies. In reality, Mimi had ignored all the things he was that didn't fit her picture of him.

Coincidence on coincidence, an invisible net drawing her into its center? Then she received telephone calls from her cousin in Prague—the new government was returning properties confiscated by former regimes to their original owners. For the Stefanik family, the first was the country estate in its entirety. Mimi instructed, "Set it up, I'll take it." Then the palace in Prague, and a possibility of the hunting lodge. Childhood memories came floating back. And, as a world she had been denied for most of her life was suddenly thrust upon her, so was a new identity: the Countess Mimi Alexandra Stefanik.

She was suddenly wrapped up in a world she had considered lost forever. It had never occurred to her that any of it would one day be hers, that she wanted it to be, until it was. With every acquisition returned to her came the sad news of its dereliction, almost its destruction. Fifty years of neglect and looting under Communist control had ruined properties and companies still owned by her. They were run into the ground and debt-ridden. In taking them back she would inherit a lifetime of work for her and her children in restoring what had belong to them before the Second World War. And what shocked her more than anything was that she did not hesitate for one minute. She wanted it all, every last possession restored to her family, including every object looted from her estates. She would seek them out without sparing herself.

More than once during those months since she parted from Jay, she nearly went back to the safe haven that being married to him had provided. It took courage not to, to fight the crisis and remain alone, adrift in the world. It was scary but exciting to begin again. She went through Karel's papers and old photographs and deeds to properties, something she had neglected since his death. Mimi began to feel curious about Czechoslovakia, about Prague especially. Who would she have been, how different her sensibilities, had she returned to Prague after the war as Mimi Stefanik? She couldn't imagine how things would have been but the thought intrigued her and caused her to follow more closely events in that country.

For a woman who is middle-aged though looks and feels young, who has her family behind her and is newly divorced, it is a necessity to re-evaluate her life. Where do you go from there? What do you do with the rest of your life? Mimi found it horrifying that, with youth receding, an awful lot of options were falling by the wayside. There had always been men in Mimi's life, but she had never gone in search of them, anymore than she had sought a lover or a husband. She had gone in search only of a father. Men had always cared for Mimi. She had come to expect and like that. Even in these strange, lonely days and nights away from Jay, she was certain a man of substance would come into her life again. She would know love better than she had ever known it before.

She wanted to fly to Prague, to seek it out, to knock on Alexander's door. But she didn't feel strong enough. When she went to him, if she went to him, it would have to be for the right reasons. To give herself up to him, and to love. Mimi found it disturbing that two men, Jay and Alexander, within a very short timespan, had called her dangerous. She wanted better than dangerous, she wanted extraordinary for Alexander.

Instead she went to stay with Barbara in Salzburg where her husband was rehearsing an orchestra. They talked about the past, their long and firm friendship. It was a happy visit, and Mimi told her about Alexander. She extended her visit to Barbara to attend a social event few outside Austria's elite are invited to. At her hostess's request, and as her house guest, Mimi was extended an invitation, since Barbara and her husband were the guests of honor. She attended a grand ball in a magnificent palace in the hills above Salzburg, given by one of Austria's foremost aristocrats, where the musical elite joined the aristocracy of various countries at a gala evening.

It was one of those affairs for which the women rifle their safe deposit boxes for jewels and men sport their decorations. Mimi found it splendid but shocking, a step back in time and into a European culture she had not experienced before and could never had imagined existing in the 1990s. Especially shocking as the man who was to be her partner at the ball was an Austrian prince, several years younger than herself, who wore the German Iron Cross, that coveted distinction from the Second World War, dangling from a Nazi ribbon round his neck.

Barbara had sought to satisfy Mimi's penchant for younger men in choosing him for her. She was not so much shocked at the young man's decoration as surprised. He was a handsome Austrian, intelligent, not unamusing, and with a reputation for liking women too much. There was an awkward moment when Barbara made the introductions. When he saw the three of them staring at the cross, he fingered it. A light came into his eyes and he told them, "It was my father's. I am very proud to wear it. The Führer himself placed it around his neck." And with that he changed the subject, encircled Mimi's waist and waltzed her into the stream of dancers.

The war had been over for nearly fifty years and all was supposedly forgiven if not forgotten. She understood, for the first time, maybe not forgiven on both sides. That seemed more than obvious for most of the men wore their Nazi war decorations pinned to expensive and well-tailored dress suits. Some women flaunted them on ribbons pinned to their sumptuous ball gowns. It was unnerving, embarrassing. Mimi felt ridiculously naive to have thought that the Nazi was gone from the world forever. The deadly glamor lingered.

The palace was one of the showplaces of Austrian baroque, luscious and filled with unimaginably beautiful objects. The young man took her on a tour of the rooms. He had been smitten by Mimi from the first moment he saw her. She did look exceedingly beautiful in an ivory taffeta ball gown with egret feathers on her shoulders for sleeves, and a décolletage that was the envy of many a woman at that ball. Her voluptuous face was all her companion needed to enslave him. The Stefanik charm, the tilt of the chin and the head moving back ever so slightly to induce a reflex action of one shoulder thrusting provocatively forward. The husky laugh and teasing eyes did the rest. He swept her from one room to the next. Mimi was impressed. Then, reaching into a jardinière for a key, he said, "In here is my uncle's study, his favorite room. Only special people are allowed to come in here."

He placed the large decorative ormolu key in the seventeenth-century lock and turned it. The room was magnificent with four enormous windows overlooking a balcony. In the far distance, a glow marked the position of Salzburg. The windows were draped heavily with ocher silk damask, lined and interlined, held back with elaborate silk tassels. The walls were hung in the same fabric, and on them magnificent paintings were arranged. The young man flipped a switch on the wall and each of the paintings sprang to life under its own light.

Mimi concentrated for several minutes on one enormous painting by the French painter David: white horses rearing against a wide landscape, beautiful women, dogs, and bold and handsome men in sumptuous military dress. A passionate, romantic painting that struck a note with her. Something about it was familiar. She stepped further back from the painting to give herself distance and bumped against the wall. Mesmerized by the painting, she hardly noticed. Her mind was tripping back in time. She knew that painting. Where had she seen it?

The young man approached her. Placing an arm on the wall, he pinned her to it with his body. He tilted her chin up and kissed her lightly on the lips. He was sexy, young and strong. She felt the physical attraction. He put his tongue in the cleft made by her breasts and licked her there. She closed her eyes, enjoying the sensation. But, when she opened them again to the painting over his shoulder, she lost interest in his advances and the pleasure she had experienced. The years fell away like autumn leaves and she recognized the glorious work of art facing her. That painting had been in their house in Prague. Mimi remembered it now as if she were five years old again and playing there in the room where it had hung, pretending she was part of the painting, that she belonged in it. It all came flooding back to her now. As a little girl she would imagine she knew all the people and animals in the painting, and act out stories about them. They had been her playmates, those exciting people in the David painting.

The young man was too anxious. He guided her hands downward: she must not miss his erection. The action was crude, she found him offensive. She stared at the Iron Cross around his neck. Disgust rose in her. She pushed him away from her with a strength that nearly knocked him off balance and quite surprised herself. Mimi was stunned. To have her childhood revived again like that, by something she had forgotten for so long. To come upon it once more in a schloss in Austria was amazing. The painting had obviously been stolen from her father. It was part of her life, her family heritage. She slapped her princeling hard across the face.

"Don't be vulgar," she told him and flounced from the room.

Mimi said nothing to Barbara or her husband and several days later returned to New York. She was angry, obsessed with the painting. She wanted it back. No Nazi was going to keep it, she had made up her mind to that. There had to be proof that the painting belonged to the Stefaniks. This was a new sensation for Mimi, anger and possessiveness over an object.

For days she searched, and was finally rewarded with a photograph of Dr. Benes and her father standing in Karel's study in the house in Prague. There was the painting in recognizable detail behind the two men. The caption underneath the photograph in the book: "The Stefanik Palace, Prague. Dr. Benes and Count Karel Stefanik, Prague, 1931." It was proof enough.

It was the painting: that had made Mimi want to return to Prague. It was such a little thing, compared to the many people who for the last thirty years had passed through her father's house and had coaxed her to do just that: take an interest in Czechoslovakia. None of them had inspired her to return. Not even Alexander and his declaration of love had reached down into her heart and galvanized enough awareness for her to endure seeing even the smallest piece of her life and home, torn away, stolen from her. War loot hanging in an Austrian palace. A visible denial of her right to have lived a happy childhood in the country and home she was born to. It was the spark that set her aflame. In a moment it had wrenched her back through a lifetime of suppressed losses.

Now, at last, she understood why Alexander had asked her to return to Prague with him. What an important moment it was for him to have his country whole and free. How blind she had been, how blind she had made herself. No, how blind fate had made her. War had destroyed that part of her life that had been Prague, killed her passionate belief and passionate love for her heritage, the country of her birth. War, and then Communism, had done their work of destruction. Now these things had destroyed themselves and until now she had hardly understood that. Oh God, the David painting had meant so much to her as a child. She had lived in the fantasy world she had created out of it. It had been such a joy to her, and now it had saved her, inspired her to return to her origins. She would get it back, would get it all back. Never again would she allow anything of such significance to slide away from her. Not if she could prevent it.

She went directly to the telephone, only to realize she had no phone number for Alexander. She knew only that he lived in Prague. She rushed up to her room and looked at his note. It was no help. She sat in a wing chair in her bedroom looking out into the garden. A warm breeze rippled the sheer white curtain. How clever he was. He had done it deliberately, he didn't want her to come to him impulsively. He was right, and until she had determined whether this really was an impulsive act, she would do nothing.

At midnight, New York time, she heard his voice for the third time in her life. She closed her eyes. Tears moistened her eyelashes, and she swallowed hard.

He said, "Mimi, dear Mimi."

"Alexander, I've been such a fool. I should have gone with you to Prague."

"No, I see now you couldn't have, you didn't understand. And you do now?"

"Oh, yes. I read your letter often, it sustains me. I have so much to tell you. So many times I have sat down and written you letters, but I never posted them. They're love letters."

"We'll read them together, in Prague, when you come. You are coming?"

"Yes," she answered. "Alexander . . ." A pause. He waited for her to continue.

"Mimi, are you all right?" he asked. She caught the note of concern in his voice.

"Fine, just fine," she answered quickly. "Maybe better than I have ever been. So much has happened. I think you should know I have left my husband. Divorced him, actually. And I am living alone, here, in my father's house."

"Mimi . . ."

"No, please, let me finish. I want you to understand. It was over for me with my husband just a few days before you came to see me. Your timing was perfect. I was ready for you to step into my life. But not aware of just how ready. So much had happened so fast. You do understand?"

"Yes, completely."

"Oh, good, because since then, without realizing fully why, I have kept making monumental changes in my life, going adrift, not knowing where. You've been in my mind. The flowers were wonderful, and your letter. When you kissed me I felt something for you I have never felt for anyone in my whole life. I felt love, powerful love. I want to feel you again holding me in your arms. I've spent nights thinking about us, wanting you. There have been dreams and fantasies, and until now they didn't seem possible. Then something inside me snapped, and I knew I was fooling myself. They were possible, those dreams and fantasies and yearnings. All I had to do was reach out and you would be there. We would make them our reality. You didn't make it easy to find you though."

"I know. I worried about that. But I wanted you to be sure, to want me as much as I want you."

Mimi felt her heart racing. Its pounding nearly drowned

out the sensuous overtones in his voice, the seductive words she had wanted to hear these many months. "I was nearly devastated when your agent would not give me your telephone number, not even an address in Prague. You will never know the relief I felt when he told me he would call you at once and give you the message that I had called. Oh, dear, I'm rambling on. Does any of this make sense?"

"It all makes sense, it's more than I dreamed possible. I've loved you a long time, Mimi, and wanted you, it seems to me, forever. There is not a woman I've made love to since I first set eyes on you that I have not pretended was you. Nor have I written a word about love and passion, nor about the bliss of erotic love, without having you in my mind and heart."

Neither of them spoke. Their emotions had to be given time to settle. And then it was Mimi who broke the silence. He did not miss the tremor of emotion in her voice when she told him, "Alexander, I want to return to Prague and come to you. But I don't know my country anymore, I don't know Prague. I was five years old when I was spirited away. I have lived a whole lifetime here, and now it's over for me. I want it all back, that Czech life that was stolen from me. I want back all my father's lands, his palaces and houses, the chapels, his paintings and all his treasures. I want it all. I feel madly possessive. I must have it all— starting with a painting by David, and then all the other things that belonged to my father and now to me. I want them home in Czechoslovakia. Seeing a painting from my childhood, hanging in a Nazi palace in Austria, was an extraordinary catalyst for me. I want to come home, that's one thing. And then I want to go to you, that is another. I don't want you to think that I am using you or how I feel about you to accomplish my return. I want you just for yourself, for no more than to love you and be with you. I want to add something to your life. I can't mix them up, the two. I think I've done that all my life, mixed up love and survival."

"I'm coming to New York. I'll be on the next plane. I can't let you go. We'll come home together. It's so exciting here, Mimi. The government is very busy returning buildings, land, works of art and businesses confiscated by the Communists and held and used by them. Everything will be yours again."

"Is it really true? I have some documents that say so, I have signed papers for some of my property already, but is it true? Have they wiped away fifty years of oppression and looting? I can hardly believe it."

"Oh, it's true."

"Do you promise I can get it all back for the family?"

"I promise."

"Then come, as fast as you can. And we will return together."

Three days later he called her from Kennedy Airport.

"Mimi."

"Alexander."

"Where are you?"

"At the airport."

"Why didn't you let me know? I'd have met your plane. Oh, Alexander, I can't believe this is happening to us."

"I didn't want you to come to the airport. I couldn't bear to meet you in public. Coming together with you again is the most private, most intimate, exciting thing in my life, and I want to share it with no one but you. I'll be there as soon as I can."

Chapter 31

Each minute seemed like an hour, each hour a day. Mimi couldn't stop looking at the clock every five minutes. She was calculating how long it would be before he got there. She was up and down the stairs half a dozen times. Everything had to be right. Suddenly she remembered Sophia and dinner. He would be here in time for dinner. Down the stairs yet again to the kitchen.

"Sophia." She didn't miss the excitement in Mimi's voice.

"You have something to tell me? Something exciting, I think?"

"Sophia, I've met a man."

"Ach!" she exclaimed. "My Gott, is this going to be trouble? I hope not."

"Will you make supper for us, something lovely, something Czech? Oh, how stupid. He *is* Czech, he eats it all the time. Just anything delicious, special. I want him never to forget this meal for as long as he lives."

"Oh, my Gott!"

"You'll like him. He's Czech, lives in Prague, and he's a famous writer. I think he loves me."

"Oh, my Gott!"

Mimi began to laugh. "Will you stop saying 'Oh, my Gott' and be happy for me?"

"I am happy for you, but . . . oh, my Gott!"

Mimi laughed again. "You've met him."

"I've met him?"

"Christmas Day, remember? We were all out walking. He was down here in the kitchen with you and Jay and some other people. Milos, too, I think."

"Ah, him. At the time I thought to myself, this man is something special. Are you sure he loves you, Mimi?"

"That's what he tells me."

"Now just one minute ... I'm thinking."

"About what to cook?"

"No. Yes, I think so ... This is the man?"

Sophia rose from the table and went to the windowsill where she kept magazines she wanted to read. She pulled one out.

"There you are, there's your Czech." And she proudly placed the magazine on the table. And there he was, Alexander Janacek, in full color on the cover. Inside were seven pages on the literary world's most respected and interesting erotic novelist.

"Oh, my goodness, how did I miss it?"

"Because you never read *Time*. And look, he's here too." Sophia handed her *Newsweek* magazine.

"When did it come out? Oh, it's last week's."

"Yes."

"He never said a word about it. I know nothing about him, Sophia."

"Oh, Mimi, how can you be in love with a man you know nothing about?"

"Believe me, it can happen."

"Quick, you read *Newsweek*, I'll read *Time*," suggested Sophia.

The two women pulled out chairs and sat down at the kitchen table to read the magazines as if hitherto starved of them. Then, without a word, they swapped.

"What do you think?" asked Mimi. "Isn't he wonderful? And he loves women. Did you read those excerpts from his latest book? They're so sexy. Oh, Sophia. His father was a count, his brother inherited the title, and they've just got back all their properties."

"Already?"

"And, look, he lives in Prague in this wonderful rococo house. And he's not married."

"But it says here he has a long-time mistress who runs his life. I don't like the sound of that. And a girlfriend," said Sophia. "Look at her."

"Well, you can just put them in the past tense."

"Are you sure of that?"

"Positive."

"Well, that's all right then."

The two women pored over the magazines. The mistress was no more than thirty-five, the girlfriend more like twenty. The article claimed that Alexander was devoted to women and the conquest of them, but had no intention of ever marrying either of the women, or any woman, come to that.

"I don't like the sound of it," said Sophia.

"I do. Sophia, I've been married. Boy, have I been married! It was a great marriage, but that's a path I don't have to go down again. I'll settle for spending the rest of my life with the man I love. I don't need a certificate to declare my right to that."

Suddenly Alexander became a reality for her, as he had been in her house that Christmas Day. He had come alive for her in those articles. She realized that she wanted really to know him, and to be the special someone who would add to his life.

"What will you cook?" she asked Sophia.

"Pigeon pie. Yes, for him, pigeon pie with a filo pastry. Pigeon pie and wild rice."

"Oh, that's inspirational, Sophia."

"And candied baby carrots."

"And for a first course? Something sexy, Sophia."

"Ah, sexy. Oh, my Gott, Mimi!"

She laughed. "Oh, my Gott," she mimicked.

"Ah, I've got it. My cold cherry soup with cream, and then fresh asparagus. Very, very *al dente*. With the lightest hollandaise sauce. Then the pigeon pie. And for dessert, pears poached in red wine and cinnamon and vanilla."

"Perfection."

The doorbell rang. "Quick, hide the magazines. We don't want to look obvious."

Mimi ran up the stairs. She checked herself in the mirror. She had dressed carefully, discarding several outfits before choosing the one she was wearing. She had wanted to look young, fresh and provocative, yet elegant and chic. She wanted to be sensuous and seductive, as erotic as hell, but not obvious. So she had chosen a fine white linen dress with a wide oval neckline that showed off her long slender neck and seductive collarbones under creamy white skin. It had enormous balloon sleeves that buttoned tightly to the wrist. The bodice hung loose over her breasts. That they were naked was unmistakable through the semi-transparent linen. The top was cut blouson-style and cinched tight with an antique Byzantine belt of silver and coral, a gift from a Greek admirer. She wore no stockings or underclothes, her body silhouetted seductively through the folds of white linen that ended several inches above her knees, accentuating long, shapely legs. High-heeled sandals of lattice-work thin white leather showed elegant feet and long slender toes, their nails painted a carmine red. She wore no jewelry except a pair of Byzantine golden earrings studded with garnets, handsome decorative antiques. Her cascades of blonde hair were held off her face with a leopard-skin patterned chiffon scarf tied around her head in a seductive knot just off-center. A perfect, chic look for a hot, early summer evening in Manhattan.

She had time for only a fleeting glance at herself in the hall mirror. For he was there, standing on the other side of the glass entrance door. She could see him clearly through the decorative wrought-iron work. Her heart began to race. She had to ask herself, was this a fantasy, or was she, for the first time in her life, taking a chance on love for nothing more than the sake of sexual passion? For merely wanting to be that someone special for Alexander. She pulled the door open. And then there was nothing to separate them.

They stood facing each other, and she remembered more than a field and their lust, that Christmas kiss: she remembered an intense beautiful young man in the Cafe Lippe.

There was a lovely light in the street, weak, soft, late afternoon, early summer light. There would be no dusk. In a very short while it would be dark. It happened like that sometimes on hot June days in New York.

They gazed at each other. The impact of seeing him was far more powerful than she had expected. He looked more handsome, his face more sensuous, more hungry for her than she had remembered. She had expected to feel disappointment, or at least a hint of it, but felt quite the opposite. He was more charismatic, more powerful. Even in his quietness there was enormous power.

For him there could be no disappointment. He had loved her too long, had admired her from afar. When she had broken down in front of him on the day of the funeral and he had taken her in his arms, he knew the extent to which she had hidden herself. He had not been disappointed then, and now, standing opposite her, he knew he never could be. For several months after he had left her on that Christmas Day, he had poured his passion into a new novel while he had waited for her to fall in love with him, to seek him out, never doubting that they would ultimately be together. He had sensed her powerful sexual yearning during those few short minutes with her in his arms, during that kiss.

It was he who broke the silence, who took her hand in his and lowered his head to place a kiss on her fingers. "May I come in?" His voice shattered the silence, the last thing keeping them apart. He released her hand, and picking up a battered leather briefcase, stepped inside.

"No suitcase?"

"Everything I need is here."

She took the briefcase from his hand and placed it on the floor, stepping closer to put her arms around his neck and look up into his eyes—those dark brown, seductive, clever eyes. He was holding nothing back, he never would. She could tell that by the way he ate her up with his eyes. She loved the hunger he had for her, and that he played no games but showed it to her, showed what he wanted from her. "Kiss me. Oh, please, kiss me," she pleaded, her heart racing.

Alexander listened to her words, but recognized in them more than she spoke. They were Mimi's desire for him. She was erotic passion on the edge, begging to be recognized and loved for it. She was Mimi with a hungry heart for those very things he himself hungered for. She was the love of his life: years of secret loving, erotic desire come to reality.

She was waiting for him as he had waited all those years for her. He took her in his arms. Nothing in his life had ever been or would be as exquisite as this moment. He had tried to make love to other women since he had fallen in love with Mimi, had satiated both them and himself with sex. Sated and discarded, again and again, when efforts to love them as he loved her failed. Because of her, because of those secret, dark and rich erotic desires she awakened in him, sexual love took on a new meaning in his life and work. She had been his in-spiration for years. Now, wrapped in each other's arms, she wanted him.

He told himself, for Mimi, I want it to be right. I want it to be so good for her, for us. I have to do this right. Because these are our lives and I am dealing with all the love and pas-sion we have stored up for each other. She knows how I feel, she understands, and now she wants me. The waiting is over.

He tilted her chin with a finger so the light could catch her face at a certain angle. He smiled at her, happiness overflow-ing, pressed his lips lightly to her cheek and then her mouth. She was trembling and so was he. His kiss was insistent. Her lips parted, tongues met and made love. He sucked gently, hungrily nibbled. The feel of her hands on his face, stroking the back of his neck, excited him. She was overwhelmingly sexy, everything he knew her to be.

He caressed her arms through the billowing linen sleeves and stroked her flesh, the long sensuous slender neck and across her collarbone. It felt good to have her in his hands again. He sensed her yield to his touch. He pressed the sides of her breasts under the linen, his penis straining against his trousers. Beneath her dress, she moved against him, acknowl-edging his passion and that their kisses were impossible to control. It was all too fast, too heady, they deserved better than this. They had had fast and heady the first time they had sex. They could do even better than that now, and for the rest of their lives.

Alexander eased off, not in retreat but merely to pause. He could feel, as she moved in his arms, her approval. That meant everything to him. Finally they parted and she slipped an arm through his. Voice husky with emotion, she gave a se-ductive laugh. "I could have at least closed the front door," she told him, and did so. "The library, I think."

He smiled back at her and kissed her again, only briefly this time. She closed her eyes and felt her heart pounding. They both knew they wanted the bedroom, but that would come later. Together, hand in hand, they stood in the hall, merely enjoying the sight of each other.

He was wearing a smart putty-colored linen suit, well-cut, elegant, probably Armani. A shirt the color of Delft blue china and a coral-colored tie of raw silk. He looked every inch the successful artist, unimaginably sexy. Love for her showed in his eyes. She felt she had never seen love like that before. Everything he was showed in his face, his body, the way he moved. Love and passion, a desire for perfection, an animal-like maleness, sensitivity, intelligence, an imaginative mind, erotic desires lurking only just below the surface of the image he presented to the world. All this emanated from him like the aroma of a very special perfume. Alexander Janacek was that special kind of man women search for all their lives.

She picked up his battered briefcase again and they walked across the hall and into the library. Mimi closed the door behind them and then stood with her back against it. He took the briefcase from her and walked further into the room. He was extremely fond of this room. It had remained vivid in his mind from his last visit here. Mimi remained leaning against the door and watched him circle the library and then turn to face her. Alexander felt overwhelmed by desire, Mimi no less so. She forced herself to put desire aside and to say something.

"You must be hungry." It sounded so banal, almost like small talk. Mimi thought she sounded ridiculous. She shook her head and turned around to double-lock the library door. Then, walking toward him, she said, "Until you came through that door today, I thought I had fallen in love with you when we got lost in sex and passion and the violence of our feelings. Then I knew I loved you when you arrived here with your Christmas declaration and Kiss. I feel a love for you that is different and richer and more special than I have ever experienced before. But I didn't understand how much, how strongly I feel about you."

She went behind him and removed his jacket. Then, taking him by the hand, and while kissing him lightly on his cheek and the lobe of his ear, she walked with him toward the large, deep sofa covered in pigskin worn soft and to a rich rust color. There they stood facing each other. Her hands were trembling as she undid the antique silver belt and dropped it on the Persian carpet. He clasped her hands in his, and then raised them to kiss first one palm then the other. Then he raised them to cover his face and gently caress it, and to touch his mouth so that he could lick them and suck their flesh gently with his lips.

"I want you too much. I've always wanted you too much. I love you, Mimi," he told her, need thickening his voice.

Releasing her hands, he opened the first button of her dress. She closed her eyes, feeling the slight fluttering of her lashes, so tense was she, so filled with desire to please him. Mimi wanted to live up to his expectations, to his love and his passion for her. She wanted to be all things to him sexually, to be all the loves he had ever had in his life or would ever want. She willed him to love her body as he loved her. She was in awe of him, holding her breath not out of anxiety but sheer determination that she should be everything she wanted to be.

He was undoing the last small mother-of-pearl button near the hem of her dress. He was tantalizing himself and Mimi as well for he had not stolen even a glimpse of her naked flesh under the dress. Now, slowly, he parted the white linen and she stood naked before his eyes. She thought she had never felt such stillness. It was as if the world stood still and all sound ceased; all life but theirs seemed frozen in time. They were more alive than they had ever been before. He raised her hand, loosed the buttons on her cuffs and slipped her dress off her shoulders, watching the white linen fall as if in slow motion to the floor. Alexander stood back and gazed at his love. He was choked with emotion. She was his. This beautiful, complex, exciting woman was his. In her stillness, naked in front of him, she was giving herself freely. A thousand times he had remembered her breasts, how they felt in his hands, the joy of sucking her nipples into his mouth. But memory had failed him. Her breasts were far more voluptuous, beautiful, succulent, with nipples more provocative, that he now sensed yearned for his lips, his mouth to suck on them, to excite her.

He caressed her long slender neck, her sensuous shoulders, traced with his fingers a line across her chest and cupped a breast in each hand, felt their weight and roundness. He lowered his head to kiss her breasts, leaving no part of them untouched by his eager mouth. He dropped slowly to his knees trailing kisses down her body to her navel, and licked her there, before burying his face in her pubic mound. It was more than he could bear. Animal passion took over. He opened his mouth, bit her, sucked her mound into it. She moved her legs further apart. He kissed the inside of her thighs. She moaned with pleasure and came.

He stood up and she watched him undress. There was an extraordinary raunchiness about his body: the chunky torso, the hairy chest, the strong arms, narrow hips, muscular thighs. Her heart raced at the sight of the long, thick, now erect penis, its dramatically large, circumcised knob. A strong, succulent-looking penis. Underneath, the scrotum: fiercely erotic in size and shape, the luscious sac filled with virility. To a woman like Mimi, who loved genitalia, it was perfect, exciting to make love to. Each held back their violent passion for sex in order to discover each other's bodies again. Like adolescents they took their time with their caresses, their fondling, until they knew once more every inch of their bodies and how they were reacting to each other.

He lay down on the pigskins and she knelt between his legs. He watched her take him wholly in her mouth and make love to him. This was not one of his dreams, his fantasies, his hopes or desires. It was real, it was magnificent. Excitement beyond anything he fantasized. The way she handled his balls, made love to his cock, revealed the fire and passion, the boundless sexual desire Mimi possessed. Lying in each other's arms, holding back their final climax, reluctant to curtail foreplay because it was so teasingly exciting, led them on to probe the very depths of their erotic souls. And there they glimpsed their own sexualized animal instincts. What bliss Alexander felt in the knowledge that he could please her erotic nature, that he would be able to transport her to a land whose divinity was Eros. He was filled with joy that Mimi had come as copiously and as often as she had by their mere discovering of each other. Each felt an overwhelming of self in the hunger they had for each other. The way they played with each other's bodies, the way they made love. No words were needed to declare this was only the beginning.

They eased themselves by slow degrees from the pitch they had driven themselves to. They were hardly composed or under control, but they did dress to make ready for dining. "This is not easy," he told her.

"I know," she answered, a smile on her lips. "Nor for me."

"Then why are we doing it?" he asked.

"I don't know," she answered him. Gazing into his eyes, she unclasped the silver belt she had just done up.

He took the buckle from her hands and closed the clasp again, patting it as if to say "That's final," and then told her, "I do. Because we are two masochists in love." They laughed at themselves. With his arm enfolding Mimi's waist, they walked from the room, Alexander telling her, "And I am quite famished for food too."

In the kitchen they dined, Sophia serving. It was a happy meal. The three chatted amicably. It had taken just one look at them to tell Sophia they had a future together.

"I've known her since a child," she announced to Alexander, as if eager to vouch for Mimi's whole life.

"I wish I had known her then," he answered.

"She's more like that child today than she ever has been since I met her. You'll be taking her home?"

"Yes," he told her, looking across the table at Mimi. Both women were stunned as he turned to Sophia and said, "Not just Mimi. You, too. I hope you'll come with us."

"To Prague?"

"To Prague," he said, and raised his glass of wine. The tears in Mimi's eyes told everything. Sophia filled her own glass again and she and Mimi gently rang in the new years of life ahead for them, touching their glasses against Alexander's.

Sophia placed the dessert on the table for Mimi to serve. She went to her room and returned dressed in hat and coat to say she would be back in three days' time. It was quite extraordinary. The old woman came to Mimi, kissed her on the top of her head, and then went to Alexander. She stroked his hair, raised his hand, kissed it and said, "I think we've been waiting for you all our lives." Then she left.

Mimi and Alexander lingered over coffee, and then arm in arm mounted the stairs from the kitchen to the great hall where he gathered up his briefcase. Together they climbed the grand staircase of the house to the first floor.

"We'll have a wonderful life," he told her, "but it may not be easy."

"What makes you think I've always had it easy?"

"I'll have my work, and you'll have the restoration of your estates, and we'll have each other. That's a full life, rich and exciting. And we'll have our country and our freedom. We'll be very happy."

"And we'll have love?"

"Yes, we'll have love."

In the bedroom they undressed and bathed. Sexual tension was sparking between them again. Nervously she stood by the window, looking out into a garden dark except for a three-quarter moon that cast its silvery-white light over the leaves of the trees and shrubs. Naked, he walked up behind her and placed his arms around her waist, kissing her bare shoulder and then her back. She shivered. His mere touch set her aflame. "Can any man be happier than I am tonight? More grateful, more in love? Surely not," he told her. "Come to bed. We'll go together on a joy-ride into sexual oblivion, down paths we took once before. We'll exchange this world for another, a place where lust takes over. There we'll die the little death, again and again, until we fall into a dreamless sleep enfolded in each other's arms."

He turned her slowly round to face him. Moonlight spilled through the window into the darkened room. The tips of her blonde hair picked up the light. It shone on her face and fell across her black satin nightgown, which clung like a second skin to her body, making her look luscious, ripe and seductive. He snapped the shoestring satin straps on her shoulders and they broke. She eased the sensuous material off her breasts and caressed them and then his face. He swept her up into his arms and carried her to the bed.

In a husky, quiet voice, she told him, "I feel the Mimi I have never known has found her life. Can you understand that?" Still in his arms, he answered her with a deep passionate kiss. They listened in the dark to the provocative sound of tearing satin as she ripped her nightgown open.

It was late morning, possibly afternoon, when she woke; she could tell by the quality of the light and the angle at which it shone into the room. She was still clasped loosely in Alexander's arms. For a long time she lay studying his features as he slept. He had been a magnificent lover who had seduced her with uncontrollable lust. They had been a perfect erotic match. A sense of deep love had guided them through adventures of abandonment to sexual ecstasy. She felt the warmth of his body against hers, its strength. He stirred. She could sense him emerging from his dreams. In a half-sleep, he pulled her closer to him, then opened his eyes. Lazily he pulled himself up against the bed pillows, and her with him. "Good morning," he said. No more. He seemed mesmerized by her.

"You're very quiet," she said.

He released her from his arms and slipped from the bed. Turning to look at her once more, he bent down and kissed her lightly on the lips. She thought she sensed a tremor in his. When he returned to her, it was with a book in his hand. He slid once more between the sheets and took up the same position: her head resting in the crook of his neck, an arm placed around her. He pulled her tight up against him. He caressed her breast, lifted her hand and kissed the palm. Then, placing her arm across him, he opened the book and read: "I saw her, this beautiful goddess, a sad child, a sensuous woman, this lady with the hungry heart. And I fell instantly in love, and knew it was forever. And now she is my life."

He looked at her and handed her the open book. The white page was blank except for those words neatly printed in black lower-case letters. Beneath: For Mimi.